CHRONICLES OF TARC

545–2

KNIGHT AND FALCON

Jiryü Räsen

PUBLISHED BY J. KASSEBAUM

Edition February 7, 2020 2nd Edition
Paperback ISBN 978-1-949359-95-4
eBook ISBN 978-1-949359-94-7
© **Jiryü Räsen**. All rights reserved.
Published by J. Kassebaum, Indianapolis.
Cover background ©Sumners Graphics via Canva.com.
#CampNaNoWinner2018

CHAPTER 1 Morning Rising

It was morning. Ilena, princess in hiding and prime witness in protective custody knew it as her eyes opened. Her nose could smell the scent of the morning air even though it was very faint underneath the smell of the sick room she was in. She'd woken up before her nurse and maid had come to see to her.

That was okay. She wanted to savor the moment. The day before had been full of completion. All of her worries for the past almost six weeks had finally resolved into the beginnings of the movements she wanted to be making forward.

Ore, her partner and her beloved, had finally openly claim her as his partner to watch over Mizi. That was a rather massive step forward in their relationship that had been very strained since Ilena had been found by them covered in rocks, nearly dead from the assassination of her Lady. Ilena's end goal was a lot more than that, but for now, she was very relieved Ore had managed to accept her even that much.

Mizi herself had finally taken her own large internal step yesterday as well. Ilena had pushed her to face herself and really open her eyes to if she would fight for her own beloved, or if she would step back and be less. When Mizi had come to her with her decision written not only in her face but all over her body, firm in her conviction, Ilena finally had found relief.

Mizi and First Prince Rei Touka, Regent of Suiran, had been in love for almost five years or more. Rei and his older brother, King Sasou Touka, had tested Mizi and agreed that if Rei wished to marry for love, he likely couldn't do better. They'd been supporting her, but Sasou tested everyone. He'd put Mizi and Rei where they could figure out how to stand together, but he'd been leaving Rei alone since then to see how he would help Mizi be able to stand by his side as his Princess.

Well...Sasou had apparently also been waiting for Ilena to show up, or something, was all she could figure. Only her push of Mizi had made her face her fears of becoming a princess and turn to walk through them towards her goal. Now that Mizi had decided she would do that, Ilena could really get to work on helping Mizi get there.

Rei had learned sooner than Ilena was ready for him to that she was his long missing cousin, princess of two countries. She'd run from her home country of Selicia when she was seven. A coup had killed all of the ruling family save her parents and herself. She'd been smuggled out of the country separately from her parents, and she still to this day hadn't seen them again.

She'd lived in hiding in the closest relation House in Suiran, Ryokudo, since she'd arrived over the mountains. While there, she'd apparently been recognized by the family from an earlier visit there when her family had passed through after Rei's birth celebration.

There had been a problem with living with the Shicchi's. They had an inborn madness that led to them being very violent and abusive. Shortly after Ilena had arrived, the old Earl had died of poison at the hands of his oldest son. A year later, that Earl's oldest son had lashed out in anger and killed his father. Because it had been unexpected, his mind had broken and he'd become mad in brain as well as in emotions.

That son, Pakyo Shicchi, was the current Earl of Tokumade. He had made Ilena his steward over the household when she was seventeen, eight years ago. That had suited her just fine. She hadn't known he knew she was the princess, but she'd already begun learning how to work with him to keep him calm so he wasn't so abusive to the staff of the manor. She continued to protect the people of the House from him as Steward, up until the assassination.

That had been rather a surprise to Ilena, actually. She knew some of the plans that Pakyo was working on presently, but that part she hadn't been privy to. She certainly hadn't expected to have a large boulder dropped on her after she'd jumped from the carriage at the first sounds of the landslide sent down on the carriage she, the Lady of Tokumade, and her maids were returning to Tokumade in.

She'd feigned unconsciousness when she'd heard the assassin walking above her to check on if she was alive or not. She hadn't expected him to come back and lever the boulder over the edge. Her heart had been in her mouth the entire time she'd watched it bounce down the slope towards her, not knowing if the next bounce would send it towards her head or away from her.

To have it land on her left hip *had* made her pass out, the crunch of the bones being more than she could take. Her only small relief had been that it hadn't killed her outright. Surely the injuries she'd received being buried under the debris from the landslide would have been sufficient? She was rather impatient for having to lie still for six weeks.

Still, if all of that trouble had been meant to put Ilena in the castle because Mizi had been close by and a Court Healer, and was known to not leave such cases alone, it had definitely worked. It had all worked within the parameters of Ilena's own plans, if not exactly how she would have liked.

The injury was worse because at the moment she would never walk or run again. That wasn't going to help her plans at all, so she was scheduled to very soon go through an experimental surgery to fix that. While she desperately needed the repair, the temporary madness she herself was going to be subjected to was going to be quite difficult. She wasn't sure the impatient her was going to lie still for yet another (consecutive) six weeks.

However, that had led to the third resolution she had needed yesterday. Rei had come to her mere days before this morning, proof in hand, demanding to know if Ilena was the missing princess. Ilena couldn't lie, since he would see the proof on her person, and he had after she'd finished her story. While she definitely wasn't ready to be tied to the Touka's as a high level political piece on their political strategy boards, it had been enough that Rei had decided to trust her - almost implicitly.

Well...really it meant he was now testing her in a completely different way. He'd finally allowed her to send for her nurse and maid to come take care of her. They knew how to handle Ilena's testy snits and childish tantrums she would descend into when far too impatient or stressed out to deal with life as a calm noble.

Even though she'd matured quite a lot in her twenty-five years, she was still very much the spoiled princess inside when things got that difficult for her. Her nurse, Leah, had experience handling those from Ilena's birth. Rio, her maid, was a sympathetic friend who still made her do her duty - a safe place to rest all royals needed when their burdens became too heavy.

They'd arrived yesterday, and she had set them immediately to work on the third goal she had in being at Castle Nijou. Rei, already a genius strategist at nearly nineteen, had figured that one out on his own as well - also far in advance of Ilena's expectations.

He'd come in and made her his Director of Intelligence far before he should have, telling her it was a restraint to keep her by his side, and that he expected to see good things out of her before he gave her the final title she would have - that of Minister of Intelligence of Suiran. Ilena had made him force it on her, since she disapproved the appointment before the other lords of the castle knew she even existed, but she'd been scolded for that and apologized already.

He hadn't been wrong in his understanding. Sasou, King of all Ryokudo for the last three years, had been running most of the kingdom for his mother, Dowager Queen Kata, since he and Rei's father had died when Sasou was fourteen. During that time, he'd watched what Ilena had done, agreed with her, then tested her. If Rei could now learn to use Ilena in the place she'd built up then Sasou would in all likelihood not oppose Rei making her Minister of Intelligence of the Region.

Sasou had sent Rei to Nijou from Ichijou only last fall to become the new Regent, replacing Kata. Rei had been learning since then how to work with the lords of the castle and Region, gaining their trust in his abilities. He obviously had the capacity to be Regent or Sasou wouldn't have sent him to begin with.

Sasou was the greatest politician and strategist of the political game that existed, as far as Ilena was concerned, although she was a very close second. She and Sasou had seriously studied the wisdom of kings and rulership, codified by their shared grandfather the King of Ryokudo two generations before. They had both been practicing it since they were four, too.

Leah and Rio were not just Ilena's nurse and maid, they were also her two close aides and assistants in her information networks - the Family and the House. Now that they were in the castle she had put them to work immediately. Today they would continue learning about what Ilena's role was within the lords of the castle. Mizi was studying with them, because she needed to know how she as the Princess and Regent's wife fit into the court as well.

Ilena's other close aide, called only Grandfather to protect him and his position, had been given leave to enter and leave the castle on his own recognizance, and been ordered to visit with her every night. That had been equally a surprise to Ilena, but had fit into the testing Rei had decided on. He wanted to see what she could do for him while she herself was still lying flat on her back. It was a test of her people, not just her.

Neither she nor they would disappoint. However, she was still teaching Rei just what she was and had in her hands so she also wouldn't just hand him everything all at once. She needed to know she could trust him with those whom she was protecting. The testing was mutual.

A knock at the door interrupted Ilena's musings. As it opened, it let in a waft of fresh air from the inner open courtyard of the medical wing. She was in one of several small recovery rooms built into the wing near the Medical Department where long-term patients could be housed out of the way of shorter-term activities, and still be seen to by the medics easily.

Her two day guards were already on the door, Ore leaving her room at the shift change having been what likely woke her up. The soldiers let Leah and Rio enter with polite "good morning"s. Ilena was more than ready to get her day moving forward. She really hated being a patient completely dependent on others for *everything* ...including when she could go to the bathroom. Still, she tried to stay kind and patient. She didn't want a scolding just yet, this early in the day.

"Good morning, Mistress Ilena," Rio smiled as she arrived close enough to Ilena's side to see she was already awake. The slender seventeen-year-old still held her beauty of her childhood, but it was now a maturing look. Her dark hair was in the braid Rio kept it in to be out of her way. Ilena was looking forward to having Rio brush her own long black hair and braid it again. Her head itched from having to lie down constantly. She would be able to sit up long enough for that today.

Ilena was pleased to see that Rio was in nicely kept clothing. For too many years Ilena had only been able to afford basic things for Rio that had barely passed as reasonable wear. Others in the Family had helped to see Rio was properly taken care of while Ilena wasn't there to properly take care of her.

"Good morning, Rio," Ilena said as cheerfully as she could manage. She was very glad to have them with her now, after all. She turned and looked for Leah, finding her slightly greying bun on the top of her head first since she was bent down to collect the tools of the morning. "And good morning, Nana."

"Good morning, Mistress Ilena," the firm tones of the short and sturdy nurse were a little more pleasant today. She must be relaxing a little now that she could actually see her charge for herself daily. Ilena knew that it had surely been very difficult for Leah to not be where she could help until now. "Let's get you cleaned up and ready for breakfast, shall we?"

"Yes, please." It came out more emphatic that Ilena had intended, but it only made Rio smile and gave Leah a reason to bustle and become happily busy. Ilena sighed in pleasure to get the usual morning routine from them. Somehow, they always managed to make her feel pampered, even though she'd not been in any kind of such environment since she'd lived in the castle in Selicia.

-o-o-o-

Mizi brushed her red hair, impatient to be going about her day today. The sun coming in the window of her second floor apartment in the Regent's personal aide's quarters glinted in gold highlights off her hair. Her green eyes weren't seeing that, though. They were reviewing the list one more time.

She'd spent a good hour after arriving at her apartment sitting at the small desk working on her assignment from Ilena. Mizi was reviewing it one more time before "handing it in to the professor" as it were. While it did feel like she was back at Kouzanshi at the University, she was pretty sure only here in the castle would she be given assignments like this one.

The list in front of her itemized everything Mizi would expect to see in a princess of the realm - any realm really. Perhaps others would find it extremely stringent, and she wasn't sure on a few if they were even considered necessary at all, but they'd occurred to her, so she'd written them down. She was already sure Ilena would tell her either way.

The brush paused, then slowly went down on the desk. Mizi paused, took a deep breath, then reached for the ribbon she tied her hair up with to keep it out of her face. As the ribbon tightened around the ponytail, Mizi's rational brain fought with her heart. *How is it that Ilena can teach me to be a princess? Why to do I believe that so strongly?*

Ilena had already proven her strengths over the last five weeks, from the time she was no longer unconscious, and maybe even before in the brief times she'd been conscious enough to talk to. In everything she had done and said to Mizi, Ilena had been a warm support to her, encouraging her, teaching her things to strengthen her. Enough so that Mizi had herself asked Rei to put Ilena at her back as Ore's partner so she could continue to have that support.

Ore had run from his duty at Mizi's side because Ilena represented something he couldn't face. When Ilena had explained that to Mizi, and Rei had dragged Ore back to stand where he was supposed to as Mizi's personal guard, Mizi had only seen one solution. She wanted Ilena, and she loved Ore as a close friend and companion. She'd made them partners, making Ore face his past so he could have a clear path into his future.

Ore did seem to be calming down in Ilena's presence. It helped that he was busy during the day in Rei's office. At the first the three of them at been at the Osterly garrison, the closest garrison to the assassination site, and constantly together. Now Mizi went in the mornings and Ore visited with Ilena at night after his duties to Rei were done.

Ilena had told Mizi early on that she loved Ore. Mizi had been happy to help that goal along as well. She felt that Ore, who was always kind and tender to her, deserved someone to love him. However, Mizi had been brought to question Ilena's resolve just a little. It was a small concern that she didn't like having in her breast, but she couldn't change it for all she kept trying.

The memory of Rei calling her into Ilena's room to hold her up while Rei looked at Ilena's bare back was haunting Mizi more than she liked. The change that had come over Rei after that had been so marked. His brilliant blue eyes had gone from distrusting and testing when they looked at Ilena to sorrow and love. As a prince, Rei loved no one that way, other than Mizi herself, and Mizi was having troubles remembering a time Rei had looked at her that way, although surely he had, right?

Rei did love his companions and aides, and in a different way his brother. Andrew in particular was one Rei relaxed around quite a bit. Andrew had been set at Rei's back by Sasou when he was young to help guide him through the difficult ages. Rei listened to his scolds and advice very seriously. Andrew protected Rei in return quite fiercely, if quietly.

When Mizi had told Andrew about that visit with Ilena, he'd listened carefully, then only affirmed that they would help Rei keep Ilena beside him. That hadn't really helped Mizi very much. She *knew* Andrew would have refused to do it if Ilena was a danger to Rei. Mizi *thought* Andrew would complain if he thought Ilena was going to come between Rei and Mizi's goal to be together. Since he'd done neither, then Mizi's niggling worries didn't have a foundation. Still....

Mizi was hoping to catch Andrew's partner Mina before she went to the Rose office, but she'd been hard to intercept recently, now that she was training her new assistant, Tairn. Mina had been with Rei since before Mizi had come to Ryokudo. Rei loved Mina as a friend, too, for all she was taciturn and could be very sharp, and he trusted her implicitly. Mizi felt she could also trust Mina's open honesty, which was why she wanted to talk to her.

Mizi took a breath, and stood up from her chair. She picked up her list and slid it into the folder next to it. She tucked that under her arm and headed out her door. She still hadn't heard Mina leaving the room next to hers yet, so she may as well get to the breakfast cart below first.

As she walked down the broad stairs she looked at the door underneath her room. That was Ore's room - when he chose to visit it. She wondered if he'd be there today. For all the four of them slept in the same wing, they didn't see each other much when they were in it. Their schedules were all different. It was a nice morning when even two of them could pause long enough to chat over a plate of breakfast.

Arriving at the cart, Mizi counted the plates. Two already. She sighed. Ore's wasn't likely one of them. He got up the latest of all of them if he'd been in his own bed, often because he'd taken a late night guard shift. Mizi had finally learned at Osterly, watching over Ilena, that it was because Ore - like Ilena - was claustrophobic and small rooms were difficult for him.

Feeling sad, Mizi made up her plate and sat in one of the chairs set up along the wall of the main hallway of the wing. She supposed she could go have breakfast with Ilena, but she'd been hoping to get that feeling settled before she faced her.

As she ate, Mizi frowned, trying to chase that feeling down so she could properly set it aside. Rei had been rather good for him and carefully told Mizi what his feelings for her were right after he'd seen whatever marked Ilena. He was still set on helping Ilena catch Ore and having the two of them walk behind Mizi.

Rei had been just as openly set on helping Mizi in her goal to become his princess just last night even, easily accepting his assignment to also write up a list of what he needed to have in the person he accepted as his wife and princess so Mizi would know what she still needed to do to get there. Mizi didn't think he had set aside his promises to her. She was trying very hard to trust him.

She knew as a prince Rei couldn't tell her everything. There were state secrets he was required to keep, and that was one of them. Both Ilena and Rei had said that Rei had to see the mark on Ilena for Sasou's sake, and until Sasou approved it, Rei couldn't say any more than he already had. Mizi wanted to support him in that. Thus the frustration of not being able to quiet the small nasty little voice in the pit of her stomach.

Mizi forced herself to swallow the last bite of fruit on her plate. With a slow deep breath out, she sat up straight and made her shoulders relax. Then she purposely stood and set her plate on top of the other dirty ones on the cart. It wasn't going to be resolved this morning. Rei and Ilena were both committed to helping her reach her goal, and she had a lot of hard to work to do to get there.

Firmly, Mizi pushed the worry down and marched herself out the door to the wing, past the two guards there, and out into the castle grounds to take herself to the medical wing. She would have to rely on Ilena's firm lessons to keep her occupied and comfort that worry until Sasou saw fit to allow her to know more.

Sasou always did things in his own way and time, not being affected by others. And, honestly, he was a terrible tease. If he knew it was affecting Mizi that way, he might draw out the suspense even longer. She was glad he was in the south in Ichijou so he couldn't know how much it was eating at her. He'd likely poke at it to make it flare up to see if he could make Mizi leave Rei's side.

She drew in another firm breath. That was enough to get her ire up to counter the worry. It was a silly thing to push against, but if it would get her through today, then she'd use it. He wasn't there to care anyway, nor would he. He would only laugh at her again and let her use him to prove her commitment to Rei.

Her shoulders slumped briefly at that thought, but then she straightened them again. The combination was enough. She had work to do.

-o-o-o-

7

Ore paused his run across the roof-tops of the castle wings and buildings to run his fingers into his short black hair, making it spike up. He was at the intersection between two destinations. The morning spring air was crisp and cool. He shivered slightly, glad he had his warm black wool cloak on. Many of his recent mornings had been full of being Rei's Messenger and Andrew combined. Doctor Elliot, the surgeon who would be fixing Ilena's hip tendon had been brought to the castle and needed a room and lab. Leah and Rio also had needed a room, and all three had needed identification and to be introduced to the gate guards. Grandfather, too. Ore had been very busy setting up Ilena's House in the castle for the last several mornings - what part of it Rei was willing to let in so far.

This morning didn't have the same requirements, so perhaps he could take a little time for himself. He pulled his hand down and looked at it for a moment, then turned for his apartment in the aide's living wing. He'd not bathed for a while, having been far too busy for it. He was early enough he could add that in this morning.

He slid down from the roof of the aide's wing to hang in front of Mizi's window, as he always did when he was entering or leaving the wing. She wasn't in her room. (He always took one quick peek first to make sure she wasn't in the middle of changing. Rei would kill him if he actually peeped on Mizi, and his heart wouldn't take it besides.) It was mostly to reassure himself she was still safely where she should be.

If she wasn't there, then she might be in her bathroom, or he'd missed her in passing. He slipped on down to his own window below hers, opened it, and slipped into his room, stepping down on to the settee below his window, then to the floor, automatically closing and locking the window behind himself.

He'd already automatically checked the room by feel, sound and smell, too, to make sure there wasn't someone waiting in it to do him in. Not that it happened often inside the castle now that he'd had since last fall to discourage the people who wanted to kidnap Mizi to use for their own ends against the Toukas or for profit.

Her red hair was enough to tempt those of the underworld. Her place at Rei's side was enough to tempt those who wanted political power. It was sometimes a strenuous job to prevent Mizi from knowing about them, but it kept his skill up and kept him fit. Plus he liked to follow her around and watch her, and even more her and Rei together.

That was going to be even more interesting now that Ilena had pushed Mizi to actually stride forward firmly to that goal. Ore smiled to himself as he stripped off clothes, dropping them as he went into the bathroom to wash himself. Ilena was as wild and independent as he was. She'd already warned him he would have to pull her back if she got too far beyond what Rei and Mizi could deal with. He'd already warned Rei he would call on everyone if he couldn't do it alone.

He was looking forward to what Ilena was going to do now almost as much as Rei was, and maybe more. He just wasn't looking forward to having to be the restraint on the willful Touka princess. Touka's were headstrong, stubborn, insufferable geniuses with cause to not doubt that intelligence.

Ore had already born the brunt of Ilena's worst, really, and just as stubbornly refused to give in to it, like he'd refused to give in to Sasou. He'd only given in to Rei because Mizi and Rei were both worthy of his skills and his honor. He'd told Rei he would only take the position at Mizi back.

Well, that had been at the beginning. Rei had been using him a lot for his own needs in the office a lot lately. Ore liked being with Rei almost as much as with Mizi, so hadn't complained too strenuously until recently. Putting together the case against Pakyo was taking all of them a lot of effort, but that was for Ilena's sake, too. And Ilena was present now to help him watch over Mizi.

Mizi herself had helped Ore see it properly by reminding him that she had chosen Ilena as his partner to help him watch over her when he couldn't do it. To be able to rely on someone else when he had too many requirements on him wasn't entirely new. He'd already hired two other hidden guards to watch over Mizi for him. Rei regularly needed him for other tasks. Still, to have one person he could rely on openly and to strengthen him was new and was something that helped him relax in a new way he'd not relaxed in for a long time.

To have that person be Ilena - who had been more headache and stress before recently - was rather surprising really. At the same time.... Ore paused, then finished dumping the rinse water over his head. He took a breath and dumped one more over him. Wiping his eyes, he turned to look at the soaking bathtub. He blinked at it, then shrugged and turned for his towel. If he took that long he was likely to get frowns from the other aides when he got into the Rose office.

He'd not heard sounds of bathing above him, so it was even more likely he'd missed Mizi. That was a little hard. He missed walking with her, and had only been able to be with her one day out of the last several weeks. Yesterday had been very interesting, though.

Ilena had called him for the first time to her side only to tell him she'd scolded Mizi and sent her out to think properly about her goals. He'd had to scold her in return for being too harsh. When Mizi had walked into the Rose office pushing the lunch cart and turned their mid-day upside down he'd been quite astonished. It had been even more fun to turn the tables and show up with Rei without announcement in Ilena's room for dinner.

Until she'd admitted her original plan was to tell Pakyo how to find him so she could escape from Pakyo to flee to the castle. Ore still didn't really like that Ilena knew he was Pakyo's youngest brother in hiding. He'd escaped from that House the night Pakyo had gone on a mad killing spree and killed their middle brother and his wife. He'd changed his name and disavowed the House. Only Ilena had been left behind, and that had been his pain since then.

Until the new pain of finding her again. That had been a shock to his system - lots of them. So many he couldn't stay by her any longer. He'd already apologized to Mizi for not being able to stay by her side, and was still paying the price for leaving by being yoked to Ilena.

Ore paused in his thinking again, paying attention to which set of clothing he was taking out of his wardrobe. He stayed far away from the formal black uniform of the personal knights to the First Prince. He really didn't like to wear it, although he was secretly proud that Rei trusted him as much as he did Andrew and Mina.

As Ore drew his second pair of his favorite outfit out of the wardrobe, he was glad once again he could rely on the castle maids to take care of him. He'd lived a lot of years with only one outfit to his name, and that mostly threadbare and almost never washed for fear it would be stolen.

He drew on his comfortable dark brown pants that let him move in his martial arts moves so he could protect his mistress. He supposed he could wear the informal black uniform today, since he'd only be in the office yet again, but he really preferred his favorites regardless. Besides all the guards knew him in this one. He got more odd looks for being in the castle uniforms.

That made him smile a little again as he drew on the cream colored shirt that was standard castle issue. He wasn't going to argue about that. A shirt was a shirt. His brown jacket with the buckles was his special requirement, though. It held the special pockets for his throwing knives.

Once the jacket was on, Ore fetched the dirty jacket off the floor and traded the knives to put them into the one he was wearing. He checked them carefully before putting each one in to make sure they were still holding their edge. They were, but then he'd not had to use them much. It was just habit from his years on the street as a freelancer nightwalker. Those weren't bad habits to keep.

The short sword in it's black sheath marked with the gold stamp of those in the direct service of the royal House was after his worn-in boots that let him climb walls easily, and didn't let his feet get hurt by the far drops from those walls. Ore buckled the black sword belt on then settled the sword in it's place, still finding it just a little odd even after the four-plus years he'd worn it. Knife was his blade - thus the *short* sword. Rei had been able to consider him that much.

That made him remember that he was getting behind on his sword lessons again. Andrew would cream him and Mina would make him pay with an immediate second bout. Ore sighed. He really didn't know how to fit in all the things he was supposed to be doing. That's probably where the two of them had gone before dawn even - to get in their daily practice. Ore really couldn't call up the care to put in that kind of insane effort just for a sword.

He already put in that kind of insane effort for his martial art and his knives. To add the short sword only made him tired. Why know how to kill in three ways when the two were good enough? It was just a decoration and mark of position for him anyway. Still, that wasn't good enough for the First and Second knight when he was the Third.

Ore sighed again and headed out his door to see if there was anything worth eating for breakfast. Somehow, he'd have to fit sword practices in again, regardless, he supposed.

The count of plates on the cart was three. He'd definitely missed Mizi, then. He sighed again, then snatched up two hands-full of things he could eat on the walk to the office and headed for the door. He managed to get the door open and closed behind him.

The guards gave him odd looks, that were just as resigned. Sometimes he went in and never came out (he left by bedroom window). Sometimes - like this time - he never went in but he came out. He just grinned at them and took a bite of his apple.

He was a few steps beyond the door when he paused and turned back. "How was Mistress when she left?" he asked the guards seriously.

They considered, then one answered, "She was fine. Determined and focused, it seemed."

"She left early for her today," the other one answered.

Ore paused. He knew Mizi had cause for both of them, now that she had a way to move forward on her goal, but early was sometimes a sign she was thinking too hard, or she'd been trying to catch one of the rest of them. He gave a nod. "Thanks." He turned back to his own path and walked on.

When he was at a place that was hidden, and he'd eaten enough to have one hand free, he went up on the roof and whistled. He had to wait for a while before one of the two hidden guards arrived where he was. "How's Mistress this morning?"

"Already to the medical wing, visiting with Head Healer Ryan," Ore was answered.

"Did you watch? Did her shoulders slump at all during her walk?" he asked. Watching the back of the person they followed was important. It was how they told what was going on inside and if they were okay or not.

"Yes. Briefly early on, but she firmed up again nearly immediately."

Ore pondered that, then released the guard to return to his post. He continued to ponder it the rest of the way to the royal offices wing. He knew that place very intimately, and the one in Ichijou even more intimately.

He slipped down onto the balcony outside the Rose office. He had to knock on the double glass doors. It was still early enough that the chill in the air had made Rei keep the doors closed, and he'd not unlocked them yet, either. The blue curtains weren't even pulled back from them yet, so Rei had likely only recently arrived, if he was even there yet.

Ore always locked the doors and pulled the curtains closed when he left in the evening, and he always left out the main doors if he was still there at night. He was usually the last one in the office unless Rei had more to do. That was his own fault, though. He was usually the last one go to get there, so had to stay latest.

This morning Rei opened the curtains, and then doors himself. Ore's eyebrow went up at him. "You're here early," Rei commented, his own eyebrow going up slightly in question. "Andrew and Mina still aren't here. They sent Tairn to pick me up." Ore frowned at him. Rei waved a hand. "It's okay. They sent along half a platoon to walk with me, too." He scowled slightly.

Ore smiled. "Oh, good. It would take that many to equal the two of them, you know." He laughed at Rei's unhappy face. "It wasn't *that* many, Master. Even three feels too much for you if it's not us."

He entered the room and left one of the doors open slightly. It wouldn't make the room all that cold to be that much, and would still give him the fresh air so he could make-believe that he was still outside instead of chained up inside to his desk. He shivered slightly.

"If you're cold, close it all the way," Rei complained at him settling into his chair covered in royal blue cushions set at his desk. He sat closest to the doors so would be cold first.

The small fireplace next to Ore's desk would keep him warm since it was already lit and would continue to burn as long as Ore added logs to it. He liked to be warm so usually kept it going longer than the rest needed it, so by mid-morning no one was complaining about the open door - usually.

Ore shook his head. "No that would be the opposite. I'd run instead. It's open so I *don't*."

Rei gave him a longsuffering look and slight roll of the eyes. "Go sit down. You'll forget as soon as you're sitting down and working anyway."

"Maybe," Ore wasn't going to commit. Sometimes only having that slight breeze kept him still. He gave a 'good morning' nod to Tairn, who was already at his desk next to Ore's and hard at work, but had lifted his head to greet him briefly.

Ore did manage to get into his work rather quickly. Sitting closest to the doors into the inner hallway, he was the first to know Andrew and Mina had arrived. He sat up to watch them enter after their perfunctory knock. Aides came and went that way. Only formal guests were introduced by the guards on the door.

"Mina," he called to her as she closed the door behind herself and Andrew. They both paused and Andrew watched as Mina walked over to Ore's desk. "Mizi's carrying a weight. She was hoping to catch one of you this morning. If you could find some time in your very busy days to pause just a moment, I think it would help ease her mind."

Mina blinked in a bit of surprise, then gave a perfunctory nod. "I'll see what I can do."

"Thanks," Ore gave her a smile, then bent to his work again. It might be a few days for Mina to work talking to Mizi into her schedule, but she would do it.

He was a little surprised when Mina asked from the same place, "Ore, do you know what it's about?"

Ore looked up again, then leaned back in his chair to ponder that question, his fingers holding his pen and tapping the end of it. "She hasn't said...but I wouldn't be surprised if it's about the changes Ilena's making around her. She's the only one of us who doesn't know." He looked openly into Mina's eyes.

He couldn't say it openly in the Rose office now that Tairn was there. He couldn't know any more than Mizi could. Andrew, Mina, and Ore had all figured out on their own that Ilena was the missing princess Thailena. They were supporting Rei, who couldn't tell them, so they'd told him they knew and he'd not had to break any confidences, nor have his brother get angry with him.

It bound them from telling Mizi, though, and that had to be hard. Ilena was difficult to understand without that knowledge. Even Ore had been able to settle a lot when he'd understood it.

Mina understood. "I'll see what I can do, but that may be hard."

"I know," Ore answered. "Please do your best."

Mina gave a nod and headed for her desk between Tairn's and Rei's. Andrew gave a supporting nod to Ore. If he could help he would also. They looked to Rei. He was frowning at the work in front of him. He'd heard them, of course, and wasn't happy that he couldn't help Mizi either.

"You're late today, Andrew," Ore teased, since he could say today what he got told most of the time. "You'll have to work through lunch and make Mistress upset with you."

When Andrew looked at Ore with a raised eyebrow, Ore smiled at him. "Yesterday's lunch was a surprising thing, no? It will be interesting to see how long Master can hold out against the determined Mistress. He was super focused after that, though, wasn't he?"

Andrew had to smile at that. "Yes, he was. I was quite proud of him for being willing to work even harder just because Mizi came on her own strength and scolded him for not eating properly."

Rei's ears went pink. Ore continued to smile at Andrew. "He'll have to work even harder now to make up for not having working lunches."

Andrew's small grin slowly came on his face and he turned to his own desk between Ore's and Rei's. "True. We all will."

There were silent sighs at that, but Ore didn't mind. He loved to watch his master and mistress when they were together. His reminder that Mizi would be coming regularly now had helped Rei recover and there was a lot of only pen-scratching and paper-turning for a long time after that.

-o-o-o-

Mizi pushed back from her desk in the infirmary of the Medical Department. It looked like her research could be left now. She'd just finished writing down her notes of where she was leaving off and what she was planning on doing next so she could come back to it easily in the future.

She looked around at the familiar, yet not so familiar space. Castle Nijou had been built up over the years to look like Castle Ichijou but there were a few old buildings of the early time when Suiran had been a frontier area with more wars against the neighboring countries.

The medical wing was set next to the castle barracks, for rather obvious reasons. They had both been built fairly early on, but received regular updates as some of the most important buildings to be kept up. So having the office spaces open enough for four desks closed off slightly by tall bookshelves set over the desks was the same here as at Ichijou.

Like the other three desks in the room, behind her was a worktable that was her own. She'd received a desk on the outside wall, so she had a window that let her put plants in it to get the sun for a portion of the day. She only had two small ones right now. Ore used her window to come and go, and as his perch while he watched over her. Well, he had before he'd gotten so busy here in Nijou.

Mizi looked out her window now and sighed a little. Yes, it was lonely not having Ore there to smile and chat with her now that she wasn't focused on her work. She hadn't really noticed all that much, since when she got lost in her work she wasn't aware of him being there - not really. But he'd become such a fixture at her side she did notice it when she was relaxed like now.

There was noise from the next room up from hers. She rose to her feet. The office had a door to the inner courtyard of the medical wing that was closed and was rarely used. Most of the people who used this office went through the open door at the inner corner that led into the laboratory for the infirmary where they prepared poultices, tinctures, and medications.

A sound from there meant Ryan was finally up and getting ready for his day. She'd come in early so hadn't disturbed him, but she needed to talk to him. She couldn't very well just walk away for the next half-year without permission from her superior.

The tousled head of black hair that was poking into a cupboard and the short stocky frame was so familiar to Mizi. At sixteen Ryan was finally starting to put on height, but Mizi would likely always look down into the eyes of the young herbal genius she looked up to so much - and she was the shortest of her group of friends other than him.

"Good morning, Ryan," she said politely.

Serious dark eyes turned her way. "Good morning, Mizi." Ryan blinked, then carried his burdens to a work table. He was never one much for words,

14

not finding conversation simple. Usually he didn't know what to say unless it was to answer medical questions. Mizi smiled. Ryan was likely to miss her and not know how to say it. That would be a little sad, too.

She walked over to his table as he pulled out a mortar and pestle. "Ryan," she hesitated, not really sure how to say it herself, actually. He paused and turned to her, recognizing her hesitation as something different. He *was* very good at that much. Even if he couldn't say things well, he did know how to be a good physician, recognizing the smallest things in others that could give him clues they might not be able to tell him.

Mizi put her hand lightly on the table. "I need to ask for a leave of absence," she said quietly.

Ryan's eyebrows went up and he immediately had a rather stricken and worried look. She sighed to herself. "I'll still be here in the castle and watching over Miss Ilena, but my goals require me to focus on a new set of research. I've Rei's approval, if you'll grant me yours."

Ryan took in the information and processed it. "How long?" he finally asked in child-like questioning.

"Miss Ilena estimates half a year or so, with duties after that, although I should be able to return to part time here then," Mizi told him as best she could.

Ryan was surprised. "Studies with Miss Ilena?"

Mizi nodded. She wasn't sure how much to say, but she didn't like keeping her friend in the dark, really. "You know I ...l-love Rei." She could feel the heat rise to say it out loud to him.

Ryan blinked, then nodded soberly.

Mizi swallowed, then firmed up and said as calmly as she could, "If I want to become his princess they say I only have that long to earn the trust of the lords. Miss Ilena has agreed to help me do that, but it will be a full-time effort between now and then." Her face fell. "I can't lose, Ryan. I have to try. It's been so long already."

Five and more years she'd been trying to grow stronger on her own. Five and more years to fall more and more deeply in love with Rei and yet get no closer to him. Five long years - two of them not even near him while Ryan and she studied at Kouzanshi university. She *had* to do this, or she would have to leave. Her hand on the table clenched as her right hand rose to cover her heart and the pain it was feeling, the fingers curling lightly around as if to hold it gently.

A warm hand came very lightly on her fist on the table. "I understand, Mizi." She blinked into the dark eyes that looked into hers earnestly. "There are enough assistants here to cover all the shifts. I was thinking of opening up another test for apprentices, but I'll hold it until you can be back to help."

"Thank you, Ryan. I'm sure if there were a medical emergency and I was needed, I would come. I don't plan on leaving forever, I just need the time right now." He gave a nod and took his hand back.

Mizi took a deep breath to recover. "I'll also still be helping with Miss Ilena's surgery and watching over her recovery. I need to go and talk to Doctor Elliot. Would you have time to do that now before you become busy?" Once Ryan got into his work, he was often hard to call back out of it, he focused so well. "Miss Ilena has asked if we could use the tincture of the Little Death again. I told her I'd discuss it with him."

Doctor Elliot was the researcher who had been experimenting with the illicit street drug. Ryan's eyes lit up. He'd read Ilena's report of how it had been used in Tokumade to protect the householders from the Earl's rage and was keenly interested in knowing more. "I'll come," he said immediately.

"Thank you, Ryan," Mizi said respectfully. They didn't have far to go. Doctor Elliot had been given a lab on the opposite side of the wing with the other castle surgeons.

The office spaces that seated four on the Medical department side held only one surgeon on their side. They were part office, having desks and bookshelves in a corner of the room, and part medical room, having a bed in the middle that could be used to work on patients that needed full surgical attention.

There was a little rivalry between the two halves of the wing, but both were essential to keeping the people of the castle healthy and alive and they were often assistants to each other on the worst cases.

Doctor Elliot's lab was about half-way down the long side of the wing on the Surgery side. Mizi knocked. They were called in and she opened the door, then let Ryan enter first and closed the door behind them. "Good morning!" Doctor Elliot was turning around from the bed, a tool in hand. A smile came on his face.

He was a thin man, already hunched over from his work. He blinked through the spectacles perched on his nose. A sudden nervous look came over his face. "Ah...."

Mizi and Ryan only just then came to realize he was in the middle of working on not a patient, but a cadaver of a woman on the table. Like most researchers, Doctor Elliot hadn't really considered his state and position when he'd invited them in.

"I'm sorry," he quickly put down his tool on the table and pulled a sheet up over the form on the bed.

"It's okay," Ryan said calmly. "We're researchers, too."

Mizi smiled. While it had been shocking to see and understand what was going on, they did understand that much very well. Ryan had been working hard to learn how to put others at ease and had used that skill very naturally just then. Mizi was rather proud of him for it. "We're sorry to interrupt," she said politely. "I'm sure you're anxious to begin helping Miss Ilena."

"Well, yes," Doctor Elliot rubbed his hands nervously together as he walked to meet them closer to the door. "Mistress Ilena is already rather impatient, and really, the grafts for the tendon I have aren't getting any fresher the longer we have to postpone the surgery. I'd very much like to have the surgery sooner rather than later. Do you know if Master Ore has been able to requisition a larger room for her?"

Mizi and Ryan both shook their heads. "He surely has, though," Mizi reassured the surgeon. "I've just not had opportunity to ask which one yet."

"Good, good. What can I do for you today?" Doctor Elliot looked between the two of them, his pale grey eyes darting between them.

Mizi presented her question. "Miss Ilena has asked if the Little Death can be used for the surgery. She thinks that the hybernative time would be the best time to perform the surgery. While I agree that it did help Doctor Bonner when he performed the surgery to set the bones in her hip, we had complications early on from the lowering of the body temperature that phase causes.

"The expected infection blossomed very quickly. Only because he had to go in and perform the surgery anyway so he could remove the infection helped her recover properly. I don't particularly like the pain phase either, since the additional pain of the surgeries seem to make it more severe, but she's told me that it's all about the same, with the surgery pain at the beginning more painful in the main."

Doctor Elliot looked away. "Yes, that phase is particularly difficult. I would imagine she wouldn't care, and much preferred the natural decrease of pain the end result gives during the day."

Mizi nodded with a little wry smile. "Yes, she does like that part rather well. I found I only needed to give her the tincture to help relive pain in the evenings. The Little Death quite helped her not feel the pain during the days."

Doctor Elliot gave Mizi a studious look. "I would like to see your research notes from that time, if I may include them with my own paper?"

Mizi nodded. "I'm sure we could sit down for an hour or so after Miss Ilena has recovered."

"Thank you," Doctor Elliot said politely. He was finishing up writing his research report on his use of the Little Death in tincture form, rather than straight granular form, for medical uses.

It was used in granular form by nightwalkers who didn't want to feel the pain of their fights on the street - or the pain of their miserable lives. Once they started taking it, if they didn't get more, they died, though, the same as if they took too much in one dose. Doctor Elliot had discovered how to wean users of the drug off of it without killing them. That was exciting knowledge that medics needed to know all over Suiran, where the drug was in highest use.

Ryan said, "If you decide to use it, I would very much like to shadow you to learn the process you've discovered."

Doctor Elliot nodded thoughtfully. "I could use one more run-through of my notes to make sure they're properly understandable to someone who isn't as familiar with it as me, if you'd be willing to be my tester?"

Ryan gave a firm nod of complete interest and Doctor Elliot smiled. He put his hand to his chin and rubbed it while he thought. "I think, since we'll be going in cleanly and in a clean room, we're less likely to have infections than in the last case, where it was a dirty wound to begin with. We'll also be here to watch her closely.

"Really, I'm more concerned about graft rejection. Those reactions can be very fast and a decrease of the body's ability to fight infections would be beneficial in that case, so that I have time to get back in and remove the bad piece and replace it." Ryan and Mizi both nodded their understanding of that point.

"Mistress Ilena is well familiar with the process of the drug as a whole and isn't afraid of it," Doctor Elliot continued. "The entire process to wean her off of it would only be a week, perhaps less, since I could use even a lower dose than what I needed to use to have the sleeptalking phase sufficient to ease the mind of Earl Shicchi.

"If you're willing to allow the use of the drug, I can calculate the amount I would need to use rather easily and have the follow on draughts prepared early." He blushed a little, "Ah, that is, if some could be obtained for me. I don't actually generally carry it on my person."

Ryan held up a calming hand. "I already have some locked in the restricted use cabinet. You'd only need to fill out a requisition form and get a proper signature." He looked at Mizi with a questioning look.

"Rei has said that he'll approve it if we all agree it could be used effectively and would be helpful," Mizi informed them.

Both men relaxed and were satisfied. If it had the signature of the Regent himself, that was sufficient. They returned to the infirmary for Doctor Elliot to fill out the paperwork. Mizi took the requisition form, saying she would take it to Rei at lunch herself and return it to Doctor Elliot on her return from lunch.

By the time Mizi arrived in Ilena's room, Ilena had been seen to by Leah and Rio and they'd finished their breakfast. As Leah pushed the breakfast cart back out into the hallway to be picked up by the kitchen staff, Mizi handed her list to Ilena, who was sitting slightly propped up for the day. Mizi sat in the chair set by Ilena's bed for her so they could talk comfortably.

"Oh, a braid!" Mizi noticed while waiting for Ilena to read the list.

"It really is the best way to manage it," Rio said conversationally. "It's really too long to be undone like it was. Mistress Ilena complained quite a lot since it took a lot of work to get the snarls out of it."

"Yes," Mizi blushed a little, "we did find the length a bit difficult to deal with. She never did ask, though," she frowned at Ilena who only shrugged since she was focused on the list.

"Well," Rio drew Mizi's attention again, "likely because she's rather particular about who brushes it."

"Since she was a child, she's never sat well for a brushing," Leah commented dryly as she passed behind Mizi to rejoin Rio in the far corner of the small room. "Rio is the first one she was able to be patient with and really train. Now it's a reward for good behavior to have Rio brush her hair."

Ilena's ears went faintly pink but she didn't comment. Mizi smiled. "I'll remember that."

Rio smiled back. "Well, and she's been willing to let me play with it as well. It's such a long length that I can put it up in all kinds of fun ways, and then be surprised at what happens when it turns out to be far heavier than I thought and what I imagined all comes tumbling right back out."

Mizi sighed just a little. "I can't get my hair to grow any longer than this," she ran a hand down the short ponytail at the back of her head.

"May I, Mistress Mizi?" Rio asked politely, her eyes brightly looking at the red hair.

Mizi glanced at Ilena. "You'll have to have it up a lot in front of the nobles," Ilena commented calmly. "If that's the only hair-do you know how to do, I'll loan you Rio for a little while. You should be thinking about what your maid will be doing for you."

Mizi froze upright. "M-my maid?"

Ilena's tawny eyes pinned Mizi in place most sternly. "Yes, Princess Mizi. A princess has more than one, but I know you need to get used to the idea. You can get used to Rio playing with your hair and talking to you about clothing now and by the time you need your own you might have some idea of what to look for." When Mizi slumped and nodded her head obediently, Ilena's eyes went back to the list, releasing her.

Mizi sighed. There were going to be a lot of changes she wasn't quite ready for. She was glad Ilena understood well enough to have a way to ease her into them. It wasn't too bad. Rio knew how to brush with a firm hand, but in a gentle way, and she knew how to keep light conversation flowing to distract Mizi.

She also made it into a rather fun process as well, since she asked for Mizi's opinions as she showed Mizi what she was doing in the hand mirror Leah produced. They managed to come up with a few simple but pretty looks by the time Ilena was ready to discuss the list. Mizi felt like Ilena had allowed the hairdressing lesson to go longer, just to get in the training for Mizi.

Ilena was rather like that. Every little thing Mizi would go through in the room would be pointing her in the direction she wanted to go, even if it was gentle and a surprise at the end that it had been a lesson.

"Now then," Ilena finally said, holding the list out for Leah to take. "I'm sure you have thoughts and questions on that list, but I'd like you to hold them for now. I want you to see Rei's list first without my comments. Once we have both lists, then we'll discuss them to put them together into one syllabus.

"For now, we're still at the beginning of even learning what we are and how we fit into the picture of the castle. Let's begin where we left off yesterday, shall we?" Leah handed a book to Mizi. "But first a quick quiz of yesterday's material."

Mizi sighed. Ilena's quizzes were very detailed, as detailed as examinations. How she remembered so many little things was beyond Mizi to know. Still, they would both have them known very well by the time they were done. It was a good thing yesterday's books had been about the castle departments generally. It was a lot of broad coverage without such details. Mizi could remember those easily. Details took more practice and study to remember.

Leah handed over a sheaf of paper and Mizi looked at it. It was the list of the names of every department head, followed by a description of what they looked like and which building of the campus the department was in and what room or set of rooms, then sublisted every person in the department and their title and roles, and *their* description and desk location. "The list of their family's and their backgrounds should come in another day or two," Leah said calmly.

Mizi could feel the blood leave her head. "The *whole* set of departments?" she asked faintly.

"The whole castle in the end, Princess Mizi," Ilena said calmly. "This will be your home and you will be the head female of it. You must know who lives here and what they do, even if you don't always remember it all in the end. We'll focus the memorization on those we must remember for sure, but you'll have been introduced in some way or the other to everyone before Rei even announces you."

Mizi swallowed. It was no wonder Ilena had forewarned her she was going to have a lot of hard work to do. The castle staff and the servants and the lords and their staff and servants all added up to a rather large number - enough to be a large village on it's own.

Still, she knew it was possible so she took a deep breath and nodded she was ready for Ilena's first quizzing question. She had to refer to the notes a lot as Ilena also asked her to now add in the "who" and "where" as they went.

CHAPTER 2 Ilena Unrestrained

After spending a morning studying together, Mizi went to lunch with Rei. Rio fed Ilena lunch in her room. Rio was cleaning up the lunch when all of a sudden she noticed Ilena's face had tears streaking down it. "Mistress!?" Rio was concerned. "What is it?"

Ilena's face scrunched up into a small child's perverse look, and from her mouth burst an infantile tantrum. "I WANT A BATH! WAAAHHH! I'm so tired of being filthy. I don't want anyone to even come visit any more. And I'm going to have to lie here another six weeks before I get to have one! WAAAHHH!"

"Well, Mistress Ilena, you could have just said," Leah said, looking at her bemused. "We have been keeping you clean, you know."

"I KNOWwww, *sob*. But it's n-not the saaa-ame! It's not a good (*sniff*) soapy scrub with a looo-*hic*-onng *hic* soothing *hic* (*sniff*) soak after. I feel like a (*sniff*) pig that's been *hi-ic* wallowing too looong. AAAHhhh!"

"It's alright, Mistress. If you think you can sit up enough, maybe we can bring in some washtubs." Leah looked at Rio with a significant look. "The room could use a good scrubbing down, too."

Rio perked up, "Yes, Mistress Ilena. We can clean out the room and have the tubs and water brought in, and the spilled water can be used to wash the room clean, too. Then both of you will be clean together."

Leah added, "And while you're not in the bed, we'll clean the bed clothes and give the bedding a good airing out."

"YEAY! A BATH! A BATH!" Ilena clapped her hands as their attempt to reverse her tantrum was finally effective. It didn't change her sudden age reversion, but cheer was better than tears. "The room and me get a bath!"

The guards outside Ilena's medical recovery room, who normally found their job quite boring, except for all of the big hats who kept going in and out, decided that today was a good day. They would finally have a funny story to tell when they got off work. The younger one, Hue, who happened to have a teen-age sister, was having a hard time stifling laughter. His older partner, Sailte, finally said, "Go on, just get it over with." The younger let loose, laughing until he teared.

When he recovered, Sailte looked at him and said, "I thought it was refreshing. At my house all my wife gets to hear from the kids is, 'NOOOO! I DON'T WANNA TAKE A BATH!' as they run off. She makes me chase them down and carry them in. We still don't know why they do it since once they're in they have so much fun we can't get them –" He cut off as the door behind them opened and they jumped to attention.

"Mistress Ilena says thanks for the laugh, she's glad she could brighten your day, and you've just volunteered yourselves to help with the project." Leah glared at them slightly.

"Ehhhh?" said Hue, not understanding how they could help since they were supposed to stay put.

Sailte knew they'd acted inappropriately and was apologetic. "Sorry. We'll help."

"Come introduce yourselves properly," Ilena ordered, her voice still petulant, but not particularly angry. "But stand over there."

One at a time, they stepped just into the room, bowed and introduced themselves. Ilena introduced herself to them, "I'm Ilena, Director of Intelligence for Regent Rei. This is my secretary Leah, and my personal maid Rio." They each bowed slightly as their names were said.

"They're in need of instructions as to how to go about requesting help from the general castle servants so they don't have to do all of the work themselves or it will be a two day process, and I don't have that kind of time. As I also need to know the house rules, since I've come from being the steward of an Earldom but haven't been employed in a castle of Ryokudo until now, please, will you tell all of us?"

Hue and Sailte looked at each other. Sailte said to Hue, "I'll leave it to you."

Hue smiled. "Okay!"

Sailte turned back to guard duty, but listened to the conversation behind him. Hue launched into a description of how the Nijou Castle household was run, sprinkled with anecdotes and commentary on specific persons. Occasionally Sailte cleared his throat and Hue went from being respectfully casual to more formal until the person passing by the room had gone out of earshot.

As he was winding down, Hue suddenly stopped and said, "But you could have just requested that the castle steward come and talk to you, or one of his staff?"

Ilena smiled at him, "I suppose, and there are many I would like to invite in to ask many questions to, but I don't think it would have been as fun to listen to." He laughed, embarrassed.

She switched to a pout, "Besides, how could I invite *anyone* here to visit when it's a less desirable place to visit than a pig sty? And who has ever seen the high office of Director brought to such a low state? I certainly couldn't bring such shame upon it." She turned to Leah, "Plleeeaaase?! Can we start now, *please*?!"

Leah sighed, "Mistress...."

"Hello! What's going on?" Mizi had returned from her lunch with Rei. Hue jumped and returned to his proper position.

"Ah, Mistress Mizi," Leah bowed to her. "Mistress Ilena was just begging for a bath."

"Not a bath," frowned Ilena. "A get-really-soapy-and-soak-bath."

"Ahh," Mizi entered the room and closed the door behind her. "And how were you proposing to accomplish that?"

22

"We were thinking we could bring in wash tubs, fill them with warm water, and have Mistress Ilena sit in one for soaping and rinsing, and the other would be for her to soak in." Leah answered.

Rio added, "We're sure it will put water everywhere, so we were thinking we could scrub the room while we were at it."

"And change the bedding," added Leah.

"Please, Princess Mizi? I'm going to have to lie here in my filth again for six more weeks. I really can't take it any more," Ilena begged her mistress.

Mizi was thoughtful. "I believe you're only just now able to sit up at all. Even if we give you your bath, you won't likely be able to sit long enough for much of a soak. Even just a thorough cleaning may overtax you." Ilena was looking crestfallen and panicked at the same time.

Mizi tried harder to mollify her. "But I can certainly understand your desire to be clean, and have a clean room. ...And another six weeks is indeed a long time. ...If you want it badly enough that you're willing to go through the pain you may have to suffer, then you may have one...in two days." That was the actual date Doctor Bonner had given them for Ilena to be able to be up and bearing weight on her hip.

"YEAY! A bath! A bath!" Ilena clapped her hands.

"Thank you, Mistress Mizi. That will give us time to prepare." Leah said gratefully. She'd been very concerned about what Ilena would have been like if she'd been refused.

-o-o-o-

Other people had other plans. Very shortly after lunch, Rei received a note from Doctor Elliot. He informed the Prince that he would be done with his research the following day and would be prepared to perform the experimental surgery on Ilena the day after that.

That evening, Rei and his aides wrapped up their summaries from the first set of cases against Earl Shicchi and Rei ordered Ore to leave the castle to retrieve the second set of witnesses, allowing him the two day lead time Grandfather had requested.

Since Grandfather would be visiting Ilena after the dinner hour, Ore thought that it would be convenient to just go have dinner with Ilena again, and be present when Grandfather arrived. Rei liked the idea of an excuse to have dinner with Mizi again...and besides, he was supposed to be making time for her, as well as following the orders of his court healer to eat and rest appropriately. So, for the second evening in a row, the two arrived at Ilena's room for the evening meal.

After they began eating, Rei told them that Doctor Elliot had sent him the note requesting that the surgery occur in two days. "We're also ready to begin the second set of cases against Earl Shicchi. I need to have Ore leave to collect the second set of witnesses at that time as well. Ilena will have Leah and Rio to watch over her and Mizi and Ryan to assist Doctor Elliot with her recovery. That should be sufficient."

He looked up from his plate to horrified looks all around the room. Then everyone objected all at once and Ilena began to weep. Rio ran to her mistress to comfort her. Rei begged for quiet. When he finally had it, he asked Mizi to be the first to explain.

"That's the first day Ilena will be able to sit up for any length of time. She's desperate for a good cleansing bath and soak. I promised her she could have one on that day. To ask any woman to go twelve full weeks without being washed thoroughly and allowed a good soaking is a very hard thing." All the women in the room nodded. "Not to mention unhealthy."

"Regent Rei," Leah added informationally, "Mistress Ilena had her first tantrum over it today." Ilena blushed.

He looked at her in surprise. "Ah, I see. And Ore, what is your objection?"

Ore rubbed his head making his short black hair stand on end, not sure how to object. He looked at Ilena. "Ah...I'd been hoping to be here for the surgery, so that I would know that she'd been properly seen to and so that I wouldn't be overly distracted from my duty."

"Hmm." Having an Ore who was no longer his own agent was a different thing for Rei to remember when it came to orders that sent him out of the castle. "Mizi, could Ilena's bath be tomorrow? I would really like Ore to leave in two days. If the surgery were in the morning to midday time frame on that day, Ore could leave in the afternoon or evening when Doctor Elliot says she's stable."

Mizi considered Rei's request. "Could we have Ore help us? The less Ilena has to do in moving around, the better. He has the strength to lift her."

Rei nodded, then had an idea. "Would you be willing to come to the office with him after the bath is done and learn some of his tasks to help him make up for the time he wasn't able to be there? Maybe there's something he can teach you that will help his desk to not become overly full by the time he returns again, even if it's something small."

"Oohh, Master, I like that idea," Ore approved.

"Yes, I would be happy to do that," Mizi was pleased with the idea also.

"Ilena?" Rei looked at her. She nodded, although she wasn't quite capable of speech yet. "Okay, then let's do that. Shall we eat now?" He smiled at everyone, and they went back to their meal.

-o-o-o-

"That felt rather like a family gathering, didn't it? With Master as father and Mistress as mother," Ore said to Ilena after Rei and Mizi had been picked up by Andrew and Mina. He had his fingers interlaced behind his head.

"Mmm, I guess. I'm afraid I wouldn't really know, though," Ilena answered. She sounded tired already.

"Has it already been a long day?" he asked her. She nodded.

"Um, Master Ore," Leah asked tentatively, "Is it alright that Mistress Mizi asked for your assistance tomorrow?"

24

Ore smiled at her. "Yes. I've been Ilena's nurse since the beginning, after all. It isn't strange to have her ask."

Rio's eyes went round and Leah looked like she would rather have heard a different answer. "It's okay," Ilena reassured them. They had no choice but to accept the odd reversal of roles.

The next morning was a flurry of activity. Large wash tubs were brought to the room. Then water, hot from the kitchen fires and cold from the castle well, was brought bucket by bucket until the first tub was full. The maids got Ilena prepared, and Ore gently lifted her from her bed and placed her in it, having removed his jacket and rolled up the sleeves of his shirt for the duration of the efforts.

"You appear to have been losing weight," he frowned at her.

"Well, it's difficult to maintain it when I can only eat a select menu daily, and I'm not active enough to keep my muscles properly toned," Ilena agreed.

Mizi frowned as she began to scrub Ilena gently. Her sleeves were also rolled up as much as possible. "Indeed, I can see too much of your ribs. I think, once you're able to eat again, we'll have to make sure you're getting food in between meals, or we'll lose you to starvation before you can recover from your hip."

"I'll see to the kitchen, then, on my way to the laundry," Leah said as she stripped the bedding off Ilena's bed.

Rio and Ore moved the desk and chairs from the room, in preparation for scrubbing it down. Leah took the bedding and dirty clothing to the castle laundry, returning with clean linens about the time Ore was moving Ilena to the soaking washtub. Rio began to scrub the room with the soapy water. Leah left the clean linens on the desk outside the room to keep them clean and joined in the young maid's efforts, saying that she'd informed the kitchen of the meal change.

Ore paused in his crouch next to Ilena to watch them, then said to the maids, "I'm sure your efforts are appreciated by the castle staff, but there's actually another option to putting Ilena back into that bed."

"Oh?" Even Mizi was curious.

"Doctor Elliot asked for a larger room, both for Ilena's surgery and recovery. I could go get the key now and she could be moved after her soak. Then she would only have to be up this once."

The ladies all looked at each other and nodded. "Yes, please, Ore, if you could do that now?" Mizi asked. The maids didn't mind cleaning the room now that they'd started, especially now that they had the reward of being in a bigger room by afternoon.

Ilena sighed contentedly as she shifted slightly in the warm water. "A bath and a bigger room. Well, maybe it's okay, then, tomorrow."

Ore smiled and put his hand on her head. "Worried?"

"Well, I have learned that the practice of a thing is always more difficult than the theory of it. I know Doctor Elliot will do his best, and I want to do my best also." She smiled bravely back at him.

"That's good," he encouraged her. He rose from his crouch and said, "I'll go get the key and open the room, then I'll come back to help Ilena out of the tub."

When he returned, the room was clean, the bed made, and the furniture returned. Towels were set out on one of the chairs, waiting to receive Ilena. He carefully lifted her out of the now tepid water, and set her on the chair. Carefully, he dried her, refusing to let the other ladies help, although the maids were scandalized. Ilena just closed her eyes and sighed happily.

When she was dry, Ore stepped back and the maids swarmed her as they helped her get dressed. When they needed her to stand briefly, Ore stepped back in to support her.

When Ilena was ready, Ore picked her up. "Well, then, Princess, are you ready for your new throne?" Leah gave him a suspicious look but he ignored it.

With the guards going before them, they made somewhat of a processional. Ore had already turned the top covers down on one of the two beds, so he just had to place Ilena carefully in the center of it. When she was comfortably settled, he covered her with the top covers.

Ilena took a deep breath and snuggled down into the bed. "Ahh...This is sooo much better. ...Mmmm." Her retinue for the day smiled and sighed with relief and tiredness. "Thank you, Princess Mizi, Ore, Leah, Rio," she said.

Almost before they could say "You're welcome", she was asleep. There'd been a lot of excitement in that one morning for a body still in recovery.

Leah and Rio promised to see that she ate when she awoke and Mizi and Ore returned to the wing their quarters were in to get changed into clothing that wasn't wet, in preparation for going to the Rose office.

-o-o-o-

When Ore and Mizi arrived at the Rose office, they found everyone but Tairn was gone from the office. Rei had official Regency business in the early afternoon he was receiving in the throne room. There was a cold lunch waiting for them, however.

After they ate, Ore began showing Mizi what his daily tasks were. Several messages and packets of reports came in so Ore also taught her how to tell which ones went to which person in the room, or were sent across the hall to the Rosebud office, although paper traffic usually went up, not down.

At some point, a message in a folder came that was bound with a white ribbon. "Don't open the bound ones," Ore taught her. "Those are for Master's eyes only. This one is from the soldiers. You can tell that by the white ribbon. It's probably related to the matter against Earl Shicchi, but we aren't to know unless Master tells us." He handed it to her to put on Rei's desk.

26

"Gold ribbon is for King Brother, Master's is blue ribbon like his eyes." He smiled at her. "If Mistress had a ribbon, it would be red, like Mistress' hair."

"What color would Ilena's ribbon be?" Mizi asked.

Ore looked at her in surprise. "I don't know? What color would Mistress suggest?"

"Hmm. Green is available.... Black would be most intuitive, but seems inauspicious." If they were going by hair and eye colors, the black would represent Ilena's long black hair. "...Purple, maybe?"

"Well, Mistress could ask her what color she would like." Ore shrugged. Mizi nodded. If she could remember, she would.

-o-o-o-

Rei's business kept him from returning to the office until nearly dinner time. They decided to eat dinner in the Rose office together, since they had missed lunch together, and Mizi and Ore were in the middle of a thing she wanted to stay and help finish. Before eating, Rei read the important messages, including the one with the white ribbon, but he didn't comment on it.

As everyone returned to work after dinner, Rei walked to the worktable, asking Andrew to pull out the maps of central Suiran. Andrew set one on the table and Rei held it down while Andrew pulled out another and they repeated the process for a third. Rei frowned in concentration and looked over the top map, his finger tracing up to the area north of Tokumade Earldom. He looked at a few other things, then flipped through the other maps, putting his thoughts together.

Rei looked up. "Do you have the reports from the field?" he asked Mina. She handed them to him. He flipped through them, reading some passages from a few, then reviewed the map again. Handing the reports back to Mina, he walked to his desk. "Okay. Andrew, get the maps and bring them. We'll go confirm a few things with Ilena."

"Ah, Master," Ore interjected, hearing the name of his partner, "we moved her to her new room in preparation for tomorrow." Rei nodded confirmation he'd understood.

As they headed out the door, Andrew said to Mina, "It feels like we're already heading into battle, just preparing for a little conversation."

Rei looked back at him, "We are. You've already seen it - she's as bad as my brother."

They looked at him, a little taken aback, then Mina said, not really meaning it, "Poor Rei."

When they arrived at Ilena's new room, Rei had Andrew pull out the map of central Suiran and place it on her lap. They commenced discussing actual locations she had seen and he had received reports of.

Andrew and Mina were progressively impressed that Rei and Ilena stood nearly toe to toe in understanding and discussing possible strategies and how to use the land, time, and resources to their advantage. It was their first time to really be in the room with Ilena when she was a fully active participant in the proceedings, save for a few very brief times before. As Rei wrapped up a point and considered which one to bring up next, Andrew asked Ilena where she'd learned how to militarily plan.

She looked up at him, and he saw a light in her eyes that reminded him sharply of King Sasou. She had decided he was testing her and had just as quickly risen to the challenge of the game as Sasou would have. He unconsciously straightened to attention in reaction. Rei sighed but didn't interfere.

To Mina, it felt like they'd just entered a list field. *It's going to be an interesting visit with this person Rei has recently brought to the castle because there is no helping Andrew.* She relaxed into fighting ready stance.

"Mister Andrew," Ilena opened with a bland smile, "do you read all of Ore's reports to Master Rei? I'm sure he's been meticulous in them of everything," there was a slight emphasis on "everything", "I've said in his hearing." *That's a fairly powerful beginning,* thought Mina.

Andrew answered, "Yes, I do."

"Then, if you'll recall Ore's report from two days ago," Rei frowned and Mina all of a sudden felt a little queasy, "you'll remember that I explained that Earl Shicchi has been steadily increasing his personal army for a number of years. And he's been keeping them active, as Ore reported from the first personal interrogation of myself by Prince Rei.

"As I'm sure was included in his report in which I explained how we learned the method of using small levels of the drug 'the Little Death' in a controlled manner, you understand already that I was almost never out of sight, or at least ear-shot, of the Earl. It is, with very little calculation I'm sure, certainly understandable that I should have learned from his own war table."

Ara! She attacked us, all four, in one stroke! I thought she'd leave it at just Andrew. Mina looked at Rei. It looked like he was thinking he might end the game of wits right there, but Andrew had practice with that sort of thrust and didn't flinch.

"Ore's report from yesterday did include Earl Shicchi's increase of his men. And certainly we have all been kept busy reinvestigating his hand in all of the cases you offered as proof for a number of weeks now. If he kept you by his side in all things, as you said, then you would certainly have learned how he thinks strategically if you were paying attention."

Andrew took a breath, then slightly cocked his head. The next was not his kind of thing - he usually defended, not attacked. He *preferred* people being straight with him, of course. "However, your report from when you were in the garrison in Osterly stated that the Earl was not known to be particularly crafty or intelligent himself. So it seemed to me that perhaps an education at his war table would have been somewhat lacking."

Ilena smiled. *Eh?* The move surprised Mina, who was used to this kind of battle. Ilena had just rewarded Andrew at a point where most who played this game would have affected a slightly offended look. "Indeed. The truth is that Earl Shicchi is one of the most predictable of strategists there is. If there is anything that could ever endear me to him, it is that one point."

Her face went back to pleasantly neutral. "However, he has the craftiness of the worst sort of wolf, make no mistake. You have been hearing me talk with Master Rei confidently about what are the possible options the Earl will consider, and a few his supporters will suggest, because I've heard them discuss at the table many times what they would do to escape this or that situation." She fell silent and looked at Andrew expectantly.

He considered what she'd said, unsure. She'd answered all the points he'd attacked with, but nothing more. She hadn't actually answered his original question. To accept it as it was was to admit defeat and lack of intelligence. To press on would be to appear to be a bully, which he wasn't.

Mina stepped up beside Andrew. "Of course, there could be no better person for Rei to be able to consult with in this matter. However, it's apparent from your ability to keep up with Rei's natural talent that you have either natural strategic talent yourself, or you've spent a good deal of time working to sharpen your skills."

She opened the door for any of us to get involved, and then made the required opening. She's testing all of us. Mina understood, although she was worried that Andrew didn't. Maybe she'd explain it to him later. She opened her mouth to continue but Ilena held up her hand.

"Pause a moment, Miss Mina." Mina was so surprised her mouth hung open for a moment. There was a bite in Ilena's eyes, like a rebuke. "Not later, now."

"Wa..'now'?" Mina was quite confused.

"Do you really want him by your side?" Ilena challenged her quietly.

Mina shook her head in confusion. "What?"

Ilena waited a moment until Mina recovered a bit more. "Doesn't he need to be able to understand so he can support you in *all* things?" Mina's heart froze. Rei shifted and Ilena shot him a venomous look. He held very still.

Mina's mind subconsciously ran through what she'd just been thinking and the conversation up to that point, looking at all the patterns and paths. One thing was apparent. Ilena was not predictable, and was therefore very likely very dangerous. How had Ilena known what she was thinking? It wasn't even related to the topic at hand.

Finally her mind began to see how the new board had been laid. If she said "no" now, she would lose, and not just to Ilena in this new conversation, but everything she was planning for her future. Ilena would end the new conversation immediately, of course, and that might feel good, but she would lose Andrew's trust and she would be admitting that a weaker Andrew was sufficient to stand by her side.

Remembering that this was the person who was determined to move Rei and Mizi forward, Mina felt several emotions run through her. Ilena was offering to do the same for her, starting here and now, without even asking. It was a prayer fulfilled, but it also made her very angry.

She wanted to throw that anger at Ilena and end the game immediately, and in the past she would have, but in this game one never allowed anger to take over until it was well considered first, and well deserved. And, ...she really was desperate. The same desperation had driven her to do a thing she had never done before and play Ore's game to cheer everyone up - and it had worked.

If she allowed herself to do another thing she'd never done before, would it work? Could she trust this person? ...Or did that matter? Maybe it just mattered what she herself wanted.

Andrew shifted, but Rei held up a cautionary finger, telling him to "hold his position". Rei could read Mina pretty well by now and had seen the emotional play go through her, even though she hadn't moved.

Mina turned to Andrew. "Miss Ilena has...offered...to turn this into a training match, rather than continue on in the traditional method of testing by words, although that will also occur as we continue, of course. By telling you this, I'm accepting her offer, which is in itself also a challenge. Thus, we are now playing two boards, as it were."

She waited until it looked like Andrew understood that much. Running back in her mind to where Ilena had stopped her and her last thought, she said, "I stepped in not because you didn't know what to say, but because she'd interrupted the typical 'thrust and parry' you were engaged in with a 'block'. She'd addressed your 'thrust', then retreated, not attacking, but also presenting nothing to you."

Andrew nodded. "That's what it felt like, yes."

"A verbal 'block' is just as difficult to overcome as a swordsman's is, when the fighting is one-on-one. I don't think it efficient to go into how to deal with it at this time, just so you understand if you're presented with it again, you'll know how to consider it." Andrew nodded again while Mina thought of how to explain the next step that occurred.

"At the beginning, your question to her was a challenge to step into the fighting list. That is, you were the first to make a thrust. She accepted it merely by the look she gave you, the one that made you come to attention." Andrew tried to hide a shudder. "Then she opened with an implied slur, followed by an unexpected attack."

Andrew's brow wrinkled slightly. "Unexpected? It sounded like a fairly normal attack to me."

"Did it? Whom did she attack?" Andrew tried to remember.

"If you'll remember Ore's report from yesterday...," Ilena prompted.

"Ah. Ore." Andrew said.

"Yes, but, harder to distinguish, she also attacked Rei, you, and me - trying to ferret out where we fit into Rei's hierarchy - did Rei let us read the report? That was unexpected because she immediately widened the challenge field to be a one-on-four challenge, with her as the challenger. It's considered to be as ambitious and potentially overly prideful as if it had been done in the list." Ilena inclined her head slightly in acknowledgment of the slight scolding.

Mina continued, "It also has the same intent. She was announcing that she desired to have the challenge to be not just a simple repartee in which she would eventually answer your question, but that she preferred to move it immediately into a test of how the four of us work as a group. Because she made the challenge with three of us present, she opened the list for any of us to answer to her at any time. If she hadn't, you would have had to fight her on your own until you lost."

Ilena raised her hand, "May I?" Mina paused, then remembering this was Ilena's offer, nodded. "Mister Andrew, your answer was flawless and received high marks." He blushed a little. "You defended all four of you very well with a smooth delivery, and wrapped it up with a light compliment. It was a delight to receive." Now, even Rei was looking at her like she was a little crazy.

"The pause before your attack let me know that you weren't as used to verbally attacking as to defense, but the method and point were appropriate and you continued to carry the delivery sufficiently well, thus the delivery, or thrust, was awarded average points."

Mina picked the lesson back up at Ilena's pause. "At the end of your delivery, Miss Ilena again moved unexpectedly. The typical defense would have been to frown slightly as if offended. But instead, Miss Ilena smiled." Mina cocked her head. "How did that make you feel? When she smiled and then agreed with you, Andrew?"

"Ah, it was...camaraderie?"

Mina nodded. "She gave you a 'reward'...mmm...like an opponent in a friendly match who takes a particularly difficult attack to execute, then pauses and congratulates you for having pulled it off well, before returning to the fight."

"Oh! I see." Andrew nodded.

"Then she followed that up with a warning and a block. Like the opponent on the list would swing his sword in a circle to loosen the hand, then step back as if to attack, yet instead sets their shield and waits to see what you do next."

"Right," Andrew answered immediately, "And I could see a way that meant 'yield' and another that would be a too-aggressive attack. I didn't want to do either."

"Right," Mina nodded. "There are always more than two ways to approach, but as I said before, against a shield it's difficult to find the path alone. However, because she'd opened the list to all of us, it was...um, legal, for either Rei or I to attack, or to make an opening to attack, to deflect the shield so that you could get through it, or to defend you and attack from another side, which is what I did.

"I stepped in, respectfully redirected her attention to me, and defended you. At that point, either you or I could have made the delivery. I was about to when Miss Ilena stopped me, picked me up and put us on a completely different list. That was the third very unexpected thing she did." Her annoyance showed.

"Hah!" Rei's fist hitting his palm startled Mina and Andrew. They looked at him, and he said, "Ah, no, sorry. I didn't mean to interrupt."

Mina, looking over to Ilena, saw she was again smiling that rewarding smile. Mina sourly looked at Rei. "Looks like you've won a point. No, you've won." Rei looked at her in surprise, then over at Ilena and saw her smile that was now an honest grin.

He smiled back. "Yes, I did," he said smugly, crossing his arms. Mina ground her teeth.

"What?" Andrew asked.

"Rei has figured out the answer to your initial question to Miss Ilena. Without actively participating at all. It is annoying."

"Why?"

Mina didn't bother to hide her frustration very much. "Because she opened the challenge to all of us, each of us must understand the answer, or yield and accept that we won't know it. He's taken himself off the board just now, thus it's appropriate to consider him a traitor."

"But that's...," said Andrew confused.

Rei said, "Now, wait...I said I was sorry." Rei hurried to explain when Ilena looked at him expectantly. "Ah...I fouled out, is what really happened, Andrew. Because I exclaimed aloud, I couldn't hide the fact that I'd figured it out and stay in the game. If a player finds the answer before others do, he or she may hide that fact and use it as an advantage to aid the others in finding their way to the answer as well.

"In Mina's analogy, it would be like as if I had seen the opponent's weakness, and then applied pressure to it so that it would become easier for you two to finish off the opponent. However, to immediately state one knows when one finds out, when on a multiplayer board, or multiplayer list, when the others don't know yet and can't see it, means that one is stepping out of the list. It counts as an individual win, but as a penalty to the team."

"If the other challengers on the board are a team." Ilena said quietly. "If they aren't, then to announce knowledge of the answer without stating what it is, is one way to excuse oneself from the game early, a 'sideways personal defense'. Thus Miss Mina's complaint that it feels like Master Rei is a traitor and the necessity he feels to apologize that it was an accident."

Andrew creased his brow in thought, "Because Rei exclaimed, he removed himself as an ally, but he wanted to reassure Mina that he still considers himself part of our team?"

"Mmm," nodded Rei.

Mina sighed. "Rei himself still has more strength to gain here as well."

Ilena raised her eyebrow, "Perhaps, but still, he's at an advanced level." She raised her hand. "Let's return to the first list, shall we? I believe we left off with Miss Mina's defense of Mister Andrew."

Rei jumped in immediately. "Mina, you said to Ilena, 'it is apparent from your ability to keep up with Rei's natural talent that you have either natural strategic talent yourself, or you've spent a good deal of time working to sharpen your skills'. Can you answer that yourself already?"

"Eh? ...Ah...yes," Mina slumped slightly. Andrew looked confused again.

"Mister Andrew, Master Rei has just played a 'helping hand' to Miss Mina, that is he's given her the one clue she needed to figure out the answer for herself. She gains no points for having the answer, but she no longer needs to fight on the list - a neutral position, and acceptable," Ilena explained.

She scolded a little, "Master Rei technically shouldn't have done it, having removed himself from the board, but because he considers himself still on the team, it could be allowed. And under the circumstances, he probably can't help himself."

"But...doesn't that leave me alone on the board?" Andrew did the calculations.

"Does it?" she responded with a small smile. "You may choose."

"Choose?" After some thought, Andrew looked up at Ilena with a bright smile and her eyes lit up. "I yield, Miss Ilena, if you will consent to another such lesson sometime when we're all free."

The bright smile went to her lips. "Done. ...Hah! That was wonderfully done, Mister Andrew. You're skills are already well honed. It won't be long before you're able to reach your goal, I think." She looked slyly out of the corner of her eye at Mina, "Especially now that you've been given a way to think about it so that your mind can be more agile."

Mina flushed, but bowed slightly to Ilena. "Thank you, Miss Ilena."

It was a bit stiffly said, but Ilena waved it aside, "It was your doing, Miss Mina." A kind smile was on her lips. "Although I think you're now stronger for having done it, yes?"

Mina thought about that. *Am I? In having done something uncharacteristically am I stronger for it?* An insight flashed through her, and she struggled to grasp it, then she had it. "Oh! I see. I see what you saw Rei."

"And what is that, Miss Mina?" asked Ilena.

Slowly she replied, "There is strength in ...unpredictability, in...."

"Doing the unexpected," supplied Rei from his answer.

"From being flexible," said Andrew. Rei and Mina looked at Andrew in surprise.

"How did you come up with that answer?" Mina asked.

Andrew grinned at her, "Isn't that how we fight best? By being able to flexibly change our patterns against our opponent? That's what you learned from watching Earl Shicchi, isn't it Miss Ilena? When we're flexible and willing to think of the 'more than two things', we find the best answers. But even better answers are found when we're able to do that together, when we're able to face our opponent as a team, flexibly."

"Ha ha! Mister Andrew has said it best! Now if you can all put it into practice, Master Rei will be very proud of you," Ilena said happily, then she narrowed her eyes, "...but I will be prouder."

It was good to see her smile, but she was so very different from anything any on them had ever experienced before. Rei said dryly, "Ilena, that was an unexpected lecture."

Smiling still, she tipped her head, "You're welcome, Your Highness. I hope it has helped sufficiently."

Rei sighed. Ilena had intentionally misunderstood him.

Ilena turned back to Andrew. "I'll answer your question, Mister Andrew, after your own manner. If you wish, you may consider it your reward.

"Earl Shicchi is and always has been my enemy, and the enemy of Ore, whom I love. However, I was his. Therefore, I chose to use it to my advantage - I learned of him and from him. While I was required to be obedient to him, I never helped him have an advantage that I did not also exploit to his detriment. Each time he planned an attack, I planned a counter-defense to his attack that he wouldn't be able to comprehend.

"I do, indeed have inborn natural talent, *and* I also have studied most diligently to improve upon it. I believe I have yet more to learn, in particular I'll continue to learn from Master Rei." She stopped and tilted her head, looking to see what effect her words had on Andrew. "I believe I've already answered to your greater concerns for me personally. But there's another thing that I must defend to you."

She pursed her lips. "In being forthright, I'm not strong. I've learned that such words are often merely boasts with no substance, or are lies that hide truths difficult to find. So for my own defense, I've brought you to an understanding in my own way. However, I can't do the same for what still needs to be defended. Rather, it must needs be the reverse. Please forgive me."

Ilena looked at Mina, including her. "When Ore wrote of how the Earl increased his men, did he include in the report what I did with the household members who were sent away?" All three nodded. "Then please understand, we had lived many years together as prisoners in that place. Because I stood in their defense as best I could, always increasing in strength, I became 'Mother'. But even a mother needs strengthening.

"Grandfather was such a one. He was the original House Steward when I came to the House. Of all the people there, he was the only one who understood fully the ways of staying alive in that place. Thus, I became his strength and he became my mentor until such time that our positions were reversed. Since that time he has been my strength and still yet my mentor. He is one I protect at all costs.

"But a defense of him is insufficient, for I bring to Master Rei not only Grandfather, but *all* of the household who love me, love Ore, love House Touka, and desire peace and prosperity for their country, for I will have none in my House who don't love what I love. To do less than that would show disrespect to them.

"In that House, we were forced to remain in a place not of our desires. In my House, I offer a place to fulfill desires, but none are required to remain. Any are free to leave with my blessing - it has no walls, nor any need of them. I can't defend them any better to you than this, Mister Andrew, Miss Mina, Master Rei, at this time. With the passage of time, you'll receive the evidence. Will you please trust my word that my House won't bring trouble and shame upon Prince Rei?"

Rather amazed that Ilena had understood on her own that he needed to know that Rei was going to be surrounded by people that could be trusted absolutely, Andrew studied Ilena closely. Her earnest face now was different than the face she'd give them during the lesson just past. It was similar to one Rei wore when he was younger.

Placing his hand on Ilena's head, Andrew said, "You're already working too hard. It's sufficient for now." They already had plenty of evidence from before and there was more coming on its own in the near future.

Mina looked at Andrew, weighing his spoken and unspoken opinion, then looked to Rei, who nodded. "Miss Ilena, you're a very formidable opponent. I am in your care," she said.

"Please take care of me," Ilena responded to them all.

Rei sighed. "Do you two remember that little conversation we had as we left my office to come here? I do believe I've completely forgotten what I wanted to talk about next." Ilena gave him an apologetic look. Rei rubbed his hand through his pale blond hair. "Give me a minute and I'll remember."

Mina looked at Andrew from the corner of her eye, "I seem to remember it being said at that time by a certain someone, that we were 'just preparing for a little conversation'."

"Mmm," Andrew rubbed his chin. "Yes, I do believe Rei was right. She is as bad as King Sasou."

"Maybe worse," said Mina.

"Oh, no," Rei was quick to correct her, "Sasou won't let you win, and won't help you make the next move, either. You sink or swim on your own merits. Also he's very abbreviated compared to Ilena, out of necessity." He sent a scolding look to Ilena. His own time was also valuable.

Andrew nodded, "That's true."

There was a knock at the door, and Mizi entered. Rei gave up and sat on the second bed. He patted it, inviting Mizi over. Mizi moved to sit next to him.

Mizi looked around at everyone. "So, what's going on?" she asked.

"We've been having a lesson on just who Miss Ilena is," Mina said dryly, "or perhaps *what*."

Mizi looked happy for just a moment to have her friends getting to know each other better. Then her look went to worried. "Ah, the warm friend or the teacher?"

Mina looked away. "Teacher," admitted Andrew.

Mizi sighed and slumped. "That's difficult. I hope you didn't do anything terrible Ilena." Her look was a cross between hopeful and scolding.

"Of course not," Ilena answered calmly. "We'll have you join in on the next lesson of that sort, but first I need to get you up to speed."

Mizi wasn't very encouraged, but Ilena didn't let her consider it any more deeply than that. "Actually, now that you're here, if Master Rei will allow the continual interruption, I'd like to make sure you're on the right path before I'm unconscious again for nearly a week. You don't have the time to waste." She blinked at Rei, who glared back.

More humbly, Ilena said, "I've told you everything that I think I can about where they'll hide." Rei relented knowing his goals with Mizi were also important.

"Princess Mizi, what is it I said you must do?" Ilena asked.

"From this time on, I must always act, believe, and see myself as a princess. Not just any princess, but Prince Rei's princess. Everything I choose to do must reflect that as already being a fact, or it will never have the chance to be a reality." Mizi answered as if she'd been rehearsing the words, and likely she had been.

"Very good. And have you been practicing that?" Ilena tested Mizi.

Mizi's answer was firm. "Yes."

"Good. Master Rei, what did I tell you you must do?" Ilena tested him next.

"I also must see her as only Princess Mizi. I must provide a place for her to stand, to welcome her into it whenever she chooses to enter it, in whatever capacity she has reached, until the day I announce my intentions." Rei was just as careful to answer promptly.

"Very good. And have you taken the time to practice thinking in that way?" Ilena asked.

Rei smiled. "Yes."

"Good. Continue to remember to think that way as often as you can until you no longer have to think about it, it just is." Ilena breathed softly for a few breaths, resting, then she looked at Andrew to give him a smile, then turned her attention to Mina. "Think very carefully, Miss Mina. How do both of these instructions apply to you?"

Mina looked at Andrew thoughtfully. She'd already started allowing Ilena to lead her down this path. So far it hadn't been too bad and she did want to know how to move things forward. She decided to trust Ilena again and worked at trying to place herself in those two positions. "I must act, believe, and see myself...as already a fact or it will never be reality. No, my goal." She looked back to Ilena. "Do I not believe it?"

"No, Miss Mina, you do not," Ilena said gently. Mina tensed. "...I see that concerns you."

Andrew was worried at that statement and put his hand on Mina's shoulder. Mina was surprised by the touch and looked at him in surprise. She could see he didn't fully comprehend what was going on, but he did understand that if she was concerned about something, he wanted to strengthen her.

She turned her face away and covered her eyes with her other hand, surreptitiously wiping away an unexpected tear. When she recovered, she looked at Rei, who looked back encouragingly. He hadn't interfered yet so if he understood what Ilena was doing, he wasn't opposed to it, which was one of her fears. Perhaps she could keep going, then.

Thinking of Rei's requirement, slowly, Mina said, "And, I must ...see my goal as if it's already accomplished and ...provide a space for it ...so it can flourish." She frowned in concentration, trying to understand what that meant.

Ilena nodded, catching Mina's attention. After looking at her for a pause, Ilena looked at Andrew and said, "When you understand that a thing needs doing that you can do, you will do it." He nodded, listening to learn her intent. "Can you understand what Miss Mina needs, Mister Andrew?"

He tightened his grip on her shoulder, almost subconsciously. Mina was so surprised she tensed. He looked at her quickly, then started to let go of her and apologize, but Ilena quickly said, "No, Andrew. You were right. You did what you were supposed to. Return to it." Confused, he tried to remember what it was he had done.

Mina was surprised when seemingly all on its own her body leaned closer to Andrew, seeking his hand that returned to her shoulder. He was almost even more confused now and shook his head a little, trying to understand.

Rei laughed softly. "It's there, so subconsciously, so automatically for both of them." Andrew's entire demeanor went to one Mina recognized.

Ilena looked at Mina. "Mister Andrew, what are you thinking right now?" Her eyes defied Mina to look away from her while he answered.

He frowned. "I was thinking, 'I'd like to support her'."

Mina began to melt silently, starting from her eyes, even though as partners that's what they already did for each other. It wasn't new, not really. It was something inside her that was new.

"Miss Mina," Ilena said gently, "can you tell that it's already accomplished? You merely need to open the space."

Mina was now trembling, and Andrew was suddenly made aware of her distress by it. Her heart wanted to deny it even still, but her mind had been shown almost enough evidence that she didn't have a way to turn away from it. He turned to look at her face and finally saw her tears. He took a step to face her more directly and stood worriedly but uncertainly before her.

"Mister Andrew," Ilena said firmly. "Let's do that again, but this time, let your body do what it will."

Andrew's arms were suddenly and warmly around Mina in a very gentle hold. "I'm here, Mina," he said quietly. It was too much and all of her loneliness over the winter mixed with all of her desires and she could only drop her head to rest on his chest and cry as he stood a warm strong companion - the only man she had ever trusted, and had come to love.

Andrew, trying to understand what his body had just done, discovered he didn't want to let Mina go. He stopped trying to figure it out and stopped thinking, instead doing what he would do when he was on the list practicing with the sword: he *felt*. Felt the flow of Mina and what was going on with her.

As he did so, his head dropped to be close to Mina's, until his breath could be heard by her ear, felt by her cheek. She tensed and he stopped moving, but didn't change position or pull away.

When Mina relaxed again, and her tears were beginning to slow. Andrew carefully turned his head to face her, shifting just enough that he could see her face, but not let go. Softly he said, "Mina, please, tell me: what's wrong?"

Mina grasped Andrew's jacket front for courage. It was frightening, but having the door against her emotions removed now she could only answer her own overwhelming need. She answered quietly, "I want you."

Andrew, who'd been waiting, balanced as he would be if he were practicing with the sword, found he was suddenly off balance with her words. He swayed, trying to stay in the "sword practice" state while at the same time comprehend what he'd just heard. "Will you say that again?" he whispered.

A little hiss escaped Ilena. Mina heard it and obediently backed her fiery emotion back down before it flared. She took a shaky breath and said, a little more normally and clearly, "I want you."

It was Andrew's turn to lose his composure. He dropped his head onto her shoulder and his arms felt weak. He turned his head just enough so Mina would hear him. "You already have me."

Mina trembled a little at the answer, finding it difficult to believe it. "Is it okay, for me to want you at my side for the rest of my life?"

Andrew paused a moment then said, "I don't know. I do know that I don't want you to have anyone else. I don't want you to leave my side. It's so cold without you." Andrew trembled. Mina wrapped her arms around him, holding him as he had held her.

Mina touched Andrew's cheek, then lifted his head so she could look into his eyes. Wiping the tears from his face with her thumb, she said, "Andrew,

I love you. Please will you consent to becoming my husband? I know it's a difficult thing to ask, and we'll need help - and flexibility - to get there, but ...will you come with me? ...Will you marry me, and be my partner - for all my life?"

Andrew was still for a while, surprise on his face, even for all they'd just said. Then it was as if he had come to awareness. He startled and looked around, his eyes seeking Rei's.

Andrew had to turn to see Rei, but he stayed close to Mina, almost unconsciously keeping one arm around her shoulders. When he found Rei's brilliant blue eyes, he relaxed. "Rei?" he pled for an answer and direction.

Holding Mizi close to help her stay calm in the midst of the emotions of the moment, Rei smiled at Andrew. "Is it what you want?" he asked.

Andrew considered briefly, then smiled gently, sadly. "Yes, but I want to keep protecting you also."

Rei nodded and looked into Mina's eyes. "Is it what you want?" She nodded. "Are you willing to work for it?"

She teared up again. "Please...," she whispered, "please let me have Andrew, too."

Rei gently let go of Mizi, left the bed and moved to stand before Mina and Andrew. He put one hand each on their outside shoulders and looked at each of them in the face with a tender look. "I hope you will be happy - for a very long time - together." He pulled them into a combined embrace and whispered into their ears, "I love you." He held them a moment while Mina's eyes dripped tears.

When he stepped back, he grinned at them, his hands moving to his hips. "Welcome to the Mother Ilena Relationship Class. Princess Mizi and I are glad to have your company."

Mizi snorted a laugh into the pillow she'd picked up to hold in lieu of Rei. Andrew shook his head and Mina rolled her eyes. Ilena sniffed ever so softly.

Andrew and Mina heard her and looked at each other with a mischievous light in their eyes. Holding hands they went up to Ilena, who looked at them with some alarm. Mina leaned over to Ilena and wrapped her in a hug. "Thank you for helping us, too. ...If you do that one more time without asking first, I'll knife you, then ask you what you wanted to say."

Ilena got a frightened look on her face. Andrew put his hand on the top of her head and gave her a kind look. "I won't let her," he promised, "but I will expect to see progress towards better restraint in the future. For this time, thank you for helping us break through that impasse we'd reached. Even I could see we probably needed a third party to help us break the patterns we couldn't on our own."

Ilena blushed bright pink. When they'd stepped back from her bed again, she told them, "I'm so proud of you. I wish you the most happiness ever."

-o-o-o-

Rei turned to Mizi, thinking to go back to sitting next to her. She was looking at him with a puzzled expression. He was about to smile at her and reach for her hand, when a thought struck him.

He was about to turn to Ilena and ask her about it when again a flash of inspiration stopped him from moving his eyes from Mizi's green eyes. Instead he put a gentle look on his face and asked, "Mizi, what is it?" He was already sure he knew.

"Ah!" Mizi looked panicked, then froze, her eyes glazed.

That was a reaction Rei had seen before. He knew he couldn't release his own gaze from her. "It's Ilena, isn't it?" he said gently. He was sure Mina hadn't had time to talk to her yet and he still couldn't say it yet.

"Ah...ah...," Mizi gulped then looked down and nodded miserably. "I keep trying, but I can't let it go." She sounded as miserable as she looked. Rei sighed sadly. He shifted, wishing once again he knew what to say.

Ilena swore very quietly. Mizi jumped and looked at her. "There! Hi, Princess Mizi!" Ilena said lightly, firmly catching Mizi's green eyes with her own tawny ones. "You need to be looking at me. Placing the Regent in the middle isn't fair to him."

Rei, released from the requirement to keep Mizi's attention, sat down next to her on the outside edge so as to not be between the ladies.

Mizi frowned, puzzled. "Remember, Master Rei called this the Relationship *Class*, Princess Mizi. It's okay to feel what you're feeling, that jealousy." Mizi's expression changed to one of surprise. Ilena nodded. "Explore that feeling. It's a very important one. Just like anger, it's a warning sign. When you let it function correctly, it lets you know that your relationship is in danger."

"Danger?" Mizi asked. Even Rei frowned, not fully understanding what Ilena meant.

Ilena answered positively, "Mmm. What are you saying inside right now?"

Reluctantly, Mizi answered. "Why does Rei love her? I wish for him to only love me." Mizi flushed pink. "They aren't very nice things, the other things that come up."

Ilena waved her hand. "They aren't supposed to be nice."

"Why?" Mizi asked.

"Because sometimes the right thing to do when you feel them is to be mean," Ilena answered almost casually.

Mizi gaped at Ilena. "How...how can that be?"

"When is it right to feel anger?" Ilena made Mizi work it out.

Mizi took a moment to find her answer. "...When there is...just cause."

"And when is it right to act in anger?" Ilena continued.

"... When...it's important to help the other party to know that they've crossed proper boundaries." Mizi finished a little stronger that time.

Ilena gave a nod, accepting the answer. "Mm. It's the same with jealousy. The two emotions are cousins. When you feel jealous, you should as rigorously analyze it as you would anger, and discard it from you if it doesn't meet the proper criteria for action.

"Not acted upon when it should be will bring harm, so you must understand how to act on it. Sometimes that means putting a competitor back in their rightful place. Sometimes it means addressing the truth underneath." Mizi nodded, able to see at least those two cases.

Ilena finally released Mizi's eyes and looked around to the rest of them to see if they were also listening. They all nodded to let her know they were. Satisfied, she looked back at Mizi, just a little sadly. "The first thing to ask is if the jealousy is because of a lack of trust, either in yourself or your partner, or both.

As Mizi considered her feelings based on Ilena's requirement, Ilena leaned back against her pillow and closed her eyes - resting, but clearly troubled. Rei, worried, looked to Mina and Andrew. He knew he couldn't move.

Mina stepped closer to Ilena. Hesitantly, she put her hand on Ilena's arm. "Ilena, what's wrong? Are you in pain?"

Ilena opened her eyes and looked at her. "Ah, thank you, yes, actually. I've been sitting up too long."

"Can we help you lie back down?"

"I feel it will make this...class...difficult if I can't properly see everyone. So I don't know what to do." At that, the others who were present for her first "class" went very still. They were now very aware that this person knew what to do.

"Don't look," Ilena said quietly, and all three resisted the urge they felt to turn and look at Mizi. Then slightly more loudly she said, "Mizi. What are you saying inside right now? I know they're hurtful things again. Please say them anyway."

Mizi pulled in a large gasp of air as if she'd been holding her breath, then closed her eyes and let the breath out. "Instinctively I want to come help you, but I'm at the same time too irritated to care. This is more than enough people to see to you when I'm put out that I can't be allowed to understand yet.

"I don't like having this emotion when it stands in the way of my goal, when I finally can see it in front of me. I know if I can be patient and wait I'll understand eventually, but it's irritating that I can't stay calm about it."

She frowned. "It doesn't help that now I'm also jealous of Mina and Andrew." She blew out an exasperated breath. "All of the things that are thrown at me by that jealousy are really pointless and I know have no sense to them."

"Go ahead and say them anyway," Ilena invited.

Mizi rolled her eyes, "Fine, but I don't believe them." Ilena gave a nod to allow for that. "Why can they just decide and get to happily be together when I have to fight so hard to get everyone's approval? Why do I have to have all those nobles who don't even understand our relationship nor even know me say I can or can't marry Rei? Why can't Rei just tell them he's made his decision and make it public knowledge that I'm his pick for his princess? Just doing that would make my heart rest, regardless of what his relationship to Ilena is.

"I know that it has to be done, and properly, or the court won't support Rei the way he needs to be supported, and I want to be only his strength. I know I need to properly earn that place by his side, or even *I* won't trust myself there." She was scowling and tears were now standing in her eyes.

"So, you're arguing with yourself?" Ilena asked gently.

"Yes."

"And it's not working?" Ilena asked even more gently.

"No," Mizi admitted miserably.

Ilena nodded sympathetically. "That's another important clue, Princess Mizi. If you can't find the argument that makes the feeling go away, there's a truth that must be addressed head on, or the relationship will fracture.

"I'm sure your arguments are valid arguments that *should* make the feelings go away. The point is that they *aren't*; they aren't sufficient to address the truth. What is that one core truth underlying all of the jealousy?"

Mizi took a deep breath. "I want to trust Rei, and even you, but I can't. I don't understand why Rei loves you. In one event, he went from distrusting you and holding you at arm's length, to not only trusting you, but loving you. Why?" Her hands clenched. "I already know Sasou has to give approval for Rei to tell me, but that's at the core of it all."

Ilena nodded. "If that is at the core, then that must be addressed openly and resolved, for all that it appears there isn't a solution right at the moment."

Mina shifted and said softly, "Excuse me please, Rei, Mizi. I'm sorry to interrupt, but may I offer a possibility?" Rei looked at Mina and nodded. "You could have Mizi speak with Ore."

Mina glanced at Andrew. "He's said some things to Andrew and I that have...made this odd evening more easy to understand, made Ilena more comprehensible. Maybe if Ore says those things to Mizi, she'll also be able to understand sufficiently until Rei is free to say more." Mina fell silent. Andrew smiled at her, glad that again there was someone else who could step in to break another impasse.

Rei thought about it, then said, "If Ore said something that helped Mina and Andrew, then it may likely help Mizi as well. Will you accept that for now, Mizi? To hear the thing Ore has to say? I do wish for you to be able to work peaceably with Ilena."

Mizi took a deep breath, and it looked like some of the burden lifted just with having something she could do. She nodded. "I'll speak with Ore."

Ilena said to Mina tiredly, "Please, will you allow Mister Andrew to help you assist me in lying down. I can no longer bear it."

Mina asked her what solution she had to being able to see them in the room. Ilena smiled in acknowledgment. "If you use the pillows to support my left side, so I'm resting on my right side, I'll be able to see into the room, although you two should move to sit against the opposite bed. Then I'll be able to see all of you." The room was rather quiet as they worked to reposition Ilena.

Rei took Mizi's hand in his and leaned his head back against the wall. He was able to relax a bit with Mina's suggestion as well. He knew that likely Ore would tell Mizi what the other aides knew and had discovered on their own. It made him worry a little, but if it helped Mizi be able to relax and trust them, it would be worth it.

As Mizi rested her head on his shoulder, he enjoyed just being with her for the moment. However, the more he relaxed the more he became aware that there was a knot in his belly. He looked at the concern that it was coming from, trying to see what it was. The direction of the conversation had pointed to it, so it should probably be addressed here, too.

When Andrew and Mina left Ilena's side and sat on the floor in front of Rei and Mizi, Rei opened his eyes and looked into Ilena's. She was waiting for him. "I also," he said.

Ilena nodded. "Then let's address it now. Even if you can't point to the exact thing, if you can talk yourself around to it, saying the words will unknot the puzzle until you can see the kernel of truth that must be addressed."

Rei grimaced. Ilena smiled with understanding. "Yes, it is an uncomfortable thing to bring these to the surface and say them out loud, but it's essential for keeping the relationship clear and strong. Sometimes they'll point to a thing not properly considered. Those should also be addressed now, before Mizi wastes a great amount of effort she perhaps shouldn't."

Rei sat up, gently enough to not dislodge Mizi sharply. He crossed his legs and frowned at the bed in front of him. When he had at least an end to the thread, he turned to face Mizi directly. She turned to face him, respecting his serious attempt to try to communicate with her.

Holding onto her hand, he smiled a wry, sad smile at her. "Mizi, I feel like you love your work as a healer more than you love me. Even to go so far as to smile as you left for two years - a very, very long time it seemed to me."

"I was angry then; even though I argued with myself and found no relief. My brother had sent you, and there was, it seemed, nothing that could be done." Rei paused, his thumb absently rubbing the back of Mizi's hand.

"While I can't fight against my brother, I felt ...betrayed... that you would submit humbly to him rather than fight to stand by my side even then. 'Did you love him more than me?' I thought on that occasion. Whether or not he may have had the best idea for how to help you on the way to your goal, I felt

...jealous... that you didn't trust me enough to choose to stay with me and let me try to do my best.

"You have many valuable traits I desire and love, however you have one that I have come to d-de...detest," he closed his eyes and squeezed her hand slightly, then took a breath and continued, looking her in the eyes and smiling the small smile again.

"Mizi, you are far too obedient." A muscle in his jaw twitched. "You have the stubbornness in you that won't let you be pushed beyond where you wish to be. But I wish that you would learn to have the stubbornness and awareness to not be pushed beyond where *I* wish for you to be." Rei stopped and took another breath. This was very hard.

He really couldn't keep all of his emotions out of his voice as he nearly demanded, "If you wish to stand beside me, then *come* and stand beside me. If you don't wish to be away from me, then *choose* to not be away. If one asks you to obediently go away from me, turn to hear *my* word and be obedient to only *me*. Go only when I say go, come when I say come. Trust me to not say either amiss." Rei stopped. He'd said what he needed to say. The saying of it helped, but not knowing how Mizi was going to react kept him tense.

Mizi sat quietly, her hands resting loosely in her lap and in Rei's hand, thinking over Rei's words. "I'm sorry, Rei, that I didn't understand. That I didn't have sufficient awareness of myself." It helped him to hear the apology, and to not hear anger or frustration at him in her voice.

"While I do love being able to help people as a healer, when I realized that I must give less effort to that dream to have the greater dream, I thought to myself, 'It's a small thing to give up'." She reached up with the hand he wasn't holding and timidly put it to his face. "I love Rei."

She dropped her hand and Rei caught it with his other hand. "If I'm overly obedient, then I would like to learn to be properly obedient to you first. If you're going to open a space for me, then I want to learn to run into it. If you say *I* may choose to stand by you, then I want to be able to choose it always."

Rei was relieved and his anger and fears evaporated. "Thank you, Mizi. I know that changes like that take practice, but I look forward to seeing your efforts. I do very much want you to be next to me, and sooner than later. I'll do what I can to help. Please always let me know as soon as possible if there's a thing I can do. I'll always listen."

Mizi turned a little pink and held his hands a little tighter. "Thank you, Rei. I will." She slumped. "If only you could take some of my lessons for me. Today was quite difficult and it was just the second day. I'm surprised Ilena's still awake, honestly. We've worked very hard two days in a row through her nap time."

They looked over at Ilena and she smiled back at them. "Oh, I'm mostly asleep now. It's good that you two can do this sort of thing so well on your own. Please don't forget into the future to talk about such things as soon as you can after they come up. It may be difficult, but life will be so much easier for you when you do."

Ilena blinked then waved her hand at them, as if shooing them out of her room, but she smiled at them kindly. "Your homework, all of you while I'm recovering, is to practice doing those things you've promised each other you would work on. I apologize for the interruption in your studies, but I hope when I return that I'll be pleased to see remarkable progress, and ecstatic delight in the eyes of Ore at the things you've done here today."

"Has Ore been sad?" Mizi asked the question they were all thinking.

"Ara, all of you!" Ilena was exasperated and rolled her eyes at them. "With all of you feeling like that, what you were before just now, how could he not? The poor man has been carrying all of you on his shoulders for how many years now! If I've done nothing else good here in this castle, I should die happy tomorrow knowing I've removed some of the burden from his shoulders - no, much of it."

Mina said casually, "Ilena, if you die, that should be an even greater burden upon his shoulders, don't you think?"

Mizi tisked her tongue at Ilena. "Ilena, you'll live, because there are people in this castle who love you."

Ilena smiled a bit of a watery smile at Mizi. "Thank you, Princess Mizi. I'll certainly hope to be up on my feet soon so I can walk with all of you. Thank you for coming to visit with me tonight - even if I was the teacher for most of it." Her eyes went to Mina. "Your practice of the first lesson of the evening is commendable. Thank you."

As the four friends rose from the bed and bedside, Andrew said, "Ah, Mina, I think that counts as another point to you, and therefore to our team."

"Yes," responded Mina, "and I think that it counts as another overall win as well."

Ilena chuckled, but really she was very tired now. They collected up the maps and bade her good night so she could rest for the next day's surgery.

CHAPTER 3 Experimental Surgery

As Andrew and Mina escorted Rei and Mizi away from Ilena's new room, they ran into Ore coming from the office. He'd just finished the work he'd needed to do to be prepared to leave the next day. Rei asked him to escort Mizi to her room before going to see Ilena, and, after saying goodnight to her, left with Andrew and Mina.

As Ore and Mizi walked to the aide's quarters, Mizi explained to Ore that she was having difficulty understanding Ilena, and that Ilena's relationship with Rei was causing her some confusion that was interfering with her ability to effectively reach her goal. "Mina suggested that there might be a thing that you could tell me that would help me understand. Rei said that it would be okay."

"Eh?! Master did?" Ore blinked at Mizi.

Mizi nodded. "He said if what Ore said helped Andrew and Mina understand Ilena, then I could hear it, too, and maybe it would help. I understand already that Rei can't say it himself."

Ore considered. "It would be perhaps easiest if I showed you. There's a thing in my room I'll fetch, if you'll wait for me." Mizi agreed. "What brought this on?" Ore asked, curious.

Mizi wasn't sure she wanted to tell Ore very much, and she could feel her face turning red. Then she remembered that Ilena had said that their relationship difficulties had been a burden on Ore. "Before I arrived at Ilena's room, something happened that I don't understand to make Andrew and Mina accept Ilena. After I came, she helped them reach the point where Mina proposed to Andrew, he accepted her, and Rei gave them his permission."

Ore was flabbergasted. "All in one evening?!"

Mizi nodded. "It was very touching."

Ore looked closely at her face. "Is that why your eyes are red?"

"It's part of it," she admitted.

"There's more?" he asked incredulously. Mizi blushed even harder. "She said things to you and Master, too?" Ore guessed shrewdly.

Mizi nodded. "She explained to me why we feel jealousy and what to do to address it. In particular, she said that to not address the truths behind it damages our relationship. She had me say things to Rei that he was able to answer, and he said things to me that I was able to answer to. ...Needing to understand their relationship is one of them."

"I see," he said slowly, mulling it over. "So, after you understand it, will Master and Mistress be able to look at each other with clear eyes again?"

"Yes," Mizi answered.

"Well, then, I'll do my best." They entered their wing. "If you'll wait for me here," he indicated one of the chairs along the perimeter of the entry hall, "I'll be back shortly."

Mizi obediently sat and waited. He brought out the Selicia history book and sat beside her. "The Ryokudo history proves the story better, but Master still has that book. Perhaps he'll let you read it." She nodded understanding. He flipped to the pages that told about the Second Princess of Ryokudo marrying the Third Prince of Selicia. He showed her the section to read. When she was done he had her skip to the section about the coup in Selicia.

Then he said, "The Ryokudo history says that the Prince and Princess were found on Ryokudo soil, beheaded. Ilena doesn't know, and it's Master's to tell her." Mizi's eyes were round. It was a terrible thing to hear, but she didn't understand why he would give her that caution. "It also says that the little princess wasn't found with them."

He flipped to the back with the family genealogy that contained the same Prince and Princess and showed it to her. "Read the names of the children."

Mizi read across the page. Like him, she stopped at the little princess and drew in a breath. The child obviously Selician, the name so like Ilena's, one of her parents an heiress of Ryokudo. Her eyes were very wide as she finally looked up at Ore. "Ilena is...her?"

Ore nodded. "Andrew and Mina already had evidence from following Master the same day I found these histories. All of us are in agreement, Ilena is this princess, alive, but until Master has the approval of King Brother, he can't speak of it. He wishes to keep her by his side because of what she's done for him already, and because she also wishes it. If he can't learn to properly use her, she won't be allowed to stay and her dreams will be crushed under the weight of her station."

Mizi took a moment to let it all sink in and correlate it to what she already knew. "She is very much like King Sasou - like the Toukas. Knowing why helps. Also, it helps to understand why she can't be placed as anything less than a minister if she hopes to stay beside Rei." She looked back at the picture of the little princess. "And, she is family. That's why Rei loves her and is tender towards her. She has no one else, and he has only known his older brother."

Ore nodded. "And, because she is a princess, there's no one better for Master to trust with your training to become one yourself."

Mizi hadn't considered that, and looked up in surprise. "Yes, that's true. But it does make me wonder...how can I expect her to stand behind me?"

"Hasn't she already said? She'll make you into someone she can stand behind." Ore looked a little rueful. "She is a Touka. Although she's kinder than King Brother and Queen Mother, she's still as ruthless. If you can't be someone she can stand behind and that can stand next to Rei, she'll send you away. The fact that she's already working with you is good, Mistress. It would be good if you can continue to stand before her."

Mizi paled, then nodded resolutely. She wasn't going to give up, and she already knew Ilena wouldn't be the first one to give up either. "I'll trust her." She stood up and handed to book back to Ore. "Thank you Ore, for explaining it to me." Ore nodded and watched as she climbed the stairs to her room and entered it.

-o-o-o-

As Ore walked to Ilena's room, he wondered at what she'd done, all in one evening. He wished he could have been there to see it, but it was enough to lighten the burden on his heart to just know it had happened.

Things wouldn't be easy for Andrew and Mina, but now they were able to move forward. It was the same for Rei and Mizi. Mizi now understood what she was to do, and the difficulties between them had likely been resolved. He would be able to leave on the morrow with only Ilena to worry his mind, and that was a large enough burden at the moment.

Indeed, it felt like she'd stepped in to support him as best she could for the coming days. He was grateful...but at the same time he wondered if he should be worried. She wasn't tactful, and was still too forceful in doing as she pleased.

As he opened the door and stepped in, he wondered if Ilena would still be awake after all the excitement she'd had, from the bath in the morning until now. He decided it would be okay if she was sleeping. She surely needed it - particularly if she was going to be ready for the next day.

-o-o-o-

Ilena came suddenly awake. She was sure her internal clock was telling her it was time for Ore to be arriving at his usual time, but her ears told her he was already there.

"Ah, you've woken up?" he asked her.

"When did you come? Did you come early again?" She felt bad she hadn't been awake for him.

"I haven't been here too long. I'm glad you were resting. ...I met Mistress on the way here and Master had me walk her to her room. It sounds like you've had a very busy day." He lit the candle on the desk and walked over to the bed to look down at her.

"I'm sorry I wasn't able to be awake when you came," Ilena apologized.

Ore shook his head. "You need to rest to be prepared for tomorrow."

"I'll have no choice but to sleep for the next week anyway. ...And rest for the following five," she said with a grimace.

He grinned at her, "True." He looked at her for a moment. "You've been busy being Mother when I'm not here to watch you, again." She couldn't look him in the eye. "Thank you." Her eyes snapped to him in surprise. "Because of what you've done, I can leave here tomorrow with only one worry to carry with me."

"I'm glad," she said softly, "although I would take that burden from you also, if I could."

He shook his head. "It's enough."

48

She studied him, then thought of the instructions she'd wanted to give him that night. "Grandfather told you last night to go to the Glass Bottle tomorrow, but you need to know what to do when you get there." Ore nodded once to indicate he was listening.

"The sign of the tavern is a green glass wine bottle with a wine glass next to it. It's fairly close to the castle, so the owners wanted to draw the upper level customers to it. You should dress appropriately." She watched to see he understood her meaning. When he sighed dispiritedly, she knew he had.

She smiled slightly. "When you ask to be seated, tell the owner, or his wife, that you're taking a trip and were hoping for a travel guide, or to talk to someone who'd been to the place you're going. Take that person with you and be obedient to them, and your way will be made smooth."

Ore nodded. He wasn't surprised to hear he would have a translator and guide again. "I wish it could be Thayne again," he said, thinking of the young man he'd gotten along with so well.

Ilena looked at him thoughtfully. "Ore, do you desire him as your man-at-arms?"

"I'm not in such a position as to have one of those," he deprecated.

"If you were? Would you accept him?"

He looked at her speculatively. "Why do you ask?"

She paused, putting her thoughts in order. "Ore, if you want him, bring him back here. You may set him to watch over me when you can't be present with me. When I can't go where you go, I'll send him to watch over you in my stead."

He blinked at her. "You're saying to use him, as Master has used me?"

She nodded. "Until I can stand beside you, let him stand in our stead."

He cocked his head. It was a comforting idea. "I'll ask Master." She nodded. It was the best he could answer. He looked at her a bit longer then asked, "What's wrong, Ilena?"

She shook her head. "It's nothing to worry Ore about," but she couldn't look at him again.

"It's not nothing." She closed her eyes and wouldn't say it. He reached out and put his hand on the top of her head, then leaned down and kissed her forehead. She was stunned. He pulled away, surprised his body had acted on its own again, afraid he'd offended her, remembering she was a princess, "Ah, I didn't...."

She put the back of her hand to her mouth and began to cry. "That was very mean, Ore. To do that when you hate me."

"Hate you?" Ore blinked. *Is that the face I've shown her?* Ore slowly reached out and, sitting on the bed next to her, lifted her and held her head to his shoulder.

He didn't know what had caused him to act like he had, but as he held her he realized that he desired to protect her like this, not just now, but always. To return to her what she'd always given to him. As he came to that seemingly surprising realization, his other arm came up around her as well. He held her close, finally feeling her warmth, smelling her scent, for the first time in a very long time. "Ilena, I do not hate you."

When her storm had finally passed, he gently lay her back down and released her, then handed her a handkerchief. She thanked him and cleaned her face. Then she reached up hesitantly, and when he didn't move, lightly brushed the side of his face with her hand, her fingertips going through his hair, her eyes looking at him still a little sad, a little hungry. Then she let go and said with a regretful smile, "I love you, Ore."

It was the first time she'd said it when awake, and using his current name. He realized instantly and sharply that it wasn't what he'd been waiting for weeks to hear. He quickly grabbed her hand before it could fall completely to the bed and, shaking his head, said, "No. Say it again, but say the name you used to call."

Her breath stopped and she went wide eyed. Whispering to herself, she said, "Oh, that isn't fair at all. What shall I do?" and tears threatened again. She could see he was serious but it wouldn't last long. As the tears dropped again, she said, "I love you, Kase," and it sounded like her heart had broken. She turned away from him, closed her eyes and wouldn't look at him again.

He stood, blew out the candle, and took himself out of the room. He knew she wouldn't rest easily this night if he stayed now. He would come back after she was asleep again. He needed Rei.

-o-o-o-

Rei had just blown out his own candle when Ore entered, announcing himself from the door when he found no lights on. He didn't want to be run through with Rei's sword as a night intruder. Rei frowned. Ore didn't sound right. He sighed and reached over to the nightstand and relit the candle. "What's the matter, Ore?"

It was indeed a sad Ore standing at the door. "I don't understand myself again," Ore said to the floor. "Ilena gave me many gifts today, and in the end, I hurt her."

"You've left her to come here?"

Ore nodded, but didn't look up. "She wouldn't look at me. I'll let her fall asleep before returning."

Rei sighed. "That may be, but if you leave it like that tonight, there won't be an opportunity to repair it before you leave tomorrow."

If anything Ore looked even more sad. Rei sighed. "Come here Ore." He pointed to a spot on the bed in front of him. Ore's eyes went wide. He was usually never allowed on Rei's bed. "Just this once, Ore," Rei clarified. He really didn't want to have to pull him forcefully out of a tree again just before he was supposed to go on an important errand.

50

Ore walked over and carefully climbed onto the bed and sat cross-legged in front of his master, still not able to look up at him.

"Tell me." Rei ordered.

Ore told him everything. Rei sighed. "You told her that you don't hate her, and then you made her call you by a name you refuse to acknowledge is your own. Are you really so afraid to let her love you, Ore? ...She scolded us, me and Mizi, and Andrew and Mina, for being a weight on your shoulders. Yet you place that same burden on her and on us."

Ore hung his head lower. "I don't know what to do. She isn't mine to have."

Rei felt a bit of impatience. "Why is it you believe that?"

Ore thought about that for a moment, then gave up. "Help me to understand it." Rei nodded. Ore took a breath. "Because she's a princess."

"That Princess claimed you long ago, and she'll make you one who can stand beside her, the same as she'll make Mizi someone she can stand behind."

Ore found the thought as disturbing as Mizi had, but ...it wasn't the reason. "Because she is Master's and King Brother's."

"And I've said she'll stand with me, with Ore at her side. I've also told you my brother wishes to see her stand at my side. He won't remove her without great reason."

It comforted Ore to hear his Master sound so confident. He didn't understand the King so well, so that had worried him. But if Rei was sure, he would trust him. "I don't understand why she wants me."

"What is it you don't trust about her yet?"

Ore shook his head, rejecting that the fault was in her. "I don't understand why she would choose me."

"Ore," Rei said slowly, "Ilena has said that she's watched over you since she chose you. It's in her nature to constantly watch and weigh those around her, particularly those who she desires to have close to her. Have you understood that about her?" Ore nodded. It wasn't all that different to how Sasou chose those he called up and placed in positions of power and strength.

"Even after all these years of watching you, she said she'll still choose you. If in all the things you've tested her in, you've only found reason to trust her, then trust her in this thing also." Rei waited. He wasn't sure there was anything else he could say to the man in front of him. After a time Ore nodded and Rei was relieved.

"Master, ...she's perfect for me. I can't not want her."

Rei lifted a knee and rested his elbow on it, putting his chin in his hand. "Is that a problem for you? That she's worked so hard to be someone that you would want to have and keep?"

"Worked so hard...?" Ore looked up at Rei finally in surprise.

Rei nodded. "In watching you, she's seen what it is you need to have in your partner, and she's worked hard to be that, all so that she may become Ore's partner. Is that a problem?"

After a few false starts as Ore tried to wrap his brain around the concept, he finally shook his head. Perhaps the only problem would be in his own insanity to not accept her.

"Ore, remember at the first dinner we had with them, she said to me that the goal for Mizi and I was that by the time Mizi's lessons were over, I would know because she would be perfectly everything I needed. I wouldn't be able to refuse her, nor would anyone be able to deny me." Ore nodded.

"Ilena has already done that work for you. If there's a thing that you need or expect, and she doesn't have it yet, it's your responsibility to teach it to her, now that she's come this far and you understand it. It's the same as Mizi asking me to consider what it is I want and tell it to her."

Ore considered that. "There is the matter you've set me to. She must be able to always come to Master's call."

Rei nodded. "That's reasonable. I think she's able to answer to you already, so you'll best be able to teach her to answer to me." When it seemed that Ore couldn't come up with another thing, he asked, "Ore, do you love Ilena?"

Hesitantly, Ore answered. "I am...coming to. She's my partner. I want to protect her. I want to see everything she has to show me. I want to hold her tightly and not let her go. It would hurt very much if she were taken from me if I were to take one more step on that path." Ore's hand clenched down as if to hold Ilena tightly even now.

"Then that's what holds you back and makes you push against her. Do you trust what I've said, that I will protect her, and you, in the position I've set for her?" Ore nodded. Rei thought a moment more. "Are you afraid you'll lose her tomorrow? That the experimental surgery will take her from you?" Ore felt it like a knife. Rei could see it in his face even as he nodded.

"*Haahhh.*" Rei wasn't sure what to do. He couldn't promise Ore protection from that fear. "Then you must go back to her and explain it to her. You'll be here to see her through it. But, Ore, I can't let you stay until she's recovered. I need you to go by tomorrow evening."

Ore nodded, but the fear hadn't left him. "May I stay with her when I return until she's recovered?"

Rei paused, then answered, "Yes. She's your partner."

Ore was somewhat relieved. He shifted. "Ilena said a thing tonight...." Rei nodded, indicating he would hear it.

"I rode with Thayne at my side once I'd recovered him. She said I could have him if I wanted it. That if I brought him from the safe house, I could have him to watch over her when I couldn't be present, and when she couldn't be by my side, she could send him to stand in her place. Like what Ore has done for Master. I said I would ask you.

"Could I fetch him tomorrow after the surgery and she's past the lucid stage of the Little Death, to have him stay with her, then leave on my errand?" He held his breath.

Rei considered it. She'd only asked that the witnesses be kept safe. If Thayne was watching over her from here in the castle, he would be as safe as she was. Perhaps that was why she'd allowed it. It was also likely that it was because he wasn't in much danger, being part of the first list.

Ah, but if Rei allowed it, it was likely Mina would want to have Tairn's younger brother also. She'd received word from her father that as soon as the Lord's Court was done, he would take her home with him. That would mean she would leave before Dane would be able to come and be trained by her.

"You may have him, but tell her that I require Dane Malkin as payment. You must bring him, too," Rei answered.

Ore's relief was very evident. "Yes, Master," he said, and bowed from his sitting position. "May I kiss you now?"

"No!" Rei kicked him off the bed. He knew Ore was feeling better now, but that didn't mean he would put up with the teasing. "Get to Ilena. Give her the kiss - she's the one that wants it."

"Ah," Ore said a little sadly as he turned to go to the door, "that's what started it."

"Then what's wrong with ending it that way, too?" Rei said with a sigh as Ore opened the door.

Ore didn't answer, but before he closed the door he did say, "Thank you, Master."

-o-o-o-

Ore decided that he'd have to wake Ilena up if she was asleep, although he didn't really want to. But when he opened the door, he knew she was waiting, although he didn't know why. He walked in silence to the candle and relit it, then turned to look at her. Her eyes were closed against the light, but when he remained quiet, she slowly opened her eyes and lifted them to look for him. They were rather red still, and his heart hurt to see it.

"I'm sorry, Ilena." He didn't move, only spoke quietly. She blinked at him, but didn't say anything. "I won't ask such a thing from you again." Her eyes lowered as she looked away. She looked very weary.

"Ilena, I've come from speaking with Master." She closed her eyes, but nodded slightly to indicate she was listening. "He's corrected me and helped me to understand my error." He moved up to stand closer to her.

He waited for her. After a moment she opened her eyes to look at him again. "I'm afraid." One of her eyebrows went up momentarily. He took a breath. "You tried to help me with it by offering Thayne, but I didn't recognize my need at that time. Master has said that I may fetch him tomorrow afternoon, after I speak with you again. I'll leave him with you in my stead until I return. Then I'll stay with you until you're recovered sufficiently.

"Master's payment is that I must also bring Dane Malkin with me so that Miss Mina has the time to train him before she must return with her father." Ilena nodded, accepting the bargain. "Ilena," he pled, "please, stay well."

She finally spoke. "Ore, will you please hold my hand tomorrow, so that I'll know you're with me when I fall asleep and when I reawaken?"

"I will," Ore promised.

Ilena closed her eyes, content, and began to relax into sleep. Ore looked at her for a while longer in the light, then blew the candle out. He paused a moment, then before he lost his nerve, he quickly stepped up to her, found her, and bent down to kiss her forehead again.

Her arms snaked around him, holding him to her. He was surprised for a moment, then she whispered, "Ore. Keep me company tonight. Even for just a little while. I don't want to let you go, either."

He paused for a moment, but couldn't deny her. He carefully lay down next to her and held her. "Live, Mother. Live for me."

She turned her head to face him, "I'll do my best, Father. Come back to me quickly."

"I will." As Ilena slipped into sleep, Ore slowly drifted into sleep himself, thinking as he did so that he was glad she'd asked. He didn't think he would have been able to sleep at all any place else that night, even in the next bed over.

-o-o-o-

It was very noisy. Ore grumpily opened his eyes. "What is it?" he frowned.

"Mmm," said the sleepy voice of Ilena, tucked down somewhere at chest level, "Marcus and Henry have finally decided to admit they know where I've been being kept, but the guards aren't willing to admit they're right. So they're devolving into an argument."

"Hehh!?" He was still trying to wake up enough to comprehend what she'd said. "...The runners from the Black Cat?"

"Did you meet them there?"

"Um-hm. I had them collect the four sets in town for me. Why are they here?" Ore rubbed his head, trying to get the blood to flow to it enough to wake up.

"I sent for them. They're working hard for me." Ilena yawned. "Someone like me isn't supposed to have favorites, but somehow those two have managed to worm their way into that position. It really means they get worked twice as hard as everyone else, but they keep asking for it."

Ore smiled. "Well, I could put them to work this morning. Shall I let them in?"

She snuggled in closer. "Do we have to?"

He kissed the top of her head. "Good morning, Mother. It's time to get up. How much time do we have until Leah and Rio get here?"

54

She sighed in resignation. "Good morning, Father. Not long, it's true."

"Well, I don't want to get into trouble with them." He carefully disentangled himself and slipped off the bed, their hands separating last, as he yawned and headed for the door.

He opened the door while scratching his head. "You kids sure are noisy for this early in the morning," he said.

They'd hopped into formal attention when the door had opened, but now Marcus of the wild blond hair and hazel eyes grinned a sly grin. "That's because Grandfather said you'd be with Mother, and we know how hard it is to wake you up in the morning."

Ore growled at them. "Don't tease the guards just to get what you want."

"We're sorry," they properly apologized to the guards.

"You can let them in when they come," Ore told the guards. "They're hers. Just trip them when they go through the door if they keep giving you trouble."

"Hey!" the young men exclaimed in protest. "We said we're sorry!"

"Besides," added Henry of the serious brown eyes and brown hair, "we're here before our shift starts, but we've got to get there soon. We were getting pretty desperate."

"Mmm? Well, your shift is starting now," Ore informed them. "If you're late tell them Ore kept you."

"Okay!" they grinned at him.

"Are you going to let Scamp and Scoundrel in or not?" Ilena's slightly grumpy voice came from behind Ore.

Their eyes lit up and Ore got out of their way. They dashed through the door, Marcus letting Henry through first. "Mother!"

As Ore turned to re-enter the room he said, "Hue, I'll need you in a bit, too."

"Yes, Sir," Hue answered. Then he grinned. "Miss Ilena certainly has a lively family. Just like her."

"Yes, she does," Ore yawned again. "They also won't let me sleep - any of them."

He went in and closed the door. While the paiges talked to Ilena he washed up and tried to finish waking up.

When he reappeared at her bedside, Henry said to him, in an aside, "It's a good thing we got here first. Miss Leah would have had your ear for a trophy if she'd come in and saw where you'd been sleeping all night."

"How would you know?" Ore asked. "Has she caught you before?"

Henry nodded. "I just managed to slip in through my window before she came up one morning, but she took one look at my bed and knew I'd been out all night. I took the liberty of mussing yours up." He winked at Ore.

Ore shook his head. "It wouldn't have mattered. Last night was different." Henry looked at him questioningly, but Ore didn't expound. "Ilena, we're going to move you, bed and all. Then I'll chase these two out and we'll get you ready for your day." Ore informed her.

"Did you see they brought me flowers?" Ilena asked him.

"Yes," he smiled down at her. "But they'd better bring more in four days. I don't want to see dead flowers on the desk when I get back, nor should you when you're finally awake enough to enjoy them." He looked out of the corner of his eye at them. They'd understood him. "Did you want to let Grandfather know about the new additions coming this afternoon?" he asked her.

"That would be a good thing to do. Boys, let Grandfather know that Thayne and Dane will be brought here to the castle this afternoon. Thayne will be with me for Ore's sake. Master Rei has asked for Dane."

"Yes, Mother," they chorused.

"Okay, lads. Each of you take a corner of the bed." Ore instructed as he headed for the door. He opened it and asked Hue to come in and take another corner, then he took the fourth.

On the count of three, they lifted the bed and moved it to be slightly right of center of the available space in the room. That was so that there would be plenty of room for Doctor Elliot to work on Ilena's left side, and still allow room for the assistants to move around her.

When he was happy with the placement of the bed, Ore sent them all away, quietly telling Marcus to let Leah and Rio know to give him another three-quarters of an hour before they came. He said the same to the guards, asking that they not let even Mizi in until the time had passed. Then he closed the door and returned to Ilena. "Okay. Let's get you ready for your day."

"You're going to do it?" Ilena asked.

"I was doing it before. I've been jealous that they won't let me do it now that we're back in the castle." He said it because of what Mizi had told him the evening before to see if Ilena had a reaction. She did, although he didn't let on he'd seen it. When she wasn't on guard and watching for it, she was actually fun to tease.

He took his time and was careful to give her the full attention he would have given her before, but this time, he also took the opportunity to watch her. Some things he thought would make her blush she took with normal dignity, and others that he wouldn't have thought could affect anyone made her squirm with embarrassment.

He decided that learning everything about her was indeed an interesting past time. But, even though he was enjoying himself at her expense, he wasn't lighthearted about it. It felt more like he was trying to learn everything he could in the last little bit of time he had with her, so that it could be etched into his memory.

When he was done cleaning her and changing her bedclothes, he propped her up in the bed, then stuck his head out the door. Good, the breakfast cart had come. He pulled it into the room and got ready to feed Ilena.

They'd sent a very light meal for her, as she would soon be entering the hibernative state, but Mizi hadn't wanted her to start the day with nothing in her because of the weight loss she'd already sustained. It would be another four days, they expected, before Ilena would really eat again.

"*Hah*," Ilena sighed. "I finally get to sit up to eat, and it's even less of a meal than all the others were."

Ore smiled at her in sad agreement. "Yes. It's true." He looked over the food that had come for him. "They gave me an orange. Would you like it?"

Ilena's eyes lit up. "Could I, please?"

He handed her the bowl and spoon and told her to keep eating, as she could now at least feed herself. He picked up the orange and began to peel it. "You seem to enjoy oranges quite a bit."

"They're very similar to a fruit from Selicia. It's more sweet, a little less tart, there. It was always my favorite. The older I get the more I appreciate the tartness of the oranges, though."

"Say, 'ah'," he said, holding out an orange section. Feeding her didn't make her blush, like it would have most other women. Rather, it made her turn into a little girl again, holding her mouth open in excited expectation, then closing her eyes to chew happily on the flavorful fruit.

He wondered if it was common for the royal youth of Selicia to be hand fed, but he didn't ask. He didn't want to make her remember things that might make her sad today. For every five bites of the porridge she ate, he rewarded her with another orange slice, until both were gone.

While Ore was putting her dishes back on the food tray, Ilena said to him, "Mistress is here. She's been waiting a few minutes already, though not long. And Leah and Rio are on their way across the courtyard."

He looked at her out of the corner of his eye. "You have very good ears, Ilena. Was it so dangerous as that?"

"Mmm...not really for me," she answered him. "It was more so that I could hear what the needs of the household were."

"Is that how you knew when someone was fighting the madness, even if it was across the house, or outside?"

Ilena nodded. "Yes. They, in particular, would make a keening sound that, to this day, I can't stay away from. When I hear it, I must answer it." She turned to look at him and held out her hand to him. "Your heart is making one similar to it now."

He turned and took her hand, then sat on the bed next to her and held her, letting her hold him once again in that position of comfort. He trembled and she slightly tightened her grip on the back of his head. "It was hard enough to go through this the first time," he said to her finally, "to have learned so suddenly who you were after your life was already in danger. But then, you were still a stranger, someone who I might once have known."

He took a couple of breaths. "This time, you're walking voluntarily into the same thing, but now I know you. Now, I'm tied to you with more than strings, more than orders. It feels like being told that Mistress has kidnappers after her again, then just saying, 'here she is, come take her'." His tears burned hot in his eyes and he held her more tightly.

"Ore," Ilena said, "I'm sorry this part is hard, but the surgery will be much better than having a boulder bouncing down the hill at me, not knowing if it was going to hit my leg or my head. I'm glad it didn't hit my head so that I can be here, with you.

"I'm going to think only of what I want. Of being able to run with Ore, of being able to walk behind Master Rei and Princess Mizi, of being able to dance, of being able to ride the wind on horseback. I want Ore to do the same. Think of the things you want after I'm recovered. Then we'll be able to have the strength for this day," she encouraged him.

Ore held her tightly a moment longer, then relaxed a little and nodded into her shoulder. She turned her head and kissed the tip of his ear. "I love you, Ore," she whispered in his ear. Then she let him go. He stood and gently lay her back down to partially sitting up, his eyes trying to say what his mouth could not. Then he walked to the door and opened it to let the other ladies in. He had his public face on by the time he opened it.

"Mistress," Ore bowed. "I'm sorry to keep you waiting." He allowed the three ladies in, saying, "I've just finished getting Ilena ready for the day. She's ready for you."

Ilena smiled at Mizi, Leah, and Rio. "Good morning. It's good to see you again, this morning." They each wished her a good morning as well, and commented that it was good to see her sitting up. Leah made a second check to make sure Ore had done his job right, and was somehow surprised he'd done a good job, even though she'd been told he'd been her nurse for some time.

Mizi talked cheerfully with Ilena for a brief while. Ilena made sure to tell her that Ore hadn't had his breakfast yet. Mizi looked at him and told him he must eat to maintain his strength for the day, then crossed her arms at him until he complied. While he ate, Mizi told them what the day's plan was.

"Mistress," Ore said when she was done, "I've spoken with Master last night. He'll let me stay with Ilena until she's recovered, after I've returned from my errand. While I'm not here, I'll be having Thayne, one of Ilena's Children I retrieved last time, stay with her for me. After I'm excused this early afternoon, I'll be going to bring him here, then I'll leave for my errand."

"Okay, Ore," Mizi said. "I'm glad you've found a way to have strength to do the things you need to do." She seemed glad that he was finally content with being Ilena's partner and was properly taking care of her.

"Rio, bring me the flowers, please," Ilena requested.

"Oh, Mistress, these are beautiful!" Rio exclaimed as she picked them up and brought them over.

"Marcus and Henry stopped by this morning with them. But you already knew that, since they're from the household," Ilena smiled knowingly at her. Rio ducked her head slightly, and smiled shyly back.

Ilena searched through the flowers, then selected a pale pink rosebud and a fragrant green. Asking for another cup of water, she put them in it. Then she gave both back to Rio to put back on the desk. She turned and looked searchingly at Ore. He took a deep breath, then nodded.

"Princess Mizi, I'm ready," Ilena said calmly. "If you'll hand it to me, I'll take it myself." Mizi poured the clear liquid into a cup. "That should last just right," Ilena said after accepting it from Mizi. She downed it like Ore would have downed a shot and gave the cup back to Mizi.

Ore put his chair next to Ilena's bed on her right side, to be out of the way of the surgeon, took the pillows out from behind her and lay her down. He sat in his chair and took her right hand in his. He smiled, remembering. "I did this for the last surgery, too. I held your hand and counted your heartbeats."

"I remember," Ilena said softly.

Ore raised his eyebrows and Mizi asked, "What?" in surprise.

Ilena smiled gently. "The fever had interfered with the Little Death enough that I was partially aware, like being in a dream. It was comforting to know I wasn't alone in the confusion; that someone was holding me anchored with a warm grasp. I was able to relax and focus on that warmth."

Mizi paled. "That was a very painful surgery, Ilena. Were you feeling the pain?"

"No, Princess Mizi," Ilena reassured her. "I was spared that, until I began to rise through the payment phase, of course. And even most of that isn't really remembered after recovering through the normal sleep phase."

Mizi relaxed a little. So did Ore. "Well, I'll anchor you this time as well, Ilena," Ore gripped her hand briefly.

"Thank you," she said softly, then she slowly slipped into sleep, beginning the descent, his golden tawny eyes the last thing she saw, her hand held firmly in his.

-o-o-o-

Ore counted Ilena's initial heart and breath rates and told them to Mizi, who made a note in her medical record. She told him to give her an update every fifteen minutes. If the rate stayed consistent, they didn't need a shorter interval this time.

Mizi looked at Ore carefully. She'd been trying to practice ever since she'd finally come to understand at Osterly that he was having troubles. He was very good at disguising his emotions, but she thought she might be starting to understand them. If she was right, he wasn't doing very well, although he was trying.

"Ore," she bit her lip.

He looked up at her, and smiled. "Yes, Mistress?" It didn't look forced, rather it looked like he was glad she was there. That was good, if she could be a support for him, too.

"Will you tell me how you know Ilena now?" She thought that if he could talk about her, it would distract him from the waiting. It would also let her know that he'd finally been able to face forward.

Ore looked at her seriously for a moment. Then he glanced down at the hand he was holding. "Leah, please go tell Master that Ilena has taken the Little Death. He would like to know it's begun. Ask for the Rose Office. Rio, go and tell Doctor Elliot and Ryan it's started also and ask if there's anything you can do to help them prepare." Both ladies bowed and left the room. They understood that they shouldn't enter the room again until he was done talking with his mistress.

When they were gone, Mizi pulled up another chair on the other side of Ilena, and placed her hand on Ilena's arm, paying attention to the slow drop in her temperature.

Ore took a little time to sort what he was willing to say out of the things that could be said. "In the history of Ryokudo, that Master has, it talks about at the time of his birth the little princess and her parents came from Selicia to Ryokudo for his birth celebration. On their way home, one of the places they stopped by was Tokumade. That princess was five at the time. I only remember her as a spoiled little girl who wanted things she shouldn't be wanting." He looked down, smiling ruefully.

His thumb rubbed Ilena's hand as he continued. "The next time I saw her, it was after the time of the coup. She was a very different person. Strong. Direct. Very concerned about others and their happiness. Alone, save for one nurse. They had crossed the northern mountains together, taking over a year to reach the house at Tokumade. It seemed like she had aged fifteen years in those three years.

"You remember that Captain Grey said that the people of Tokumade respected her at a young age...it was from nearly the time she came. She was able to stand up to the Earl's father, even before she had to learn to stand before the Earl.

"From the time she came, she made it her duty to comfort those who the Earl's father punished, those whose minds were breaking from the treatment they received at his hand. ...Even mine." He paused and smiled a small smile at Mizi. "I told you before, that she healed me then. She healed everyone who needed it.

"Then, the Earl and the Earl's father had a fight, and the Earl killed his father, unexpectedly. He was already one of those who was teetering on the edge of having his mind broken from the treatment of his father. The death of his father broke it." Orc was speaking matter-of-factly, but Mizi had a creeping feeling of horror coming over her.

"He became worse than his father, because his outbursts were unpredictable. One night he went on a killing rampage, killing his second brother and his second brother's wife, and others. I could no longer take the madness, and ran from the house. Later, I missed Ilena's comfort, but remembering it gave me strength."

Ore paused and counted again, then gave Mizi the data. She recorded it, writing in her lap. Ore picked up the story again. "When I came to the castle and saw Mistress, your strength reminded me of her strength. Master's firm kindness reminded me of the same in her. When I saw that there were others like her, in a place I could be safe, it was difficult for me to leave. You both taught me that I wanted to stay close to Master and Mistress.

"I was afraid to return to Tokumade, still fearing for my life. I was very glad when the Earl didn't insist on speaking with us two months ago. ...I'm sorry I didn't attend to you when you were there in the fall. Master allowed me to have other things to do, so that I wouldn't have to enter the house."

"Ah! That's perfectly understandable," Mizi reassured him. "It was difficult to face him as someone who wasn't ever of that house. I can imagine from your point of view it would be impossible."

"...Still, I am sorry," he said quietly. "Like you, I didn't know Ilena was the steward. We didn't see her there this spring because she was already in Osterly, and I hadn't been back until that time. I didn't fully recognize her at the landslide site because so many years had passed. It wasn't until the Captain and his men were talking about her and said her name that I had any idea she was even still alive.

"To have heard she was also the right hand of the Earl made me question reality. Given how I knew the Earl to be, it was very difficult to believe she hadn't also been corrupted somehow in that amount of time." Mizi nodded her understanding. It would certainly be a reasonable assumption.

"The conflict between what I remembered her being like, and what I thought she must have become was what caused you the most difficulty in Osterly. I apologize for that difficulty."

"But, you've resolved that now?" Mizi asked, looking at him.

He nodded. "I learned much from her as she answered Master's questions about what she'd done. And I learned much from her Children as I collected them several weeks ago, about what kind of person she's become. I've been relieved to learn that she is still the same as she was when I left Tokumade, only stronger. The Ilena of then, and the Ilena of now, is someone I can walk beside, although I must help her learn to hear Master and Mistress. She is still very willful."

Mizi smiled. "I imagine that at Tokumade, that was a strength."

Ore nodded. "It may well be difficult to find the balance - allowing her to be strong, yet also teaching her to bow her head. Likely she will only bow her head to Master and Mistress, in the end."

"Do you think she'll learn to listen to me?" Mizi asked, a little surprised. "I think she's already very respectful of Ore."

"Yes, Mistress. She'll listen to you when she feels you're ready to hold her in your hand with strength. She'll teach you that strength. ...She already hears me because she wishes to have my good will from the beginning. If she hadn't decided it for herself, she wouldn't be.

"Even Master and King Brother can't hold her in their hands yet, because she hasn't willingly given herself to them, although she supports them with her strength in the place where she's placed herself."

Mizi thanked Ore for telling her his story and they sat quietly for a while. When he took the next count, and she'd recorded it, he said she might let in the maids, if she liked.

She went to the door and, when she saw they hadn't arrived yet, she let the guards know that they could be granted admittance. Then she and Ore sat and talked of a few light things, both of them glad to have some time in each other's company again, even if for only a short while.

-o-o-o-

Everyone arrived all at the same time an hour later, and preparations for the surgery began in earnest. For Ore, the time of the surgery this time was like the last, being lost in the counting to ensure that they understood the stress to Ilena's body. Holding on to her like a drowning man, willing her to stay alive until it was completed and beyond. For Mizi and Ryan it was a time to learn and understand things they didn't have much opportunity to see, and a short time of focus as they prepared the glue to hold the graft together.

Doctor Elliot made sure to be very careful with his workings. In the end, he did decide to remove the egg sack and tube from Ilena on that side. The egg sack had been torn badly and the fluted end that was near it had been damaged as well. He felt he should follow the midwife's recommendation and err on the side of caution.

Ryan was able to get Ore's attention long enough to explain to him what the surgeon had done. Ore nodded, but wasn't surprised. The two of them shared looks of resignation for the emotional storms that were to come. Leah and Rio, having heard earlier from Ore about it as well, also sighed. If all went well, their Mistress would live and walk again, but they would likely have a battle ahead of them to get her through the recovery.

The repair the field surgeon had tried hadn't worked. Doctor Elliot had to cut the pieces of tendon off that hadn't worked, but he was able to save enough of the tendon connected to the upper front leg muscle to connect to the piece he would be adding. The bone set well and the glue seemed like it would work also.

He stitched the tendons together enough times for it to look like it would hold. He was glad he'd set the glue first, though, because stitching the tendons together put some unexpected stress on the bone graft. It didn't look like it would be too bad if they made sure she wasn't moved at all for the first few days.

In order for that to not happen, he'd brought with him a stick that was thin but sturdy. He had them place it down her left side from just under the left breast to the left knee. They wrapped strips of cloth around her to hold it into place around her ribs, belly and around the left leg. It acted as a body splint so the hip was held in place. After the six weeks were up, she could slowly work the muscle and tendon and stretch them back out. It was the bone graft that needed to set correctly first.

When Doctor Elliot was done, he carefully set everything back in place, but he had a special way of setting it so the skin wouldn't heal just yet. He wanted to be able to get back in quickly if the body typing had been incorrect. Rejections were problematic, and quick re-entry could be essential. Once he was sure the graft had been accepted by her body, then he could allow the exterior of the body to re-heal.

He did have to say that the work Doctor Bonner had done in reconstructing her hip was very good work. He could see where some of the joins were, but for the most part it was very well repaired - even for the fact he'd been setting a woman's hip and not a man's. Doctor Elliot was quite relieved by that. He'd been worried he might have to break it and wait another six weeks before performing his experimental surgery. He was glad he wasn't going to have to mention that possibility to Ilena, or the Regent, now.

When he was done, he put an external cloth over the wound site, explained to Mizi and everyone who was going to be Ilena's nurse how to care for it, then left it to Mizi to finish binding it. He was quite tired, but pleased with how it had gone. He washed his tools and repacked them. Then he and Ryan went over one more time their plan for if the graft was rejected.

They'd decided against using the Little Death in a second dose on top of the first. They would just take her off what she'd had that day. If she needed follow-on surgery, Mizi would make the pain killing tincture she'd made for Ilena before and they would give that to Ilena just before going in. Ryan assured Doctor Elliot that it could be remade each morning and evening so that it would be ready if it was needed. If she didn't need it, then that was okay, too.

Doctor Elliot put his hand on Ore's shoulder, waiting for his attention. When Ore nodded, he said, "I'm going up to see Master Rei now to give my report. He stopped by this morning and said I should do it personally; that it was okay for you to just stay with Mistress Ilena."

Ore glanced at him briefly. "Thanks." Doctor Elliot nodded and patted his shoulder. Taking his leave, he went off to see the Regent.

Ryan gathered up the supplies and ingredients that needed to be taken back to the medical offices. Rio helped him with the things that were too much for him to carry alone, and they went to the infirmary to return them.

Mizi asked Ore for Ilena's vitals when she was done with the bandaging, which Leah and Alice had helped her with, and recorded them in the medical record. The ladies cleaned up the rest of the room. When everything was done, they collapsed into chairs. Rio walked in shortly thereafter pushing the lunch cart.

Mizi looked at it, then at Ore. "I think I would like to take lunch outside in the courtyard. Would you ladies please join me? Ore can eat in a bit." They'd seen her look, and agreed they would like to eat outside as well, so out the cart went again, the ladies with it.

When they were gone, and he was alone with Ilena, Ore finally collapsed on the bed, his hand still holding hers. He was glad Doctor Elliot had said the surgery had gone well, but it hadn't been very good on his heart. He was quite strung out. Sitting on the chair, the top half of his body draped across her bed, he dozed lightly, his mind and body trying to recover.

-o-o-o-

Ore came alert as his body recognized the change in tempo in Ilena's body. She was coming out of the Little Death and approaching the sleep talking phase. He continued to lie halfway on the bed, but he propped his chin up on his arm and waited.

"I don't think I can do that," was the first thing she said.

"What can't you do, Ilena?" he asked her. Involving himself in her dream conversations had nearly become second nature.

"I can't tell you where Kase is."

"Hasn't he run away?" Ore asked.

"No, he's just hiding."

"Oh? Do you know where he is?"

"Yes. I'll find him when Ore's ready to let me find him."

Ore's eyes flew open wide. "You're impossible, Woman." He didn't expect an answer. She was about out of time.

"...Of course I am. If I was easy, I'd already be –"

Was she already asleep? "Dead?" he asked just to be sure.

"Worse. The cause of a war."

He stared at her, then realized she'd moved to the next phase. Quickly he called for the guards to send Mizi in. She arrived just as Ilena was beginning to moan in pain, Ryan, Leah, and Rio behind her. Ore had moved to the left side so he could support the wounded hip.

Mizi took the right side. Together, they held Ilena down as her body arched in pain, although she fought it less this time than she had with the last surgery. Ore wondered if it was because she'd been started on a lower dose, or if it was the splint Doctor Elliot had put on her.

When the pain cycle was over, he quickly walked back around the bed and took her hand again. This time, he sat on the bed next to her, so she wouldn't

64

have to work so hard to see him. The tears started to flow and Mizi, who had traded places with him, pulled out a handkerchief and wiped her face.

"Mistress, will you give her the next dose now?" he wasn't sure how the cycle would go this time.

Mizi shook her head. "I'll give her the first decreased dose to take her off of it tomorrow morning, then again in the morning the next day, then they'll go to this time after that. Doctor Elliot said if the after-tears dose is given this close to the first dose, she'll build up too much in her system too fast."

"Ah, I see." Ore felt the hand in his squeeze his hand. "Good afternoon," he said to Ilena.

"I'm still alive. That's good," she said and slowly opened her eyes.

"Yes it is. Doctor Elliot says the surgery went well. If the graft takes, he says he'll be very pleased."

"That's good. Are you okay?" she squeezed his hand again.

"Yes, now that you're talking to me," he smiled at her. "Is the pain bearable?"

She considered it. "Yes, I guess. Pain is pain, after all."

"True," he said. "But if it feels like coals again, let us know immediately, if you can, okay?"

She nodded. "Ore, the rose and plant I pulled out this morning. Do you see them?"

"Yes."

"Take them and put them in your jacket where they can be seen. Take them with you and remember me. They're all I can send with you." She was fading into sleep. "Ore," she whispered, and he leaned down to hear her final words to him that day.

He kissed her cheek. "Good night, Ilena. I'll be back as soon as I can." He sat with her a few minutes more, not really wanting to go, trying to make it look like he was making sure she was really sleeping. Then he gently let her hand go and walked over to the desk.

He cut the stem of the rose short enough that he could slip it through a buttonhole of his jacket pocket. Then he did the same for the fragrant leaf, tucking it behind the rose. He looked at Leah and Rio. "I leave her in your care." They bowed to him.

He turned to Mizi. "I'll return as soon as I can, Mistress. Please watch over Ilena and yourself while I'm gone, for you'll have none of those Master has set behind you to do it for you."

Mizi was a little surprised that he would be concerned for her, too, at this time. "I will, Ore. I'll give you my strength, too. ...I'll spend the time I'm not here in the Rose Office. That way Rei, Andrew, and Mina can watch over me while the two of you can't."

"Thank you, Mistress." Ore bowed to her. He took one last look at Ilena, then left the room and the castle.

CHAPTER 4 Bringing New Strength into the Castle

Ore had ordered for Fenrier to be ready, so it wasn't long before he was on his way to Falcon's Hollow. On the way, he used the hour hard ride to calculate the passage back. It was a good distraction for him from the other thing his mind kept wandering to.

At some point he patted his horse. He was glad Fenrier loved to run as hard as he did. They didn't get to do it often when Mizi was with them because she wasn't very familiar with horses, but when Ore was sent out as Rei's Messenger, they ran for the sheer joy of the run.

When Ore slowed down to approach the guard station, he realized he'd left without lunch. Maybe there would be someone in the kitchen who could throw something together for him.

"Sir Ore! We didn't expect you today." The day's guards had come out of the station when they saw a rider coming down the road, but he had to be closer before they saw it was him.

"It was decided late last night," he told them, his signature relaxed grin on his face. "That's what I get for being the Regent's Messenger - woken in the middle of the night with new orders and sent out to strange places without warning." They grinned back at him.

Then, a little more serious, he told them, "I've been sent to bring two of them up to the castle, Master's orders. Then I'm off to collect the next set. Has everything been okay at the house?" He hadn't received a daily report for two days and had expected one to arrive today.

"Yes, sir. Things are quiet here, just a few to turn away every so often. Everyone at the house has settled into a nice routine. They're all calling it their 'vacation home'. Most of them are picking up hobbies to keep themselves busy. The ones that aren't have actual jobs to do."

"That's good. I'd hate to see problems crop up due to boredom...like in the soldier's quarters," he waggled his finger at them. "I know what you guys do when you're on down time."

They laughed, embarrassed. "Well, we're trying to be good," they claimed.

"That'd be nice, if it was the truth," Ore said. "Well, I'll wave on my way out." He kicked his horse into motion again and headed at a run down the road towards the house.

The sound of a horse arriving wasn't too unusual, but it was rare enough that everyone that heard it looked for the source. Thayne and Foster were the first to recognize the horse and rider. Thayne ran out towards Ore while Foster started passing the news around that Father had come. Enough clamor went up that even Captain Garen came out to see what was going on.

Ore slowed a bit, then leaned down and extended an arm to Thayne as Fenrier came up by him. Thayne grabbed his arm and leaped up behind him as Ore pulled him up. "You're coming back with me," Ore said to Thayne. "Get

Dane and meet me in the kitchen. I've got to talk to the Captain first, but I haven't had lunch yet."

"Got it," said Thayne as Ore pulled Fenrier to a stop in front of the crowd that had gathered at the main entrance to the manor home. Thayne slid off as soon as they were at a full stop and headed for the kitchen, grabbing Dane's arm and pulling him along.

Foster took Fenrier's reins and Ore jumped off. "I'm not to be here long. Saddle Thayne's horse, and pick one out for Dane." Foster was surprised, but nodded, and led Fenrier to the stable.

Ore picked up three-year-old Thom, who was headed for his leg, and threw him in the air. "And how's Master Thom today?"

Thom grabbed Ore around the neck when he came back down laughing. "Hello, hello!" he crowed. Sallie trotted up to him and held out her hands for Thom. "Thom, Father's here on business. Come here." Thom went.

"I'll come play in a few more days, okay, Thom?" Ore promised.

"Okay!" Thom nodded.

The adults all got interested in that comment, but Ore was grabbing up seven-year-old Micky, who was prepared this time, and throwing him in the air next. "Have you been having a fun adventure so far?" Ore asked him as he set him down.

"Yup!" Micky said. "Grandpa Roy, Mat, and I get to go exploring up in the little caves every day with Mister Robert and Peter!"

"Hoh? There's caves are there?"

"Yup. We're making some of them bigger so we can play fort and the girls can play house. Mister Robert knows how to do it so they don't fall on us." Mat was nodding enthusiastically, too.

Ore smiled at them. "That sounds like lots of fun. Maybe I can come up and see them some time." He looked around for Robert and caught him trying to hide a blush. Ore was glad he'd found something to do that helped the Family as a whole. It must mean that he finally felt part of.

"You can't stay long? That's too bad." Elandra said with the signature pout she liked to show him.

"Are you keeping busy doing good things?" he asked her, really already knowing the answer since the Captain kept him updated.

"Yeah," she sighed. "I might even forget how to be a bad girl at this rate."

"Well, that's not all bad," Ore said, and she mock frowned at him. "Your workload is going to double, though."

"Eh?" she was surprised.

It looked like Ore had everyone in the Family group he was going to get. He turned to the Captain. "I need to talk to you first, to make it all official, but I'm going to ask the Family a question before that. Are you okay with me making it all confusing?" The Captain nodded a bit resignedly. Ore turned to the Family. "I'll explain after I talk to the Captain, but I need your approval for one thing first."

Everyone got quiet and listened. "How do you feel about a very few of you being taken back, for reasons of the Regent, with the approval of Mother, and the rest having to stay?"

Everyone was very quiet with their thoughts for a while. Robert raised his hand. "I'd like to stay. It won't bother me if someone's needed by the Regent."

"I'd leave in a heartbeat, you know that," Elandra said, "but you were right. Sitting on the stable roof is really nice."

"If Foster had to go, I'd want to go with him, and Thom, too," Sallie said. "But if someone was needed, that's okay with me." Betty and Roy nodded. They'd want to stay together, too.

Ore could see that Peter was torn by that. He'd want to stay with Robert, but he'd want to go with his adoptive family. He called to him, "Peter, I know you'd just be happy wherever there was food, as long as it wasn't onions you'd have to peel." That got a few chuckles. "That isn't what I want to know. How would you feel if someone else was taken and you weren't?"

"The same," he shrugged. "If they're needed, then they need to go."

Rose was the last one in the group. Ore looked at her. She smiled. "It's okay. We all feel the same."

"All right then," Ore said. "Gather everyone and meet me in the dining hall in about fifteen minutes and I'll fill everyone in at once."

They nodded and began to scatter. Ore turned to the Captain, "Let's go to your office."

It didn't take long for Ore to tell Captain Garen what his orders were. "Why did you ask them if it was okay first? It's an order from the Regent, isn't it?" Captain Garen wanted to know.

Ore paused for a moment. "They're a family, right? It isn't right to cause them friction without knowing it. If any of them was going to get jealous, or worried they were going to be betrayed, your job would be a lot harder. And...they're part of Mother's household. Her rule is that it's a House with no walls, no restrictions on leaving it if you want.

"She's asked them to let her bend those rules by asking them to remain here peaceably. Yet, now she's also asking them to let her break her own rule again and bring two back. We can't afford to mess with their loyalty to her. That's what's keeping them here and happy."

Captain Garen nodded. "Yes, that makes sense. ...You said you'd be back soon?"

Ore nodded. "When I deposit the two boys where they belong, then I'm off to pick up the next set. I'm sorry I can only tell you I got eight names this time. I get to find out just what ages and how many people that really means this time before I go, but I don't find out until tonight. So I won't be able to give you any more heads up than that, like last time. Sorry." The Captain shrugged. "We should be back faster since I just have to pick them up, not hunt them down. At least, that's the goal." He grinned ironically.

"Well, they'll probably settle in just as quick as this group did. At least that's what they claim," Captain Garen smiled back in a similar vein.

"Okay," Ore stood. "I'll go talk to everyone and let them know what's going on. I've brought news for them, too."

"I'll come tag along," the Captain stood as well. "I've decided my hobby while I'm stuck here is to write up my research on how a group of families becomes a family group, and doesn't kill each other in the process."

Ore laughed. "Well, you'll have to come meet Mother sometime then, and interview her. She's the glue, you know."

"Yeah, I've kind of figured that out." Captain Garen looked at him out of the corner of his eye as they walked down the hall for the door to the servant's quarters where the soldiers were garrisoned. "You remember I asked you when you left last time why they called you Father, and you were playing along?"

"Mmm, yeah, I guess I do." Ore opened the door and they walked out into the yard.

"You said to ask them, so I did." Captain Garen said with a little shrug.

"Did they tell you?" Ore asked.

Captain Garen gave a little shake of his head and gave Ore an odd look again. "Not directly. But I have noticed that you're almost as much glue to these folks as Mother is."

Ore looked at him. "Somehow, I already knew that. I just don't know why yet. ...Except Mother's decided I'm Father, so everyone accepts it."

"It's definitely more than that. In listening to them, it also has to do with why you naturally 'play along' with the title."

Ore paused internally. That struck a chord deep within him that resonated with Ilena's sleep talking earlier. *I'll find him when Ore's ready for me to find him.* He wondered why the two fit together. He pondered that as they entered the house.

He told the captain to wait in the dining room with the others, then went to the kitchen himself. There he found Thayne, Dane, the cook, Bill, and a plate of food set out for him. "Ah, food! Thanks Bill, Thayne," Ore said. He sat and began to eat quickly. "We'll go into the dining hall in a bit. Bill, if you'd go ahead and go now...." Bill bowed slightly and left the kitchen.

Ore thought while he ate. Dane looked at him curiously, wondering if they should really also be there. Thayne saw him shift. "It's okay Dane. Father can only do two things at once. Right now that's eating and thinking. He'll talk once one of the those is done."

Ore rolled his eyes at Thane, but kept eating and thinking. Actually these two would have the answer for him, *if* they'd tell him. Or at least another clue. "What does Mother expect me to become?" he asked them, swallowing down his drink. He caught the look they passed between each other. "Don't answer it now. Answer it once we're on the road. Then you'll have had time to decide how much of the answer you can give me."

"You're really taking us out?" Dane asked.

Ore nodded. "Do either of you have a problem with the fact that Master and Mother have called for you?" He was careful to keep his voice neutral.

"No," they both shook their heads. He could see that they were firm in their commitment to serve both.

He stood. "Good. Come hear the news, then gather up whatever you've got to bring. Foster's getting your horses ready." He led them to the dining room.

Indeed, everyone but Foster, Alice, and the four little children were there. Ore took the central area inside the square of tables, where he'd stood just before he'd left them. "Master and Mother have called for Thayne and Dane to be brought to the castle. They'll be protected there and have specific jobs to do that only they can do.

"I don't expect them to return here, although if any of you wish to visit with them at the castle once this is all over with and you can go home, that would be acceptable. At that point they will be free to leave the castle when their duties permit it. My understanding is that these are permanent assignments."

Everyone looked at Dane and Thayne in excitement. They were looking stunned, but not completely opposed to the idea. Sallie looked at Thayne with that sad but proud look all mothers look at their grown sons with when they move up into full adulthood and leave home. Ore reminded himself he'd have to give him time to say his goodbyes to her and Thom, who would miss him terribly. It was good Peter and the other young boys would be here for the young lad.

"Also," Ore continued, "this evening I begin the collection of the next eight-plus witnesses." Everyone looked at each other with knowing looks. He closed his eyes halfway. "This time I actually get Grandfather's help." Dane laughed and Thayne smiled.

"I'm sure you'll take good care of them. I'll stay a short while to give them the same speech I gave you, and if we're fast enough I'll stay to visit for a few hours. I would like to stay longer, but...I have further news about Mother."

Everyone got very alert and very quiet. He didn't realize it, but they could see that the light he shone with was shadowed slightly as if by a thin cloud. "Doctor Elliot performed an experimental surgery on Mother's hip this morning to graft a new tendon onto the hip bone and the natural tendon in her leg. The surgery went well.

"If the graft isn't rejected by her body, she'll be able to begin learning to walk again in six weeks. She's allowed him up to three tries, as it's painful both physically and mentally. She's already teetering between testy and tantrum from the first six weeks she was required to remain immobile on her back." There were looks of sympathy around the table.

Roy and Betty looked at each other in worry. Sallie looked worried, too. She looked over to Roy and Betty and some unspoken communication went between them.

"Master has approved Grandfather to visit every evening, and has allowed Leah and Rio to come sit with her and brave her tantrums so that Mistress doesn't have to." There were satisfied nods from those who knew the maids. They were pleased she would have the support.

"And, Master has made her his Director of Intelligence." He carefully watched their reactions to that news. Dane sat upright in his chair in shock. Many looked surprised. A few nodded, as if they'd expected some sort of news like that eventually.

As his eyes passed over the captain, he noticed that the captain himself was shocked by the news. Ore smiled inwardly. He would have some interesting new data for his research now, if he was really doing it.

"That's everything I have for now. Thayne and Dane, gather your things quickly, then say your goodbyes. Peter, help Thom. He'll be losing his big brother for the second time." Peter nodded. "I'll be at the stable waiting." Ore turned and left the dining hall. He wondered who of the line of people following him would reach him first.

Captain Garen reached Ore first just outside the house. "He really did that? He made her Director of *Intelligence*?"

"Who put together all these witness all those years ago, Captain Garen?" Ore asked him. "And kept them loyal to herself until they were needed?" That stopped the mouth of the Captain. "Continue to do your research, Captain, but begin to dig a little deeper, open your eyes a little wider." He left the captain behind.

No one else caught up to him before he reached the stable, but when he turned around after checking on his horse, he was surrounded by the two couples of the group, Sallie and Foster - who had been filled in quickly by Sallie - and Roy and Betty. He looked at them quizzically. "What can I do for you?"

The individuals of the group shifted until an unspoken spokesperson was chosen. Foster crossed his arms and Roy said, respectfully, "Father, you are not okay."

Ore grimaced. Of course. These four would know it. "No, not really, but Master's done his best to give me what I need in the middle of having needs of his own. He allowed me to stay with Mother through the surgery.

"Ilena's given me Thayne, with Master's approval, to watch over her while I'm gone. He'll stay with us in the same capacity I've stayed with Mistress for Master." Foster nodded his approval.

"When I return to the castle, Master will allow me leave from my duties until she's sufficiently recovered - which will likely be when she starts to throw her tantrums and I'll wish to escape." He smiled a lopsided smile. Foster grinned back at him. Roy hid his smile, but it was knowing all the same.

"That's good," sighed Sallie. "To be sent out on the same day...," she shook her head. "I'm glad that Thayne can be a support for you. I think of all of us he's wished the most to not be here, but to be where he can be of use to you.

"Thom will be okay. It was different when Thayne was meanly stolen away and we were all sad. For you to take him, Thom will be happy to share his brother and we'll be happy with him. It will help that we can tell him we'll visit Thayne later."

"That's good to hear," Ore said.

"If it's okay with you," Betty said carefully, "we'll explain it to everyone after you've gone. Then they won't press you more than you can bear when you return. There will be other times we can visit with you that your heart won't be weighed down and your desire conflicted."

The other three nodded. "It would be wise to allow it," Foster said, looking at him meaningfully. Ore remembered that he'd been through the loss of one wife already.

Ore nodded. "You may tell them after we're gone."

Betty and Roy each extended a hand to him. Not normally physically demonstrative, except with Mother, he paused. Then he took their hands in his. This was Mother's world. They pressed his hands to extend to him their strength, then they released him and left.

Sallie threw her arms around him and gave him a hug. Ore tried not to be too distressed. Then she stepped back and Foster took Ore's forearm in his big hand. "Mother is strong. Rely on Thayne. He won't fail you." Ore nodded, and they, too, left saying they would go find Thayne and say their goodbyes. Sallie called to the children and they said that Peter had already collected Thom.

As he watched them walk off, Ore felt Elandra's presence above him. He looked up and into her face that was peeking over the edge of the roof. She grinned at him. "It's very quiet up here. If you'll join me, I'll promise not to say or do anything."

She was right. That really was where he wanted to be right now. "You promise?"

"Yup," she was just as serious as he was. Ore was on the roof quickly. He found his favorite view and sat down. After a while, the peace of the openness and the distant sounds of people began to seep into him. He noticed that even Elandra's quiet presence was surprisingly calming. It was good to know he wasn't alone at this time. After some time had passed, Elandra said quietly, "They're coming."

He looked over to the house and saw that she'd been sitting so she could watch out for them for him. He slid over to the edge of the roof. "Thank you," he said to her.

"Take care of her for us," she requested.

"I'm doing my best," he answered before he slipped down to the ground.

Dane and Thayne tied their bags to the backs of their saddles, then looked at Ore expectantly. He smoothly climbed into his saddle, and they followed suit. They took one last look around Falcon's Hollow, then followed behind him as he led them out onto the road. The guards waved them through as they passed the station.

Ore estimated they had about two hours they could be out, but first he had things to say to the two he'd called out. So for now, he went at a somewhat slow trot. Fenrier wasn't pleased. He liked to either take it at an easy walk, or run hard. It was difficult to get him to take the middle speeds. Ore forced his way - Fenrier could use the practice.

He motioned to the two other young men to come up on either side of him. He found it interesting that when the Family was all together, he really did think of them as being much younger than him, or he as much older. When they were like this, it was more like what they really were, all young men roughly the same age.

"Dane, Master's taken your brother Tairn into his office where he is studying under one of his direct aides, Miss Mina, the heiress to the Yosai Earldom. Her father is now requiring her to spend half of her year at Yosai to learn her duty. Master, of necessity, has need of two who can take her place when she can't be at Castle Nijou." He spoke directly ahead so both could hear him. Now he looked sideways at Dane. "It was you and your father's example to me that decided him in the choice."

Dane was looking pleased and surprised. "It takes two to replace her?"

"Yes. Miss Mina is excellent at everything she does because she feels she can't afford to be bested by any man, as the sole heiress of the Earldom. However, that makes her loss to Master more difficult to compensate for." Dane nodded.

"I wasn't present for Tairn being called up, but Miss Mina's told me that she was careful to call Master to remembrance that he already had one heir he would lose, and he was calling another. He calmed her by saying that he was only calling Tairn for the time it took Miss Mina to train her second understudy to be as efficient as she. That way he'll only have to continue to look to one permanent aide." Dane was still listening politely.

"You'll need to work hard. She returns with her father to Yosai after the Lord's Court this year, and will likely not return again until next spring. Tairn should be able to help you with the work, but she isn't putting as much effort into training him in her methods as she will with you."

"Wait. *I'm* being called up to be Lady Mina's eventual replacement?" Dane was flabbergasted.

Ore nodded. "The stacks on my desk need attending to as well. If Miss Mina gives you any time to rest at all, please help Mistress with my stacks. She's only had one day of training."

"Lady Mizi is in the office?!" Dane's eyes were even bigger.

"She requested it. Ilena's allowed it temporarily while she isn't available for her training. When Ilena recovers, Mistress won't be able to help me as much, I'm afraid. She'll be very busy with just as difficult a task mistress as Miss Mina, learning to be Master's Princess." Ore put on a sad face. He really would have liked to have more of Mistress's help.

"Mother's doing what?"

"Mistress has asked Ilena to help her become Master's Princess. Master's been unable to do it himself, so the matter has been taken out of his hands by the two Mistresses." Ore shook his head. "Ilena warned me that she was going to be difficult. She was not lying."

Dane worked to wrap his head around the news. He shifted uncomfortably. "Umm...has my brother said anything?"

"Yes. He's told us he's King Brother's man and you are Ilena's. Master says that's fine. If he forgets to tell a thing to his brother, Tairn may tell him. If something comes through the office you believe Ilena should know, you may tell her. He doesn't want something important to go missing."

"Ah, I see." Dane seemed to be feeling very enlightened.

"Is that why you were so surprised that she's been asked by Master to be his Director of Intelligence?" Ore asked.

"Yes," Dane affirmed.

"Mmm, well, Ilena made it very obvious what she wanted her place to be. When she's finished proving herself, Master will place her where she belongs."

"Wait." Thayne protested. "She's been given the Directorship while she's still in testing?"

Ore nodded. "Master understands that King Brother already recognizes her skills. That isn't what Master's testing."

Now Dane was surprised again. "The King already knows she's a ...."

"Yes. He's been watching her and their networks cross in several places. ...It's how she found me again, she says," Ore said calmly.

"Oh," Dane said faintly. Then after a pause, "Then I should be able to work with Tairn. It's always been a difficulty for us that he couldn't understand her place in the workings of Ryokudo. That has never mattered to me."

"Yes," Ore said smiling. "He was as surprised as you when he and Master talked. I think he was muttering just yesterday that he was wishing you could come soon and help carry the burden that is Miss Mina."

"Will it be that hard?"

"Yes, but it will be well worth it." Ore looked at him with Father's eyes, although he didn't know it.

"All right, then," Dane nodded, finally content.

"Actually, they were going to wait until all of Falcon's Hollow was released to bring you to the Rose Office, but you were Master's price for me to gain

Thayne. Master has been waiting for that excuse for some time. He hated to be the one who owed Ilena. But then you would have had only your brother to train you for most of a year...or you would have been sent to the Earldom to train with Miss Mina there. Mister Andrew didn't like that idea, though, particularly now that they're engaged, finally."

Dane had ever so many questions. "What? Isn't he the close aide to Prince Rei that no one believes would ever leave his side?"

"Of course. It's likely he still won't leave Master's side, although they have yet to work out their plan. But if he does, I do hope Master doesn't make me stand in his stead. I have enough difficulty with the little, in comparison, he has me do. Ah, but already Mister Andrew is giving me other tasks of his own to complete...and he already has the entire Rosebud Office to call on, while Ore has no one other than an untrained Mistress." Ore was sad again.

Dane held up his hand to slow down the words that kept pouring from Ore. "Um...if he does that, Father won't be able to stand in the place Mother wishes to place him."

Ore looked at him sharply for a few seconds. "We'll come back to that," he said shortly. Dane nodded, although he was surprised Ore was willing to put off the question he'd asked earlier.

Ore directed his attention to the other young man with him. "Thayne, Ilena has given you to me. She asked at first if I should like you as my man-at-arms." Thayne gave a start. Ore found that interesting. "I told her I wasn't in a position to have such a thing. She said that she would give you to me to stand in my place beside her when I can't stand there, and that she would send you with me when she can't go with me. Master approved, if Dane was brought as well. Thus here we are." They both nodded.

"When we arrive at the castle I'll take you both to your quarters and give you your keys, then introduce you to Master. We'll leave Dane there in the cold ungentle hands of Miss Mina and the desperate embrace of his brother," Dane was looking a little pale. "Ah, sorry, Dane. It isn't that bad, really." It didn't look like he was going to believe Ore.

"And I'll take you, Thayne, to Mother. The location of her room is secret. You mustn't let anyone know you know of her, or where she is." Ore looked at him directly, his eyes fierce.

Thayne nodded, "Yes, Sir."

Ore turned the same look on Dane. "Yes, Father."

Ore continued. "I'll introduce you to her guards and Mistress. Mistress, Leah, and Rio are sitting with Ilena. You'll also sit with her in my place. Typically my watch is the last watch from the eleventh hour until breakfast is served.

"Always be respectful of Mistress. Because you're in my place, I'll expect you to also stand behind Mistress as she has need, for during this time neither Ilena nor I are there. She's promised to spend her time away from Ilena at the

Rose Office where Master can watch over her. You will at the very least see she arrives there safely.

"If she knows when you should go to fetch her, you should also see her away. But if you take her to her rooms at night, never enter them or Master will send you away immediately. Call for Miss Mina. Her rooms are next door to Mistress'." Ore paused. It was a lot of instructions all at once.

Thayne nodded his understanding again. Ore sighed. "I'd originally thought I would like to have you with me again. Ilena would send you with me, being as concerned about me being gone as I am about her being alone. But my need is greater than hers, and I'll have another guide from Grandfather." He almost missed the look that went between Dane and Thayne.

"Ah, there are others of the Family in the castle - I'm sure many I don't know yet - but Thayne, you'll remember Marcus and Henry, the runners from the Black Cat." Thayne nodded. "They've arrived since Master let Ilena speak with Grandfather. She's called them to do her work.

"This morning they arrived outside her door to wake us up. I've told the guards they may be admitted, but for the first week of her recovery, only those who are required to assist her should be admitted. If she's strong enough after that, we'll see. I've required them to bring her a gift in four days. It's to remind her to get better for my sake.

"Now, Dane, let's have the answer. I asked 'what does Mother wish for me to *become*', you said '...in the *place* she wishes to put me'. They are two different things. Which one will you answer?"

Dane considered it. "I don't think I may answer the first one. I'll answer the second." Ore nodded, and Dane continued. "I think perhaps you may already know it, although it hasn't been said yet.

"A high level court appointment requires many staff, and most importantly, the one who stands next to the one who is in the highest position. In the case of the Department of Intelligence, the person who stands at the first level must be completely loyal to the crown, or regent, lest they plot and execute the downfall of that crown or regent.

"The second to that person must also be of the same level of loyalty. Not only because they know all of the information, but because they fulfill the will of the highest level person."

After some deciphering, Ore said, "Because Master will put Ilena in as Minister of Intelligence, she will put me as her Assistant Minister, in order that I may carry out her and Master's will."

Dane nodded. "You've understood it."

Ore nodded. He could see it. He could also see it conflicting with what Master wanted if they didn't agree early where Ore should be placed. It was good Dane had told him. He'd tell Master about it, so that they could set Ilena's expectations appropriately.

He remembered what Rei told him, *"That Princess claimed you long ago, and she will make you one who can stand beside her, the same as she'll make Mizi someone she can stand behind."* Just as Mizi must become a princess to have a princess stand behind her, just as Ilena must become a minister for a princess to stand beside the Regent, that Princess Minister couldn't have some stray dog picked up out of the gutter to stand beside her, whether or not he was the assistant minister, although that position would also not be handed to any stray dog.

In his thinking over lunch, he'd come to understand that she would bring his own past back to haunt him again. But Dane was right, it wasn't his place to tell Ore. Ilena would tell him in her own way, in her own timing.

While she might say she would wait for Ore to be ready to reveal Kase Shicchi's hiding place, he knew she wouldn't wait if it was detrimental to her plans to wait. He needed to become prepared or he would have to fight against her very hard. He didn't want either at the moment.

He shook his head. "I'm done with my speaking. Let's hurry to the castle." He finally allowed Fenrier his head and he leaped ahead at a run. The others hurried after him, their horses just as happy to stretch their legs and feel the freedom of the speed.

-o-o-o-

Rei had told Ore to quarter Dane in the same wing as his other aides, so Ore had given him the room next to Andrew's. Ore pointed out whose rooms were whose. The lower corner room on the right closest to the stairs was his own, then Andrew's, then Dane's. The rest were empty on that side. Above were Mizi's, then Mina's, then the rest empty. The rooms on the other side of the wing were all empty, and were suites - two bedrooms to either side of a main sitting room or office.

The central area was a great hall with seating around the edges. A breakfast cart was brought there early in the morning for the aides to eat from before they went to work in their respective offices. The stair rose up at the far end from the main entrance to the hall and a set of doors at the landing led out into a small private garden where the aides could go to relax on their down time.

The private garden was used most often as a private trysting spot for Rei and Mizi when he had the time to walk her to her rooms. Of course private was relative. At least one of the knights was always with them unless Rei sent them away. Then they stayed just inside the door where he could call them if he needed them.

Outside the hall, on the castle side, the door was guarded by two guards. They prevented unwanted entry into the wing, and if any aide needed anything, they could let the guards know. Ore had introduced both Thayne and Dane to the guards when they'd entered the wing.

"Here's your key, Dane. Go explore for a minute. I'm going to stop by my room while I'm here." Ore hadn't been back for a while and he needed to get properly dressed for going to the Glass Bottle that night. That took a little longer than he expected. He didn't want to wear his dress formals, and his normal castle uniform wasn't quite right either.

He finally settled on his one 'costume' that he kept to get into such nice places. He didn't like it very much. Maybe he should ask the castle clothing department to make him a new outfit that was more comfortable.

Thayne whistled when Ore came back out and Dane looked at him approvingly. "You dress up nice!"

Ore tugged at his jacket, then checked to make sure the rosebud and greenery were set firmly in place. He'd worried he might have lost them on the run back, but he hadn't. "I'm meeting my guide at the Glass Bottle."

Dane nodded, understanding. "That should go over fine there, but are you going to have to wear it the whole trip?"

Ore looked at him aghast. "Absolutely not! I have other things packed, of course."

Thayne smiled at Dane. "Don't you remember what he wore into your house? He seems to keep various costumes around with him everywhere he goes."

"Well...this is my only costume. The rest are real work clothes." Ore said. "Let's get moving to the next thing. In the interest of time, Thayne, I'll take you to your room later. It's closer to Ilena's."

To the people who saw them pass in the hallways, it looked like a new lordling had come to the castle with his two men at arms behind him. Ore would have been horrified to know. The few times he greeted people he knew, they had to look twice to understand who it was they'd seen.

Even the guards at Rei's office door almost didn't let him in at first glance. It wasn't until he gave them his "do I need to be angry with you" look that they believed it really was the Ore who tortured the Regent so much. Before they knocked and announced them, Ore introduced Dane and Thayne to them, so they could have correct passage into the room later.

Mina opened the door to let them in. She stood in the doorway a moment sizing up the three young men. Then she said to Ore, "You look more like what I was expecting than them. I don't think I can let you in."

"You want this one," Ore pointed to Dane. "Are you going to let Master greet them or not?"

Mina moved one step and turned to let them in, then closed the door behind them. Rei was still sitting at his desk as it wasn't a meeting, but he'd put his work aside for the moment. Andrew was standing next to Rei's desk and Tairn was standing at his own desk, looking very relieved to see his brother enter the room. They gave each other careful nods of greeting when Dane first entered the room.

Ore led them up to Rei's desk. "Master, this is Dane Malkin, second son of Earl Malkin. This is Thayne of Wexford." He indicated each of them in turn.

Rei greeted them both in proper order, then addressed Thayne first. "Thank you for coming to stand behind Ore for Ilena's sake. I'll entrust her to your care while Ore is gone. As I'm personally interested in her welfare, I wish you to understand that if there are any significant changes in her status, you will please inform me right away."

"Yes, Regent," Thayne bowed.

Rei turned to Dane. "Dane, you'll stand with your brother to support Mina. In my office, please refer to me as Rei. Thank you for showing mercy to Ore when you first met him. You have my gratitude for forgiving me as well, and being willing to come with him."

"It's my honor," Dane bowed.

Rei glanced at Andrew who took his turn. "I'm Andrew Marciel. Welcome to the Rose Office. I'll have your castle staff badges for you by tomorrow afternoon, however without having Ore here, Thayne, it may be a few days before we can get yours to you. You understand that we can't send a paige with it."

"Ah, that," Ore said, shifting. All the regular's eyes turned to him. "This morning two of Ilena's who've come since Grandfather began coming arrived at her room barking to be let in. It was a disturbing alarm clock for this morning. Ilena said they were finally admitting they already knew where she was so they could wish her well before the surgery.

"Their names are Marcus and Henry and currently they're working as castle paiges. If you need to send messages between here and Ilena's room, you may use them. Ilena said they're used to hard work. Apparently they keep asking her for it."

Rei, taking the news in that she'd indeed started acting right away, was pleased. His eyes lifted in a minute smile. "See to it," he said. He looked at Mina, signaling it was her turn to speak.

"I'm Mina Durand. I hope you'll be able to learn quickly what I have to teach you, Dane. Tairn has proved most helpful. I look forward to working with you also."

Dane bowed to her. "Please take care of me."

"Then, please come over here. This will be your desk." She placed her hand on the table that was set perpendicular to her and Tairn's desks. It already had several stacks of documents on it.

Ore waved a "good luck" wave at Dane as Dane gave Ore a "good bye" look. Ore was about to take Thayne off, halfway back to the door, when Rei called him. "Ore."

"Master?" he looked curiously at Rei to see what he needed.

Rei looked at him closely. Ore's eyes were worried, but they weren't shadowed, and his shoulders held the burden of his partner, but he was no longer unsure of himself. Rei nodded. "So, did you end it with the same kiss as you began it?"

Ore blushed a bright red and everyone in the room looked at him in shock. Even Rei had only expected an off-hand comment like usual. Ore had been so suddenly filled with a confusion of emotions he wasn't sure how to respond. Rei also noticed that fact.

It was obvious to him...Ore had, and it had probably been received well. If it had been otherwise, Ore would have easily deflected the comment. "Ah," Rei said contritely, "I'm sorry. I shouldn't have teased."

Ore, still not really knowing what to say for the first time in a very long time, finally settled on a quick retreat. He bowed to Rei. "We'll take our leave." He turned and led a still shocked Thayne out of the Rose office.

After he was gone, Andrew looked at Rei. "You've managed to make Ore mad, I think?"

"I wonder?" Rei said. "I certainly didn't expect such a strong reaction, or I wouldn't have said it."

"Who did he kiss this time?" Mina asked.

"This time?" Andrew asked, not understanding since he thought he knew Ore didn't go around kissing people generally.

"Wasn't it Rei last time?" Mina said as if she was keeping score.

"He didn't!" Rei protested vehemently.

Mina just gave him one of her signature cool looks, and Rei knew she was punishing him for having said it and making Ore mad. He sighed and rested his chin in his hand. He would have to remember to apologize to Ore again properly when he returned.

Dane looked at Tairn, wonder and questions in his face. Tairn shrugged, saying, *yes, that's typical of this office.* Dane smiled a little. Even if Mina was a hard taskmistress, he would enjoy working here.

-o-o-o-

After walking in silence for a while, Ore asked Thayne, "How would you go about getting Marcus or Henry to know you needed them?"

"Ahh," Thayne was startled out of his thoughts by the question. "...Like this," he pursed his lips and whistled.

Ore quickly memorized the whistle. "That's an interesting way to communicate with them. Would you do that for any of Mother's Children in the castle?" Thayne shook his head. Ore crossed his arms. "Thayne, for someone who supposedly was stuck in a back country hunting lodge, you seem to be particularly knowledgeable about Ilena's household matters."

Thayne flushed. He'd been found out. "You said earlier that Tairn admitted to Prince Rei that Dane was an agent of Mother's. I...am also one. She had me be sure to stay at the hunting lodge this last season particularly in order to be taken up by Viscount Delay, so that I could learn what his intentions were.

"Prior to that, I was stationed mostly in Kouzanshi. However, Marcus and Henry are never far from Mother. I learned that way of contacting them when she would visit there."

"I see," Ore said. He wondered how far away the whistle could be heard from and how long it would take Henry and Marcus to arrive. He was surprised when they rounded a corner and Marcus was in front of him, with Henry running up behind him.

"You called?" Marcus grinned at him. Henry was trying to catch his breath. He must have come from far away. They'd been very fast to respond.

Ore passed them and kept walking. "Well, I had Thayne do it this first time." They fell in behind him. "While I'm gone, Master will need trusted hands and feet to deliver information between the Rose Office and Mother's room. I've told him about you. You're being assigned to his personal paiges.

"Please inform the paige office. If they need corroboration, you may let Mister Andrew know you need notice sent down. That's one of his jobs." He said it just because he was glad it wasn't going to be his job this time, and he wanted to pay Andrew back for pushing that onto him these last few days.

"But you can't say you're being assigned to Mother, just to Master." They nodded. "Make sure you properly introduce yourselves to the Rose Office and Master so they know who they're trusting. Thayne," Ore pointed at him with his thumb, "will be with Mother while I'm gone. Be obedient to him."

He watched from the corner of his eye as they gave Thayne serious looks, then they nodded to Ore again. "Ah, and, you may deliver gifts to Mother, but this week, at least, you aren't to disturb her."

"Yes, Father," they both said obediently.

"Off you go, then," Ore said casually, and they took off towards the part of the castle the paige's office was in.

Thane followed him quietly for a while, then said, "I was right before, you know. You are a natural."

Ore would have shrugged it off, but it clicked into place with the other pieces he'd been considering that day. Ilena was going to put him in a high place, and Thayne was telling him it was a place he naturally fit into. Ore sighed. "I'm thinking I would rather not be, right now. I'm still not sure I'm ready to fit into that place."

Thayne looked at him, then smiled his secret smile. Ore wanted to wipe it off his face, but held himself still. "Have you been paying attention to the path?" Ore asked him. Thayne nodded.

Ore pointed down a hallway to their right. "Going this way will take you to your quarters. You're in the same wing as Leah and Rio. I thought it best to keep you all together. Here's your key. The room number is on it." Ore handed the key over and Thayne looked at the number, then put the key in a pocket. "You'll have to learn the way later. Maybe one of the ladies can help you find it. For now, we go this way."

Orc turned to the left, then took the next right. "This is the medical wing and infirmary." It was a rectangular building, with rooms around the perimeter accessed from the interior, then a covered hallway area concentrically set within that perimeter.

In the center, as was the case with most of the wings, was an open courtyard, divided into three sections by more covered walkways that joined the opposing long sides of the rectangle. At the ends of the crossing walkways were exits from the wing that took pedestrians out to other parts of the castle.

"This side," Ore motioned to their left, "is the medical offices, infirmary, and healers, with the gardens and greenhouses on the other side. That side," he motioned to the right, "is the surgeons. Doctor Elliot has his laboratory and office in that room." He pointed to a specific set of rooms about at the half-way point on the right-most side of the rectangle from them.

"If Mother has need this week, that's where you must go to fetch him. He'll be standing close by until he's satisfied that the graft has been accepted. He says a rejected graft is a very serious thing and will need his immediate attention." Thayne nodded soberly, marking the office well.

They were nearing the end of the left hand side they'd been walking down. "These doors," Ore indicated a set of doors that had two guards set on it, "are the entrance to the offices proper. This is where Ryan, the Head Healer, and Mistress work. I don't know how much time Mistress plans to spend here this week, but if she wants to work here, bring her without her knowing it." They turned the corner and began to walk up the short leg of the wing.

Half-way up was another guarded door. Ore stopped in front of it. "Sailte, Hue, this is Thayne. He's standing for me while I'm gone. Do not interrupt his work." They nodded and looked at Thayne closely. Thayne nodded a greeting to them, and looked them over as well.

Ore paused, then added, "The two brats from this morning are being assigned as paiges between the Rose Office and here. Feel free to confirm they're on Master's business if you think they're here for fun." The guards nodded. Hue's eyes sparkled. He likely thought it would be fun to have them come by to visit now and again.

Ore took a breath. He considered not entering for fear his presence would wake Ilena up. Then he realized that was just an excuse. She would have already heard him talking, even with the door closed, and probably from most of the way down the wing. She wouldn't be pleased with him if he left without saying goodbye.

He'd learned that from Master and Mistress. Not that that had stopped him before, but he still had to introduce Thayne to Mizi. He nodded to Sailte, who knocked on the door, waited a pause, then opened it.

Ore led Thayne into the room. It felt small again, because they'd decided to leave Ilena's bed in the middle of it. They would move her back against the wall after Doctor Elliot declared her secure.

Mizi and Rio were in the room. Mizi had a book in her hands, as always, and Rio was hand stitching some cloth. Ore noticed Ilena was still breathing peacefully, but he was sure she was already beginning to rouse. It didn't make him happy. He would rather she stayed asleep.

Mizi stood when they entered. "Ore, was your trip successful, then?"

Ore nodded, "Yes, Mistress. This is Thayne of Wexford. Thayne, this is Mizi, Ilena's mistress." He remembered what title she'd claimed for herself in cases like this.

Thayne bowed respectfully. "Mistress Mizi. Please take care of me."

Ore saw Ilena shift her hand slightly and the corners of her lips seemed to pull up a little. She liked Thayne as well, he could see. That was good. "Mistress, I must leave it to you to instruct Thayne. Rio, I've pointed the way to the wing you're housed in. If you could be sure he understands how to get there?" Rio nodded.

Ore sighed. Ilena was nearing fully awake. He turned and looked at her. "It would be better if you stayed asleep, you know," he scolded her.

Rio hid a smile and Mizi looked at him in surprise. "She's awake?"

"Almost. She can't bear to have people in the room she hasn't acknowledged. Go say hello, Thayne." Ore motioned him to Ilena's bedside.

By the time Thayne was at Ilena's side, she did indeed have her eyes open. "Welcome Thayne," Ilena said thinly, still very weary from her ordeal, but a smile was on her face and in her eyes. "Thank you for coming."

"Mother. ...Mistress Ilena," for some reason using her correct title for his position made him blush. "It's an honor to be asked to serve."

Ore knew it was true. "His own mother, Sallie, said he'd been pining, wishing he could be here in this place."

Ilena looked at Thayne closely. "Have you had a desire fulfilled, Thayne?"

Thayne blushed deeper. "...Yes, Mother."

"That's good. Then it's a full circle." Ore didn't know what that meant for sure, but the words made Thayne's face go soft. Ilena let her eyes close briefly. Thayne stepped back, making room for Ore, looking at him expectantly.

Ore sighed internally. He hated saying goodbyes. The one he'd already said earlier was enough for him. He worked up his courage, then stepped to the side of the bed and looked down at Ilena.

"I'm sorry, Ore," she said, "for waking up and making you do this again."

He stared at her for a moment. Then he shook his head with a small, wry grin. "Ah, well. It was inevitable, having to bring Thayne in. Also, I knew I would leave you feeling sad if I didn't come in with him. I didn't need you crying more tears on my account."

She looked at him and smiled. "Thank you for desiring to decrease your own burdens."

"Was that supposed to be a slight?" he furrowed his brows at her.

"No," she continued to hold her smile.

He gave up and his hand reached for hers. He really was going to have to do something about that, having his hands do things without his permission. She accepted his hand and held it warmly, then she gave up and fell back to sleep. When he was sure she was asleep, he let her hand go gently and turned back towards the room.

Mizi had her head tucked into her book. That meant she was embarrassed, but her expression was happy. Well, if he'd made her happy, that was alright. Rio was pragmatically back at her sewing. Thayne was watching him with an interesting expression on his face, but Ore couldn't quite interpret it.

"One thing I've learned is, when all else fails, hold her hand and she'll fall asleep. I'm not sure I like the thought of you doing it, but if you need it, now you know, too." Ore told Thayne. "I'll leave you to it."

Thayne bowed. "I won't fail you, Master Ore."

Ore nodded at him, then bowed to Mizi. "Mistress."

"Have a safe trip, Ore," she smiled at him.

He smiled at her, then finally was able to escape the room. Once he was through and beyond the door, he paused and looked back. At least with this leaving he was leaving Ilena much better protected than for the first, and...he knew he would be coming back.

CHAPTER 5 Second Set of Witnesses

Ore walked into what was indeed a high class eating establishment. The Glass Bottle was completely different from either of the other two places run by Children of Mother that he'd been in. This one reeked of money. It surprised him. He wouldn't have thought of it at all from his previous experiences, but then he remembered Elandra. Based on everything other than her, he wouldn't have expected her either.

A proper waiter welcomed him, sat him in a seat along the wall as he requested, and took his drink order. Ore ordered from the high end of his personal favorites, glad the castle was covering his expenses.

He looked around the room. There weren't too many other customers at the moment. Quiet conversations were going on between well-dressed ladies and gentlemen, the majority of them middle-aged. Ore suspected it didn't ever get very rowdy here.

After a while, a well dressed waitress appeared with his drink and an excellently prepared meal. She was polite, but she didn't stay. He began to eat, wondering at what point he would be helped with his other need. After the first few bites, he decided it wouldn't be all bad if it was after he was done eating. In the end, it was after he ordered his after-dinner drink.

This time his drink was brought to him by a distinguished gentleman, greying about the temples. In manner, he reminded Ore of Tairn and Dane's father, Earl Malkin. "I hope you've enjoyed your meal," the man said. "I'm Mister Holloway, owner of this establishment. Is this your first time coming?"

"Yes, it is," Ore said. "The food was quite excellent, thank you."

"If there's anything I can do for you?" Mister Holloway asked.

It seemed to Ore that this place must be, at best, an undercover location. It was no wonder Ilena had given him a specific thing to say. "Well, actually, there is. I'm about to embark on a trip, but it's to a place I haven't been yet. I was hoping to find a guide who might be able to go with me, or at least who could tell me about the place before I leave. Would you be able to help me?"

"Hmm," Mister Holloway considered. "I might be able to. One of my customers is a merchant, and he happens to be here tonight. Perhaps he's traveled to where you're going. I'll ask him if he'll speak with you."

"Thank you very much," Ore said gratefully. He hoped that would be the right person. He had no idea where to say he wanted to go. Then on the heels of that thought, he knew instinctively where to say, although he didn't know if anyone else in the Family would know of Ilena's ties to that place.

He sipped his drink and watched as Mister Holloway walked to another table across the room and spoke with another man, probably in his mid-thirties. That man nodded, stood, and followed Mister Holloway back to Ore's table. Ore stood to receive him politely. "This is Raine Marciel. He's consented to speak with you."

"Thank you very much," he said to both of them and Mister Holloway left them to their conversation. Ore asked Raine to sit, sitting himself.

"So, this is the new young lord I heard about today," Raine said. "You've just come to the castle today, and already you're leaving?"

Ore raised his eyebrow. He wasn't quite sure what Raine was talking about, but decided to play along. "Yes, well, I was just there for a brief visit this afternoon. I've business elsewhere I must attend to. I was hoping you could help me with it?"

"I hope I'm able to. I've traveled extensively as a merchant. Where is your business?"

"Well, it's along the North road in various places, but I was also hoping I could hear a little about Selicia. I've heard they have a fruit very similar to oranges, though less tart and more sweet. I was wondering if that was a product that could be procured and shipped to Ryokudo, say...at least to Castle Nijou?"

"Mmm," Raine rubbed his chin. "I've tried that fruit myself. It's called mikan. It is indeed very good. It's also a delicate fruit, not suited to transport through the mountains, except at the height of the warm season. You're asking at the right time, though. If I sent a party now, it would be able to bring one shipment that would arrive at the castle towards the end of the summer. That's a bit of an expensive proposition, however, for one box of fruits that are similar to what we have here."

"Are there other products of Selicia that could be brought and sold to cover some of the expense?"

Raine smiled. "You're familiar with the trade of merchanting, I see. Well, yes there are, of course. Hmm...I could bring you one crate of mikan but it would be less expensive if you could order several. The fruits are fairly small, easy to peel, and can be eaten very quickly. Even three crates would hardly satisfy if there is more than one or two in your House you would be sharing them with."

Ore considered him, and wondered if he could expense it to the castle. "How much for three crates, then?" Raine named a price. Ore blinked. He couldn't help it. "*Hahh*...that is rather a lot for just a different variety of oranges, isn't it. How much for two crates?" Raine named another price that was more than two-thirds the original cost for three. Ore wasn't surprised. "How well do they store? If I were to hold back a crate, how long would it last for?"

Raine considered. "We'll have to purchase them still green off the tree so that they ripen slowly during the transport. That will affect the quality a little bit, but only native Selicians who've had freshly ripe ones would notice the difference.

"If they were kept cool, they might be able to be stored up to another month past the time they were delivered, I would think. You would want to be careful to check them daily or every other day and pull any that looked like they were molding or shriveling."

"Only a month...," Ore couldn't see paying for three crates for only a month of potential eating.

"Well, they tend to be eaten quickly, as I said. It might be hard to get even three to last that long." Raine was trying to drive a hard bargain.

Ore shook his head. "I think I would have to settle on two crates. We could eat the first with abandon, perhaps, but the second would have to do for the rest of the month."

Raine smiled. "Done. I actually have a caravan preparing to go that way in the next week or so. I'll add it to the list of things to have my agent pick up." He paused, tilted his head, and asked, "Is the interest in this fruit for any particular reason?"

"It's Mother's favorite," Ore said neutrally, watching Raine as he took the last sip from his after-dinner drink.

Raine was a consummate merchant. The only reaction he had was to freeze very briefly with a slight widening of the eyes. But that was enough of a reaction for Ore. He put his cup down. "Now, as to my other business on the North road. Will you be joining me?"

"Ah, yes, I think I would be. I understand you prefer to travel quickly."

"Yes, I do. I'll need to change clothing to proper travel clothes before we leave. I anticipate we'll travel most of the night before stopping. Can you keep up?"

Raine shook his head. "That won't be necessary. If you're done here, I would be happy to show you to my office."

Ore looked at him surprised, then nodded and stood. The waiter who had seated him walked over. He said that Mister Holloway had instructed him to let Ore know what the charge was, as it was his first time there, and named a price. Ore handed it over, memorizing it for next time - if there was a next time. This was too expensive a place to come on his own purse.

Raine had a carriage, and he rather forcefully suggested that Ore tie his horse to it and ride with him. Ore could only oblige. He was almost starting to wonder if he was being kidnapped. As they entered the carriage, Ore asked him the question that had been burning in him since Raine had been introduced to him. "Are you, perchance, related to Andrew Marciel?"

Raine smiled as he sat down opposite Ore. "Yes. I'm his cousin. Our fathers were brothers. Mother gave me to know she was wooing me partially because of my relation to him. Ours is, for the most part, a business relationship. Fortunately for her, I'll be charging her less for the business we'll be conducting next because you've made it a lucrative night for me."

Ore groaned slightly. "I'll be sure to let her know that her mikan should be treasured, then."

Raine gently laughed. "I think that if they're her favorite, she'll already do that." Ore agreed. She probably would. At least, he hoped so.

Raine changed topic to the task before Ore. "Because you were able to give Grandfather a three day notice, most of the people have already arrived here in the city. We're still waiting for the farthest out person to arrive. We expect them to be here midmorning. If you would rather meet that person at the crossroads you waited at last time, we can let them know we'll be doing that. Then if they arrive there first, they'll wait for us to get there. Which would you prefer?"

"How long will it take to get everyone moving in the morning?" Ore asked while trying to wrap his brain around the sudden speed of his job. He had a sudden thought. "And, can we stop at a soldier's station in town along the way to your office this evening?"

Raine nodded and called an order to his driver, then considered. "There are twenty people already here - and three more coming tomorrow - so it will take us about a couple of hours to be ready to go, I would think, from the time we rise. We'll be going by caravan, so it should only take a few hours to get to the crossroads."

Ore frowned. "That's more total people than last time, for fewer names given. But I'm most concerned about your caravan. I can't allow any of your drivers to travel with us once we're on that crossroad. And I can't guarantee when you'll be able to get your wagons and horses back."

"Of course," Raine said smoothly. "The cost of the rental of the wagons and teams is included in the charge to Mother. They'll be needed to return the Children to their homes when they may return."

"Ah, I see." Ore said. "But that's an entire caravan season's worth of time."

Raine smiled. "This caravan is transporting people, rather than goods. The wagons and teams will be gone the same amount of time as if it were goods. The profit is the same to me."

Ore looked at him, amazed, then shook his head. "Very well. Thank you for your assistance. I think I would like to meet the remaining group at the crossroads." Raine tipped his head in acknowledgment.

The carriage pulled to a stop and Raine looked out the window. "We've arrived at your requested stop."

Ore looked too, then stepped out of the carriage, leaving Raine behind to wait. He went into the town guard station and walked into the head's office with only a perfunctory knock on the door. The on-duty sergeant looked up at his knock. As had been happening to Ore since he'd put his costume on, he wasn't recognized.

He pulled out his Regent's Messenger badge. "I need to send an urgent message. Please have a soldier take it immediately and directly to the castle message office. May I have paper and pen?" The sergeant nodded and searched his desk, handing Ore a small stack of paper, then a pen and ink. He rose and headed out his door to find someone who could take the message.

Ore quickly wrote a note to Captain Garen telling him how many people would be coming, and informing him they would be there by dinner the next night, and that there would be more wagons and horses to house. They might want to consider building another barn just for the wagons to be protected - they were rentals, after all.

He folded the message, then folded another piece of paper around it and wrote the code name for Falcon's Hollow on it, and added the symbol for immediate delivery. Messages to and from Falcon's Hollow went by bird, so that a human wouldn't be tempted to give away the location, and the bird went to the guard station, not the quarters themselves, in case the birds were tracked.

When Ore was done, he walked back out of the office and found the sergeant again. He was standing next to a guard who was ready to go. Ore handed the paper over. "If you can't deliver it, destroy it, but you aren't going that far, so it should be okay. Just take it to the castle message office." The guard nodded and headed at a trot out the door. "Thank you, Sergeant," Ore said, then left and returned to the carriage waiting outside.

"Ready, then?" Raine asked as Ore sat back down in the carriage.

Ore nodded. "Thank you for stopping." Raine waved it away.

Very shortly, the carriage stopped again. This time Raine led the way out of the carriage and held the door for him. "Welcome to the offices of Marciel and Crane Trading Company. My partner is also not one of Mother's Children. I handle the northern routes, and he the southern and water routes."

Ore followed him into the building. Raine took him past the outer business offices and upstairs to the third floor of the four story building. "The lower two floors are actually one tall floor behind the offices," Raine told him conversationally. "That's where we keep the cargo in transit and the wagons.

"There's a stable behind where we keep the teams that we're preparing for the current caravan. The top floor of this building is my living quarters and rooms for the drivers to stay in when they're in town. This floor is for when we have passengers traveling with the caravan."

Ore could see that it was divided like an inn would be, with bedrooms on either side of a hall, but before that, just at the top of the stairs, was a larger anteroom where the travelers could gather while waiting for departure. There was also a small kitchenette in the far corner of the room. Several women were washing dishes as if the group gathered in the room had just finished eating their dinner.

The entrance of Ore and Raine caused a hush to come over the room. Ore counted nine adults, four teenagers, and seven children. Quietly he asked Raine what the complement of those still coming was.

"Two adults and one infant." Ore nodded and moved to step forward. Raine stopped him. "I'll remove myself to my rooms. We'll begin preparing the wagons at first light. There's a room here for you for the night. Your horse is being seen to and your bags should be brought up shortly."

"Thank you," Ore said.

Raine bowed himself out, heading back downstairs first, and Ore turned back to the room. Everyone was now sitting quietly in family groups, waiting for him. Ore suddenly wished he could have changed first before visiting with them. It was harder to get into the character of Father while wearing finery. Then, remembering Dane and Thayne's advice to just be himself, he mentally shrugged.

"Hello," he smiled his disarming smile at the group. "This is quite unexpected for me. Last time I didn't have Grandfather's help. This time I've received so much help I'm feeling a bit lost." There were kind grins from the adults in the group.

"Thank you for being willing to travel to me. It's been very helpful. However, not knowing who is who, I'll just have to call down my list. When you hear your name and we've had the chance to meet, please introduce me to whomever you've brought with you. After we've all met, I'll have a few things to say, then we can all get a good night's rest before tomorrow's journey. Mister Raine tells me they'll begin preparing wagons at first light, and we'll meet the last family on the way."

He called the first name on his list. A ruddy man stood. "I am waiting to hear the words of Father."

Ore paused, a sudden emotion choking him, then he said, very gently, "Mother has sent me for you." Even the children went still, sensing the reaction of the adults. The man paused, not sure he wanted to interrupt Ore's attempt to recover. "Go ahead," Ore said gently. The man introduced his wife and five children - two teens, and three younger children. Ore greeted them as well so that he could remember their names.

The man sat down and Ore called the second name on his list. The same process was repeated for each of the names, with one person not being present, being the one they would pick up the next day. When they were done, there were three single adults, one married couple that, like Roy and Betty, seemed to be a duo that had received aliases, two of the adult witnesses were married and had children - one being the first man called, and one was an adult man with children but no spouse.

"I'm pleased to meet all of you," Ore said. "I look forward to traveling with you tomorrow. So that you may know, the place you're going is in the countryside with sufficient open space for the children to run and explore. There's a boundary we ask that you not cross for your protection, but it's not difficult. There are already eleven adults, two teenagers, and four children there who are waiting for your arrival. I'm sure they'll help you feel welcome very quickly.

"When we meet up with the final family, we'll be leaving the North Road and heading down a crossroad. At that point no one but you and myself may travel with us. I would ask that anyone with experience driving a wagon please assist with driving our wagons to your new summer vacation home." He paused. "I'm sure that you wish to hear about Mother. Please be patient until you arrive tomorrow for me to be able to tell you."

There was a knock on the wall and Raine put Ore's bag just inside the room. Ore nodded his thanks and Raine left again, this time going upstairs to his rooms. "That's all I have to say at this time. If I could be pointed to an empty room, I would really like to get out of this costume now that my real clothes have arrived."

He got sympathetic grins from several of the men and teenage boys, and surprised looks from many of the women who probably thought that was what he looked like all the time. "Next time I tell Grandfather we aren't meeting at the Glass Bottle. Master is going to die when he looks at the bill for this trip. And it's even going to be a shorter one than last time." He got a few chuckles.

One of the older teens stood and collected Ore's bag and his mother led Ore down the hall to one of the rooms at the end. Ore was glad it was a corner window room. Those were the ones he could sort of breathe in. An inner room he couldn't at all. He thanked them by name as they left, then he changed quickly into his comfortable traveling clothes.

When he was done, he rested on the edge of the bed, his arms resting on his knees. "*Haahh*...Mother, I'm not sure this is really better. Will they be able to trust me if they haven't had the time and experiences to learn who I am?" For a moment, his heart cried out for her.

He held the rosebud, twirling it by the stem between his fingers. It wasn't going to last much longer. They never did. He pulled out the fragrant green with his other hand and held it to his nose and breathed in its scent. He knew from working with Mizi that it would dry over time and still retain the scent. He was glad Ilena had given him both.

He sat a moment longer, then took a deep breath and put the two plants back into his jacket buttonhole as he walked to the door. He wanted to spend time in the common room talking to people. It would at least pass some of the night away. He wasn't likely to be able to sleep even after that, though.

-o-o-o-

The next morning, Ore was up and readying his bag as soon as he heard the wagoners above him preparing for their day. He was the first to arrive in the common room. Putting his bag near the stairs, he put water on to boil, then walked up and down the hall knocking on doors to let everyone know it was time to wake up. By the time he had the morning tea made, Will and Francis, this trip's aliased couple, had come out as well, each carrying a bag.

They put their bags down near his and joined him in the kitchen. They immediately began pulling out dishes and preparing a simple meal, explaining that they (also) ran an eating establishment in one of the smaller towns so were used to that kind of schedule and work. Ore had wondered. They'd gone to bed early enough he hadn't had time to talk with them the night before.

As he sipped his cup of tea, they told him they had arrived two days before, in the middle of the day, about the same time most of the people who lived outside of town had arrived. Those who'd been in town to begin with had come just yesterday, wrapping up their work since they could come more last-minute. The families with children had come in the evening the day before just before dinner as they'd taken the longest time to get everyone together.

The other single adults were the next to arrive in the kitchen and they poured themselves cups of morning tea. One woman helped to get eating utensils and plates out. The smells of breakfast were beginning to make Ore hungry. He hoped it was making the kids hungry as well. It would help wake them up.

A little while later, he heard the first patter of feet coming. He leaned out from the table where he was sitting to look down the hall. It was one of the little girls. "Good morning, Alexis!" he said cheerfully. "Are you hungry? Breakfast is just about ready. Signora Francis is there juice for the littles this morning?" The little girl had stopped and was looking at him solemnly.

Francis smiled at him and poured a glass of juice and handed it to him. He put it on the table in front of his place, then stood up. Bowing to Alexis he said, "Your Highness's juice is ready. May I help you into your throne, Princess." Alexis' eyes lit up and she ran to jump into his vacated chair. "Signore Will, is the Princess's plate ready yet?"

Will glanced over at them and smiled. "In just a moment, Your Highness."

Alexis smiled and kicked her legs happily as she drank her juice. "And did you sleep well enough, Princess Alexis?" Ore asked her.

She nodded. "I got to sleep with Mommy. She doesn't turn and kick like Sarah."

"Ohh, then you got good sleep. That's good. We have traveling to do today. Are you ready?" Ore leaned his folded arms on the table to talk to Alexis.

"Mmm," she said noncommittally. "Are there any kitties where we're going?"

"Hmm." Ore thought about it. "I don't know. But there is a stable with horses, so there probably are mice. Where there are mice, there are bound to be kitties, don't you think?"

"Well, maybe. Horsies would be okay. I don't like mice, though." Alexis made a face.

"Yeah, I don't either. They eat my things up and make them into their beds. It wasn't fun the day I lost my favorite scarf to a family of mice. I was very sad." Ore frowned sadly to make his point.

Alexis nodded wisely. "Yeah. Mommy hates them, too. They ate her favorite winter skirt last fall."

Ore shook his head. "That's too bad."

The sound of other youngster feet could be heard coming down the hall. "Don't run!" called the already frazzled mother. She had the youngest, a two year old, in her arms. Her husband was behind them carrying the bags.

"Quick!" Ore called the other two children. "Come hide behind me!" They ran past him, then turned back around and clustered between him and Alexis. "Good morning Princess Sarah, Prince Peter. Are you ready for your juice this morning as well?" Francis was already putting the glasses on the table.

George, one of the single men, was bringing over another chair that he set at the end of the table, around the corner from Alexis. Ore picked up Peter and set him in that chair with his juice. "Your Highness. Juice for you. Signore Will says the food will be ready shortly." Peter gaped at Ore for a moment, then saw Alexis' contented face. He shrugged and picked up his cup. "And Princess Sarah, here is your juice." Ore put it in front of Sarah who had climbed up in the seat next to Alexis.

"Thank you," Sarah said politely.

"You're very welcome," Ore bowed properly to her. Her eyes got wide.

"Are you from the castle?" she asked. "You were dressed very nice yesterday when you came."

Ore smiled. "Yes, I am, actually. But I only wear those clothes on special occasions. Like when I get to meet a Prince and Princesses like you."

The girls looked at him in awe. Peter looked more like he disbelieved him. "Are there any other girls where we're going?" Sarah asked him.

"Yes, one a little older than you. She'll be very happy to have you two Princesses join her. So far it's only her two little brothers and another little boy, although there is a teenage girl who watches them."

Peter perked up. "Two boys?"

Ore nodded. He could hear another group of young people headed down the hall so he held his next comment until they could hear it, too. "Yes, three boys, an uncle, an older brother, and a grandpa. All of them working on carving out a couple of caves up in the rocks. One for the boys to have as a fort, the other for the girls to play house, or whatever they want."

"Woot!" It was one of the older boys from the single father family which tended to more rambunctiousness. "Sweet! Caves!"

Ore looked into worried parent's eyes. He smiled. "Don't worry. The stoneworker Robert of Pence is the one working on the caves. They'll be as safe as safe can be." The parents relaxed. "You guys can help out when you get there," he added to the boys - two teens and an older child.

The early adults had vacated the chairs at the table and the younger boy snatched a seat. Francis handed out glasses of juice and tea and refilled the earlier set. Ore continued to entertain the children, and the last family arrived shortly, rounding out the group.

Children filled the last set of chairs at the table and full plates were handed round. The group thanked the cooks and made the plates empty again quickly.

When the meal was done, the mothers quickly washed up the dishes and several others dried and put them away, everyone helping with the chores as if they were already a family group.

They were just about done with the dishes when Raine came up the stairs to announce the wagons were ready. The men and teens not helping with dishes gathered up bags to carry down. Ore got the regiment of children put together and marching down the stairs. They found a full caravan getting ready. Three wagons were waiting for the family members.

Ore put Sarah, Peter, and Alexis in one wagon, having Sarah hold the baby that he'd carried down. He had the other family, being three children and two teens in the second wagon. Then he put the three older boys in their wagon. He had the single woman go with Sarah and Alexis' family, and the two single men with the boys. That made it roughly seven per wagon, with the ones they'd be picking up going in the last wagon, bringing it's total to slightly more than that.

Fenrier was saddled and waiting with the wagons. Ore pulled his bag from the pile, tied it onto the back of the saddle, and rubbed Fenrier's nose. Then, just because, he hugged Fenrier's neck. He wanted to climb on a roof. Instead he climbed onto the back of his horse. He wanted to run with it. Instead, he waited patiently. When the last of the dishwashers came down, he told them their assigned wagons and they climbed in.

Raine came up to him. "If you want to get going, you could have your men go ahead and drive them now. Or you can wait and go disguised with the full caravan." He winked.

"How much longer before the caravan goes?" Ore asked.

"Probably another hour," Raine admitted. "We're still loading."

Ore nodded. "Then we'll go ahead and go."

Raine gave him directions for getting out of the city from where his office was, which of course was convenient to the gate since he was a merchant. Ore thanked him one more time, then called for everyone's attention and let them know they would be leaving now, and would one volunteer per wagon take the reins?

When each wagon had a driver, Ore led the way through the streets to the gate and onto the North Road headed west. His horse danced once they were on the road. Fenrier wanted a morning run. Ore patted him. He did too, but it wouldn't happen that direction.

-o-o-o-

Ore spent the trip to Castle Road paying close attention to the road around them, looking for signs of ambush or attack - because he should, and taking turns to talk to everyone as they went - because he wanted to keep himself distracted. He'd decided to not push the speed. It was likely they'd have to wait again.

He was surprised all over again when they arrived at the crossroads to find that the little family was already waiting for them. He waved the wagons to turn down Castle Road before stopping and rode up to the family. It was a young man, his young wife, and an infant. He was a bit surprised they were so young, but he figured he probably shouldn't be.

He welcomed them in the name of Mother as was required, then asked them to climb into the last wagon, and thanked them for being ready to be picked up so early, apologizing for their hardship and the wait. They waved it off and settled in. The little caravan got going again and Ore talked to them for a while, getting to know them.

He headed to the front of the line, thinking about what path to take and feeling the road. There was a good ambush site ahead, and it wasn't a secret from last time they'd taken this road, as given by even Raine knowing it. Just past that point, they could take a detour to the inn the first group had eaten dinner at, and it was getting close to lunch time. He couldn't feel anything ahead just yet.

He dropped back to the back and worked his way up the line, quietly telling each driver they were going to take the next stretch at a run, then make the turn, and pick the speed back up again. The excuse he told them was that the little kids were getting hungry and lunch was far enough ahead they needed to put a move on.

On his signal, the wagons, in order, picked up the pace to a fast clip. They did have to slow some to take the corner, but he kept up the pace until they were getting close to the village that had the inn. He had the wagons slow to cool the horses down and went ahead into the town to check and make sure things were clear there.

As he was just entering the town square, a tall youth saw him and came running up to him. He stopped and the youth grabbed his saddle. "Father, you need to keep going. You're being expected at the inn, and it isn't good."

Ore looked at him closely. It was really too bad they hadn't taught him how to recognize Mother's Children yet. But he looked like he was telling the truth. "Everyone's hungry," he answered back. "And we've no food with us."

The youth chewed on his lip. "Detour them around town to the north. Ma'll feed them. I'll catch up to you in a second."

Ore nodded and turned his horse around. Sadly, he thought he'd been seen. They might not get to stop even at the lad's mother's house. But as he left the square, he could hear a commotion. Maybe the person who had seen him was being kept quiet? He ran Fenrier back to the wagons and waved them onto the little lane that split to the north.

"We've got trouble waiting for us in town. We're going to an alternate lunch option - which means eating while we travel, I suspect." A few of the women looked troubled, but no one complained. He had the drivers pick up the pace a bit again, although the small country road was a bit more dangerous to travel at high speeds.

Pretty soon the youth he'd seen earlier came crashing through the trees in front of him. Ore leaned down and pulled him up onto his horse and rode up to the side of the last wagon. "William, is he legitimate?" Ore asked the father of the teen boys.

William looked at the youth, then smiled. "Yes, he is Father."

"Thanks." Ore rode Fenrier to the front of the line. "Tell me when to turn off," he said over his shoulder. "Did you delay the spy who saw me?"

The youth nodded. "The other Children, they're making it difficult for the enemy to get out of the inn. They'll keep the road clear, too, until you've passed beyond far enough, but you should take the next detour you can to get off that road. We thought we got them all last time you went through, but we missed one. You'll have to take this town off your list for next time."

Ore shook his head. "We'll be doing the last set different anyway. Probably won't ever see you again. But thanks for your help, and let everyone else know, too."

The boy shrugged. "Mother's got a regular route. You'll learn it eventually."

"She actually sees everyone? Most of the first set haven't seen her since she adopted them."

"No, she has certain places she visits regular. Most of the ones you're collecting she's been protecting by *not* visiting them. Likely she's dying to see them again."

"Yeah, likely she is," Ore agreed.

"Turn left here. The house is just up there," his young guide instructed.

Ore obediently turned Fenrier up the narrow passage between the trees, watching before and behind as they went. As the way opened up into a clear area surrounding a small house, he had the wagons turn around so they were facing the lane they'd come up, in preparation to head back out. "Please stay in the wagons. The Family in town is keeping the attempted delay delayed. We shouldn't put any more strain on them than we have to."

The boy had slid off as soon as Fenrier was just still enough to not step on him, and run into the house. Now he came back out and asked for help from two. The two oldest teen boys jumped down out of the third wagon and ran into the house. In just a little while, the three of them came back out with large baskets of fruit and bread and three large wheels of cheese.

They handed them into the second wagon and ran back inside. The children in the wagon and their mother quickly divided up the food and ran the portions to the other two wagons. The three boys came back out with two jugs of liquids each, giving two to each wagon. Ore would have been grateful if it was just water.

He reached into his pouch and pulled out enough coin to cover the food and a little more and rode up to the youth. "Thank your family. And here, this is to make sure you'll make it through." Ore wouldn't accept refusal.

The boy took it and thanked him, then Ore got them going again, turning left at the lane to continue on the north detour. "Hold the food until we're where we can slow back down," he instructed as they went. "Would hate to waste it with spillage, when it was half their winter savings. How many swords do we have?" All the men, all the teens, and all the women raised their blades.

Ore was very surprised. "Well, then. By all means use them if you need to. Children, to the center of the wagons and lie down. Play hide-and-seek until I tell you it's safe to come out. Millie, you lie down, too, with the little one. She'll stay quiet that way."

The young new mother nodded and moved to be obedient. Her husband looked at Ore gratefully. "Teens, sit down and around the littles. Hide the fact you've got blades until your opponents are close enough to surprise attack and win against."

One of the teen boys waved Ore over. "Take me up to the first wagon. The kids there don't have a guardian." Ore held out his hand to steady him for the step over to Fenrier, then trotted up and he crossed back over into the wagon with Sarah, Peter, and Alexis. "Hello Prince and Princesses. I'm your guard for the next part of the trip. I'll keep you safe," he said. Ore smiled. He must have overheard Ore at breakfast that morning.

He was called back by George. "They need another man there, too. Take me up." Ore nodded. That was just a little trickier since George was an older man and not quite so nimble, but they managed and got him into that wagon. After a bit of discussion about skills and experience, he stayed as sword for the wagon.

Ore's senses were heightened. Nothing was on or around the road they were on. He moved far enough ahead that he could warn the wagons in time to stop or run, whatever was needed, but he was careful to not get too far ahead. When they got back to the main road, he pulled off on the town side and waved them to turn away from the town, keeping at high alert.

He did briefly see a head pop up that waved a signal. William, who'd seen it also, said it was one of theirs saying the enemy wasn't on the road in their direction from town yet.

Ore had them pick up the pace to as fast as the horses could go and still continue for the whole trip. Now he was worried about which detour to take. How far had they been followed last time? He didn't want to take any of the south detours. That would put them too far from the house...but he also didn't want to go straight to the house from here. If someone did follow them that could be very bad.

When they approached the next crossroads, another head popped up. Ore sighed. Did the Family already know where the witnesses were being kept, or was it just because they were still near the town? He moved ahead of the wagons again to talk to this head, because it looked like it wanted to talk to him.

This time it was a teenage girl, thin as thread. Her face was very serious. "You've got enemies on both roads, but they're expecting the main road straight ahead. I've already sent the few who could come, up the north fork to start picking them off. Head that way.

"And then I'd recommend straight to the house. Not because they won't follow you, but because we've got a message on it's way to the guard house. If you head for the house, you'll get reinforcements faster."

The wagons were to the crossroad and Ore waved them north. "How do you guys know where it is?"

"We live here," she grinned at him. "Can't keep things secret when you're busy running all over the place around here."

"Well, I guess I'm glad of it, then," Ore said. "Thanks." He rode quickly back up to the wagons. "We can expect an ambush ahead, she said, but it's less than the other option. We've got reinforcements already on their way there."

He considered the options. There was the "run through" method Ilena had suggested with her travel from the Osterly barracks to Castle Nijou, and they were already moving fast so that might work. But if they had reinforcements, even a few, with as many blades as they had the opposite might almost work just as good. Stop a few feet away from the near edge of the ambush and make them come to them....

Ore whistled the wagons to stop. They were a bit surprised, but were obedient. He had the first wagon shift over to the far right of the road, the second wagon pull up as close to the first as it could, then the third up against the second so that they completely blocked the road from side to side.

"It's lunch time, everyone. Kids, you can sit up to eat, but stay where you are, okay?" When he got *"you're crazy"* looks from the moms, he smiled. "You know Mother works by doing the unexpected. We're going to give the reinforcements time to whittle down the ambush in front.

"Then we'll continue slowly in this configuration, the center wagon just a little out in point. If they still want to stop us, we'll charge through. Their horses won't stand against a charging wall.

"If they decide to come to us while we're eating, all the littles should go into the center of the center wagon. We'll concentric circle the teens, women, then men around them."

Everyone older than twelve nodded, and they got busy getting the lunch out. Ore stayed on Fenrier, but he was brought food. Everyone ate quietly. That made Ore feel better, too. They wouldn't draw unwanted attention that way.

For as long as they ate, he never felt anything out of place along the road, before or behind. When everyone was ready and things were cleaned up, Ore stayed put just a little longer, letting everyone digest a bit. If he could wait just long enough, the soldiers would be that much closer to where they were.

Suddenly he heard a piercing cry he was familiar with. He looked up in the sky and saw one of the royal messenger birds circling high overhead. He smiled. Rei had gifted every one of his aides with the bells that called the birds, and then told them they always had to wear it. It was insurance to keep the people precious to him safe. To see one now meant the soldiers were close, following the bird hunting for Ore.

"All right, everyone. That's our sign. Let's go at a slow walk. That will give them time to get even closer. When I give you the signal, I want you to yell and make as much noise as possible. We'll do a vocal attack at the same time as we charge through them. That will also tell the soldiers how far they have yet to come to get to us.

"Once we start the charge, don't stop it until I tell you. That means we'll charge through the soldiers, too. Got it? I'll be behind you so you don't run me over and I don't outrun you. Center wagon out front just a little; side wagons, put your noses at about midrib."

They got going at a walk, the teens making the kids lie down again. The men not driving the wagons took the outer front perimeter, the women backing them up, and the teens stayed beside the kids. Ore loosened up his throwing knives and his short sword, and kept his ears and eyes to the road in front of them.

There was movement in the trees finally. Eight men stepped out onto the road facing them. Ore wondered at them for a moment. He caught a brief glimpse of a face and hand signal those eight couldn't see. One of the men turned to Ore with a smile. "That's all of 'em." He said it quietly enough the ambushers couldn't hear.

Ore smiled back. "Pick it up to a fast waltz, keep in time. Don't stop. As a matter of fact, act like you don't see or hear them until we're just on them. Then shout with one loud voice. If the horses bolt, let them, but keep to the road." The people before him gave tense nods.

Fenrier snorted. He didn't want to be behind the slow wagons, even though they were increasing in speed now. That was another reason he was there. Ore did keep a watch behind them, just in case.

Now the people in front of them were making demands...now they were shouting...now they were highly confused...now everyone on the wagons was shouting as loud as they could, the little kids, too. It was enough to make the infant cry and her noise just added to it all.

Five of the eight ambushers moved fast enough to throw themselves off the road, but three were caught by the outer wagons, the horses having indeed jumped ahead at the noise. Fenrier kept up just fine. Ore threw a couple of knives at those who'd managed to leap to one side, then turned and threw another few at the ones still up. Then they were out of reach of the ambushers who were in the process of being ambushed by the reinforcements sent earlier.

He let the wagon horses keep running and shortly they came to, then passed through, the soldiers. One turned and caught up to him to get orders. "Send a few farther on to see if we can get witnesses to who set up the ambushes - there were multiple. The rest should turn and form up with us. We'll go straight to the house."

The soldier nodded, then fell back to relay the orders. Shortly the beat of the soldier's horses coming up behind them got near. Ore called ahead for the wagons to slow and return to a staggered single file. As they got into the new configuration, the soldiers surrounded them. Once there were enough at the tail end, Ore moved up to the front again. Everyone gave him grins as he passed, and he grinned right back.

-o-o-o-

There was no further incident on the way, but Ore remembered Ilena's other comment...that one should always be prepared for the second surprise ambush, so he didn't relax until they were finally inside Falcon's Hollow. That was a noisy affair: all the kids making noise and people milling about. Ore decided to stay on his horse until things calmed down a little. He might be heard better if he needed to say anything.

A larger portion of the soldiers had peeled off at the station, going back to the road and back down towards the town. He'd told them what had happened, that both at the inn and along the next main road down other ambushes had been set up. Once the witnesses were considered safe, it was necessary to investigate further. Ore was glad there weren't too many extra horses around with all the people going here and there.

He leaned on his pommel, watching everyone mingle, a smile on his face. Millie was as excited as Sarah that there was another girl her age to play with, and was doing a good job of including Alexis, too. The boys, new and old, were already making plans to go up to the caves.

Ore sidled over to them. "Make sure you ask your moms," he told them. "They'll worry otherwise. And Mat, make sure you explain the rules about where they can and can't go." He looked at the new boys. "Make sure you follow that one rule over all the others, okay? It's the one that keeps you and your parents safe." They got serious and nodded at him.

When he nudged his horse away, he could hear them beginning to tell their story of what had happened on the way in. While he wasn't interested in becoming a hero, so he hoped they didn't do that to him, it had been exciting, and as Ilena had said before, fun - because the plan had worked and none of the people he was caring for had been hurt.

Still...even this trip had been very haphazard. He finally decided it must be because of the lack of communication, even as it had been before. If he'd know it was going to be such a caravan, he would have had a guard detail to begin with. And, if he'd known they would need lunch food on the way, he would have had some available.

He sighed. He also needed Ilena to initiate him into the Family. There had been at least three times that if he hadn't had an interpreter available, and one he hadn't at the first, he could have gotten them into great trouble for trusting someone he wasn't supposed to.

Someone touched his leg. He looked down. It was Foster, looking up at him. "Do you want to go inside and rest? I'll water your horse." Foster offered.

"I'd rather you came and joined me," Ore said. "Is there someone else who can take Fenrier?"

Foster looked at him curiously. "Yes. If you'll let me, I'll take him in and pass him off. Shall I leave your bag on him?"

"Yes. I won't stay long, although I could since we got here so much faster than I expected." Ore answered.

Foster went sober and shook his head. "You shouldn't. We'll take care of them. What you should do is get back." Ore nodded, understanding Foster was thinking of him and Ilena. He slipped down off his horse, promising Fenrier they'd run for real in a little bit.

Captain Garen had been waiting for the chaos to die down and for Ore to come down from his horse as well. He walked over as Foster took Fenrier towards the stable. "I was glad your message came before the word came that your path was blocked. If I hadn't gotten it we wouldn't have believed the other message."

Ore nodded. "They surprised me in the village, too. I asked the second one who popped up if everyone knew where this place was. I'm not sure they *all* do, but all Mother's Children who live in the area do. She said the circuitous route we took the first time alerted all of them we were in the area, and it wasn't hard for them to figure out where we'd ended up. In her words, 'we live here'!" Ore rolled his eyes a little.

"And the first boy who caught me going into town and rerouted us said that we'd been given away the first time by the stop at the inn. He said they'd tried to filter out all the spies on their way out of town, but likely missed one."

"So, it worked, then?" Garen asked, folding his arms.

"Yes, if we've drawn out all the possible ambushers in this round, and can get hold of enough prisoners who will talk. We've seen what they'll do for themselves, and I've also got a good handle on the weaknesses in the system, I think," Ore answered.

"Good." The captain looked fairly satisfied.

"Did you know they'd armed themselves to the man, woman, and teen? But not the little kids." Ore said approvingly.

"Did you get to see them in action?"

"No, thank goodness." Ore laughed. "I think if I hadn't been able to think my way through, Ilena would have washed my ears out with many choice words. I'm sure she'll get a thorough report by sometime next week. We were, after all, under close observation for that test by more than eight men from her Family. They left us eight to see what I would do. It was a bare minimum, so it was pretty obvious."

"Ah," was the only comment the captain could give.

"I do hope you're letting them keep their weapons?" Ore raised an eyebrow.

"Yes. They always carry when they go out of the house, and when the boys go up to the caves there's always an extra they don't know about that trails after them. With this many more men and teens, I suspect they'll be a lot less worried about that trip because more can go with them. ...It's actually good this group came so quick. It was hard for them to explain to the little boys why Robert couldn't take them up there. You took their two best defenders, you know," Garen smiled a little at Ore.

Ore raised a hand of defense. "Yeah, sorry. But these kids are good, too. Just sending the teens will keep them plenty safe, if they aren't directly attacked by the main force."

"Do you expect one?" asked Foster from behind them.

"Yes, Foster...but, then, you lot do too. That's one of the things I want to talk to you about," Ore said without turning around. "Shall we? We'll go to the old lord's office."

He led both of them, asking the folks he passed to collect in the dining room in a half hour, and to spread the word that all but the youngest should be present. When they arrived at the office, Ore sat behind the desk. Both men stood before the desk. It felt strange to Ore to be sitting in the seat he usually expected Rei to sit in, and in the same way.

He felt a shudder of premonition go through him. *Oh, no, not again.* He'd just taken another step in the direction Ilena wanted him to go in, and all without thinking about it beforehand. He put his hand over his eyes for a moment. When he looked up again, Foster was smiling at him, although Garen was wondering if he wasn't feeling well. Ore sighed. "Wipe the grin off your face Foster. Yes, she's winning. That doesn't mean I have to like it yet."

Foster grinned bigger. "I'll tell her that, shall I?"

Ore frowned and scolded, "No. Not yet. I'll tell her when I'm ready."

"She marked you, you know. You could have asked deeper questions on the way anytime." Foster pointed to the rose and greenery in Ore's buttonhole.

"Yeah, I figured that's what it was, but I wanted to see more first. Now I'm ready to ask. And you're one who can answer, I'm assuming. Thayne admitted yesterday afternoon he's an agent, too. That makes you a manager."

Foster shifted slightly. "Ah, that's a close enough description, I suppose. Area captain might be closer, though."

Ore nodded. "Is she expecting to keep this place? And are all of you anticipating staying for good to run it?"

Foster's eyebrows jumped up. "Wow. Jump right to the deep questions, is it?"

Ore shrugged. "Master already figures it, too. The pattern was too obvious in just the first set of you, and how fast Robert got to work on the caves."

Foster blinked at him, then settled. "Well, if you've got that much info, then yes. To both. There will be some who'll go home, but the majority already signed up long ago."

Ore frowned slightly. "But that begs the question about all the wagons and horses. Are they really rentals or is she going to keep them?"

Foster shrugged. "I don't know. Mother doesn't tell anyone *all* of her plans, you know. But she does intend to make this a horse ranch."

Ore's eyebrow went up. "She really does? It doesn't have quite enough land for that does it?"

Foster shook his head. "That's part of the things I don't know."

Ore thought a bit longer. "The lack of communication thing is annoying. Both times, that has caused problems for us - for me. We can't afford that next time. I'll be bringing them directly here as fast as we can, and leaving as soon as they're past the guards, who'll finish bringing them in. We don't want anything interrupting the run."

Foster nodded, as serious as Ore. "The testing's over. Once they come attack here directly, everything will be set from our end as well." He paused. "We'll need to know how many you want kept alive. We don't intend to leave any more than that alive when they come. We don't want any coming back."

Garen looked at Foster. "Wait. That isn't what you guys look like normally." Foster gave him a wolves' grin. "Yeah, that. I guess there are teeth there." He went from almost mock-surprise to a shrug. "Well, I, for one, am looking forward to what you're all going to do. We'd like a sampling in case they send in waves from different Houses, say one or two from each section. And how much involvement do you want from us?"

Foster's wolfish grin remained. "Make it look like you'd had a party to celebrate the end of your work. Then fill up the house. We'd like you to protect the kids and Freida. If we do all the outside work, they'll think three times about coming back."

Garen nodded. Ore smiled. "I told you so. Just because Ilena's Family is full of light, that doesn't mean it doesn't have a dark side, too." His smile dropped and he looked at Foster with a common bond. "You can't live through what we've all lived through and not have one." Foster nodded agreement.

Ore all of a sudden realized - *that's why Mother is a moon, not a sun. She has a dark side, too.* A part of him relaxed, having understood that. He wondered briefly if it was as dark as the bright side was ever so bright.

"The other thing I need to know is how to recognize Family. I hit the town watchman alone. I took him with me, but had to get verification after we were already committed to a path that could have taken us right *into* an ambush. That's not going to fly any more." His tawny eyes were piercing.

Foster bowed slightly. "I can do that for you. You can get practice seeing on the folks who are here. But the Captain doesn't get to know." Ore nodded. Garen looked disappointed, but not surprised.

Ore asked his next question. "Ah, a curiosity, but why the rush this time? I enjoyed having the time to get to know all of you from the first set. I was hard pressed to get the little I did this time." Foster looked a bit caught in a bind.

"Ah, don't give me the excuse. You're the kind that can't do it." Ore leaned on his arm. "So I guess I'll say it. They can't not talk to me and there's things you don't want the castle to know yet, that they know. You liked the written option so well, after all. It was easier to edit the stories." Foster reluctantly gave a nod.

"Do keep them coming. They make great reading, and they're a nice bedtime story for Master, who needs such things in his life. I can't say you should change it, because I know I'm the one caught in the middle; however, I personally don't like it." He frowned.

Foster paused, then said, "We'll make you an unedited copy and gift it to you at the right time. Would that be sufficient?"

"That would help, but that's not why. ...If I'm supposed to eventually really be 'Father', how can I be that for people who don't know who I really am? Last night and today were barely enough time, honestly. As I see it, it's only going to get harder to have time to talk to folks individually like we did."

Foster looked at Ore fondly. "You know, that's one of the things we find endearing about you." Ore looked at him surprised, then the tips of his ears turned red. Foster laughed. "It's too late to be embarrassed about it now. I think you'll find the time, Father. It's just not now. It's how Mother feels also. When she visits she is so happy, when she leaves it is always too soon."

Garen shook his head and smiled. "You see, I said it was you yourself as well. Here's an example."

Ore was confused, then shrugged. It was who he was, and that was supposed to be okay. "Captain, go ahead and go on down. We'll be there shortly." Garen tipped his head, then turned and left the room.

-o-o-o-

When Garen entered the dining room, everyone looked over and got quiet. When no one else entered with him, they went back to quiet talking. He took his seat, and looked at the new families. The first arrivals had sprinkled themselves throughout and were answering questions and generally meeting the new set.

In some cases the new ones were telling the story of their journey, in particular the teens. The one teen girl, who was the only one other than the staff family daughter, Alice, was getting attention from all the teen boys. Except Peter who, it looked like, had taken one look, turned bright red, and hadn't had the courage to look again. Garen smiled. Peter really did have troubles with women.

Within ten minutes, Ore and Foster entered the room. Ore took center stage as usual; Foster took one of the first chairs available. Ore repeated what he'd said for the first arrivals: how long they expected it all to take and why, that the captain would be taking their testimonies, repeated the house rules, and reintroduced Bill and Lilly and explained their roles.

"I've already given the news about Mother to those who were already here, but I can now tell the rest of you." The new arrivals sat up expectantly. "She's alive and in a protected location. Her hip was crushed in the landslide.

"She has just yesterday undergone an experimental surgery to replace a tendon that under normal circumstances would be unrepairable. Doctor Elliot is optimistic. She sends her love and her gratitude for your willingness to come and to help Master. ...Master has made her his Director of Intelligence for her first appointment.

"Foster has agreed with me that the testing phase is completed. In a little bit, he and Captain Garen will discuss with you what the guarding arrangements of Falcon's Hollow will be. Foster has already told us you wish to bear the brunt of the flood that's coming.

"While I agree with the philosophy that if the household can prove itself you're likely to be left alone, I'm reluctant to completely agree with the plan he's proposed." In general the eyes of everyone were bugging out.

They'd really not expected him to be so blunt about what had been going on underneath the surface. Still, it was only proper thinking to assume that the lords these witnesses would bring down wouldn't just sit quietly by to be handed over to the new Regent for trial and conviction.

"If you're thinking that with the few of you, you'll survive unscathed, that's suicide. They know how many of you there are here, the same as they have a good idea of how many soldiers there are here. So it stands to reason you're expecting help from the Family in the surrounding area.

"That's fine. We won't stand in the way of that. However, I would rather that you accept a portion of the garrison as brothers-in-arms upon the field. Come to an agreement of just how many are needed to protect the house, then allow the rest to dress as if they were on vacation also.

"I ask for two reasons. One is because if I must come back for one of you to take you for a funeral, Mother will not recover, nor will I. The second reason is because we expect Little Death users. I don't expect any of you are anymore, since you're no longer under the care of Doctor Elliot or Mother.

"Just to be clear, if any of you do use it to get through the fight, you'll be carted to the castle and thrown into the jail. Master and I will not tolerate its use other than for strictly supervised purposes." He could see they understood. It was probably the only order he and Rei had given them directly. "But because we expect them to come, please accept the aid of additional trained swords.

"I'm sure at least two of you are medically trained. We have enough medical supplies to set up three or more different stations around the Hollow, so you can quickly get an injured comrade to medical attention. I'd hoped to run with you as well, but Mother's need is more important than my fun. Perhaps at a later time we may run together.

"Be well, and stay alive. We'll leave the next step to you." Ore smiled at the people sitting around the tables, then nodded to Garen, turned, and left. He rode hard, both he and Fenrier glad to be doing it.

CHAPTER 6 Graft Rejection

When Ore returned to the castle, he wasn't sure if he should report to Rei first or check on Ilena first. He finally settled on checking on Ilena first. He was back earlier than expected. Perhaps Rei could forgive him.

As he walked into the medical wing, he heard a door close and saw Hue turning back to his place. Wondering who had gone into the room, Ore's steps quickened. Halfway down the long leg, one of the guards outside the medical offices entrance caught sight of him.

"Sir Ore," he called and urgently motioned to Ore. "Mister Ryan and Doctor Elliot've just been called at a run." Ore broke into a mad run, challenging the speed of his own horse. Hue had the door open again by the time he got there, and closed it immediately behind Ore.

Catching the scene in the room in a single glance, Ore slipped past Ryan and Mizi as he shed his jacket and tossed it on the other bed, and put his hand on Thayne's arm. Thayne looked up at him, then quickly side-stepped out of his way.

"Chair," Ore ordered him. Thayne quickly grabbed a chair and pushed it up behind Ore so he could sit. Ore had already registered Ilena's pained face and the careful but quick way Doctor Elliot was re-entering the surgery site, his expression one of worried concentration.

By the time he was sitting, Ore already was halfway through his standard count. He frowned and put his other hand on top of Ilena's heart itself, and restarted the count. Finally he counted the breathing rate, but for the rest....

"Breathing labored, heartbeat extremely irregular, temperature significantly high." He quickly calculated. She should be past the pain payment and into natural sleep. "Thayne, how long into natural sleep did symptoms start?"

"Her breathing became labored about an hour and a half into the natural sleep state," Thayne answered immediately.

"Did she complain of burning or pain in the lucid phase?" Ore asked.

"Some pain, but she didn't think at the time it was beyond what was expected for the day after the surgery." Ore nodded. Whether it was confusion, or hadn't set in yet, it would have been the same.

"Ore?" Mizi stood next to him her eyes wide in surprise. Then she quickly recovered, "Here, the pain and infection fighting medication. Try to get it down her, like at Osterly." Ore took it and immediately began pouring minute amounts into her. "Thayne, take this cloth and keep her cooled down. Start at her forehead for now. Ore, uncover her as soon as you have hands. We'll need to cool her chest down to prevent damage to her heart."

Ore nodded. "Thayne, watch what I'm doing." Thayne placed the wetted cloth on Ilena's forehead, then watched closely what Ore was doing.

"I've got it," Thayne said when he understood the process. Ore passed the little vial to Thayne, then watched him administer two more drops. That satisfied him Thayne knew how to do it well enough to not drown Ilena.

He moved to the other side of her from Thayne and began untying the upper part of her surgery gown. When she was uncovered, he picked up the cloth from her forehead, pulled the water bucket closer to him, and began putting water on her chest.

He was concerned. He could tell even better now that her breathing was troubled, and the water was evaporating within seconds, even when he was allowing it to dribble on her freely. "Mistress, she isn't sweating. For a fever this high, is that normal?"

"Yes, Ore. That's why we need to do it for her." Mizi was busy helping Ryan prepare a poultice.

Ore occasionally alternated cooling Ilena's chest with putting water on her hot forehead and down her neck. At the ten minute mark he moved to putting water on her with one hand, and held her wrist with the other to get the next count. He announced a count, and shook his head. "But it's still mostly erratic. That's the closest count I can get. No change in temperature." He went back to two handed substitute sweating her.

"Done," Thayne announced.

"Put the vial on Mistress's tray," Ore told him. He waffled a moment, then gave up. "Sit in the chair and hold her hand. She gets slightly lucid at times like this and it helps her. I need both my hands for this." He showed Thayne how to feel her pulse and taught him how to do the count, doing it with him at the next ten minute mark so there was a corroborative number, the same way as when Mizi had taught him.

At the next ten minute mark, he did it with Thayne again. They were in agreement that the heart rate was normalizing. Ore brought the temperature level report down a notch as well, but he didn't stop putting water on her. It was only evaporating slightly less fast.

Then, Ilena moaned and twitched slightly. Doctor Elliot froze and Ore looked up at him. "Miss Mizi, the pain medication either hasn't taken effect or is insufficient...though the pain reduction effect of the Little Death should be beginning to help as well."

Doctor Elliot sat up and stretched his back, looking at Ryan and Mizi. Then feeling an extra presence, he looked around farther and finally registered Ore's presence. "Ah?"

"Just got to the wing as you entered the room," Ore said. "My other job is finished."

The surgeon nodded and turned back to the healers. "I've unstitched the tendon. Your poultice seems to be calming the heat in her natural tendon well enough. It's the bone. Is there a way to dissolve the glue? I think the glue is providing a barrier for most of the interior bone surface, but that also means it isn't coming out easily."

Ryan and Mizi looked at each other, then rapid-fire spoke the language unique to the medical field. Ryan nodded and Mizi leaped up and sped out the door. "She's getting the required ingredients," Ryan informed the surgeon. "It will take about seven minutes to prepare."

Doctor Elliot nodded and put his head back down to his work. After a couple of minutes, he stopped again, and sat to wait. Thayne reported the next heart rate count. Ore followed it with the breath rate and temperature report. Doctor Elliot considered the numbers. "It sounds like the infection fighting medicine is working as it should. I told them to make it very strong. But bones...they register so much pain...."

"Take...it...out!" Ilena gasped weakly, surprising them. "Already ...hurts ...damn ...bad –" Ore could see she was grinding her teeth against the pain. "Pain will stop ...if it's out!"

"Yes, Mistress Ilena," Doctor Elliot said, "But we're waiting for the tincture that will dissolve the glue. I can't just take it out without doing damage that will make it impossible to repair."

"Four more minutes for Mizi to have it ready, Ilena," Ryan told her. "Please wait a little longer."

The air hissed through Ilena's clenched teeth. Ore picked up her close hand. "Ilena. I'm here." He squeezed her hand and she clenched it back. He had to shift his fingers in her hand slightly so they didn't get squeezed off. "That is rather a lot of pain, isn't it? But it won't last long." Ilena whimpered.

"Do you remember what you said to me before the surgery? That you would get through it by thinking of what you wanted to be able to do after it was successful? Can you think of one of those things right now? Just one, to hold onto?" He paused. It looked like she was trying. "When you've thought it, take a deep breath and let it out, letting the pain out with it. Keep thinking of the thing that's going to keep you going right now."

When she started taking deep, ragged breaths, and her clenching grip eased slightly, he began putting the water on her again, a little at a time - mostly on her brow. Strangely, it looked like she was getting cold. He frowned. "Doctor Elliot, she looks cold, although she's still hot to the touch."

"Put a separate damp cloth over her chest. That will hold in enough heat but still cool as it evaporates," Doctor Elliot ordered.

Ore looked down at his busy hands, then up at Thayne. "Get the second cloth," he told him. Thayne nodded and disengaged his hand from Ilena's. He found a cloth and wet it in the bucket. He wrung out the cloth and lay it across her chest. Fairly quickly, her shivering stopped. Ore nodded. "That did it."

They continued to keep the damp cloths on Ilena, and Ore continued to hold her hand as she breathed through the pain. Finally Mizi came back in the room and handed a ceramic bowl to Ryan. He smelled it and looked at it closely, then nodded and handed it to Doctor Elliot. "Pour this carefully around the join. You may want to test an edge to be sure we've used the correct ingredients in their proper measure for what we made before."

Doctor Elliot nodded, then took out a little tool that he used to pour the liquid onto the hip bone. As it began to work, Ilena's breath hissed again and she tensed up, but with effort she was able to pull it back and let the dissolving agent do it's work.

After a few minutes, he was able to wiggle the graft, then finally pull it out. He put some of the agent on a cloth and wiped the hole clean and smooth, doing his best not to damage the soft marrow inside the bone. Then he smeared a thin layer of the poultice he'd put on the tendon in and around the hole. "You can start making the glue now, Mister Ryan," he said, reaching for his second graft option.

Ilena had gone very pale. Thayne frowned. "Master Ore, I can't feel her heart rate very well. Can you check it for me?"

Ore put down the cloth he was holding and felt the wrist of the hand holding his. Then he was grasping her hand as her grip failed. He couldn't get a heart rate either. He slid his hand under the cloth on her chest and still couldn't feel it. "Mistress...," concern colored his voice.

Mizi put her hand on Thayne's shoulder and he stepped aside for her. She moved the cloth covering Ilena's chest and put her ear directly over Ilena's heart. Everyone was very still and quiet while she listened. "It's faint." She checked Ilena's breathing. "She's unconscious again."

Doctor Elliot grunted. "Probably too much pain to handle. But keep watching her heart doesn't stop altogether."

"Ore," Mizi said gently. "Use the vein on her neck. It will give you a better count than the wrist."

Ore very gently felt along Ilena's neck until he could feel her faint pulse. It was surprising how hard it was to get just the right touch to find and feel for the heart rate in the neck, although it was more definite in that location. It was also a difficult angle to maintain for long. He had to shift several times before he found a sufficiently comfortable position. No wonder they usually used the wrist.

Thayne, noticing, brought him the chair so he could sit again. When he was sitting again, Ore wiped the sweat from his brow with the back of his arm, surprising himself. He quickly rolled up his sleeves, then took up his post again.

Doctor Elliot said, without looking up, "Now, Mister Ryan, please." Ryan handed over the glue. The surgeon quickly got the bone graft positioned and set, placing the glue poultice in place over the join. While it set, he selected another piece of long tendon, removed it, and laced it through the needle he had ready and carefully heated clean over a candle fire.

When Ryan declared the glue set, Doctor Elliot looked closely at Ilena's tendon and sighed. He placed more of the poultice on both sides of the natural tendon and worked it gently in through the fibers as best he could, then began stitching the graft tendon to it.

Ore frowned. "Her heart beat has decreased again. And the rate is very low."

Doctor Elliot nodded. "How deeply is she breathing?"

Ore watched. "Shallow."

"Talk to her, close to her ear. See if you can get her to revive enough to get her back to regular, if pained, breathing."

Ore looked at Mizi, feeling lost. He couldn't do it and everything else he was doing, including trying to hold himself together.

Mizi knelt beside Ilena, put her head close to Ilena's, and began talking to her. Her quiet but firm voice washed over Ore as he focused on feeling for Ilena's heart beat and the changes to it. Then he remembered he was also supposed to be watching her breathing. His head came up, but Thayne's hand came down gently on his shoulder. "I'm watching her breathe," Thayne said. "You do what you need to do." Ore nodded gratefully and left that task to him.

Gradually, Ilena's heart rate returned to a soft, regular beat. He gave a report. Thayne followed it with a positive increase in her breathing. Ore could tell Mizi was now including praise in her running words to Ilena. He smiled slightly. If anyone could talk a person into living, it would be Mizi. He knew *he'd* respond for her.

He lifted Ilena's hand he was holding, put it briefly to his cheek, then without letting go of her hand rested his head on his raised hand, his eyes still closed in concentration to feel the faint beat of her heart in her neck.

Doctor Elliot tied his last knot, set the needle down and made one final check on the glue and the bone graft, checking to see everything was the way he wanted it. Then he carefully put everything back where it belonged. "Master Ore, is Mistress Ilena's heart-rate strong enough I can have Mistress Mizi back?"

Ore thought about it as he made another count. "It's not back to normal, but I think so."

Mizi said a few more things to Ilena, then stood and went to help the surgeon wrap the bandages. Ore opened his eyes and looked at Ilena's face. It wasn't quite as pale now. "Has her breathing increased again?" he asked Thayne.

"Yes," answered Thayne from behind his head. "It seems to be steadying at about a normal deep sleeping rate."

Ore watched her chest rise and fall gently, counting. He was getting worn out enough he wanted to put his head on her chest to feel that rise and fall, and fall asleep to it. *That's right. I didn't sleep at all last night, did I?* He shook himself and announced the breath rate.

"That's better," Doctor Elliot said. "I'd like it kept there. If she can sleep at that level for the next twelve to fourteen hours, that would be good."

"Master Ore, how do you count the number?" Thayne asked.

"It's like counting the heart rate, but you have to count for a little longer," Ore explained it more fully and had Thayne practice out loud a few times.

"Okay. I'll do that, now," Thayne said.

Ore nodded. Still holding on to Ilena's hand, he put his arm down and rested his head close to her ear. "Good girl. You were obedient to Mistress, and you're still living. Doctor Elliot's done. You rest now. You've made it through the worst of the pain." He squeezed her hand. "Whatever it was you were holding onto to walk through it, I hope it comes true for you."

-o-o-o-

Tap. Tap. Tap-tap. Sasou looked up briefly to glance at the door to the wide balcony that ran the full width of the Royal Office of Ichjou. It was kept closed at all times unless he really was in the mood for fresh air.

He nodded to his closest aide and Kingdom Minister of Intelligence, Lord Barret. He was also the closest to a friend Sasou had, the guardian originally assigned to him by his father before his father had passed away. If anyone could be said to be a surrogate father to Sasou, it would be Lord Barret, although the relationship was not quite that. Really, closest aide summed it up best.

Lord Barret rose from his desk at the other end of the King's office and went to the door. Sasou paid attention out of the corner of his eye as Lord Barret spoke quietly with the person outside the door, then turned to him.

Sasou looked up at him, a lock of pale gold hair falling over his right eye. He preferred to have his eyes hidden from the world he judged constantly. It kept what he was thinking a mystery. Most people found his direct bright blue eyes too piercing and fiercesome anyway.

"It's a message, written, from Miss Ilena." Sasou motioned for Lord Barret to let the messenger in. He watched the messenger keenly. It was the one who usually came.

Ilena was respectful and made it obvious so he didn't have to worry about different random people coming to that odd door. She was the only one who had messengers that came that way, so he'd already known it was from her. The fact it was written was what caught his interest. He hadn't received a written message for a few years now.

The messenger bowed before his King on one knee. He already had the message out, having shown it to Lord Barret. He didn't hold it out right away, though.

"My King, Mistress Ilena has had her experimental surgery yesterday. The surgeon was pleased with it. She came out of it well enough to speak with Master Ore before he left on the Regent's errand to retrieve the second list of witnesses. He delivered them to the safe house today and is returning to be by her side." Sasou nodded, sufficiently pleased with the report. It was good to know Rei was still studiously focused on his most important task of the moment.

The messenger held out the message and Sasou reached out to take it. Just before he had it in his hand, it was withdrawn slightly and he paused to look at the messenger, just a little confused.

The messenger had frozen and his head was turned towards the slightly open balcony door, the expression on his face going from respectful to stricken. Sasou froze in turn and his breath came in short bursts until he managed to get it back under control. His heart was another matter. It was tight and beating rapidly. The tension made it to his eyes as they tightened.

Finally the messenger turned back and bowed his head. "I'm sorry, Your Majesty." His voice broke and he had to swallow and breathe once to recover and calm. "I've just received word that Mistress Ilena has gone into rejection of the graft, and the surgeon and Head Healer have been called to come immediately."

Sasou's hand, still reaching out for the message, balled into a fist. "Is the word still coming?"

"Yes."

Sasou carefully opened his fisted hand and took the message in front of him. "Stay. I'll send a response with you." The messenger understood, bowed his head obediently, then rose and went to stand against the wall across from the open balcony door to wait on word from Suiran and his liege.

Sasou went to sit at one of the chairs set along the balcony wall, but at a distance from the open door, in order to read his letter from the person he was worried for, wondering what would have prompted her to write a letter just before she went into surgery. His plan had been to keep the messenger in the corner of his vision, but he became enrapt in the letter instead.

King Sasou,

Rei has been much more capable than you led me to believe. The depths of his capacity to search out meaning and understanding have exceeded my expectations by three-fold. I expect him to easily solve the current trouble and to have little difficulty with the next, although there are yet things for him to learn. Myself, as well.

The rose has of herself decided to become the apple tree, finally. I did have to point her head towards the light, but she has of herself, without knowing who she asked, requested that I train her up myself. But you will have already heard it for yourself.

Please pardon me for moving quickly at this time to strengthen you. My experimental surgery is scheduled for earlier than anticipated. I've set Andrew and Mina together in one night, and the third tree of the garden and the apple tree face each other with clear understanding, also in that same time. The sapling I nurture has been allowed to inform her what he and the other aides have already figured out for themselves so that I may not be hindered in helping her immediately.

Sasou twitched, both at her reference to her surgery and that the intelligent people at Rei's back had not needed anything other than his own actions to understand what Ilena was to them. He could forgive it, since it hadn't been Rei or Ilena who'd said it, and he knew that aides who knew their charges well enough to deduce such things were of the better ilk.

Her moving quickly wasn't surprising. She always moved to ensure that if she ended up removed from the board things were placed in the best possible position they could be at the moment.

As for the garden as a whole, I feel constrained to warn you that you have left yourself open to a deadly weakness. Sasou's heart thumped once, very hard. *If you cannot do what my sapling has done, at the irritated requirement of his mistress, and face your past properly, your future will be shortened - rather dramatically, actually.*

There is an orchid you have placed to become a sapling, and even labeled as such, but have neglected to tend to to ensure it becomes the tree you intended at the first. Because you have neglected it for two and a half years now, it is withering and becoming stunted. Please remember that to flowers, and saplings, time passes with each day and season and the threats to each are more dramatic.

The timing and strength of older trees is much different. It has led you to complacency. Your sapling, in your neglect, is being watered with poison and being given false sunlight by the enemies of the gardener. Because you have planted it next to the greatest tree in the garden, the roots of that tree are also being poisoned just as surely.

It is not dead yet. It can still be retrieved, carefully dug out and replanted, or the enemies of the gardener removed and clean water and nourishing food given to the sapling and it will learn to grow in the way you originally intended. You must understand why it is you have neglected it, and bend your mind to the timing of saplings and flowers if you wish to see it recovered.

If you cannot set it correctly and properly in a proper environment to see to it's strengthening by the time you wish to come and see with your own eyes the second tree and it's growth, even more damage will come to the garden, for the garden of the third tree will become uprooted with the whirlwind.

If you continue to refuse to heed the words of your assistant gardeners, the great tree in the center of the garden will fall, toppled by the enemies of the gardener within one year, two at the most. Can your second and third trees hold the weight of the garden? And if the second one falls within that time because of weaknesses that are still in it that have yet to be shored up, will the third be able to carry the entire garden on it's own branches?

Would you see the garden ravaged by your enemies, Master Gardener?

114

In Service,
Ilena

The paper in Sasou's hand shook, even though he was sure his hand was steady. He quickly put the message down in his lap and turned his head to look out the balcony window, although he wasn't seeing it. He rested his chin in his hand, his elbow up on the back of the chair he was sitting in as if he were merely pondering a casual correspondence. He had never received as severe a scolding as that from Ilena in all the times he'd been scolded by her. Nor one that frightened him so much.

Lord Barrett had been scolding him regularly for the past year to pay more attention to his wife, Queen Aryana, and with more frequency and harsher words for the past half year or so. Ilena was right that he thought in decades more frequently than in months or days.

Two and a half years. Has it really been that long? Sasou was privately horrified he'd neglected his wife for that long. Within the first year and no later than in the second they should have begun working on an heir. Why had he postponed it?

His mind shied away from the answer. He sternly pulled it back. If his own fear was the weakness that was going to destroy all of Ryokudo, he would punish himself until it was rooted out. He could not - *not* - allow himself to be the destruction of the kingdom he had charge over.

He flailed himself with the issue until he had an understanding of what it was about himself that he needed to correct, then he turned to his aide. "Lord Barret, begin to tighten the noose around those who are poisoning the ears of my wife."

Lord Barret looked at him soberly for a moment. "Will you step in yourself?"

"Not yet, unless you need me to unearth proper evidence. I don't want to step too quickly and make them run and hide." Lord Barret nodded. He looked like he would rather the King moved faster than that. Sasou looked at him, then finally allowed, "Within four months, Lord Barret, we will see to it." A time frame was better, even if it was still long in the lives of average citizens and people of the world.

Lord Barret gave Sasou a bland scolding look. "I'll send to let the Queen know that you'll be joining her after dinner. The breakfast cart will arrive at her rooms the same time it would for yourself."

Sasou blinked, but in the face of both his aide and Ilena's letter, he couldn't openly refuse. Instead, Sasou looked at Ilena's messenger. "What further word has come?" The messenger was a bit pale, but the word was not death, not at this time. Sasou went to his desk and took up a pen and put it to paper.

Dearest Ilena,

Please do not die. Your messenger arrived at the same time as word of the graft rejection. The garden cannot stand so well without the strength of the second tree, the same as it will stand the stronger for the saplings' growth. I will properly tend to mine, as I watch you tend to yours and that of the third tree. Let them take care of you properly as well.

S

He wanted to carry it himself, for just a moment. He paused, holding still until that moment passed, then bound the message and took it to the messenger. Lord Barret saw the messenger out. It was a long time before Sasou was able to return to his work. His weaknesses had been shown to him all at once and it was a difficult thing to recover from.

-o-o-o-

Ore woke slowly. He was resting on his arms on Ilena's bed, still holding her hand. He could feel something covering his back. He reached up and felt it. It was his jacket, laid over him. He relaxed again. It was nice to just rest there, although it wasn't the most comfortable position.

He listened to Ilena breathe. It sounded like she was sleeping well; his count was completely unconscious. His hand lifted, and he gently passed it over her forehead, brushing her hair. She felt nearly a normal temperature, perhaps still just a little high to fight off any remaining infection. He was glad it wasn't as bad anymore. He sighed. It had been a crazy two days.

Ahh...I still need to see Master. He couldn't quite lift his heavy body yet, but then it did it for him. *Really. How does that work?* He was looking down at Ilena as he grabbed for his jacket before it completely slipped off his shoulders.

She was covered again, both by clothing and clean bed covers. He remembered what she looked like before and his hand reached out to rip them off again. *No!* This time he did make his body do what he wanted it to. Somehow the compromise was to place his hand on top of her chest over her heart.

He took his hands off of her, turning away from her and clenching his hands into fists. He knew he was just finally having a reaction to nearly losing her. When he felt in control again, he shrugged on his jacket. Then he turned back to her and kissed her forehead, running his fingers lightly down her arm as he returned to standing upright.

"Master calls," he said softly, then turned and quietly left the room.

"Ah, you're awake, Master Ore," Thayne was waiting outside the room. He pushed his sturdy frame up from a relaxed lean on the nearest pillar of the walkway overhang to stand upright.

"What time is it?" Ore asked him.

"Two hours after the dinner hour."

Ore nodded and finished doing up the last couple of buckles on his jacket. "I must report to Master now. Go and sit with her. She's sleeping well. I'll return in a few hours." His hand gripped his jacket front as he finished the last buckle. It still wanted to rip the covers off Ilena.

He closed his eyes. What did it really want? It wanted to see her chest rising and falling again. To lay his ear to her heart. To know by touch that she was really still alive. He wanted to be lying next to her, holding her again, feeling her warmth. He wanted to hear her tell him anything, even if it wasn't a nice thing. His jaw clenched.

A warm, solid hand gripped his shoulder. "Father," Thayne's gentle voice called him. "She's alive. She will wait for you."

Ore opened his eyes and looked into Thayne's grey-blue eyes. They held understanding and warmth. Thayne gripped Ore's shoulder just a little tighter for a moment, giving him strength. Ore drew himself up slightly and nodded.

Thayne released him as he turned to walk down the hallway towards his Master. Both men knew that no other call could have called him away from his partner at that time.

-o-o-o-

Rei set down the last document on his desk as he walked past it. He hadn't been able to be still for very long, ever since he'd received word from the medical wing that Ilena had rejected the first graft. He'd had to tell himself repeatedly that he had to trust in the people he'd placed there, that his presence would be more distracting than useful.

It didn't help. He wanted to be there, too. Andrew and Mina both had done their best to support his decision to not go, even as he knew they would have let him go if he'd have said he would. There were a few times Andrew had opened his mouth to say, "go", and Rei had glared at him until he'd shut his mouth again.

He'd been glad to hear the news that the surgery to remove the graft and replace it with another had been accomplished. He'd been shocked to hear Ore had appeared just as they'd begun.

When Mizi explained that Ore fell asleep by Ilena's side just after they put her bandages on, and even before they'd finished cleaning up, he'd both felt very jealous - but only for an instant - and very relieved. Her partner had been there for her in her time of need. If Ore had been so tired as to fall asleep as soon as she'd been stable, it had to be because he hadn't slept all night and had hurried back to be by her side. Ore would come to him when he woke.

Mizi had come for dinner, needing his support after the surgery. He was glad she came. He needed her support, too. They took their time at dinner, five of them. Tairn had begged off to other tasks before dinner, but Mizi, he, Andrew, Mina, and Dane had all sat together giving each other strength as they hoped for strength for Ore and his partner.

Rei had been intrigued by the depth of emotion Dane held for Ilena. In person, it was pretty obvious how deeply she'd affected the second son of Earl Malkin. He'd thought back to Dane's story of how he'd met her, one of the ten Rei had read from the people at Falcon's Hollow, each one as intense and amazing as the others.

Dane had been on the wrong path that many second sons get onto. Bad friends, choices that led to the others in the family to frown on him, choosing to not care even though it made it all hurt worse. Like Rei, he'd always deeply respected his father and brother. He just couldn't see how he would ever be useful to them, or what his purpose was. It wasn't something he couldn't recover from with the right guidance.

Then Dane found himself caught in a trap he couldn't free himself from. His bad friends had betrayed him to a master nightwalker. They'd slowly led him down a path into a web he hadn't seen and the master struck suddenly, paralyzing him. He was told his only way to move forward was to betray his family, and in such a way it would destroy his father's House. He would have nothing to return to, once he and they had been completely drained.

Tairn, being an agent of the King, had already felt the tremors. He'd confronted Dane, and Dane had rejected him, saying he would handle it on his own. Tairn had tried to follow him and protect him, but that particular master of the underworld wasn't the one who Tairn had his eye on, and Tairn lost Dane.

When Dane had been missing for three days, he put out word on the light network - that of the regular town guards and soldiers. When Dane had been missing for two weeks, he had, in desperation, begun asking the nightwalker informants and any informant he could find not in the King's network.

Ilena's dark network was one who heard of the search and was the source that found Dane. He was being kept and used by an ally of Earl Shicchi's. The Earl had already had two alliances that he had scrubbed clean. Ilena hadn't held sufficient power over the Earl yet to prevent those deaths, but she felt she could prevent it that time. Then she learned that ally was holding Dane.

Instead of preventing the Earl from scrubbing that House, she'd allowed him to do it, going with him. She found Dane just before the flames reached the place he was kept prisoner and pulled him out of the building to a darkened area of woods.

She asked him if he wanted to live, wanted to help his family be strong. Was he willing to do his best to stand beside his father and brother, who had searched long and hard for him? Would he take a task for her that would bring him and them strength and support his family in their chosen path?

To him, she was an answer to his pleas in the darkness and pain of the room she had freed him from. He had fallen to his knees and begged her to tell him what to do, tears flowing freely from his eyes. She'd held him and whispered in his ear what she wanted him to do.

It was the same as with the others. Remember what had been done. Tell when he was asked to tell to the person she asked him to tell. Stand next to his father and brother. And if he needed something to do that would bring him purpose, live for her. He'd agreed, then he'd passed out.

118

When Dane had come to, he was back at his father's house. His wounds had been tended, and he'd been freed from the Little Death. He wept in grief and relief.

A month later, Ilena had come to Nakaba and greeted him. His father had seated her at the place reserved for a guest of honor. Then she asked them for a favor. She had someone who needed a place of safety where she could be cared for. Would they allow said person to come to their home and be cared for by Dane?

Dane said yes without reservation, that he would take care of whomever it was. Because he agreed, his father also agreed. One week later, a carriage came bringing Freida, already into her eighties. Earl Malkin's heart was softened immediately upon seeing that Ilena had asked him to care for someone who certainly deserved great and tender care. Dane had only had his own certainty validated, and from that time had served Freida with tenderness.

At dinner, Dane had told them how hard it had been for him to not know if Ilena had survived the rock slide. He'd been grateful that Ore had been able to tell them when they arrived at Falcon's Hollow, but even before then, when he'd watched Ore - from the funny episode of his unnecessary ploy to get him out of his father's house, until they reached the safe house - he knew, somehow, that she was okay and that she was being watched over.

"I didn't know why, really, he'd been given the title of 'Father' until I was able to be with him for that time. I was glad I could be part of the first group and come to understand it. I'm glad she has him watching over her."

Mizi had nodded. "I'm glad he's now willing to watch over her. She's had to work hard. But I think it was because he could talk to people like you that he was finally willing to really look at her. Before then, he wouldn't trust her. Thank you for that, Dane."

Dane had looked at Mizi in some surprise. "Ah..., but I didn't really do anything."

Rei smiled a small smile. That was how good things were done: good people just living their lives right having a positive influence on the world around them. He'd chosen his close aides so he would be influenced rightly on his own path.

He was standing beside his desk, his hand still on the document he had put down, looking out his windows towards the city, his back to the door, when it opened then clicked closed. He turned his head slightly. He knew that presence. "Are you back, Ore?"

He heard the soft footfalls of his sworn man approach, then the rustle of his clothing. Ore had knelt before his back. "I'm sorry for going to the side of my partner before coming to Master."

Rei sighed quietly. "I would rather you had come to me first, but I would have sent you right away. I'm not angry. How is it you were able to return so quickly?"

"It's as Master suspected. They didn't want me to speak with the witnesses. There are things they will say to me that they wish to edit before the castle hears."

"...Will they keep those things secret from you always?" Rei asked.

"No. They're willing to tell them to me at a later time," Ore confirmed.

"What do they wish to do next?"

"They will defend the hollow, both from within and without. I've encouraged them to consider using the soldiers to their benefit by letting them know we expect the use of the Little Death. ...And I forbade them from using it themselves in your name and my own." Ore was quite firm and his dislike of the Little Death laced his voice.

"Do you know what they're planning?" Rei wanted to know the specifics so he would know what to plan.

"Not yet." Ore had confidence he would learn of it eventually, one way or the other.

"Dane said today that he didn't understand why you'd been given the title of Father until he met you and talked to you on the journey, and he was glad to be given that opportunity. Have you learned it yet?"

"No. I still only understand that I'm to stand beside her. But Dane did say what place they expect me to stand in."

Rei turned and faced Ore. "What place is that?" his eyes held the piercing look of a hawk.

Ore didn't move from his fully formal humble kneel, one knee on the floor, one fist supporting his bowed back and head. "When you place Ilena in the position of Minister of Intelligence, they expect you to place me in the position of Vice-Minister of Intelligence, so that I can carry out her and your will."

"...They wish for you to be the blade in her hand?"

"...I believe so."

Rei was quiet for a while. It perhaps couldn't be unexpected. "Is she already moving?"

"Yes."

Rei's eyes flashed. Ilena was moving many pieces on her board: Mizi, Mina and Andrew, Ore, and even himself. Moving everyone into stronger positions. And her household was moving as well, stirred by her own hand. "What did they say about Falcon's Hollow?"

"They expect you to gift it to her. Most of them will stay, having chosen 'long ago' that they would," Ore answered.

She was moving on a board she had set up long ago. Long enough ago to have witnesses for him from the time things happened. Long enough ago to want the land he hadn't known he would use for her sake. "What does she intend it for?"

"Horses."

"Horses? Is that why so many are coming? Even though it isn't big enough?" That was a surprising addition to the tally of clues he was holding.

"They don't know why, only that it is so. There are things she won't tell them."

That was a given. So he would have to ask the right questions at the right time to know, but he could feel it now. Feel that the test she was expecting had been set just as long ago as she had decided to be his shield. Feel that it was big enough to encompass the entirety of Suiran, and very likely all of Ryokudo. "Ore, she's already said something important to you. What is it?"

Ore looked up at him in surprise, then thought back through all the time he'd been gone from his master, these last two days. "When she was in the sleep-talking phase of the Little Death after her surgery yesterday morning, she said that there was a fate for her worse than death. It was the fate of being 'the cause of a war'."

That was it. War. Not just internal conflict. External conflict with another nation. It would come from Tarc - Rei had already guessed that. But now he knew: she was at the center of it. Tarc knew she existed and wanted to use her as it's pawn.

"Yes, that's the answer," he said aloud for Ore's sake. "She's setting the board into a position of strength, with sufficient protections around herself, so that she can't be used by Tarc when they come to war against us." He looked at Ore, who was still looking at him. "Will you protect her in that place at that time?"

"Yes," Ore said. His whole body and demeanor was in agreement. She had indeed already moved Ore into being ready to be placed in his position.

"Very well, we'll give them what they expect. Are you already prepared?" Rei's piercing blue eyes bore into Ore, to see into his heart.

"...," Ore gave the barest of sighs. "Yes."

Rei smiled sympathetically. "Then, I'm ready to hear your report." Ore stood, settling into his semi-formal stance, feet shoulder-width apart and hands lightly clasped behind his back, and began his detailed report.

When Ore was done with his report, Rei considered. He'd already asked about most of the important things in the report, but there was something in it that had stood out to him. "When Foster said that, after the direct attack, 'everything would be set' from their end, was he talking just about a sense of being secured after that, or was he saying more?"

Ore considered the feel of that conversation. "He was saying more."

"So there's a plan they'll be in place to execute....?" Ore shook his head. He didn't know what it was yet. "...Perhaps it has to do with the horses?" Rei shook his head. "Keep that as a question to answer." Ore nodded.

"Ah, Ore...," Rei rubbed the back of his head and Ore relaxed. The official part was done. "I'm sorry I made you angry. I shouldn't have made your concerns a public joke."

"Well...that is true, but I wasn't angry."

"You weren't? It seemed that way." Rei was puzzled, but perhaps he could be relieved?

Ore put one hand behind his neck and looked away, over Rei's shoulder. "Ah, well, a quick retreat just seemed the proper thing to do at the time. But if it made you consider yourself, then that's okay."

"Mina scolded me." Rei admitted. "I was too curious."

"You were curious, Master?" Ore turned his attention on Rei. "Would you like me to kiss you, too, so you understand?"

Rei blushed, remembering Mina's words, and scowled at Ore furiously. "No! Of course not!"

Ore looked at him narrowly, putting his hand on his hip. "Well, I think one day you should just let me do it once. You won't have to be curious any more after that. Besides, your words say no but, –"

"NO, Ore!" Rei cut him off.

Ore sighed. "It was just on the forehead, Master. She's still only my partner."

Rei wanted to protest. Ore's blush had said more than that had happened, but he was already in trouble enough, so he kept quiet. "I know I said you could be with her, but when the reports come in from Falcon's Hollow, will you come and help with them? That much I will need you to do." Ore nodded. He wasn't surprised to be asked to help with that.

"Then we're done." Rei knew Ore wanted to get back to Ilena's side.

"Where are Mister Andrew and Miss Mina?" Ore asked.

Rei waved a hand. "They excused themselves, knowing you were coming."

"Have they decided what they're going to do yet?"

Rei had to take a minute to figure out that Ore must have been told about their "lessons" with Ilena. He shook his head. "They haven't said, but maybe they're considering it tonight."

"That would be good. ...You also need to be done with work. I'll walk you to your rooms." Ore turned towards the door and looked at Rei expectantly.

Rei shook his head. "They said they would come back for me. I have a thing I still need to do."

Ore looked at him closely. "You're not going to run, are you?"

"No," Rei laughed. "I've promised Mizi a written list. I need to finish it."

"Well, if it's for Mistress...," Ore winked at Rei as he headed for the door. "Good luck." He let himself out.

Rei had gotten a good start to his list, but had reached a state of confusion when Andrew and Mina returned to the office. "Still working hard?" Andrew asked him.

"Did Ore come?" asked Mina.

"Yes," Rei answered both questions at once, still slightly distracted.

"What are you working on?" Andrew asked.

"My list for Mizi."

"Are you having troubles?" Mina asked.

"I'm not sure what's required knowledge of a lady of the court," Rei admitted with a sigh. "I have no sisters and my father died when I was young enough that I only saw Mother in her role as Queen and Regent. Somehow I feel I'm lacking knowledge."

"Then I think you can expect Miss Ilena to fill in those gaps," Mina said pragmatically.

"Oh, is that so?" Rei considered that, then wrote one more line. "That should do it." He set his pen down and put the document in a folder to give to Mizi at lunch the following day. Then he rose from his desk and headed over to join Andrew and Mina.

As he reached them, he looked at Mina. "Did you discuss it?" She nodded. He looked at Andrew. "Is there anything you need me to do?" Andrew smiled and shook his head.

"Let me know if you do." He made them promise, then continued to walk towards the door. "Let's go then." Mina opened the door and they walked out of the Rose office, and headed for Rei's rooms.

CHAPTER 7 Anxiety

Ore was in a hurry to get back to Ilena - at least a part of him was. The part of him that wasn't ready to give up yet wasn't. So, even though there weren't a lot of people around at that time of night, he was going slow enough to practice seeing Ilena's Children. It being the later hours of the evening, he decided to detour to some of the more populated areas for that time.

He started with the study room and library. Neither were that full at that time of night either, but those who had extra studies would be there. After walking around for a while as if he were looking for books, or a particular person, he finally shrugged and gave up - at least he seemed to.

Three for sure, but who was the fourth? There had been someone that had responded positively, but wasn't marked the way he expected. *Was it one of King Brother's?* It had seemed to be that way. *Could it be one of the crossover points of contact?* He knew he'd have to ask to know for sure.

He could stop in and take a look at whatever evening activities the lords were participating in, but he wasn't ready to step into that realm unprotected by Rei just yet, so he skipped that one and headed for the servant's wing. Since he needed a purpose to be there, too, that late at night, he took a slightly meandering route towards Leah and Rio's rooms. He hadn't seen them at all yet and he was curious as to why.

He didn't get very far from that wing before he started seeing the Children. The night time janitors were heading out for the various wings with their buckets and mops and rags. Over a third of them were hers. Fully half of the ones he saw were like the one he'd run into in the library. Not hers, not "just janitors".

The whole servant's wing was like that, and he was only seeing maybe a third of the ones housed in the castle. There were many who lived in town and came to the castle for the daytime shift, and he was mostly seeing only night staff. He would have to see how the night shift compared to the daytime shift, but it made him nervous.

He found his way to Leah's room and knocked. She came to the door relatively quickly. Good, he hadn't pulled her out of bed. "Master Ore?" She was supremely surprised to see him at her door and stiffened in some concern.

He instantly recognized her mark, but noticed it was a bit different, accentuated, and he looked a little more puzzled than he otherwise might have when he answered her. "Why didn't I see you this afternoon?"

"Ah! My apologies, Master Ore." She bowed deeply, apologizing as if she'd deeply offended him. "Rio and I were sent to retrieve Doctor Elliot and Mister Ryan, and were told to wait outside until the surgery was completed. You were asleep by the time we were called in to help with the clean up.

"Mistress Mizi gave us orders to only stay until dinner, watching over Mistress to make sure that she slept well. She stopped by on her way to dinner with Regent Rei, took our report, then said when Thayne returned we were excused for the night."

Ore listened patiently, then raised his hand. "I'm not angry, Miss Leah."

"Oh. Well.... That's good, but...," she petered out.

"What is it?" he invited her to say it.

"You were looking so serious," she said a little weakly. It wasn't really a normal thing for Ore to have come visit her at her quarters.

"Ah, Foster taught me how to see today. I've been looking as I came to speak to you, and I've seen several things that concern me I have no answer to. It's that," Ore explained.

"Oh? May I help you?" Leah relaxed just a bit.

"What does your mark mean? It's different," he asked first.

Leah paused. "It's because I was Mistress's nurse at her home before."

Ore nodded. He understood that meant it had significance because she'd been with Ilena since Selicia. "There are others in the castle who are marked, but are not of Ilena's Family. Who are they?"

Surprise ran across Leah face, then she shook her head. "No, I shouldn't be surprised. You ran in the underworld long enough. You know how to see them already, and you've had your eyes opened to the mark of the light side networks. They are either King Sasou's or the Queen Mother's."

"The Queen Mother's?" Ore hadn't considered such a thing, nor had Ilena mentioned it. But as he pondered it, it did make sense. She'd been regent here for many years and would also need to know what was going on in her own house. "How can one tell which is which?"

Leah looked at him just little impatiently. This was not really the place. Then she leaned forward. He gave her his ear, and she whispered it to him. He nodded. He'd seen the distinctions. The Queen Mother's people slightly outweighed the King's in the castle. "Is it normal for nearly *all* of the staff to be part of one network or another?"

Leah shook her head. "It's because there's still a shifting of responsibility. If Mistress is confirmed, eventually the larger portion will be hers, with only maintenance levels from the other two, although the Queen Mother's portion will still be more than the King's."

That made Ore feel better, but it made him want that to happen just a little faster. "Doesn't having high concentrations of three different Families cause greater opportunity for conflict?"

"It could, but the other two groups were already working together for a time, so had a balance. Mother knew we would be putting pressure on the system so ordered extra care from us." Leah reassured Ore. "They're also testing us, so for now they're just watching, for the most part. There are some who we may turn to for aid when needed."

Ore had a thought. "How many of Mother's Children were here before she came?"

Leah didn't smile, but her eyes glinted just for a moment. "A smaller number that was sufficient to gather information."

Ore hesitated for a moment, then accepted that answer. It wasn't like an exact number from the past was important now, nor would he know yet how to interpret it. Likely Ilena had a similar number in Nijou Castle. "Thank you for letting me disturb you," Ore said to Leah.

They said good night, and Ore continued on his meander, this time headed for the castle garrison. He wasn't sure what he would find there. Most of the guards on night shift he'd seen weren't marked at all - just a very few - and of those, he had yet to see one that was Ilena's.

He was a familiar presence in the guard area. Rei frequently sent him there on business. He waved or chatted easily with the off duty soldiers who were still awake. There were a few more of King Sasou's men here, and quite a few of the Queen Mother's, although still at a smaller percentage of the garrison as a whole, but again, he found none marked as Ilena's.

Then, as he was leaving, he ran into a junior soldier just coming in. "Ah!" exclaimed Ore before he realized it. The soldier looked at him curiously. Ore quickly said, "Could I please speak with you over here for just a minute?"

The young man courteously nodded and followed him to a nearby place they could quietly talk without being overheard. "You're one of Mother's Children?" Ore wanted to confirm it first. The young man nodded. "Can you tell me why I've seen no soldiers other than yourself who are her Children?"

"I'm sorry, Sir Ore, but I'm not authorized to answer your questions. You'll need to ask one of your guardians," the young man apologized respectfully.

"Eh? I have guardians? Ah, this is a matter of ranking, I suppose? I'm probably even your junior...but in a different line?" Ore tried to puzzle it out.

The young man shifted as he considered what he could say. "Mmm...sort of. The people who'll answer your questions are the people authorized to answer them. It prevents confusion."

"Oh." So, he was seeing it as ranking because only highly ranked Family members had the authority to answer his questions. "I think I see. Well, thank you for explaining at least that much. What's your name?"

"David Tellius," he bowed. "It's a pleasure to meet you."

"Thank you, David. I won't keep you any longer." While Ore walked back towards the medical wing, which wasn't very far away, he continued to watch, but he also was thinking.

Foster had answered his questions, and he was an "area captain". Dane and Thayne answered his questions and they were both "agents". Leah had answered his questions. He didn't know her title, but it was likely very high since she was Ilena's secretary.

Would he be answered by any area captain or agent, or just the ones assigned to be his guardians? He regretted not asking what David's rank was. That might have told him. At the time it had just felt like he was a lower rank.

When Ore turned down the hallway to Ilena's room, he took the time to look at the guards on her door. Hue was unmarked, but Sailte was marked as one of the King's. That surprised Ore. Maybe the King really did know her and have a marked interest in what happened to her.

He looked down the hall. One of the guards at the medical offices door was the King's, the other was one of the Queen Mother's. That seemed to be a case of both sides working together to protect a valuable asset.

Ore stopped in front of Ilena's door and looked Sailte in the eye. Sailte's eyes were questioning for a moment, then he bowed slightly. "Thank you," Ore said. Sailte hadn't expected that, and his eyes were a little wide, but he smiled. Ore put his hand on the door knob and went in.

Thayne was standing by the time Ore entered. He had a small candle lit, but was hiding it behind the flower vase so that the room was mostly just ambiently lit. "She's continued to sleep peacefully, Master Ore." Thayne said. "Was Master Rei angry?"

"Not particularly," Ore answered. "I've come across some questions on my way back. Will you stay and answer them for me?"

"Of course, if I may." That answer held new meaning for Ore now, although the original meaning surely still held true as well.

"Why are there so few soldiers that are also part of any of the three Families, and why have I only seen one that is part of Mother's Family?" Ore settled on the edge of the second bed where he could see Thayne and motioned for him to sit in his chair again.

"Oh, you've seen that there are three Families?" Thayne raised an eyebrow of surprise at Ore as he turned the chair so he could see both Ilena and Ore. He sat in the chair as Ore answered.

Ore nodded. "Miss Leah explained that to me. I stopped by to speak with her briefly."

Thayne gave a nod of understanding. "In general it's because it's both unnecessary and difficult to recruit soldiers. A man becomes a soldier often because they're already loyal to a particular crown. If asked to give information a soldier will answer without question. If they gain important information, they'll immediately report it. Thus it's unnecessary to ask them to become faithful - they already are.

"It's also difficult because they're naturally suspicious of anyone who's not within the proper chain of command. They therefore must already have a strong loyalty to the person who asks them to become part of the network. Or someone already in the network must go into training, pass the testing, and be assigned to the place you need them. That's a long process, and they aren't guaranteed to be placed where you need them."

Ore lightly clasped his hands together and ran one thumb slowly over the other. "I ran into David Tellius. He's done the latter?"

Thayne smiled. "Yes. We're very proud of him for performing well enough in his class that he was able to be selected for duty at the castle."

"Do you have any others here in the castle?" Ore asked.

"A few." Thayne didn't want to be pressed for more information in that area, Ore could tell.

Ore moved on to his next question. "I asked David a question and he told me that he wasn't authorized to answer me because it would cause confusion, and let it slip I have 'guardians' who are authorized to answer them. Is it based on a ranking system, or a selection system?"

Thayne leaned back in his chair and stretched his feet out in front of him, crossing them at his ankles. "Mmm...a bit of both. Only those who have the ability to determine what Mother is ready for you to hear will answer you, thus by ranking, but it's by selection because we're the ones she's chosen to place in your path.

"If Mother hadn't sent you to collect us, we wouldn't be authorized to answer you, but only those of us ranked high enough can answer you. Because Mother has given me to you, it's her way of saying that I'm to be not just your guardian, but your teacher for this time. Dane may answer certain questions now, even as Miss Leah did, but in the main it's expected that you'll learn from me, and from Mother of course."

Ore nodded, "It did feel that way, that I should bring the questions to you or to her. What are the rankings?"

"Child, Paige, Agent, Captain, and the Immediate Family."

"Would David be a Paige or an Agent?"

"He's an Agent."

That was consistent to what Ore had felt. "You and Dane are Agents, and your father is a Captain. I would assume Miss Leah is part of the Immediate Family." Thayne nodded. "Grandfather as well." Thayne nodded again. "What is Miss Leah's title?"

Thayne shook his head. "Only Mother can tell you that. She protects the Immediate Family the most."

"I don't feel very protected," Ore complained.

"You've been very protected, Father," Thayne remonstrated. "No one but Family knows who you are, and they would die before they told an outsider. The Family as a whole was only shown who Father was beginning last fall, and that's also a protection for you. When you're seen, every member knows it's their responsibility to ensure your safety."

"That has been my burning question from the beginning," Ore said dryly. "How does everyone know what I look like?"

Thayne smiled. "Mother sent the word to everyone that, 'Father will be taking a pilgrimage to every lord's house on the North Road in Suiran this fall. He will be standing behind the red-haired Princess. Learn his face.' Everyone in Kouzanshi, including myself, immediately knew who you were. She'd already had us watching both of you.

"There was one who knew your route and when you left. That word was spread and everyone worked to be somewhere along your path so they could learn your face. She recalled me to my father's house after she gave that order but before you left Kouzanshi, so I was able to make sure they also knew when and where to be looking for you."

Ore shook his head. That would have been a massive undertaking, even if it was he that had, in the main, gone to them. "It's hard to believe I didn't notice anything."

Thayne rubbed his cheek a little. "Perhaps you did and ascribed it to something else. Being watched by the eyes of a light network feels different. You don't seem to feel it much. You're hyper-aware of dark eyes, of course."

Ore nodded. He'd been distracted by his fear of Mizi having to go visit Tokumade for the first half of the trip, or more. And he'd not particularly noticed being watched at Kouzanshi, except occasionally by shadows. They'd probably been part of the Earl's network. "Well, I'll have plenty of opportunity to practice here now, but already just from looking for it tonight, I'm uncomfortable. It will take me a while to settle to this new feeling."

"It may help you to remember that the dark eyes hold death in them, light eyes hold no ill will for those who haven't earned it. They're merely observing. That can be how you distinguish between them," Thayne tried to be helpful.

Ore remembered back to Osterly, when he'd delivered the word that the steward had died to the Little Death. Many of the eyes that had been looking at him were that - just observing. "There were an awful lot of you in Osterly, then, at that time."

Thayne chuckled quietly, shaking his head. "Yes. We were unable to prevent them from coming to see for themselves, even though there was little to see except you. Thus, you became the subject for many conversations at that time."

Ore sighed. "So it's a gossip chain too?"

Thayne smiled. "It's hard to stop gossip, especially when that's all there is, but we distinguish very carefully between information and gossip so that there's no confusion."

Ore quickly pinned Thayne with a sharp look. "That's the second time today I've heard that."

Thayne put on a firm face and folded his arms. "The sole purpose of an information network is to transmit accurate information from one place to another. If we couldn't maintain careful, trustworthy information transfer, our efforts would be in vain, and we wouldn't be worthy to walk next to the networks of the King. Confusion is the enemy to an information network. There are many structures in place to prevent confusion, but now is not the time for you to learn those details."

"Even though I have the title of Father, I understand that I'm not yet Father. Among the other rankings, where am I?" Ore moved on to another of his questions.

"Still Child, of course," Thayne grinned, "but you're now in training for Paige, since she marked you yesterday.

"You're already at the advanced stages of training because you bring with you your prior experience which helps you learn very quickly the things of the light network. And because you ask pointed questions to understand that which you don't understand. But you'll need to learn a few things at her knee before you graduate from your lessons. I won't be able to tell you everything, because you're Father."

Ore nodded. That made sense. "There are things that Foster couldn't say that I already knew, and it's because I stand between Mother and Master, and answer to Master. At what point will I have to make the choice between them?"

Thane frowned. "It's our goal that never has to happen. If it does, you must let us know right away, before you must act on it. If it needs to go all the way up to Mother to correct, we'll take it to her, or you may. The further on the path you choose to go, the easier the way will be. After all our goal is to stand to support Master Rei. If there's a conflict, that's a problem."

"Yes, that would be." Ore said darkly. "Then, if I feel conflicted, I'll confront it."

Thayne sat up and made a half-bow while sitting. "Please do."

"I'm done with asking questions," Ore said. "Have you learned where your rooms are yet?"

"But that was another question, Master Ore," teased Thayne. He answered it meekly when Ore glared at him. "Yes, I have."

"Then get out. I'll stay here until Master calls for me. You should familiarize yourself with the castle until then. If I need you I'll send one of Scamp or Scoundrel to fetch you."

Thayne stood and bowed, "Yes, Master Ore. Good night." He left and Ore turned to look at Ilena.

-o-o-o-

Ilena was still sleeping deeply. It seemed so unnatural that she hadn't woken even briefly when he came in, nor had stirred, nor commented during his and Thayne's entire quiet conversation. There had been several moments where he'd expected her to interject witty or caustic comments, but they hadn't come.

Ore rose from the second bed and prepared himself for sleeping. He lay down on it again when he was ready, and thought about the day and the conversation he'd just had, but before long he was sitting up again.

Ore sighed. He'd held himself back over and over, night after night while testing Ilena, his distrust anchoring his resolve. Two nights ago that had been breached because of his fear. After having participated in the day's crisis, a part of him couldn't trust she was okay, couldn't relax.

"Indeed, what a child I am," he chided himself, referring to both his fear and his station in her household.

He tried again, rolling himself into his blanket and facing the wall. He used her soft breaths as his lullaby and forced himself to relax into at least the nightwalker's light watchful sleep that would give his body some rest.

He'd been sleeping that way for several hours when there was a light knock on the door. He rolled slightly to see who was entering. "Ore?" It was Mizi whispering quietly.

He rolled to standing, his blanket still clutched around him. "Mistress?" he whispered back.

"I've brought Ilena's next dose of the pain reducing medication. She'll be needing it shortly. It must be administered every twelve hours." Mizi left the door open slightly so she had enough light to see by to work.

"Have you stayed awake all this time?" he asked as he walked over to join her at Ilena's bedside.

"No, I've woken recently to make it. I'll return to bed after she's taken it," Mizi answered.

"That's good." Ore was relieved she'd rested properly.

Ilena shifted, catching Ore's attention, then groaned quietly. Mizi lifted Ilena's head while softly speaking to her, telling her who she was and what she was giving her, like she'd done after the second surgery at Osterly garrison. Then she put the vial to Ilena's lips and carefully poured it for her. Ore could see that Ilena was aware enough to swallow it obediently, if slowly.

Mizi lay Ilena back down, handed Ore the vial, and quickly checked the wound site for telltale heat. "That's good. She's still at an acceptable temperature."

"May I know it, Mistress?" Ore wanted to know so he would know if it became elevated, but he was afraid to touch Ilena without permission.

"Yes," Mizi took his hand and guided it to the places she was touching to measure. Ore was glad it was dark enough to hide his blush. Mizi holding his hand on any day was just as dangerous as him touching Ilena tonight would be. He hoped Rei never heard of it, but then again he could probably use a good scolding right about now. He tried hard to focus on the temperature he was supposed to be remembering.

When Mizi let go, Ore hid his hand in his blanket, holding it close to his heart. "Thank you, Mistress. Do you know what symptom it was that sent for the Doctor to come?"

"It was like at Osterly, when she had the infection, but her fever came on very quickly," Mizi answered.

Ore nodded. He'd been in the room for that before. "I'll recognize it. Shall I walk you back?"

There was a soft scuff at the door. "That won't be necessary, Ore."

Ore turned in surprise. "Master?! What?"

"Mizi told me at dinner she'd be coming down. I told her I would help." Rei walked into the room and up beside Ilena. "After all, I still haven't seen Ilena yet."

Mizi explained to Ore that Andrew and Mina had told how Rei had restrained himself from coming down during the surgery and they'd approved the unescorted trip as a reward. It made Ore nervous that his master was unescorted, and very glad he'd behaved.

Rei was looking at Ilena. Her face showed some of the pain she was in. He brushed her forehead with his hand, as if wishing to banish the pain. She turned towards the touch, then her eyes opened blurrily.

Both men recognized it. She'd looked at them like that before, the first time she'd spoken to them, the time Ore had grieved for abandoning her. This time, Ore had nothing to grieve for, save her pain. He felt, rather, that this time he had things to be grateful for.

"R-e-i."

He smiled at her and put his hand on her arm, squeezing it briefly. "Ilena."

"Tha-nk you." He nodded, then nodded towards Ore. Her head turned slowly.

She saw Mizi first. "Prin-cess."

Mizi leaned down and gave her a light hug. "You'll be better soon," Mizi said to her.

"Yes," Ore heard her answer but he couldn't see her face because Mizi was standing to block her. Mizi looked up at Rei with a worried expression on her face.

"Ore is here, too, Ilena," Rei said to Ilena, wanting to encourage her. Mizi moved to let Ore through, trying to not show him a worried face.

Ore reluctantly moved to stand close to Ilena. He was worried about what he would do. He looked into her eyes that were once again fighting to stay open. Ilena's hand lifted and Ore took it by reflex. Her eyes closed. "O-re," she sighed.

She relaxed as much as she had, and as suddenly as she had, when she'd passed out before on the surgery table. Ore was immediately alarmed. Mizi felt for Ilena's pulse on her neck and counted, then left her hand there, monitoring.

She looked up at Ore. "Do you remember that Doctor Elliot said that we should talk to her to keep her present enough until she had the strength of herself again?" Ore nodded. "I want you to do that this time, until she stabilizes again." He looked at her, lost and uncomprehending.

"Ore," Rei called to him. Ore looked into the blue eyes that anchored him. "Your night two nights ago with Ilena didn't just end with a kiss on the forehead. What did you do that allowed you to leave?"

Ore swallowed in fear, to answer that question to Rei. "She...she asked me to stay with her, that she was afraid, too."

Rei nodded, then held his hand out to Mizi. She walked around the head of the bed to take his hand, and he began to lead her out of the room. At the door, he looked back at Ore. "Do it again. Keep her here. Keep her alive."

"Ah, no, but...," Ore tried to say as Rei shut the door behind them. Ore trembled. He'd just been ordered by his master to do the very thing he'd been holding himself back from doing. He wasn't sure how to take it.

He'd wanted a scolding, something to help him pin himself down on the other bed. Even his mistress had ordered him to stay by her...again. It was the second time. The second time for everything. Could he help her stay alive this second time?

He bent down and said in her ear, "Ilena, I'm afraid. I'm going to stay with you. Will you stay with me?" He carefully sat on the bed, afraid of shifting her too much, and slowly lay down next to her, his blanket still wrapped around him. He reached around her and placed his hand on her neck, finding her heartbeat. It was indeed as low as before. He shuddered.

He knew he didn't know what to say, but there was no one else here to hear him say it. He opened his mouth and the words he'd been holding inside for the last two months, the last thirteen and a half years, began to flow out of it and into her ear.

He told her how much he'd appreciated her strength at Tokumade, her loyalty, and her kindness. He told her he was sorry for abandoning her, that he still couldn't understand why she didn't hate him, but that he was grateful she didn't. He thanked her for being his warmth and strength through all the dark years.

He thanked her for being there to protect him at the battle and bind his wound so that he could live. Told her that the scar was a reminder that she'd always been watching over him, had always remained his strength. His heart had been missed and she'd bound it and protected it. Would she continue to protect it, continue to be his strength, bind it again by living, by staying by his side?

He told her he'd stayed with Rei and Mizi because they reminded him of her, because he'd seen her in them. They wanted her to live, had ordered it. She must be obedient to Rei and Mizi in all things, but especially in staying alive for them.

He reassured her that serving them wasn't a burden, but was light - a weightless service. Even he hadn't expected it until he'd accepted it and found it to be so. He would help her, would be her strength until she understood it for herself. Rei would protect her, and he, Ore, would help.

She needed to still help Mizi stand by Rei. No one else could do it. She couldn't leave after making that promise. He'd been waiting so long for them to get together, and she was the only thing that had come in answer to that desire in all the years he'd followed Mizi. He was so glad she had, even if it meant she was going to be difficult. He would live with that if it meant that Mizi would finally get to stand by Rei as his Princess.

"In a very short amount of time, you've become the source of great change in this place. There's still much you have left to show us, you must show us, else we'll be lost to war and ruin." The pulse under his fingers jumped. It had been slowly increasing in intensity, but her reaction to that comment said that she was, at some level, really hearing what he was saying. Her worst fear - being the cause of a war - had awoken her to a state of being willing to fight to live, finally.

Ore sighed in relief and rested his forehead on her head. "I love your Children, Mother." He told her. "And they love you. They work for you because they know your cause is just. They'll help you win the fight to prevent war from coming, but they need you at the head. Only you know how to direct their efforts. I'll help you. Master will help you, but we can't do it without you.

"You still have things to tell us that we need to know in order to prevent a war we know nothing about yet. We'll protect you from your enemy, so that you can't be moved. All of us will. We want you, and we want you in the place you've chosen to be." He couldn't tell if he was moving into the realm of half-truth now or not, but he was certainly already desperate.

Ilena's heartbeat was much stronger now. He remembered Mizi rewarding her last time. He kissed her temple and praised her, encouraged her some more, and held her to him, saying, "I'll stay here by your side tonight. Let my presence bring you courage and strength. Sleep to recover your strength, but stay with me. Stay alive."

Her hand twitched and he took it in his. She faintly squeezed his hand, then turned her face towards his, and fell into real sleep again. He faded into the sleep of semi-awareness, her breath on his face his anchor.

-o-o-o-

When Rei and Mizi left the room, Rei said nothing, but led Mizi quickly towards her quarters. She could tell by how tightly he was holding her hand that he was very worried. He was careful with her on the stairs up to the second level, but he was still in a hurry.

There on the landing, he stopped and turned to her. "Mizi...," he started, but then couldn't find words.

She wrapped her arms around him and held him. "It's okay, Rei. I know why you love her. I know it's frightening to think you might lose her, but she loves Ore. She'll hear him calling her and will listen to his voice."
134

Mizi allowed Rei to hold onto her for strength and courage until he was ready to stand on his own again. They sat on the top step, side by side, holding hands, talking quietly until they couldn't stay awake anymore.

Rei saw her to her door. Then, using his master key for the wing, stumbled into Ore's room and fell asleep on his bed. It was the cause for quite some excitement the next morning and a scolding from a very worried Andrew, who was cut off in the middle by two frowning women who stood to protect Rei. Rei was glad for it. He'd gotten to sleep in for once, which he desperately needed by now.

-o-o-o-

Ore and Ilena were discovered first by Leah and Rio, coming for the morning nursing. They weren't all that noisy, but Leah chose to shake Ore by the shoulder and demand that he remove himself, at least to the other bed.

He opened one eye and rolled it to look at her. It wasn't a kind look. "Master and Mistress's orders. We almost lost her again last night."

Leah let go suddenly and froze. "Ahhh." She finally remembered to breathe, letting it out in a long sigh. Rio had her hands to her mouth in shocked dismay. "I'm sorry. Is she okay now?"

Ore closed his eye and put his hand on Ilena's heart and counted. "Yes. She's still sleeping."

Leah stood quietly for a moment, then said, "We should still get her ready. Doctor Elliot will be here shortly to check on her status, and Mister Ryan will follow after to bring her next dose of the Little Death."

Ore woke up for that. "No!" he said lifting his head and turning it to look at Leah. "She won't survive it today."

Leah held up her hands. "That is for the two of them to decide. You must speak with them. It is our duty to see to the morning tending."

Some inner part of Ore was impressed. Leah was standing up to him while he was in protective mode. "I can do that," he said dismissively, putting his head back down next to Ilena's. "I've been doing that for months. Go tell them I won't allow it today during the day. If she's strong enough tonight maybe she can tolerate it."

Leah looked at him in dismay. Finally she looked at Rio. "Stay with them. I'll go and speak with the doctor and healer."

"Send a message to Master, too. He'll be wanting to know she's still alive," Ore ordered. "He's probably sleeping in my bed." And that was how they found Rei that morning. When asked later how he knew, Ore answered with a shrug, "It's what I would have done. And, wasn't it the safest choice?" No one could argue with that.

-o-o-o-

Leah returned some time later and quietly told Rio that the two medical staff were in conference. They, having been told that Rei had himself come down with Mizi, were considering asking him for his input into the matter.

Thus it was with relief they welcomed Rei into Doctor Elliot's laboratory when he suddenly appeared, Mizi and the other two constant shadows behind him.

"Tell me what's happened," Rei ordered.

"Miss Leah says Master Ore is refusing to move from Mistress Ilena's side, and has refused to allow her to take the Little Death at her morning dosing time. He says if she's strong enough by evening, he may allow it then." Doctor Elliot summed up the current situation.

"Ore has never liked that she's been on the Little Death," Mizi said sadly.

"How is she doing now?" Rei wanted to know.

"We haven't been in the room, but Miss Leah says he checked her heart rate and said she was sleeping," Doctor Elliot answered.

"Well, that's good enough news," Rei did look very relieved, as did Mizi. "What are the options for the Little Death?"

Doctor Elliot looked at Ryan. "We're in agreement with Master Ore that her body won't likely be able to handle the strain of the hibernation state so close to the time she was already weakened, and the pain payment will also be too stressful.

"However," Doctor Elliot looked worried, "she and I spent long months carefully calibrating the timing and amounts. She was given a minimal dose to begin with this time, but it's still high enough she can't just be taken off of it. I could delay the dose for a time, but the pain payment will be greater, rather than less."

"I know when to administer the pain reducing medication in relation to the administration of the Little Death dose in order to most effectively reduce the pain of that payment time, although it still only affects a portion of it." Mizi offered.

"You do?" Doctor Elliot was surprised.

Mizi nodded. "Yes, I experimented with it when we were in Osterly. It was difficult to bear her cries."

Doctor Elliot brightened. "That's wonderful. May I have a copy of that research?" Mizi allowed he could.

Rei cleared his throat to return the topic back. The three researchers discussed options and timing for another twenty minutes before finally settling on the best time and dosing. Mizi and Rei argued for not just delaying the doses but also reducing the number of them.

Only Doctor Elliot knew exactly how much additional difficulty Ilena was going to have in the end, since he'd already had to live through it multiple times during their original research, so when he pushed back on certain things, they deferred to him, sometimes with obvious reluctance.

When they were wrapping up the meeting and beginning to summarize the plan they would take to Ore, Rei sent Mina over to warn him they were coming.

-o-o-o-

Mina knocked once on the door to Ilena's recovery room and entered, as was their standard entrance into the office. She had to admit it was rather shocking to walk into the room to find Ore lying next to Ilena in her bed, his arm wrapped protectively around her. He'd always been wild, but the new emotional openness was raw - particularly because she understood it completely.

"Ore, Rei is coming." She had to stare into his tawny eyes, or she would have to look away from them and talk to the wall. "He wishes for you to be ready."

Ore continued to stare at her a moment longer, then he reluctantly let Ilena go and sat up. Mina sighed an internal sigh of relief. Only Rei's name could get him to move, and she'd already learned that when it came to Ilena, sometimes even that wasn't sufficient.

"Master Ore, will you please allow us to take care of her now, before the Regent comes?" Mina thought Miss Leah was very brave, but then the people of Ilena had learned how to face the madness of the Earl of Tokumade.

Ore slowly turned his head to look at Leah, and considered the question. Then he looked down at Ilena and his face softened slightly. "I'll help you," he answered. "Miss Mina, please tell them we'll need fifteen minutes to have her ready."

"Very well," Mina left them to it and returned to Rei. That room was just standing, preparing to go. Mina stood in the doorway, blocking it as a sign to them. "Regent Rei, Ore and Miss Leah request that you allow them fifteen minutes to complete the morning preparations for Miss Ilena."

"You were able to get him to move, then?" Rei's question was firm, testing Ore through Mina.

Mina hesitated, wanting to answer the underlying requirement properly. "No. It was only your name that moved him; however, I was afraid even that wouldn't be enough."

Rei's eyes widened and Andrew showed a reaction as well. "It's nearly as bad as that?" Rei asked. Mina nodded soberly.

"As bad as what?" Mizi wanted to know.

"As the time he ran away from you and her and we had to forcibly remove him from his tree to bring him back, Mizi," Andrew quietly explained.

Mina nodded. "He has the same wild look to him now as he did then. Miss Leah is very brave to be willing to stand up to him when he's like that."

Rei was on that bit information quickly. "Did he listen to her?"

Mina nodded. "It was she who requested they be allowed to prepare Miss Ilena. He considered it, then agreed."

"*Haaah.* It's a good thing she's come to the castle, then, if they'll both listen to her. I think I need to ensure she remains my ally." Rei looked significantly at Andrew. That meant, *schedule a time for me to meet with her*.

Andrew nodded. "We'll wait in the courtyard for them to be done." Mina opened the door and the committee recessed for the moment.

-o-o-o-

Everyone in the courtyard turned when Miss Leah opened the door and invited them into Ilena's room. Mizi and Rei entered first, Andrew and Mina following to stand behind them against the wall. Their presence was a message from Rei to Ore.

Ore was sitting on the bed next to Ilena facing the incoming guests, one leg tucked up under the other, still only in his shirt and pants. His boots were still under the other bed, his jacket draped across the back of one of the chairs. His dress was his message to them - he would not be moved from Ilena's room that day.

Rei had to agree with Mina's assessment. Ore wasn't being rebellious – after all he'd been told he could stay already – but he had the look about his eyes and in his posture that were exactly like what he'd been like when he'd fled to the castle before. He would listen to what Rei had to say, but if he disagreed with it he would fight it.

Ryan entered the room, but stayed near the door, looking sad. Doctor Elliot had come in just before him and, when he passed Mizi, both he and Mizi walked to Ilena's left side. Ore said nothing, but watched them as they examined Ilena and Mizi took her vitals. They turned and reported to Rei that she was stable and resting deeply.

Ore shook his head. "She's already waking up. It will just take longer."

"How do you know, Ore?" Rei asked.

"I've learned it from being with her every night. Her breathing patterns change. There are too many people in here at once, and she's concerned." His tone was one of merely exchanging information, but the feel in the air was that he would rather they left so she didn't wake up.

Rei decided not to argue it. If Ore was right about her waking, they would know. He was right about them being here - the sooner they all left, the more rest Ilena would have. "Ore. They've worked out the best plan they can for the most benefit to Ilena, balancing the requirements of the Little Death with her fragile state. Hear them out."

Mizi took a deep breath. It had been decided she would be the spokesperson given her relationship with Ore and Ilena and his current state of mind. "Ore," she called to him, and he turned and looked at her. "We agree that she can't handle being given the morning dose of the Little Death this morning. However, the longer her dosing is postponed, the greater the pain of the payment.

"We'll ameliorate it with the pain reducing medicine, but the correct balance must be maintained. If we postpone it too long, it will have an insignificant effect. We also feel that we must reduce the number of doses to the minimum necessary to minimize how many times her body must be stressed." Mizi took another breath. Ore, so far, was listening.

138

She went on to tell him the exact schedule they'd worked out. It was aggressive. Doctor Elliot and Ilena had used the method the first time they'd experimented with removing her from the Little Death. He hadn't liked it because her pain had been significant and the timing was tricky. It was only Mizi's research with the pain reducing medication that had swayed him.

The selected method also would put Ilena in a shortened hibernative state due to the extremely low doses of the drug. That was seen as a benefit to her current situation, but it changed the timing of everything, so constant monitoring would be necessary.

As Mizi neared the end of her explanation, Ore glanced down at Ilena and took her hand, but stayed silent until Mizi was done. When she was silent, he sat and considered it, then looked back down at Ilena. "Do you agree with their proposal?" he asked her.

"It is carefully thought out," she answered thinly. Everyone else in the room was surprised. Ilena even still looked asleep.

"Can you live through it?" his voice was harsh and demanding, even though he didn't raise his volume.

"Ah, Ore, only the gods can know such a thing...," she said with a sigh. Then, when he squeezed her hand, she slowly opened her eyes and looked around for Doctor Elliot. "What is the next dose?"

The surgeon told her the specific amount they'd decided upon. She looked like she was calculating to him and Ore, but to some she looked like she'd fallen back to sleep. "I can't say what effect the hibernative state will have on me, but without the pain reducing medication I wouldn't survive the pain payment. ... It is indeed aggressive. If the dose could be administered even that half-hour before...it would be helpful."

"What sign is there at that time?" Ore asked.

Ilena considered again. "No, you would be able to tell, Ore, but I don't know what sign to tell you. It feels like a beginning of becoming agitated that slowly increases to extreme pain."

Ore looked at her, thinking. "...Yes. I've seen it before. ...But will you be conscious enough to take the dose?"

"Yes, at that time there is lucidity, similar to now, but it's overcome by the pain eventually, so the window is short, maybe ten minutes at most," Ilena answered.

Ore looked back up at Mizi and Doctor Elliot. "Both medications can be made ahead of time, but by how much?"

"Twelve hours at the most for the pain reducing medication, and it's effectiveness decreases after about eight." Mizi said.

"Three to four days for the Little Death," answered Doctor Elliot.

"How long do you expect between doses?" Ore asked.

Doctor Elliot pursed his lips. "She won't begin to have withdrawal symptoms today until some time this evening. Thereafter, I don't know, but it will be less than a day between for each because they are such low doses. Indeed, I expect the last two doses to be needed about half a day apart, although they should be as far apart as possible. That's the part that worries me the most. Her body may not have sufficient time to recover in between the doses."

"But," Ilena interjected, "those two doses have the little pain, and the shortest hibernative effect." Doctor Elliot nodded, agreeing that she was right.

"How shall I know if she needs the final dose? Will it be as before, with a session without tears?" Ore asked one more question.

Doctor Elliot shook his head. "This is a different process. You'll have to wait to see if she has the withdrawal symptoms one more time. They could come within four to eight hours of the previous dose. If she has no more pain payment, she's done, but she should still be monitored until she awakens naturally.

"This is the process most peace officers use on addicts when they know what dose was initially being taken, and that last dose is often the one that is administered incorrectly because they can't tell that it's needed, nor when. If you can tell it, I'll let you do it. I almost missed it the first time." Doctor Elliot turned a little pale just remembering.

Ore was still. He looked down at Ilena. She opened her eyes and looked at him, then gently pressed his hand. "When you're off of it this time, you will promise me to never take it again," he stated. He looked at Doctor Elliot, "And you will promise to never give it to her again." Doctor Elliot bowed.

Ore looked at Rei. "Master, I won't be able to come by the time the reports arrive. I expect them to arrive two mornings from now. Perhaps by the following day I'll be able to come."

Rei paused, thinking. That would be four witness reports for each of Andrew and Mina, but they could do that in one day. It was the packet of daily reports that Ore summarized for him that he was mostly wanting Ore for. He supposed he could do them if he couldn't wait for the one day. He nodded. "Ilena's survival takes precedence. You'll send me updates after each dosing." Ore nodded.

Rei walked over to Ilena, also on the far side of Ore, and placed his hand on her head. She opened her eyes to look at him. "You, Ilena, will live." His blue eyes were icy hard. "You have many things to tell me yet that I'm waiting to hear."

"Yes, Regent." If she'd been standing, they could feel she would have bowed. Then she smiled at him slightly and sighed. "Master Rei, you are too quick for me. I'm having great difficulty in keeping ahead of you."

"Good," Rei said. Then he relented. "But I'll wait until after the lesson to hear the details of the test. One worry at a time is sufficient."

"*Haahh...,*" she smiled as she closed her eyes. "Have I told you I love you yet? Ore, kiss Master Rei for me." Her voice faded away at the last as she finally gave up and fell asleep again.

"Ah!" Ore held up his free hand in self-defense at Rei's look. "I think she misspoke. Surely she meant to ask Mistress to do it for her!" Mizi turned red. Mina and Andrew looked at each other and smiled with their eyes. Ilena had broken the combative air at the end and reminded them all they had won as a team again.

Andrew and Mina approached Ore. Mina hugged him, then moved aside and Andrew placed his hand on Ore's shoulder. "We'll handle the reports if necessary," he said to the surprised man, "but don't be gone too long. Your desk is already groaning and we don't have the time to help it. It would be a shame to have to use it as firewood from it splintering."

"You'll have to use the floor if that happens," Mina said dryly, but she had a slight grin on her face.

"Thank you," was all Ore could think to say, "but I wouldn't mind using the floor, or even the tree."

"No, I imagine not," Rei said dryly as the others laughed, "but Mizi would."

"Well, no actually, I wouldn't," Mizi contradicted him. "I'm quite used to working on the floor with Ryan and I've been in trees for my work since I was quite young. However, I'm not sure how we would get the stacks of paper to not fly everywhere, once we'd figured out how to get them up there."

Finally both Rei and Ore smiled. Even Ryan smiled, remembering a time Ore had helped him collect papers that had been blown by the wind, including up into a tree. "Mizi," he said in his quiet voice.

"Yes, Ryan?" she was always quick to answer him when he called.

"I'll make the medicine and bring it to Ore. You should go with Prince Rei to help Ore preserve his desk."

"Are you sure?" she asked him, concerned about his time.

Ryan nodded. "I would like to do it," he said.

Mizi nodded. "Okay, Ryan. I'll leave it up to you."

"I'll bring it in a few hours," Ryan looked at Ore, trying to display the earnestness he was feeling.

Ore gave him his signature grin, that came so easy because he always used it to hide what he was really feeling. "I'll be counting on you, then, Ryan." For Ryan, he would be gentle. Ryan nodded, bowed to Rei, and left the room.

Doctor Elliot spoke up. "I'll also go and prepare the doses. I'll make sure they're clearly marked and understandable, and explain them to you when I bring them." Ore nodded, his face serious again. The surgeon bowed to Rei, then left the room, following after Ryan.

Mizi explained to Ore when he should administer the pain reducing medicine in relation to the Little Death for the best effect, then paused uncertainly. "Ore, is it okay?"

He looked at her, his head tilted a little. "Mistress, I would like to say to you that it is. I'm angry, but there's little I can do at this point except what must be done. We must get to the other side, the same as we've done before in Kouzanshi.

"I have Miss Leah, Miss Rio, and Thayne to help me here if it's needed. What you can do in the office will help me, but if you need to come here, I'll not turn you away. She is also yours, and it was your call she answered to yesterday."

Mizi looked at him with gratitude. "I will come, then, for tonight at least."

Ore smiled gently at her. "You don't need to stay for the pain payment, but if you'll come for the time she's in the hibernative state, I would be grateful."

Mizi's hand was at her heart again. She nodded, then looked at Rei expectantly. He looked at her and put his hand on her head and smiled. He turned to lead the four remaining out the door, then looked back at Ore. "I'll leave it to you, then, Ore." His eyes both pled and ordered.

"Shall I expect to see you suddenly again, Master?" Ore asked him seriously.

"...Most likely," Rei said as he turned away. He headed for the door.

Andrew frowned at Rei's back. "Will you at least go to your own bed afterwards, Rei?" he complained.

Ore looked in surprise at Mina. "Did he sleep in my bed after all?" he asked her as she turned to be the last out the door.

She looked back at him. "Yes. Andrew was crying by the time your message came. He said he should remember to kiss your feet for knowing, and then cut you for not telling him sooner."

"Ah, Mister Andrew needs to be knowing our Master better, then doesn't he?" Ore said wisely.

Mina smiled her faint smile. "I think he knew. He just couldn't believe it. Rei has rejected Ore so many times, after all."

Ore smiled a knowing smile at her. She closed the door behind herself, and Ore's smile turned into a sad look. "But Master needs Ore, too," he said sadly. He reached down and put his hand on top of Ilena's and rubbed a finger with his thumb. "And Ore and Master need Ilena," he whispered.

He lay back down and held her again, his eyes closed but not sleeping, just listening to her breathe, thinking of the time when she could run with him. Leah and Rio exchanged looks, then settled in for another quiet, long vigil.

-o-o-o-

"Was Ore really like what he was that time?" Mizi asked, referring to the time he had abandoned his duty to her.

"Yes," Rei answered her.

"He seemed willing to listen and discuss it, though," she said, trying to understand.

"If he'd disagreed, even an order from me wouldn't have swayed him," Rei said. "It seemed to me even Ilena had to work hard."

142

"I think," Mina spoke up, "this time the room was his tree. Before, he would listen to us or to Rei if we went to him, but he wouldn't come down. If he wasn't in the tree, he couldn't be found."

Andrew nodded. "It seemed to me to be that. We wouldn't be able to move him from the room except by force. But this time, it's different."

He was looked at in surprise by more than one of his companions. "It's different?"

"This time we may all support him." The silence of agreement met his assessment.

-o-o-o-

Ilena shivered and took a shaky breath. She'd been having confusing dreams where things and people would shift in strange ways. Ore, Rei, Mizi, and a certain young man kept shifting in and out. She would reach for them when they appeared, then they would disappear as if made out of smoke she'd disturbed, and cruel laughter would echo around her. She whimpered in fear and desperation.

A strong, warm hand slid under the back of her head and lifted it. Ore's voice came to her through the disturbing images in her mind. "Ilena. I'm going to give you the next dose now, then I will, in a few minutes, give you the pain reducing medicine. Please drink it."

His voice sounded so sad. She wanted to reach out and comfort him, but she was all of a sudden having to pay attention to swallowing. It helped her push away the dream a little more. Then she was being returned to the bed.

She lifted her hand, looking for Ore. He'd turned away to give the cup to Mizi, who'd come about a half an hour before, after the office had finished eating dinner. Ilena found his shirt and grasped onto it. He turned back and gently removed her hand from his sleeve so he could turn to face her, surprised she wasn't very willing to let go easily.

"I'm here, Ilena," he said to her. Then, when she let go of his hand and reached for him again, he took her hand and placed it over his heart. She clutched his shirt again. "What is it?" he asked her and passed his hand over her forehead.

She shivered again. "Don't...don't let him take me away. He is ...always laughing.... Don't disappear." Her grip on his shirt tightened in desperation.

Ore leaned over her and put his forehead on hers. "I won't. We've promised, Master and I. We'll protect you from him, but you must live so that you can tell Master the things he needs to know."

Ilena's head moved against his in a nod. "Together... together we can defeat him."

"Then we'll do it, together." Ore promised. Ilena finally relaxed, but she didn't release him from the grip she had on his shirt. Ore lifted his head. He could see the pain was starting to rise within her. "Mistress," he warned her.

143

"I'll do it," she said softly, and placed her hand on Ore's shoulder, gripping it to support both herself and him. Ilena would have to go through pain twice for each dose. Once for the withdrawal symptoms and again for the payment. The medication they would give her wasn't for this pain, but for the next.

Giving her the Little Death now would calm this pain and cover it with the hibernation state, but it could take up to fifteen minutes for it to enter her system. Doctor Elliot had explained that because she wasn't eating due to the surgery, it would likely take effect much faster than that as her body absorbed the liquid and the drug quickly. They would have to make sure she had the medication before she slipped into that state, but it couldn't be given too soon.

Mizi released Ore's shoulder, then she picked up the vial and walked around to Ilena's other side. Ilena shuddered again. This time it was in physical pain, and she gasped. She breathed with the pain instinctively for a while, then clenched her jaw against it.

Ore slipped his hand under her head again, readying to lift it. He rubbed his thumb against her jaw. "Ilena, you need to allow us to give you the medicine. Can you relax just a little?"

She shook her head. Ore looked at Mizi. She was looking concerned. "Be prepared, Mistress," he warned her. She nodded and knelt by Ilena, preparing to give her the medicine.

Ore continued to rub Ilena's jaw, trying to get it to loosen. Then he leaned in very closely to her ear and whispered very softly, so only she could hear. "I will have to kiss you very passionately, then." He got the reaction he was looking for. Ilena's jaw dropped open in surprise.

He immediately lifted her head and guided Mizi's hand to her mouth. Mizi quickly put the vial to Ilena's lips and tipped it. Ilena almost didn't get it swallowed, she was still so surprised.

When Ore laid her head back down, Ilena called, "Nana?"

Leah looked up in surprise. "Yes, Mistress?"

Ilena opened her eyes and looked angrily at Ore. "Remember this: when I am first able, I owe Ore a sharp rap to the head. Several of them."

"Oh, my. And he had been doing so well, too...," Leah sighed melodramatically.

Ore's eyes danced. "That was very effective."

"You are still very mean, Ore," Ilena narrowed her eyes at him.

Mizi looked from one to the other, sitting back on her heels. Finally she decided she didn't really want to know what he'd said. It would only place her more in the middle of their fighting again. She sighed. "Really, Ore. Was it necessary to go to that extreme, to make her mad again?" She looked into Ilena's eyes. "Though, I will have to agree with him. It was very effective. So much so you are very awake right now. That's unexpected."

Ilena flashed a slight grin. "That is true. I wonder what he'll have to try next time, though...?" Then she turned back to Ore, angry again. "But if you try that one again, you'll have to follow through for as many times as you've said it."

He looked at her mildly. "Is that supposed to frighten me?"

She puffed up her cheeks and narrowed her eyes, looking just like a chipmunk, but not a cute one, rather an angry one. She let it go suddenly and soberly looked at him, and into him.

She sighed, and winced in pain. When she recovered, he could see she'd taken the first steps into the hibernative phase. She said softly, "Ah, Ore. Have you moved so far since I've been able to look at you?" She raised her hand and touched his face with the back of it. "I'm sorry."

He reached up, slipping his hand between hers and his face, then wrapped his middle finger around hers. Her hand slowly pulled their joined hands down to the bed as her eyes closed and she slipped into the descent. He sighed and put his other elbow on the bed, and rested his chin in his hand, watching her move further and further from him again.

Mizi shook her head. "Did she just forgive you?"

"No. She just asked me to forgive her, did you not hear it?" Ore smiled at his mistress.

"I heard it, but I didn't understand it," Mizi admitted.

"Well...that's okay. She understood it." Ore was looking at Ilena again.

"*Haahh*...," Mizi stood and dusted nothing off her knees. "I'm feeling like Rei sometimes feels." She looked at Ore sharply. "So, have you settled it then? Or will that happen again next time?"

Ore raised an eyebrow. "Well, that will have to depend on if she remembers it or not, I think."

"Ooore...," Mizi actually whined at him, slightly, but it was there.

Ore looked at her in surprise, then seriously shook his head at her. "If she doesn't remember it, I won't do it again when she can't. But she does have to remember it. Master told me it's my duty."

Mizi sighed. "All right. I'll accept that." Behind them, Leah smiled.

CHAPTER 8 Rei's Test

By the time Ilena was starting to come out of the hibernative state, Leah and Rio had both retired for the night. They had asked if Ore wanted Thayne to come and he'd said no. He looked at Mizi. "Mistress. Ilena is beginning the ascent. You should leave now."

Mizi considered his words. They were dismissing her, but she had the right to stay, both as Ilena's medical provider, and as her mistress. She stood. "You must have a reason for wanting to be alone with her, but I won't go far. I'm concerned there may be complications, so I'll wait in the courtyard. Call me."

Ore nodded, and watched her as she left, then looked at Ilena again. They'd once again set a candle behind the vase to give gentle light to the room that wouldn't be disturbing. Her features were softened by the light and by the fact that she was lying down. He wondered if he would recognize her when she was finally able to be upright, forgetting he'd actually seen her sitting up just a few days prior.

In his imagination, what she looked like wavered. When he thought of the steward, he pictured someone with hard, cold features. When he talked to one of the Children about Mother, he saw someone with a quick smile and tender eyes. The woman in front of him was a mix of the two. Her face could go hard and cold very quickly, but just as fast it could show tenderness.

She loved to smile, but was apparently a consummate player of the court games. That required not showing any strong emotion at all. He couldn't picture that, but Rei, Andrew, Mina, and Mizi had all assured him she was very capable of it.

He was about to touch that face that had been either so still in sleep or marred by pain for the last three days, remembering the emotions he'd been able to see when she had reacted to his teasing the last time she was awake, glad for them, when she took the first breath that heralded the sleep talking phase.

He stopped and put his hand back down. This would be the last of the longer sleep talking phases. The rest would be too short for conversations. It was the one thing he *would* miss about the damnable drug. It was why he wanted to be alone with her, although of course it didn't mean she would say anything useful.

"Ore? Ore? ...Where are you?" For a moment, he couldn't say anything. This was the first dream she'd ever had that included the present him from the beginning. "Where did you go?"

"I'm right here," he said quietly. "What do you need?"

She took a sharp breath, as if surprised by his "appearance". "Ah! Are you there?"

"Yes. What can I do for you?" he asked again.

She frowned. "Tell Rei.... Tell Rei.... It's important."

He was about to ask what he should tell Rei, when he remembered that she was supposed to have blocked that kind of thing from being spoken. She would likely not be able to tell him at this point. "What is the key?" he asked instead.

"When it's time, when he asks the question, only Ore's voice will be heard. Both must be there, but only Ore will be able to ask," Ilena answered.

"Okay. I'll tell Master. Do you know the question?"

"Rei knows the question. He said he would wait."

That had to referenced what Rei had said that morning - the test he would be facing after they took care of Earl Shicchi. "Okay. I understand."

"...What is Ore's question?" That was a little surprising, but he was perhaps grateful to be asked.

Ore paused, then asked quietly, "Does Ilena love the Ore of today?"

"...Yes. Very much so. But Ilena is afraid." It was said quietly.

This time, Ore did touch her cheek lightly with the back of his fingers. "Ore is afraid, too." Did he have time for one more? "Why did Ilena make Ore to be Father?"

"...."

Ore put his head in his hands. He wondered if he was too late.

"...Ore," it was Mother's voice. "You already know."

Ore's eyes went wide, and his heart lurched. "When did I understand it?"

"When you first loved my Children." He knew it. He could feel it from his depths.

"You're right," he answered, "but I didn't know how to see it."

"Do you now?"

"Yes," he whispered.

"Good. ...I love you, Father. Please continue to love my Children."

He took her hand. "I will." She slipped away. He lay his head down on his arms at her side, glad to be alone with her, wishing it would last...that the next phase wouldn't come.

But come, it did. Her breathing changed. He slowly got up and walked around the bed. Her breathing increased until she was gasping, then she cried out in pain. He put his hand on her, to let her know he was there, but as of yet, she was not arching in pain. She gasped again and again.

Ore growled at her, "Stay - alive!" To him, it looked like she was fighting against the pain. Fighting to not cry out, but it was still just the beginning. She finally gave way again. "Ah...ah...AAHHH!" Her jaw clenched and she hissed.

The door behind Ore opened, then closed. He ignored it until the person spoke. "Ore, what can I do?"

He turned his head and looked at his master with a heart filled with sorrow and anger. He pointed to the opposite side of the bed, where he'd been before.

"Stand there. When she begins to arch because of the pain, we must hold her so that she doesn't damage the hip."

Rei obediently moved into place. Ilena was continuing to hiss in pain with each breath. Rei looked at her curiously, then at Ore with the same expression. "I thought there was more than this?" he carefully tendered.

"She's fighting it." Ore said, his voice bleak and pained. "She shouldn't be aware enough to, but she is. ...There are things I must tell you, when it's over."

Rei nodded. Ore saw a tremor go through her and he placed his hands to support her hip, but waited other than that. Rei followed his example. She tremored again when Rei touched her, and she moaned three times, then cried out a sound like that of a falcon in great pain and distress. That time, she did arch.

Ore, practiced, held her left hip. Rei, surprised at his first experience almost let her slip, but his fighting reflexes caught her. When her body slightly relaxed again, Ore saw her begin to fight against it again. "No!" he almost yelled it. "Fighting it will wear you out faster. Let it run it's course." She gave a faint shake of her head. "Damn it, Woman! This is not the time to be difficult. You do NOT have the energy. Relax, and let it run it's course! Save your energy for staying alive."

Both men felt her slowly answer him. As her mind relaxed its control and the pain began to sweep through her, the body tensed again in reaction to it. But now, instead of crying out, she began to weep. Rei looked up at Ore. Ore was staring at Ilena in almost surprised horror, telling him that was also unusual behavior.

Ore shook his head, trying to recover himself, then looked at Rei. "Come take my place." Rei quickly moved around the bed. As soon has he'd taken Ore's place, Ore moved to her head, wrapped an arm around her, and held her.

The door opened again. This time it was Mizi. She hurried to the bedside and took the place Rei had just vacated, putting her hands into place, in her practiced usual position. She looked at Ore, then Rei in concern. "The pattern was different. What's happened?"

"Ore said that she's aware enough to fight it. He told her to stop fighting it, to just let it run its course so she doesn't unnecessarily wear herself out. When she let go, she began...that." Rei gestured with his head. "Ore doesn't know either."

Mizi answered him with a horrified expression. "She's aware?"

Rei nodded soberly. "When he first told her to let it run it's course, she refused."

Mizi's grip on Ilena tightened momentarily and she paled. "The pain price comes before tears, after which is awareness. They aren't supposed to be mixed together. I don't think even Doctor Elliot has seen this."

Ore wasn't paying attention to their words, although their sounds and voices washed around him, helping anchor him. He thought back to Ilena's dream, the one that had been so different. There had been two voices who had seemed to speak to him from that dream state. The latter one was Mother....

"Who is it?" he asked into her ear. "Who is it that's awake?" His voice was desperate.

Ilena gasped a few times, trying to gain sufficient control to answer. "Thailena," she answered.

"Why? Why do you fight it? Why are you here?" Ore was so confused.

"I fight. I fight to live ...as I wish to live. ...Ah...ah –" Ore turned his head away to protect his ear. Mizi gripped Ilena tighter and Rei followed suit, remembering he was on the important side now. Ilena arched and screamed a long scream.

She shuddered as it wound down, then began to shiver. Mizi looked around and grabbed the top covering off the other bed and threw it over Ilena, giving her another layer. The shivering didn't lessen.

"Mistress," Ore gestured quickly to his jacket, requesting it. She pulled it off the chair and handed it to him. He wrapped it around Ilena's head to keep in the heat there, too, then wrapped his arms around her again. She soon stopped shivering, although tremors still went through her, causing her to moan each time.

"What caused the wall to be breached?" Ore asked Ilena. "Why are you here?"

She turned her head towards him. "Because Ore and Rei are nearly ready. The question has been breached."

Ore dropped his head to the bed. "Damn. We did move too fast for you, then?"

"It's of no consequence. When you're ready, you're ready. It's only I who'll hold you back, in this state."

"This state?" He turned his head towards her again.

"I must be able to ...run and ride ...before the next ...phase ...can begin." Her body was beginning to build up to it's limit for the pain again; her breaths were coming in gasps.

"Can I do it for you?" he almost begged the question, but he would have to wait for the answer. He turned his head away.

This time her scream was a lower "Aaaarrrggghhhh!" of almost frustration, and her jaw clenched again. Rei and Mizi noticed she didn't arch as much as the last time. Mizi looked at Rei in small relief. "She's beginning to come down from it already," she told him.

Ore shrugged the helpful comment off in frustration. He still wanted to hear what Thailena had to say, but she would probably not be available after this for some time. He asked her again. "Can I do it for you, if you can't run or ride?"

"Sorry, no. You can help...though," a tremor went through her, interrupting her words. She gasped for a few breaths, but her body didn't tense.

He asked her, "How can I contact you again? I want to speak with you again."

"When everything is in place, ...the walls will be gone. ...I'll come again ...when needed ...before then." The last was whispered faintly. Ore knew she was gone. He clung to her - his princess. As her shudders faded, his began, and he sobbed the same as he had the first day Rei had come to Osterly. But this time, the arms that comforted him were Ilena's.

"Ah, Ore," Ilena said to him as she put her arms around him. "I'm sorry. I wanted to not have to have you go through this again. ...It's okay. I will live. I'll run and ride with you again."

He heard her words and wondered, "Did you hear? Are you aware of what the parts of you who are locked away say when they come out?"

"Whispers. Remnants. When I'm in states like those. They're louder now than they used to be. If I speak it so I can hear it, I remember. ...But they are always me. I'm whole. It's only the information that is locked and keyed." Ore shivered. Tears were still dripping from his eyes. "What do you need, Ore?" she asked him.

"Princess," the word was ripped from him. "I need my Princess." They were speaking to each other quietly, but Rei and Mizi couldn't help but hear, in the now quiet of the room. They looked at each other in wonder, not understanding really why that was his answer.

"I'm here, Ore. You don't need to seek me to find me. I've come to you. I promised you I would. I'll not willingly go away again." Ilena spoke gently to calm Ore's distress.

He nodded and held her tighter, but he began to calm. Then as she began to fade, he said to her, "Do not do what you did last night again. Don't walk away to where you are hard to reach. You've found me, but you've also promised to live. Don't forget it."

She turned her head towards his face, her lips brushing him on the cheek. "I won't," she breathed. Her arms gently released him and he sat up, wiping his face dry. "Thank you, Master Rei," Ilena said quietly and slowly, then she slept.

Mizi reached out her hand for Rei. He took it then, stretching to reach at the farthest point, he walked around the bed to her side. He held her briefly. "She'll sleep now?" he asked quietly. She nodded into his shoulder. He sighed. "I wish I could feel like that was safe, like she was okay now, but after last night, ...I agree with Ore."

Mizi pulled back slightly and smiled at him. "Ore will be with her again. She'll stay for him, like she did last night."

"Well...just in case...," Rei let her go, stepped over, and bent down close to Ilena's ear. "Ilena. You've also promised me you'll stay alive. Don't forget."

Ilena twitched ever so slightly. "I'll take that as your positive answer." Rei said. He stood again and looked Ore in the eye. "You have things to say to me?" Ore nodded.

Rei sat down in the chair and set Mizi on his lap so that he could still look at Ore and wrapped his arms around her middle. She blushed a little, but, remembering her lessons with Ilena, decided to go with happy instead of super embarrassed. "Let's hear it, then," Rei said to Ore.

Ore raised his eyebrow. "Can it be informal, then? I don't think I can do anything else with you holding Mistress like a child's toy."

Rei grinned at him. "Okay." Mizi couldn't keep the blush down at that, but she didn't move.

Ore somehow managed to gracefully balance himself sitting on the head of Ilena's bed, one leg tucked in and one outstretched around her head, facing Rei and Mizi. He placed his fingers gently on her neck to monitor her heart beat while he spoke.

"Mistress was here for the first part. When Ilena began to enter the time to be given the dose of the Little Death, she first was in a disturbed dream state. After I'd given her the dose, she was afraid - I think from the scenes in the dream. She said, 'Don't let him take me away. He's always laughing. Don't disappear.' and she clutched at me tightly.

"I told her that we promised we would protect her but that she needed to live so that she could tell you the things you needed to hear. She agreed and answered, 'Together we can defeat him', so I promised we would do it together. Then she entered the expected state of pain before we administered the medication. It's important because it followed her into the following states."

Rei looked at him surprised. "Is that why things were different?"

"Yes, I believe so, but they were all triggered by your comment to her when you left this morning," Ore answered.

Rei thought, trying to remember. "The one where I let her know that I knew what the test would be?"

Ore nodded. "You triggered a locked question."

"I thought I might, ...although I didn't expect it to have such far reaching effects. ...So her dream was about the person who knows her in Tarc?" Rei asked.

Ore nodded. "I believe so. It felt that way when she spoke to me. That is, it wasn't the same as when she speaks of the Earl or her uncle."

Mizi looked at him surprise. "Ah...?"

Rei looked at Mizi, trying to decide what to tell her. "Master," Ore warned, "Ilena believes it's wrong to keep Mistress lacking in knowledge." Rei nodded.

He explained it briefly to Mizi: "The Earl protects himself by having other people who look like him do some of his works. One of those people Ilena learned by accident was her uncle, a bastard son of the Selician King's second wife whom he banished to Tarc. He is an evil man and knows who she is.

"I believe he was the one who placed her in the position of being rescued by you and Ore so that he could claim he'd 'gifted' me with her so that he could request the army of Ryokudo to support his bid for the Selician throne. He has no rightful claim and I don't intend to speak with him on it.

"Ilena herself hates and fears him, more than the Earl." Mizi nodded, looking sad. Ilena had very little family left, and much of what she'd had contact with in her life sounded like it had been very bad.

Rei continued, "It sounds like her dream may corroborate my theory that there's another force within Tarc that's also using the uncle, even as he's using the Earl. It's that force that is the test she's preparing me for. In my parting comment to her, I was letting her know that I understood that there was a test, that it was coming from Tarc, and that person also knows who she is and is intending on using that knowledge, and her, against us. But that's all I know so far.

"I was also letting her know that I would wait to hear more until after we've dealt with the Earl and her uncle. ...That's why I'm surprised it triggered more information immediately."

They both looked at Ore. He nodded and continued his report. "When she began the sleep talking it was immediately different. She spoke my name and asked for me, seeking me. Not the past, but the present."

Rei breathed in a sharp breath. "The barrier was broken?"

Ore nodded, then explained to Mizi, "She's explained to us that, in order for the secret things she was protecting to be safe while she was under the watchful eye and ear of the Earl, she learned first to hide away the important information behind locks that need specific keys. When I ask her a question, she answers it because I'm a key. It's the same for Master. If anyone else asked her those questions, they wouldn't receive an answer."

Ore paused, focusing for a moment on Ilena's heart beat, but it was normal. "Once, Master asked me to ask her a question, specifically relating to her uncle. He'd threatened her with death if she told anyone who he was, or their relationship, so she double locked it. Because I asked her the question, she was able to see the second lock, but couldn't give me the answer. Master was with me at the time, and was the second key, so we were able to unlock both and hear the answer.

"For Master to let her know he was ready for the next piece of detailed information about the test, he unlocked one of the locks." Rei looked at him expectantly. Ore nodded again, answering his nonverbal question. "She wanted to tell me, in the sleep talking phase, that it's double locked. She said to tell you it's important. The second key is that only my voice will be heard after you ask the question. I will have to relay any questions to her."

"So...we'll both have to ask each question in her presence? She'll have to hear us both ask?" Rei confirmed.

"Yes."

"That is very tightly defended information." Rei was rather amazed.

"Because she was answering questions in the present, I asked her another one." Ore looked down at Ilena's sleeping face and brushed her hair with his hand, running his fingers lightly over her brow. After a moment, he looked back up at Rei. "I asked her why she made Ore to be Father. The one who I'd been speaking with could not, or would not, answer me. I thought perhaps she had passed from the sleep talking phase, but then Mother spoke to me." He paused significantly, watching Rei's face.

Rei's face moved quickly from confusion to amazement. "She's separated the information based on what role she plays?"

Ore nodded. "The timing between the sleep talking phase and the pain payment phase is very short. At first I was confused as to why she would be fighting the pain phase. Normally she wouldn't.

"I think she's always at some level of alertness through that phase, now that I've seen this, and she's mentioned before she remembers some of the times. She already naturally knows that to let it run its course is best, having lived through it many times. So I didn't understand why she would fight.

"It was when Master touched her, and she reacted to it, that I understood. She was fighting it for my sake, and then for both our sakes."

"...The last 'person' I had spoken to was Mother. I didn't want her to jeopardize herself for us, when she needs to live for our sake, not weaken herself, so I commanded her to stop. But she refused. ...Mother wouldn't have refused.

"I wanted to know who the other was. Who controls the information that Master needs to know to protect Ryokudo? And, what would she tell me? So I needed to let you help her while I talked to her."

"It's the Princess, then. I heard her tell you," Rei said.

"Did you hear all of it?" Ore asked.

Rei quickly went back through that time in his mind. "Mmm...no. What did you ask her when she answered, 'It's of no consequence'?"

"I asked what had breached her sleep talking wall, and she answered it was because your comment had breached the question and we were ready to hear the answer. I asked if we'd moved too fast, remembering her response to your comment. That was her answer to that question."

"So if I wanted to ask it now, she would give me the answer?"

Ore nodded. "But she also said that being able to act on the answer would have to wait until she can run and ride again."

Rei frowned. "That sounds like a connection to her wanting Falcon's Hollow for horses."

"Yes," Ore agreed. "I think when you ask the question and we unlock the second lock, you'll be able to ask her that question and she'll tell you."

Rei nodded. "Because it's part of the solution to the test. But because it's behind the double lock, no one else will be able to tell us." Ore nodded soberly. Rei thought about what else Ilena had said. "What did she answer you at the end, when you asked her how to contact her?"

"She said that 'when everything is in place the walls will be gone'. She will 'come again when needed before then'. Though afterwards she said that she is whole. It's contradictory." Ore's brow wrinkled, not really understanding those words.

"No, she said that it was only the information that's locked," Rei answered it. "She was saying there will be more information to be said, either just the answers to the next question, or to others. Each time we seek information that's locked, she'll 'come again when needed'. When all the information that she's protecting has been said, there won't be a need to protect it any longer, and the walls will be gone.

"But I wonder what constitutes 'everything in place'?" Rei chewed on that for a moment. "I feel like it may mean more than preparing for the test. Her board includes Mizi becoming Princess, and I haven't been able to see how that fits with the test. But it does fit with another thing...."

Ore and Mizi looked at him questioningly. Rei looked at Mizi. "I think to her, 'everything in place' means that she's received confirmation that my brother will let her stay in the place she wants to be in. Even over protecting myself and Ryokudo, she wants to protect the place she wants to be in - beside Ore, behind Mizi, supporting and shielding myself. There are questions still to be asked and answered in that field, even if she has answered all the ones relating to the test."

Mizi sat up. "She answers my questions!" The men looked at her, curious. "There have been a few questions I've asked that she's answered differently, like what you've been describing. When I asked her how she felt about Ore it was like that.

"I found it curious that it felt the same as when Ore and I both asked her to tell us how it was she came to be on the Little Death, although I don't think that was locked information." Ore shook his head, agreeing with her. "But I think answering my question - it was locked information, some portion of it."

"Do you remember now what you asked her and what she said?" Rei asked. It had been long enough ago he didn't expect much.

Mizi concentrated. "It was right after Ore left to not return." Ore flinched slightly. "I asked what she'd done and she said she'd answered his questions truthfully. But then, she looked, well, ...*into* me and said 'I see that you care for him, thus I will tell you'. Looking at that now, it feels like that was the unlocking of a lock." She looked at Rei and Ore to see if they believed her.

They both nodded. Ore said, "That's one of her gifts, to be able to see into the heart of a person. She already knew about you from watching me and watching Master. She tested us similarly before she would answer the first questions we asked her. It could be possible, certainly, that she's keyed some locks to you."

"Each of the things she says that were locked contains important clues, Mizi. While it's possible the things she said then are overcome by events, if you can remember anything, I would like to know," Rei requested.

Mizi nodded. "She answered that question with 'he's not so much angry as he is afraid, because I know his distant past and his present, and he never wanted the two to meet'. She said that she'd never meant to cause him pain, that because he'd refused her by saying he wasn't the person she believed him to be, to her he wasn't.

"I asked her why Ore was so afraid of his past and she answered that it was because his past was full of darkness and death and for anyone to know of his present connection to that past was to present to him his own death. Ore has himself said things to me since then that tell me those were true words.

"I asked her if she was a danger to Ore. Her answer relieved me, but seemed odd. She said 'no' and, 'My only role in this life is to be a protector of others. I've protected Ore since we were very young. He won't die, and most assuredly he won't die because of me. If I can't help him understand because he will not, then I'll continue as before - protecting him from a distance without any acknowledgment. The one does not require the other.' The answer was so odd I've remembered it.

"I asked one more question. I asked, 'what is Ore to you?' She seemed surprised that I'd asked her, but she answered 'the man I love and wish to stand next to the remainder of my days'. She fell asleep right after that, but I couldn't believe that she would love Ore with that wish yet at the same time be okay with him never acknowledging her while she protected him from a distance."

Rei looked at Mizi shrewdly. "Was it after that conversation that you decided to ask for her, to stand as Ore's partner?"

Mizi nodded. "Yes, but I had to look at Andrew and Mina first to see that it could happen that way. I was trying to think of some way to help her, while also helping him."

"She set the stage for the first, and most important move with her answer. She knew who she was talking to," Rei leaned back a bit and thought. "*If I can't help him understand because he won't, then I'll continue as before - protecting him from a distance without any acknowledgement. The one does not require the other.* ...Ore, I have answers to the remainder of what she said, but does that one have meaning to you?"

Ore blushed a little, although the light wasn't strong enough for anyone to tell for sure. "Yes, Master. When I talked with Thayne last night before sending him away, one of the things he said was that she protects all of her Family, but her Immediate Family the most.

"I complained that I wasn't feeling very protected, and he scolded me, saying that not only had she not let anyone know who I was until last fall, when she let everyone know who I was at that time everyone understood that wherever I was, I was to be protected. It doesn't matter to them that I do or do not know who they are."

"That's the 'protecting him from a distance' side, then." Rei said. "*The one doesn't require the other.* Then what is the former? 'If I can't help him understand because he won't'?"

Quietly Ore said, "It's referencing my title as Father again, but this time in regard to what it means."

Rei looked at him, wide eyed. "She told you?"

Ore nodded. "I asked her why Ilena made Ore to be Father. She answered me, 'you already know it'." He touched his chest over his heart. "My heart answered she was right, but I still couldn't - didn't - want to see it. I asked her 'when did I understand it'? She answered, 'when you first loved my Children', and she asked me again to love her Children."

Rei was still confused and waited for Ore to explain further. "They're like me. They've lived in the darkness, have tasted of her love and light, and they thrive or fail based on her life and light. When I'm with them, I have compassion on them, the same as she did and does. I desire to protect them, the same as she does. When they speak of her, I understand them. Many of them who know me have said that we're the same, or similar. They learn to love me very quickly as they love her.

"It's a direct reference to her prior statement, 'My only role in this life is to be a protector of others'. I am Father because she wishes to protect them. She's set them to protect me, the same as they protect her, and she's set me to protect them...from her own eventual death or when she's taken from out of her place to be put somewhere far from them. I am Father because I can be to them the parent she may not be able to be.

"Even if I didn't come to understand, or wouldn't stand in that place, if they all believe that is what I am, they will still have a parent to cling to. If she lives and can stand in her place, we'll be Father and Mother together to them, and they'll be none the wiser."

Mizi looked like she was trying to not cry. Rei was stunned. "Even before she knew she was going to be harmed and placed with us, she was protecting them that way?" Ore nodded. "Why? Why would she already know...? Was it because she'd finally removed the last good out of the house?"

"Maybe..., but I'm afraid," Ore said. "It's the rest of what she said to Mistress. That she's protected me since we were very young is true, but why did she say 'he won't die, and most assuredly he won't die because of me'? I don't believe it's because of the Earl, nor even the uncle. It is Master who will ensure I don't die at their hands."

Rei's eyes went wide. "The force in Tarc knows who *you* are?"

Ore shook his head. "I don't think so. I don't know anyone from Tarc, nor have ever had an opportunity to. I think it has to do with the position she placed me in from the beginning, and her desire to protect me the way she has since we were young. Master, what does the force in Tarc want with her and Ryokudo, or Suiran?"

"To own it, and rule it as his own, the same as he rules Selicia. A puppet government would be enough for him, but Ilena stands in his way." Rei answered automatically, then went back and thought about what he'd just said, and his eyes got as round as Ore's were after hearing that.

"Oh, my. If he has to get to Ilena, he has to go through you. Whether he'll use her the same as the uncle, to grant him legitimacy for both kingdoms, or whether he'll remove her after removing me because she's a thorn in his side, it doesn't matter. He doesn't have to know who you are. If you've been placed to protect her he has to go through you."

Ore nodded. "You have answered my fear. She said it. Before she can become the cause of a war, she'll remove herself as a playing piece on the board. She'll sacrifice herself before she'll sacrifice me, and probably before she'll sacrifice you." He placed a hand protectively on Ilena's head.

Rei and Mizi both went pale. Rei's hand went into a fist. "She can't. I won't let her have the need."

Ore asked gently, "If that was the solution King Brother asked for, because she is too high ranking a piece, even higher than he is, would you be able to say 'no'?"

Rei paled even further. "Why do you say that, Ore?" he said in a quiet, strangled voice. "Why do you place her higher than he is?" His brain didn't want to accept it.

Ore looked sad. "Because she can make one man into a king of three nations."

Rei closed his eyes and was quiet for some time. Mizi turned and put her arms around him and held him. He buried his head into her shoulder and trembled. Mizi looked for anything to say, then she said simply. "Rei, Ilena already knows. She's already begun moving to prevent it. She herself said that she'll live if she can, standing in the place she wishes to stand. That's where she *wants* to be.

"We've promised to help her be in that place, so we've already promised to protect her from that fate. It's not wrong of her to desire to protect her Children...and all of us. All good parents think of their children's futures, but that doesn't mean such things must come. As you want her to trust you to protect her, you should also trust her, that she wants to protect you and her desires."

Ore added his support. "She said to me, when I asked her why she was fighting the pain of the Little Death, that she fights. She said she fights to live as she wishes to live. Everything she does is so that she can do the thing you've said. She fights always and most to protect her desire to stand next to Ore, behind Mistress, and supporting and protecting Master.

"In her dream, she said he is 'always laughing'. She sees him as formidable, but she said that 'together', we can defeat him. If Master, and Ore, and Mistress, and King Brother, and Mister Andrew, and Miss Mina, and the Family are all fighting together, we can defeat him."

Rei took a breath, then another. "It isn't a burden I need to pick up today," his voice was muffled in Mizi's shoulder. "It will wait. She'll let me know when time shortens, and we have until she can ride before we must begin to act."

His voice was getting stronger as he listed the position they were in at the moment. "I can think of things that will help as time passes. But for now, it's important to take the next step, that of removing the Earl and uncle, lest they remain his allies and additional thorns for Ryokudo."

You could just give her to one of them. That would remove her from the board, a sacrificed piece, but still living. It was his brother's voice. Rei shook his head at the phantom of his brother. That would not be living. Sacrificed, yes, but not living.

"You're right, Ore, my brother did just ask if I would sacrifice her, as if he'd been standing here." Mizi tightened her grip on him. She was afraid of the King, even though she would face him directly if he pressed her. "He said, why not just give her to one of them? That would remove her from the grasp of the man who would be emperor. She would be a sacrificed piece, but still living."

Now it was Mizi's turn to tremble, but Rei lifted his head and looked at Ore, his face dark and his eyes piercing, as he'd looked when he'd gone looking for Mizi when she'd been kidnapped. "I will never do that. Ilena has thought of a plan, has a solution. She's come to me, trusting me to be able to make it even better. She's sure of her path, although it may be rough.

"I'll help to make it smooth. We'll grant her desires. She won't be sacrificed. That would be my failure. The test will only be acceptably passed if we can place her where she desires to be. I'll ask you again. I will take her with me. Will you support it?" He looked at Mizi as well.

They both nodded. Rei stood, his strength restored. He continued to hold on to Mizi's hand. "While I don't know yet why having you as my princess very soon is part of her plan, let's work on it very seriously." Then he paused and looked at her again. "Besides, it's already too late for me. I wish I could take you to my room tonight. I'm sorry I'm impatient. Thank you for supporting me tonight."

Mizi squeezed his hand. "I'm also impatient, but for now I must wait on Ilena to recover. Although, I'll do all I can while I wait. But...," she smiled at him, "I won't come to your room tonight."

Rei smiled back at her. "I didn't expect you would. Let me walk you back to your room, though." She nodded.

"Be safe," Ore called to them as they left. And after the door was closed, added, "...although it would be nice if you didn't behave for once."

158

He lifted himself from the bed carefully, prepared for bed, and once again lay next to Ilena, placing his fingers again on her neck to feel her life blood still moving through her - proof that she was keeping her promise. He sighed. What a complicated woman. It was a good thing she was his.

-o-o-o-

Rei walked Mizi back to her room. He'd come to support Ore during the hardest time for Ilena on purpose. It was his way to want to experience what others were experiencing so that he could understand them. He knew Ore hated the Little Death, and he'd received reports about it, but hadn't seen it himself. Visiting when Ilena was living it had seemed a good opportunity for multiple reasons. "That wasn't a normal pain cycle, was it?" he asked Mizi now.

She shook her head. "Even for her that was very mild. Because she's on low doses, her pain cycles are lesser than a regular user, or so I've been told. Her very first cycle I experienced was excruciating, for her and for us. She screamed for over five minutes, or so Ore says. It took most of his strength the whole time to hold her from re-injuring her hip.

"It felt like an hour. Even the next four nights were bad, but not as bad as that first one. It wasn't until the doses became very low that they became more like this one. Even then, this one was odd. That's why I came in. I was worried about complications, and that you and Ore weren't able to come tell me."

Rei had met Mizi outside the room when he arrived. She'd told him that Ore had asked her to let him be alone with Ilena for the sleep talking phase. Because Ore had told her to not come in unless there were complications, Rei had told her he would go in for her when they heard Ilena's first cry.

"I wouldn't have thought Ilena was aware, today or any day, during the pain phase. She said that it fades during the time of sleeping afterwards, though, so perhaps I shouldn't be so surprised." Mizi continued.

"It's hard to think that someone we care about must understand they are going through such pain," Rei said gently, remembering a certain Ore who had said something similar to him.

"Yes, that's true," Mizi agreed. "...It was odd to me because once the screams start in earnest, they don't stop until they taper off at the end, even if the time is short. For her to be able to do what she did just now...I don't understand it. She was obedient to Ore, wasn't she? She stopped fighting it, it seemed to me?"

Rei nodded. "There seemed to be something different to me, but it was my first time seeing it. I wonder, like Ore, if she really is whole...but I don't know if there's a way to tell."

Mizi frowned. "It didn't seem to be that to me. It seemed to be more...like the effect of the drug was actually less. Like when she was coming off it before. I wonder if it was because she was given the lowest dose that Doctor Elliot could give her? ...I'll look at her medical record tomorrow and compare this evening's dose to what I was giving her before and see where she would have been then."

Rei looked up thoughtfully. "That would be good to know." They'd arrived outside her door.

He gave Mizi a goodnight hug and kiss, then *didn't* enter her room when she did. He did go wake up Andrew and have his overanxious aide walk him to his room. He suspected Andrew had been waiting up for him, or had been listening for him, anyway. At least, he wasn't surprised when Rei knocked, and quietly just accompanied him.

"How are they doing?" Andrew asked him once they were on their way to Rei's rooms across the castle campus.

"It was milder than they expected," Rei answered. "Mizi thinks it's because the dose was so low, but she's going to confirm it tomorrow. Ilena was able to come through the hibernative state fine. Ore still isn't better, though. He may need extra time to recover. I wish I could say he could have it. ...He told me that he'd spoken to Mother during the sleep talking phase and she told him why he was Father."

Andrew raised an eyebrow. "He didn't like it?"

"Not really. It's so if she can't stand in the place of her choosing, her Family still has a parent to watch over them, although he doesn't have to do anything. She placed him to be merely a figurehead if that's all he's willing to be, but I don't think that's all he'll settle for anymore - not now that he's become involved with them. They're also his protection if she isn't able to be here to protect him."

"She doesn't believe you'll protect her?" Andrew tested.

"She set it up before she knew when or if she would come, last fall," Rei hedged.

"Mmm. But that doesn't answer my question, does it?" Andrew pointed out.

"I don't know." It was the only answer Rei could give to the question. He wasn't so sure right at that moment he *could* answer it.

After Rei was in bed, he lay there thinking. While he hadn't lied to Mizi and Ore, he hadn't told them everything either. He didn't know why Ilena wanted a Princess Mizi as soon as possible, but he'd all of a sudden been presented a reason why *he* should want it.

Ilena was a temptation for anyone in power. Even his own brother would divorce his queen wife if he had within himself an ounce of a desire for empire building. Rei was pretty certain that he, Rei, had no desire for empire building himself. Ilena probably believed it too or she wouldn't have been planning on coming to him. That didn't mean he didn't comprehend the temptation.

The sooner he could marry Mizi, the sooner his intentions with regard to Ilena would be understood. His brother was likely looking for that, and once the lords knew, they would most certainly be looking at it.

Rei groaned and rolled over. If the lords found out before he was married to Mizi, or at least made his intentions to marry her very clear, they might scrap the list in his desk and put Ilena on a plate for him, cousin or not. Although...he might be able to be protected from that if he appealed to Sasou and his brother openly sided against Ilena as a potential mate. He sighed. There was an awful lot to do in as short an amount of time as possible.

It was like his own goal right now. He was carefully planning and setting up the nets that would trap more than the Earl. Once they were all firmly in place, he would close them quickly so the fish he desired couldn't escape. It was the same with Ilena. She'd been planning for the same thing for most of her life already.

Rei paused. She'd said that Tarc had been just as patient in bringing down the ruling family of Selicia. The person behind that work would have seen her survival as a useful addition to his plans. Why not go for three countries when you're already in conquest mode and a helpful tool comes along?

Rei considered. He personally knew very little about the governance of Tarc at the current time, at least to the depth he needed to understand in order to face the coming test. He could ask Sasou for information, but he would have to word the request such that he didn't imply Ilena and her network were insufficient to support him.

Rei sighed again. He really hated sending letters to Sasou. There should be some other way without having to ask the next question to Ilena. He pondered a little longer, then fell asleep in the middle of a thought.

He was still thinking about it in the morning when he walked into the Rose office. He was a bit late from his second interrupted night in a row. He looked around the office and saw Dane and Tairn huddled together over one of their desks. He stopped, staring at them. Ilena had already given him the tool he needed. He started walking again. "Dane, come to my desk, please." He got lots of surprised looks for his sudden order.

Rei sat down at his desk. Dane arrived obediently in front of him. "I need information on Tarc and its current governance. To the point of detail of names, roles, and responsibilities. Ages and family situation would be appreciated if obtainable. I'm coming to you because Ilena is currently unavailable. Please see that I receive the information as soon as possible."

"Rei, will that be in addition to his other duties, or are you reassigning him for a time?" Mina asked for clarification.

"In addition to." Rei looked at her as if it should have been obvious. She blinked.

"Yes, Rei," Dane bowed, still saying the informal very carefully, still unsure he should be. "We should be able to have the report to you sometime tomorrow."

"I can't just have Ilena's most recent one?" Rei pressured him.

"It no longer has that level of detail." Dane's answer was smooth and without pause. Rei was impressed and his mouth quirked up slightly.

"I see. Well, then I'll wait if I must, but it's of high priority." He dismissed Dane by pulling out his first document for the day.

Dane bowed again and returned to his desk. He wrote a quick message and took it to the paiges outside the door. Then he returned to his discussion with his brother. Mina surreptitiously looked from Dane to Rei. Rei was satisfied. Well, she was too, if that's all the distraction it had been for her precious assistant.

CHAPTER 9 Recovery

Ore was brought to awareness by the heartbeat of Ilena. It had increased in tempo and strength. As he continued to increase in awareness he checked her breathing. She was in pain. There was a knock at the door. He heard Rio - her footsteps were lighter and more energetic. "Good morning, Mister Ryan."

Ore was up off the bed and standing behind Rio, pulling the door open wider, before Ryan could finish saying good morning. He saw the vial in Ryan's hand. "She's just now needing that, Ryan," Ore said cheerfully. "Your timing this morning is excellent." Ryan blinked at him, then smiled his slow, shy smile. Ore moved out of the way to head back towards Ilena, making sure Ryan was following him.

"Really, Master Ore. You shouldn't appear at the door in such a state," Rio scolded him as she also reentered the room.

"And what state is that?" he asked her over his shoulder, winking at Ryan, who had already recognized the teasing twinkle in Ore's eye.

"A mess," she sighed. "You've only just come from sleeping, after all."

Ryan looked worried. "Did I wake you?"

"No, no." Ore waved his hand. "She did," he pointed with his thumb at Ilena. "She's in pain." Ryan walked quickly over to Ilena, spoke to her, and helped her drink the medicine.

Ore watched Ryan as he gently brushed the hair back from her forehead, then placed his hand there to confirm her temperature. He put the vial in a pocket and put his other hand on his own forehead to compare. "Not too high. That's good." He checked Ilena's heart rate while watching her breathing. He nodded in agreement with Ore's assessment. "It's good her heart is stronger today," Ryan said quietly.

Ore looked at him knowingly. "You like Ilena."

Ryan blushed, then looked frightened. "Ah, but it isn't like that! She's already said...."

Ore looked at him curiously. "What did she already say?"

"When we first met...," Ryan couldn't look up, "she said that I shouldn't think of her that way. That Prince Rei wouldn't give her to me. That's when she told me that I should go visit the Scholar's Tavern. ...I've been thinking I'll go back this next week, actually." Ryan finally looked up at that last statement.

Ore smiled at him. "That sounds like fun. Will you go yourself this time?"

Ryan paused, then nodded. "I thought I might. It would be a good experience for me." He was actually looking strong, or so thought Ore.

"I think it will be a very good thing for Ryan," Ore said encouragingly. He felt Rio shift, and had a thought. "What day will you go?"

"My next evening off is next Prince's-day. I'll go then," Ryan answered.

"Good luck, then. Drink one for me, okay?" Ore requested.

Ryan looked at him aghast. "I can't do that, Ore, or I won't make it home."

Ore laughed. "You don't have to drink my drinks, Ryan. Well, then make a toast to me, so I'll have been there in name at least."

Ryan smiled. "I'll do that. If you need anything else today, please let me know."

"I will," Ore promised. "Thanks for bringing that over." Ryan waved as he left the room.

"Will you be wanting Prince's-day evening off, Miss Rio?" Ore asked nonchalantly, not quite looking at her.

"If I went it would be to take your name in vain, Master Ore," she answered.

"Ah, I'm not liked, ehhh?" He looked over his shoulder at her. She ignored him. She was working on a document of some kind, he could see. Well, it wouldn't do to have her not liking him, but it also wouldn't do to provoke her. He left her alone and got himself ready for the day.

It occurred to him it was perhaps a bit late in the morning. "Ah, perhaps it is that, unlike Miss Leah, Miss Rio doesn't know how to make Ore let her do her duty to her Mistress, so Miss Rio is distressed?" He was looking at her, his head tilted to one side questioningly.

Rio looked up at him swiftly, shock on her face. "H-how would you know that?"

Ore smiled. "Because normally Miss Rio is very quiet and hiding in the shadows, but there is no Miss Leah here today. She entrusted Mistress to you but you aren't sure how to go about getting it done."

Rio snapped her mouth shut. "Well, it would be something like that, yes." Her eyes flashed.

"I don't bite, Miss Rio. You can hit me in the head with a book if it suits you. That's what Mister Andrew does." Rio looked disturbed. "Just please don't do what Miss Mina does."

"What is that?"

Ore narrowed his eyes at her. "...No, I don't think I'll tell you. You're the kind that would do it." His face went back to jovial. "Well you'll have to pick what works best for Miss Rio to wake up Ore."

He paused and got a little more serious. "Rio," her eyes went wide, "I understand you care for Ilena also. I may be grumpy or worried, but really, I'm not any different than anyone else in the Family. If there's a thing you want or need to do for her, I won't stand in your way, nor be offended. You may tell me." She stared at him with round eyes for a moment, then nodded. "Shall we get Ilena ready for her day together, then? And I'm sorry to have slept in."

Rio put aside her document and rose to join him. "Thank you, Master Ore. Though... that's the first time I've been able to experience Father for myself."

164

As Ore removed the covers from Ilena, he answered her, "No, Miss Rio. I'm always Father. That's the first time you've looked." She had no answer but to ponder on his words.

-o-o-o-

Ilena felt herself waking up. It was a rather surprising sensation, and she observed it for a while. Strange things ached about her middle areas. She felt her face wrinkle a little in reaction. She decided she didn't like that and made it smooth out again. She took a deep breath to ease the ache some, then decided she might open her eyes.

Ore was sitting on the bed next to her, taking up all her view. His chin was in his hand, his elbow resting on the knee he had tucked up under him. "Good afternoon. Have you joined us again for a bit?" His eyes were twinkling and his tone was a bit teasing, but she thought he looked more just a regular happy.

"It seems I have," her sleepy surprise came through somewhat. "You seem pleased. Have good things happened?"

He shrugged. "You waking up is a good thing. You've been doing an excellent job of staying alive this time."

"Oh? Well, that's good then." She rested for a bit. It seemed to take some energy to talk.

"How are you feeling?" Ore asked.

"I ache about the middle, seemingly in odd locations. And I'm weary. But otherwise, it's perhaps okay," Ilena answered.

"Doctor Elliot found a few more things left over from the landslide injury that Doctor Bonner missed. Perhaps those corrections are what you're feeling in addition to the expected pain," Ore offered.

"Perhaps." She thought she'd like to close her eyes now, and they obeyed.

"Are you going to sleep again so soon?" He actually sounded disappointed.

"No...I don't think so. Where are we in the cycle?" She wasn't really sure what her body was going to do this time any more than the last time.

"...We don't know." Her eyebrow lifted in question. "You still should have two more treatments, minimum. Doctor Elliot expected at least one more than that. But based on your reaction to the amount you were given yesterday evening, they're guessing you may only need one more. They don't know which of those one doses to give you. They're still debating it."

"Ehhh, I've developed a resistance, have I? We postulated that might be a side effect from the long term use of it. ...I wonder if Doctor Elliot remembers that?" she murmured.

"I'll ask him, but yes, that does seem the case," Ore agreed.

"Well, then, the minimum dose should be sufficient. If my body needs it, it will have it. If it's sufficiently resistant, it will be the last necessary dose." It didn't particularly concern Ilena much either way.

"Just like that, that's the answer, huh?" Ore said blandly.

Ilena decided she didn't have the energy to answer him. "Is there something we can do about the fact that I don't have any energy at all?" she asked instead.

"Well, food would help with that, but are you hungry at all?" he wondered.

Her stomach gurgled in answer. She blushed lightly. "Not until you asked, although Mistress Mizi's tea sounds better. The one she made for me the first time."

"Well, if you can stay awake long enough, I'm sure I could ask for that to be made up easily enough."

Her stomach requested it again. Ore did laugh this time. "Okay. I'll go and ask." She felt his hand lightly brush hers as he rose. For some reason, she seemed to want to call him back, but it would take too much effort, so she didn't.

For a while she just floated in a peaceful state, sounds occasionally entering her ears. At some point it occurred to her to wonder if she'd been left alone. That was an odd feeling. She hadn't been alone in a very long time - well as far as being in the presence of someone went.

Her curiosity finally won out and she opened her eyes again and turned her head slowly to look around the room. She was pleased that it was a decent size. There was another bed nearby. It didn't look like it had gotten much use. She wondered idly for a moment where Ore slept.

She craned slightly to finish looking around the room and caught sight of a pair of legs under a skirt. She recognized that. She closed her eyes and smiled. "I'm glad to know Rio will still keep me company, even when I'm not much company to be with."

Ilena floated in quiet peace for a while longer, then the smell of the tea woke her again. She opened her eyes. Ore was holding the tea, standing nearby, a concerned look on his face. "What is it, Ore?" she asked him.

He shook his head and wiped the expression off his face. "Are you ready for some tea?" he asked her.

Ilena answered politely, "Yes. It smells very delicious."

He pulled a chair up beside the bed and with careful practice helped her to drink it. At some point, he turned to Rio and gave her some order, but the words didn't penetrate well through her focus on the tea and her weariness. Rio left the room on whatever errand Ore had sent her on, and shortly thereafter Ilena finished the tea.

When he'd laid her head to rest on the bed again, she thanked him with a smile. He put the teacup away, then placed his hand on her head, looking at her very seriously. "Ilena, can you hear me?"

"Of course, Ore," she said.

"Will you let me test you?" he asked her

Her brow creased slightly in confusion. "Yes. Is something wrong?"

Ore paused. "I'm not sure, yet. Will you close your eyes? When you hear my voice, raise your right hand. When you hear any other noise, raise your left hand, okay?"

"Okay," that was easy enough, if she could work up the energy. "But is it okay if I don't lift them very high? They're heavy today."

He smiled. "Just enough so I can see them is fine."

"Okay." She closed her eyes. He lifted her hands and placed them on her body so they would be where he could see them and she wouldn't have to move them much.

"Okay, let's test it. Raise your right hand." She did. "Now your left." She did that as well. "Good, I'll be able to see that. Let's begin, then."

She could tell that he was starting with distance, so when he moved out of her word comprehension range she told him, "I can still hear your voice, Ore, but I can no longer make out your words." There was a pause. She wondered idly what the range was, but she was too weary to open her eyes. She continued to raise her hand when he spoke, then she could make out words again.

He'd asked if she could hear his words. "Yes," she answered. He moved around asking the same question. Each time she could, she answered with a yes. When all she heard was the sound of his voice, she merely raised her right hand.

She heard Ore sigh. She raised her right hand again, and grinned. "Ah, you will tease me?" he asked. "Even at such a time? ...Well, I guess it's good you're in a good mood at least. You may open your eyes."

She sighed and slowly opened her eyes to find faces surrounding her on all sides. "Ah! It's that bad, is it? What's the range, Ore?" She turned to look at him.

He was standing next to her the closest on the right side, a serious expression on his face. "Four feet to hear my words. If I speak anywhere else in the room, you hear my voice only."

Ilena looked around the people gathered around her bed again. There was Rio, wearing her very worried expression, Ryan. Then on the other side, Doctor Elliot, Mizi, and on her other close side, Rei. "You spoke in my presence again, didn't you?" she asked him. He nodded, then looked at Ore. She turned to look at him as well.

"We thought it would make no difference if you were sleeping," he explained.

"*Hahh.* Ore, even you know my ears are open at all times. The question may not have been asked," she turned back to Rei, "but if the topic is discussed, that is sufficient to prepare me to receive the question."

Rei's mouth moved, then Ore's voice came to her. "What shall we do, then? Can we reverse it until a more appropriate time to ask the question?"

"I don't know what we'll do, but how is there a more appropriate time than the time at which you are prepared to receive the information?" Rei paused. She could see he didn't really like that answer.

She hesitated, then said, "Master Rei, it will already have to wait until next time I wake up. I'm too weary to remain awake much longer. You're concerned about a thing that needs your careful attention. As long as there are holes in your understanding, will you still be able to focus on that thing, or will it worry you? A burden can be easier to set aside when it's fully comprehended."

She paused to rest, blinking at him. "It's possible that if the topic isn't spoken again by you or Ore in my presence, then it will settle back in the darkness until the time you wish to discuss it, but I don't know. I set the keys, but didn't put time constraints on them."

Rei's mouth moved again, and again Ore's voice followed. "Would the information rest if it was commanded?"

Ilena shrugged. She caught sight of Doctor Elliot's mouth moving. He'd helped her, perhaps he had a suggestion. The room was getting dark and she could no longer keep her eyes open, so she didn't. She walked the path back to sleep and darkness as gracefully as she had walked it to awareness, although she thought she heard a sound just before sleep claimed her.

-o-o-o-

"Do you think she heard it?" Rei asked Ore.

"Yes," Ore answered. "She said it herself."

Rei sighed. "How is it?"

Ore tilted his head, "It's a skill, or perhaps several skills, that we can train ourselves to in order to protect ourselves from predators. When I sleep lightly it's like that. Any sound will rouse me immediately. ...Normally, Ilena's hearing is three to four times the distance of mine and it's impossible to walk up to her without her knowing.

"When Miss Rio told me to be very quiet and see how close I could get to Ilena before she noticed, I thought she was joking, but she looked so concerned I did as she requested. She never did hear me walking in the room. She smelled the tea. Then, as I fed the tea to Ilena, Miss Rio spoke to Ilena, even until she was shouting, and Ilena had no reaction."

Rei turned to Rio. "What happened that made you think there was a problem?"

"After Master Ore left to retrieve the tea, Mistress Ilena lay quietly for a while, then began to look around the room. When she finally saw that I was here, she said, 'I'm glad to know Rio will still keep me company, even when I'm not much company to be with.' I asked her if she'd been feeling lonely, but she didn't respond to my question. It's not like Mistress Ilena to not know when there's another person in the room, but she had to see me to know I was there."

168

"It doesn't seem like her to let a question go unanswered, either," Rei frowned.

Rio nodded. "At first I thought that she was merely still tired, but then I dropped my book on the ground. It was quite loud and startled even me. Mistress Ilena, however, had no reaction to it. I spoke to her again, asking if she would tell me if she was awake, and she didn't answer, but I could see her moving slightly, as if she were. So when Master Ore came in shortly after that, I asked him to experiment for me. She'd answered him well enough before he left, after all."

Rei nodded. "Thank you, Miss Rio." He looked at Ore, then Doctor Elliot and Ryan. "I don't believe this is permanent, nor is it due to the other things she's going through. I'm sorry to be its cause. Ore," he turned back to his sworn man, "let me know if this happens again. If what we tried doesn't work, there'll be no help for it but to ask the questions."

Ore nodded, then, seeing Rei was preparing to leave, hurriedly said, "She also gave the answer to the other issue Mistress brought to us this morning." Everyone gave him their attention. "Ilena wasn't surprised, and said that early on she and Doctor Elliot postulated that one of the side effects of her long term use of the Little Death would be that she would develop a resistance to it.

"She said that it would be only a matter of giving her the lowest dose next time. If her body needed it, it would be present, otherwise it would be the last dose. It felt like she meant it would be the last dose regardless."

Doctor Elliot nodded. "I was wondering if that was the case. She thinks the lowest is acceptable?" Ore nodded.

Doctor Elliot shrugged and looked at Ryan. Ryan looked at Mizi, who sighed. "All right. Ore you may give her the lowest dose when she needs it. Is the second of those doses already prepared, in case she should need one more after that?" She looked at Doctor Elliot.

He nodded. "Ore already knows which ones they are." He pointed to the shelf that held the closed bottles, for Rei's sake.

"All right. But, Ore,..."

"I know," he smiled at her, "if there are any complications I'll be sure to let someone who is very close by know immediately."

After the other four people left, Ore looked at Rio. "With Ilena, I'm never quite sure if I'm hearing good news or bad news. It seems with her, one always picks up a two-sided coin."

Rio nodded. "We've learned that it therefore doesn't pay to get too excited about anything, one way or the other. It's just our duty to see she doesn't roll off the cliff."

Ore laughed. "I see how it is you're able to sit with her, then. I'll remember that. ...Actually, it's what I have to do for Master and Mistress, too. They'll try to get themselves into trouble with no thought for themselves otherwise." Rio gave him an odd look, then excused herself to her chair again. Ore returned to his vigil by Ilena's side.

-o-o-o-

Ilena began to show the first of the withdrawal symptoms about two hours before she had the evening before, just before the dinner carts were to be delivered. Ore collected one of the lowest dose containers and sent Rio to tell the infirmary they would need the next dose of the pain reducing medicine immediately.

He was glad to know that Ilena was about done, but he felt like it was backwards. If she was resistant to the drug, wouldn't she need more to be able to have it help? Then he remembered that had always been the reaction of the city police, to give more when it looked like their attempts to get the users clean wasn't working, and it usually failed. Ilena had always instructed them to use far less.

He opened the container, waited until he was sure it was just the right time, and lifted her head. "Ilena, it's time to take your last dose. Here you go." He put it to her lips, and she refused. His heart skipped a beat. "Ilena, there isn't much time, please take it." She refused again. He lay her back down. He swapped hands holding the cup, and took her middle finger in his, in their years-old signal. Was she now unable to hear him as well?

He watched as she forcefully pulled herself awake. Her hand let go of his and she reached for his head. He put his ear close to her mouth. "Half. Tell Doc..tor Elliot...make it half." It was barely whispered.

"Are you sure? How can you tell?"

"Smell."

Ore jumped up and ran for the door, he reached it just as Rio opened it. "Stay with her. Hold her hand," he called to her as he ran past.

Doctor Elliot wasn't any more pleased with Ore's request than Ore had been with Ilena, but Ore was insistent. She wasn't going to take anything else. While it was steeping, and they were too, Doctor Elliot asked Ore why he believed her.

"Well, I don't smell anything at all," Ore admitted, "but she always smells it before she takes it. She smelled the tea from halfway between her bed and the door. It's like her hearing...much better than most."

"Hmm. Well, I never did have to take it, myself," Doctor Elliot admitted. "I should ask her to write it up, if she can."

His timer finished and he poured the required amount into a clean container for Ore and sealed it. Ore was off and back at the room as fast as he could go. He was glad the guards could open the door for him. It meant he didn't have to slow down until he was beside the bed. He took the side opposite Rio, who was holding Ilena's hand and sweating slightly.

Ilena was already pained. Ore lifted her head. Her jaw was tight, but when he put the cup to her lips, she paused, then greedily drank it. When it was gone, he set her down, then dropped onto his knees and rested on the bed in relief.

170

"I'll say it again: gods, Woman, you are difficult! Doctor Elliot wants a full report on how you can tell how much you need by smell as payment for that."

Her hand lifted, then rested on his head and across his back, her angle being a little awkward. "Thank...you."

"Just live," he said wearily. "If you really want to thank me, then live."

"I don't know, Master Ore," Rio said from the other side of the bed. "If she lives, she'll just keep running you ragged. Are you sure you'll survive?"

Ore smiled, and then Ilena laughed. It was a laugh mixed with pain, but a laugh nonetheless. Ore raised his head in surprise, then looked at Rio, who was just as surprised, but then smiled in delight. Ore smiled back. "I guess it worked, eh?"

He shook his head. "Definitely a coin with two sides, every time." He put his head back down, enjoying feeling Ilena's touch, listening to her breathe through the pain. It wasn't as bad this time, that was good. "Ah!" he looked back up at Rio. "The pain medicine?"

Rio shook her head. "Mister Ryan had come and gone by the time you arrived again. She's already had it."

He relaxed again. "Ryan's a good man," he said.

"Yes, he is," said Rio.

Ore smiled into his arm. "I thought so. You want Prince's-day night off?" He peeked over to Rio and saw the blush. "You've got it. One of the other three of us can handle it, I'm sure. ... Although I'm glad you were here today. You've been a great help. Thanks."

He missed seeing her blushing a deeper red. "I'm sorry I didn't look to see Father in you before," she said to him. "I've been properly considering it today. The fault was mine."

"...Well, if it helps you to be more capable of doing your duty now, then that's good." Ore said forgivingly. "I didn't need you rolling off the cliff, too." *Pfft!* Rio tried to hold it in, then just couldn't. As she laughed, Ore smiled. It felt good to know another of his Children understood.

Ilena's hand moved until she was caressing his cheek, then ran her fingers through his hair, subconsciously clutching gently when she reached the spot she always felt for. He closed his eyes, happy. Ilena sighed as the pain finally left her. Ore thought she sounded happy, too.

When Ilena came up later that night, the sleep-talking phase was about as short as Ore had expected. She only said, "Ore, thank you for loving my Children."

He answered, "Thank you for teaching me, Mother." Then she was gone.

He decided to stay lying next to her. At that low a dose, the pain shouldn't cause her to arch enough to damage her, and he could hold her otherwise just as well from here. He waited, listening to her breathe.

He was going to miss being at her side during the nights after tonight. He wondered what he should do about that. The other bed was really where he belonged, but it would be a cold place. Well, he would still be able to hear her breathe, at least.

He felt her shudder. Then again. He held her close. "Don't fight it. It will be short tonight," he said quietly in her ear. The child in him still wanted to cry, though.

Her breathing deepened as the intensity increased. Then she moaned, a sound that wrung. The deep breaths were frequently punctuated with moans for several minutes, then they faded and she returned to shudders for about another minute. Ore watched her face, looking for the tears.

Ilena's eyes opened and she looked at him, lying beside her. "Oh, is that where you've been sleeping? I wondered. The other bed hadn't looked very used."

He lifted his head a little to look at her curiously. "Ilena, you didn't cry."

She yawned. "No. I don't suppose I would. That was the last gasp of the rain cloud." She snuggled into him. "Now it's just the boring wait. ...That I do wish I could skip."

"Have you really taken it so much you just know these things now?"

"Mm hm." She nodded into his chest. She sighed. "I'll write it up proper when I can sit up again...or maybe I'll make Elliot take dictation some day when I'm bored."

"Well, that would be a good thing." Ore put his head back down. Then he wondered how short the alert phase would be, since everything else had been shortened.

"Ore?"

"Mmm?"

"What are you going to do?"

Ore considered it. She was probably talking about her first comment again. He sighed. "That night...no, that day, after you rejected the first graft, I was like a child who'd been frightened and couldn't be reassured. I wanted to hold you, to have you tell me you were okay. I lay on the other bed, making myself sleep as before, listening to your breaths.

"Mistress came in the middle of the night to bring you the next dose of pain medication. I'd been thinking a good scolding by Master would be a great help when he came in to see you. That's when you tried to walk away from us for the second time." Ore shuddered and Ilena reached up a hand and grasped his shirt.

"Mistress ordered me to speak to you, to bring you back as she had the first time. Then Master made me tell him how I'd been able to leave after the initial surgery. He ordered me to do it again, and they left. Instead of being scolded and nailed to my proper place, they'd ordered me to be the child I was inside." He was quiet. She was still awake, waiting.

Finally he said, "You came back for me, but because you still hadn't spoken to me, I wasn't satisfied. Today, when I knew you were about to wake up for the first time for real, that part of me was very happy, and again this evening, when you woke for me during the withdrawal pain, I was happy again.

"If you're finally whole again, free from the Little Death, I don't need to stay here after tonight. The other bed will be enough." He closed his eyes and willed his child's heart to be quiet. He was an adult, and she was not his in that way.

"Thank you for being my warmth and my anchor these nights." Ilena responded. Ore wanted to kiss her. He held very still, fighting himself. Perhaps even staying tonight was dangerous. "Ore, you have chosen to be Father?"

"Yes," he was glad for the distraction of another topic. "I will love your Children, and will care for them when you cannot...and when you can."

"That makes me happy," Ilena said. "And it makes me happy if it makes you happy."

"Mm. It does," he whispered, and his heart hurt, knowing why she'd done it. "Ilena."

"Hmm?"

"While you're fighting to stand in the place you desire, please remember that we are fighting with you. Please trust Master when he says he'll protect you. ...Do not sacrifice yourself unnecessarily. Remember that it's only by working together with everyone that we can win."

Ilena held very still. "I-I'll try, but I'm very afraid, Ore."

He squeezed her to him briefly. "I know. We'll need to show you, so you can learn to trust that you aren't alone anymore. If there is anything you can learn from these last few days, I hope it's that."

She stayed still a moment longer, then nodded her head. "I'll consider it."

"Good." This time he did reward her with a kiss on the head.

They lay quietly for a while, then as sleep was reaching for them both, Ilena said quietly, "Next time I wake up, I'll give you the last list." Ore squeezed her shoulder in response. That would complete her bargain, other than her personal testimony before the Lord's Court. There would be a long six weeks in between.

-o-o-o-

Doctor Elliot came to visit Ilena the next morning after Leah and Ore had prepared her for the day. He very carefully inspected the incision and the site. There was no excess heat, redness, or swelling. Letting out a careful breath when he was done, he said he was slightly optimistic that the graft was taking this time.

He questioned her and Ore heavily on her reaction to the previous night's dose of the Little Death. Ilena was quite insistent that she wouldn't need any more, and made him the promise that if he would come take the dictation, she would tell him everything about her experience with the drug. Of course everyone agreed it should be after she had regained more strength.

"Actually," Doctor Elliot said, rubbing the back of his head, "Regent Rei stopped by this morning to receive the report from last night and talk with me a bit. He's asked me to put together my research into a preliminary report for him to review. He wants to see it published in the end, and he wants me to continue with it. While it isn't surgery, it is research I'm most familiar with, so I've agreed."

"I'm glad you've found a new patron," Ilena said to him. "I hope he's more acceptable to you than the previous one."

"Well, you were a very good patron to have," Doctor Elliot rejoined. Ilena grinned. "However, I'm glad I won't have to experiment with the Little Death on you anymore. He's asked me to use it on prisoners to see if the sleep talking phase can be used for interrogation purposes, and if a dose that will allow that affect can be found that has a minimal amount of pain effect.

"He would also like to know if it's possible to remove from the drug the pain payment phase, and maybe the hibernative state although that isn't as necessary, but still maintain the reduction in feeling pain later. That would be useful for things like surgeries and other medical purposes. Mister Ryan said he'll help me with the latter research. I'll be glad to have his experience."

"It's nice that what we've done before can be used by the Crown, now," Ilena said.

Doctor Elliot nodded, then stood. "Master Ore, I would think if there were to be any troubles with the graft, we should see signs today...maybe into tomorrow at the latest, but to not have had any into today I think is a good indicator it's taken."

"I'll send for you if there are any signs." Ore promised.

Doctor Elliot bowed slightly and left the room. Ore looked at Ilena. "Well, it's good to hear more optimistic news, even if it is cautious. Though," he sighed, "I'm not really in a hurry to return to my desk. I'm sure it's piled very high."

"Well...only more will pile on it," Ilena said pragmatically.

"True," Ore looked away pensively. "I wonder how Mistress is getting along?"

Ilena said, cautiously, "You could go see. ...If there's anything you would like to accomplish you could bring it here. I'm afraid you'll be very bored here, otherwise."

Ore looked at her, wondering. "Are you trying to be rid of me?"

Ilena shook her head. "I've just been thinking that Ore has been caged for many days now."

"Ah!" Ore was surprised. "I suppose it has been days, hasn't it? I hadn't felt it. ...Well, I'll consider it. Maybe if you nap well again and I feel restless

I'll go briefly, but I would be displeased if you should go into rejection while I was gone."

"Well...I suppose it isn't for me to say what my body will or won't do in that regard, but I don't think it will," she answered.

"I will consider it." His words were final, and she subsided.

Leah walked in, pushing the breakfast cart in front of her. "Well, now, Mistress Ilena, Master Ore, it's time to eat."

"Me, too?" Ilena asked surprised.

Ore nodded. "You were able to take the tea yesterday. Today we'll try 'thin gruel', flavored with...mashed and thinned dates," he looked at it closely, smelled it, then stated what he thought it was.

"Oh!" Ilena's eyes were round. "It's sweet, even."

"Well, you are nothing but bone any more, Mistress," Leah said, a frown on her face. "I'm told you'll be getting three meals today, but if there are no further complications, tomorrow they'll be sending five. If you can stand it, we'll likely give you an evening after-dinner snack as well." She tucked two pillows up behind Ilena's head to lift it enough she could eat.

"Leah! I'll become fat, lying here without moving, if I eat that many meals a day!" Both Leah and Ore frowned at her. "Well, I'll do it until I've at least recovered my energy. Then I really think it should go back to three meals a day until I'm able to properly move about," she compromised. "Besides, gruel and porridge six times a day for six weeks will be more unbearable than the three times a day it was before, no matter how many things they try to disguise it with." She made a yuck face.

"Of course, Mistress," Leah said, not committing to anything. She made up three plates of the normal food, that Ilena was trying hard not to drool over the smell of, and Ore offered Ilena her first bite.

"Well...it isn't as good as what you're getting to eat, but it is better than what it could be," Ilena said after swallowing it. She ate a few more bites obediently, then looked at Ore. "Isn't this constant nursing of your partner becoming a burden?"

Ore raised his eyebrows at her. "Should it?"

Ilena blushed lightly. "I suppose not," she mumbled.

He paused the spoon above the bowl and looked at her. "Is it so hard to understand, this having a partner?"

She blushed deeper. "I'm sorry."

He looked at her for a moment more, then offered her the spoon. For once, she was embarrassed to be fed by him. He pondered the cause while she ate. He finally said, "I'm sorry if I surprised you last night."

She looked away from him. "Well...after hearing your explanation, it was understandable." She blushed again, then shook her head. Ore wondered what she'd been thinking of, but thought if he pressed forward it likely wouldn't go good places. He didn't want her to dislike it, but if it was needful he'd do it again even if she did, so it didn't really matter. He kept quiet while feeding her, and she eventually calmed down.

When she was done, he looked in the bowl. "Well, you've eaten more than half of it. That's good for your first meal." He put the bowl down and picked up a cup of water, holding it for her to drink from to wash down the gruel.

"Would you like to lie back, Mistress Ilena?" Leah asked.

Ilena shook her head. "That was rather a lot. I'd like to sit up a while longer, I think." She rested with her eyes closed until Ore had finished his meal, but her hands were more restless than usual he noted as he watched her.

"Ilena, has the room become too small?" he asked her as he set his dishes on the cart.

She looked up at him in surprise. "Ehh...perhaps." She considered. "I do feel a little anxious. My mind wants to be up and moving, I suppose. Although now that I've been fed, my body is drowsy again. It's uncomfortable."

He smiled at her. "I suppose it would be. Sleeping again would be best, then, I would think."

She took a deep breath in lieu of sighing. "Well, before that, if you'll get paper and pen, I'll give you the list."

He nodded and went to the desk, retrieving the supplies, but staying there to use the hard surface. "I'm ready," he said since she couldn't see him.

Ilena gave him six names, all of them at places he recognized. They were still in their Houses, or very near them. It would indeed be difficult to extract them without their absence being noted. While he pondered on that for a moment, Ilena was quiet. He was about to put the pen down when she spoke again.

"Ore, would you be able to pick up one more? It isn't someone to go to wherever you're keeping everyone else, but if they could be taken to a safe place, a small town some distance from where they are now, maybe?"

"Tell me more," he said simply.

"It's a mother with three children. I've promised to keep them safe for someone who cares about them very much. They aren't related, but they do know my name."

He pulled out a separate piece of paper. "Who is it?" Ilena gave him a name and place as with the others. "How will she know she may go with me?" he asked her.

Ilena paused. "Are you still a Messenger?"

He looked up. "Yes."

"Show her your medallion. She'll go with you, I think, if she hears my name and knows you've come because of me."

Ore put the pen away and put both pieces of paper in his jacket, which was on but unlatched halfway for the casual but "living as normal a life as could be lived in this room" atmosphere. He returned to sitting next to her, and took her hand in his, feeling for her heart beat and counting it out again. She was still doing well, and was indeed becoming sleepy. Her eyes were already closed. "Are you ready for the pillows to be moved?"

"Yes," she answered quietly, her breathing slowing. Leah came to the bed and removed the pillows while Ore held Ilena's head then put it back down on the bed. As he moved his hand from behind her head, she turned her cheek into it. He left it there briefly, his eyes soft, then he slowly released her and sat back in his chair, taking her hand in his again. He slowly brushed the back of it with his thumb, until he knew she was asleep.

"*Haaah*," he sighed sadly. "It is difficult, isn't it?" He sat and looked at her a little longer, then stood, gently releasing her hand. "Miss Leah. I am going to go out. I'll have Thayne come sit with her while I'm gone."

"Yes, Master Ore," she said quietly.

Ore walked quietly out the door, making sure it closed quietly behind him as well. He went into the courtyard and whistled. He was a bit surprised when it was Thayne himself that answered a few minutes later. He was leaning against one of the pillars, one foot up on the pillar, so Thayne relaxed and walked up to him. "Things are quiet?" he asked.

Ore nodded. "Have you heard the latest?"

Thayne grinned. "Since the surgeon visited this morning. It sounds good."

"Well, it's better now. Two nights ago, not so much." He looked up into the small square of blue sky above. "I need to go see Master for a while. Go and sit with her. Watch for the signs you saw before. I'll return quickly."

Thayne nodded, and Ore jumped up to the roof and vanished. Thayne sighed. He was glad his master was outside again. He just wished Ore could be free of his burden. He turned, nodded hello to the guards, and went in to sit in his master's place.

-o-o-o-

"Ah!" Mizi stopped suddenly on her way to drop another document off at Andrew's desk. Andrew looked up at her, then in the direction she was looking.

"Ore's here, Rei," Mina said without looking up.

"Mmm," Rei said, busily writing.

Ore smiled at Mizi. She seemed to be having a hard time believing she was seeing the apparition crouched on the banister. She shook her head to recover and put the document on its pile on Andrew's desk. Andrew smiled a her. "Rei has to have an office with a balcony just for him," he told her. "That's his door - mostly."

"And I have to coax him through it, too - mostly," Rei said as he put down his pen and stretched. He pushed away from his desk and walked to stand leaning on the glass balcony door frame with his arms crossed, the opened dark blue curtain a warmth next to his side where it had soaked up the morning's sunlight. He looked closely at Ore. He looked okay, but he still wasn't ready to come work. That was alright. He could talk from here. Rei nodded.

Ore reached into his jacket, still not quite done up all the way. He pulled out two sheets of paper and held them out for Rei. Ore wasn't planning on staying long, then. Rei pushed away from the door frame to go take them. He looked through them, then looked back at Ore.

"The long one's the last list. The single is a request. Not Family, but she takes care of them. She wants to know if I can move them to a new home in a safer location - not the safe house."

Rei considered, then put the list in his jacket and handed back the single. "Let me know when you're going to go move them. Make sure it doesn't conflict with the plans." Ore nodded and put the paper back in his jacket. "...What did the surgeon say?"

Ore looked back up at him and paused, thinking. "He thinks there's a likelihood it's taken. If it isn't rejected by tomorrow evening he'll relax."

"Do you want to stay 'til then?" Rei asked him. It was a day longer than they'd previously agreed.

Ore looked indecisive and Rei could see the sadness on him that Thayne had seen. "Let me see how she is tomorrow morning."

Rei turned and leaned on the banister next to Ore. "What is it?" he asked him.

Ore looked down at his hands, hanging relaxed between his knees. "I'm not sure." He turned his head slightly towards Rei, but didn't quite look at him. "When she woke up last night, she was clear of the Little Death, but I'd stayed where you told me to stay. It surprised her."

Ore looked down again and Rei leaned forward and looked around at him, waiting. "I don't know what to do again." Ore finally admitted. "I told her you and Mistress had ordered it. That I'd be in my rightful place again starting tonight, assuming the graft holds."

"Well, that is the safer place to be," Rei said dryly, up-righting himself.

The tips of Ore's ears turned red, but he sighed. "I know that, Master."

"You want to stay?" Rei asked him a little surprised.

"That's why I don't know what to do. ...And it feels like she doesn't either. For the first time, today she was embarrassed when I fed her. I apologized for surprising her and she was able to calm down, eventually."

"She didn't like it?"

"No...I think it's that she did, but she still believes...," Ore paused.

Rei lifted an eyebrow. "Well, do you?"

Ore put his hand to his head and gripped his hair, then closed his eyes and dropped down off the banister to stand leaning on it the way Rei was. He opened his eyes, crossed his arms and scowled slightly at the floor in front of them. "When I'm with her, no. I'm Ore, Father, partner. But when I come out and see the sky," he looked up into it and breathed in and out a breath, "it isn't time yet."

"You're sad for her sake?"

Ore closed his eyes. "She is very alone, Master. Even with us fighting with her, she is alone. I asked her to learn from this experience that she isn't any more. She could only say she would consider it." He looked at Rei. "I don't know what it will take to convince her, how long. Since she was very young she's been alone, with only Miss Leah, and her memories of Kase to keep her company." His eyes were very sad.

Rei looked at him compassionately. "I know. I wish to fill that emptiness for her, too. It will take her time, though."

"I wish I had a thing for her, like she had for me in sending me to meet the Family, that would help her see it." Ore said wistfully.

"Well, I think she'll find it. She has Ore by her side to show her."

"And me, too." They looked up. Mizi was standing in the doorway, her hand curled over her heart, her other fist clenched at her side.

Rei smiled at her. "And the rest of us," he agreed.

Mizi walked out to stand before Ore. "When I came to this place, to Ryokudo, there was only Rei, with Mister Andrew and Miss Mina by his side to walk with me, and often they were far away. However, I was determined to walk my own path and they supported me. Now I'm with them and they are with me, and there is Ore, too, and now Ilena. I'm not alone in Ryokudo.

"Ilena is determined to walk her own path, and it's with us, too. She'll come to understand it because she desires to understand it already. If we support her, she'll feel it."

Ore was looking at her with his mouth partially open. He closed it now and smiled at her ruefully. "Mistress always says things well."

"Ore," she hesitated, "if it isn't time yet...to make her yours, then it isn't." He raised an eyebrow at her for even being brave enough to talk about it. "But you also shouldn't leave her alone if you worry she's lonely." She caught sight of his expression and got a bit of a saucy expression on her own face. She'd already lived five lonely years standing near Rei but never yet quite next to him.

He looked away first and nodded. "I understand, Mistress." He took a breath. "We'll follow in Master and Mistress' footsteps." He leaped back up onto the banister, preparing to go.

Rei moved to stand next to Mizi and took her two little fingers in his first two fingers. She moved to hold his whole hand with hers, and gave it a little squeeze. Ore looked back over to them, and seriously said, "But we can't wait as long. There are things we must do for Master and Mistress that can only be done with us being together properly."

Rei nodded. "I'm working for that, Ore." He looked Ore in the eye, promising him.

Ore blinked at him, then turned and leaped up to the roof, leaving them standing together on the balcony. Mizi sighed. "I'm glad we don't have to wait much longer, either."

Rei turned to her, smiling, and gave her a kiss. "Me, too." He put his arm around her and they walked back through the open balcony doors together.

"You forgot to give Ore his work," chided Mina when Rei and Mizi reentered the Rose office.

Rei looked at Mizi. "I think it might be a good idea if you trade back with Ore tomorrow. I think I'll be able to tempt him into working, given what came today."

Mizi agreed. "It will be good for him to remember there are others here who care, too."

Rei nodded. "I think so."

CHAPTER 10 Princesses in Training

Mizi returned to her chosen office chores. They were slight, compared to the many things to be done, but she was learning many things, and the others reassured her that even that little was helpful to them. As she worked, she always kept her eyes open for the thing that she could do, as Ilena suggested she do, not that she expected to find it here right away.

She'd discovered that currently most of the documents coming through the Rose office were related to Earl Shicchi's activities. She'd seen some of the other documents that were shunted across the hall to the Rosebud office, and they looked interesting, too, but she hadn't had any ideas from them yet either.

As she was walking back to the Rose office from delivering some of those very documents, she was waylaid by a minor lord. "Lady Mizi, I was wondering if I could have a bit of your time?"

She sighed internally. This was the third time she'd been waylaid that day. "Well, the office is quite busy right now, Lord –?"

"Prosley. Lord Prosley, Lady Mizi. I won't take much of your time, really. I was just wondering if you might bring up with the Regent the matter of the drought in the central sections of Relant."

"Well, Lord Prosley, what have you done so far about the drought in the central sections of Relant?" She tried to look as if she might actually like to hear it.

"Ah, well, we've been bringing in watcr from the surrounding areas, but that's getting to be a more expensive process than we anticipated. I was hoping the Regent might be willing to provide some additional funds for the benefit of the people in Relant." He gave her a hopeful look.

It was always a request for the Regent to approve more funds for some project or other. "Are the people paying for the water themselves, Lord Prosley?"

"Well, they are paying for some, but I've been using the land coffers as well."

"Hmm, and is it the wells that have gone dry? Or the rivers and streams?"

"The wells in the main. There are some streams, but not many," Lord Prosley answered.

"How long have those wells been in use for?" Mizi asked.

"Since my great-grandfather's time, but they've never gone dry until now."

Mizi felt like she might consider strangling him. "How much rain have you been getting?"

Lord Prosely's brow furrowed. "Well, less than normal these past three years, but some. The crops have been thin enough we haven't been able to meet our quota to the castle, but we have had just enough for the people, thank goodness."

Mizi held on to her temper. "Lord Prosley, have you tried drilling new wells, say on the other side of hills or streams, or on the far side of the towns?"

"Why should we do that when we have perfectly good wells already?" Lord Prosely took his turn to be impatient.

"Because, Lord Prosley, that has been a very long time. Even with rain, most wells only last two generations to maybe a third before they become dry. The larger the population, the faster they become emptied. Did the city wells dry up before the others?"

Lord Prosely blinked. "Why, yes they did, actually."

"Then, Lord Prosley, I suggest you have the people turn their energies to finding new locations to put new wells. That would be time and money much better spent than continuing to import water."

"Ah, I see.... Well, perhaps I'll consider that," Lord Prosely muttered.

"If you'll excuse me, I need to return to work." Mizi turned away.

"Ah! Please let Sir Andrew know I won't need to speak with the Regent after all, if you could," Lord Prosley requested to her back.

"Certainly." Mizi sighed inside. They all ended like that, too. She reentered the Rose office. "Andrew, please remove Lord Prosley of Relant and the drought of the three-generations-old wells from Rei's schedule."

"Certainly," Andrew said, absently reaching for his schedule to make a mark. Then he looked at it again. "Ah, Rei, she's cleared your meeting schedule, again, for the second day in a row."

"Why are they coming early?" asked Mizi. "Why don't they just wait until their meeting time? And yesterday I couldn't help Count Blakely. Rei had to listen to him."

"It seems to be something about if they're standing around and they can grab anyone to hear their plight, they might get special consideration," Mina answered her.

"You could have helped Count Blakely if you'd understood a little more," Rei said, his fingers interlaced before him. "You understood it well enough once he'd both clarified his position, and I added the information I had."

"Well, I suppose." Mizi wasn't too sure.

Rei looked at Andrew, then Mina. Andrew smiled at him. Mina nodded. "Mizi, would you be willing to help me with such things in the future? If we get you the list of petitioners and the pertinent information relating to their cases? You've been handling them quite admirably." Rei had a hint of a twinkle in his eye.

"If it becomes a matter you can't handle, you can still say you'll bring the matter to Rei's attention," Andrew reassured her. "There are always a few even he must research after he's spoken to them."

"It also puts your face before them," Mina said, looking at her pointedly.

"We could give her the Lotus office," Andrew said introspectively. "I could continue to handle the scheduling until Miss Ilena's recovered. In the end, she would likely be the better source of information for the cases anyway."

Rei looked at Dane. "Dane?"

Dane looked up from his work. "I haven't heard anything she doesn't know about yet, and a few things you missed, so that's probably about right."

Rei looked at him with a raised eyebrow. "Should I ask you to do it for her until then?"

"Ah, no." Dane looked a little horrified. "I think Mina has me plenty busy enough right now."

"You can't have him, Rei. Not for that, if you want an Earl sitting in her place." Mina didn't blink.

"Well, we'll have to keep using the Rosebud office for that, then. What do you think, Mizi?" Rei asked.

"Ahh...well, I *have* been looking for something I could do. If you think I could do that..., but I think I should ask Ilena first. I don't know what she has planned for me and what the schedule will need to be."

"Well, all the more reason to trade with Ore tomorrow, then," Rei said. "The Lotus office is right next door, so if you would need us, you could come, or send word. Also, you would still be close by for lunches." He was pointing at the wall to his left that had a small shared fireplace in it close to the hallway. Mizi had wondered what room was on the other side.

"Actually," Tairn put his chin in his hand thoughtfully, "having the Director of Intelligence also be the secretary for the Princess who you give that power to will greatly decrease the fraudulent requests. It has its benefits. And starting it now means she'll have a very good grasp of the workings of the Region early."

"And a good feel for each of the lords as well," Dane added. "I think Mistress Ilena will be pleased, really."

Mizi flushed. "Well, I'll speak with Ilena tomorrow, then."

"Excellent," said Rei. "Let Andrew know when you plan to start and he'll get the information and schedule to you. In the meantime, we'll get the Lotus office open for you." Mizi nodded, feeling overwhelmed but proud at the same time.

-o-o-o-

Ore was pleased to return to a room nearly as quiet as he'd left it. He was also pleased to not be bringing work back with him. He had to admit, though, after having even a short break, he didn't really want to lock himself up for very much longer. Just because Ilena had to be didn't really mean he did if she was feeling better.

Thayne had vacated his chair when Ore walked in, but Ore waved him back into it and sat on the bed on the other side from him, being careful not to jostle Ilena overly much. He gently touched the side of her neck, finding the heartbeat, and counted while he watched her breathe. She was still sleeping and everything seemed to be within the acceptable ranges.

He looked up and saw Thayne was watching him. He smiled. "It's become habit, eh?"

Thayne slowly smiled back. "It does appear that way. Are you going to greet her that way when she's finally up and walking?"

"Not likely."

"You could always disguise it as a hello kiss, you think?" Thayne teased.

"Hm," Ore pictured it. "That could actually work. I wonder how long it would take her to catch on?"

"Probably only once," Thayne shook his head at him.

Slowly, Ore said, "I don't know.... She seems to miss things for a while when it's me."

"Really?!" Thayne's face showed his surprise. "Not much gets past her."

Ore looked at Ilena's sleeping face. "No, that's what even I would think. But since she stopped being constantly on guard, it's become interesting."

"Hmm," Thayne wasn't sure.

"Master Ore, it's when you think such things that you need to be worried," Leah said from her corner.

Ore looked at her, "Oh?"

Leah looked up at him from her work. "If she's letting you take something now, be assured she'll demand payment later."

"You think she knows?" He hadn't thought she'd noticed at all.

"There's very little that she's not aware of. You do know what world she's lived in up until now," Leah scolded just a little.

He thought about that. "True enough." To survive in the world of predators and prey, one never let their guard down or looked the other way without a good cause. "Do you think she lets me tease her because she knows she's so difficult, then?"

Both Leah and Thayne looked at him in surprise. "It's actually possible," Leah said slowly.

Ore snorted. "Ah, you're both so serious. She's difficult because she is Ilena, and I tease because I am Ore. Miss Leah frowns at Ore's antics because she is Miss Leah, and Thayne teases Ore because he is Thayne. There doesn't have to be meaning and calculation behind everything just because one is very good at doing it."

Thayne grinned. "Well, I for one like your simplemind- ...I mean simpleness."

Ore mock frowned at him. "I think we need to test your strength. It surely must be greater than your intellect."

Thayne continued to grin, but sat back in his chair. "Are you feeling better, then?"

"When was I an invalid?" Ore asked him, deliberately misunderstanding. Then he abruptly changed to wistful. "Though, really, now that I've said it, it would be enjoyable."

"I'd be happy to spar with you any time," Thayne said, his eyes lit up with anticipation already.

"Well, not today," Ore said, "but there should be an opportunity sometime in the near future. Did you become comfortable with the castle while you were on vacation?" He unconsciously began playing with Ilena's hair that had been lying on the bed near his hand.

"I did," Thayne answered. "They wanted to toss me out for saying I'd gotten lost at the Queen Mother's quarters, but other than that, it was a pretty quiet walk."

Ore nodded. "She keeps to herself, her staff with her."

"She's well protected," Thayne said. "Her Minister of Intelligence - ah, Ilena calls them her 'Uncles' - is a serious man who has little room for play. She's told us all to not step on his toes. I hope I didn't do that when I was exploring over there."

"I understand he was somewhat pleased someone from the Family had the capacity to even try," Leah answered. "If you have need, he'll hear you."

"Oh? That's surprising," Thayne said. "Well, I'll remember it then."

Orc looked at Leah with some speculation. "So, you really are in that position to Ilena, then. I thought it was Grandfather."

Leah tipped her head at him. "Consider it more carefully, Master Ore."

It didn't take him much time. "Ah, yes. You're inside, he's outside." He nodded to himself. "Why are the two of you alternating days? You and Rio?"

"While Mistress Ilena is unable to act for herself, we will. Until she becomes, as you say, difficult, it's not necessary for us both to be here. And when you and Thayne are also here, it's even less needful."

"Is it even necessary for Ilena to be here?" Ore was just curious.

"It's only necessary for *her* to be here. The rest of us are extra." Leah said. "You've asked that because you haven't seen it yet."

Thayne nodded. "She's very formidable. The rest of us must run very hard to still be able to see her in the distance."

Ore raised his eyebrow. He thought about that. If she was constantly running ahead, watching over her would be very much like watching over his Mistress. Then he thought about the two of them together. "Ah, then I think, Thayne, that I'll need you to stay very close to her, especially when she and Mistress are together. Mistress is very much that way as well. They are bound to get into great trouble together."

He looked over to Leah. "Miss Leah and Miss Rio, too, will need to be careful that they don't become two coins rolling off the cliff together."

Leah smiled. "Rio told me about that. It's an apt description."

"Yes, I liked it too." Ore was satisfied with himself. "It was nice Rio could finally relax yesterday. Ah, and I've given her next Prince's-day night off."

"So she said," Leah said coolly.

"I shouldn't have?" Ore asked.

Leah paused. "...No, it's okay. It was merely surprising."

Ore tilted his head. "The castle is not a prison, Miss Leah. Even you may have a day off if you have need of it. Only Ilena can't, and that's more because she's not allowed to move because of her hip."

Leah looked at him surprised. "Thank you."

"Is there a time you would like to go?" Ore asked.

Leah shook her head. "I'll let you know if I should need to." Ore shrugged.

"Does that mean I get days off, too?" Thayne asked.

"Didn't you just?" Ore asked.

"Aw, that's mean. You said to stay where you could call me." Thayne pouted.

"Yes, that's the way it is," Ore nodded in sad commiseration. "When one is assigned to follow such a one, the leash is rather short. Only orders lengthen it slightly for a short time."

Thayne studied Ore. "But you don't regret it."

Ore's eyes sparkled. "It's fun to watch them."

Thayne slowly grinned again. "Well, yes, I understand that."

"But even still, if Ore needs to run, Master will have compassion on occasion. If you find yourself in that place, you must let me know. It's not good to choke a good man to death just because he must have a short leash."

"Thank you, Master Ore," Thayne said gratefully. "I'll be sure to let you know."

"Good," Ore said. He looked down in some surprise. His fingers had become quite entangled in Ilena's hair. There was quiet in the room for a while as he worked to free them without waking her up.

Ore bent down to untangle a particularly difficult knot from around one finger, amazed at how entangled he'd become, when he suddenly heard an angry sound from very nearby. "Ore!" He froze. "If you're going to wake me up, at least pay attention while you're doing it!"

He sat up suddenly, wide eyed. "I didn't mean to wake you up."

Ilena narrowed her eyes at him. "Then that is worse, Ore. Do you not understand that the scalp is very sensitive? Every stroke, twist, and pull, Ore. *Every one* has pulled me awake, and it feels like you are only making it worse. Nana, come free me of his nimble thoughtless fingers." Ore was panicking, and also looked to Leah for help. She hurried over and began gently disentangling the pair.

Ilena looked over to Thayne. "Take your Master out and exercise him. Get in a few good thumps for me, if you can. I already owe him several and he has just earned a few more." Ore waved his free hand, his mouth unable to protest. His hand was suddenly freed and it bounced up. He flexed the fingers in more mild surprise.

Ilena narrowed her eyes at him again. "Ore. Get. Out."

"Yes, ma'am," he finally said. Thayne walked out behind him, putting his hand on Ore's shoulder in sympathy.

-o-o-o-

Ilena sighed in frustration as the door closed behind the men. "He didn't mean any harm, Mistress," Leah remonstrated.

"He's smothering me, Nana! Every time I've woken up, it's he who's been here. Where is Mistress even? And surely Master Rei has need of him elsewhere. It's not necessary for him –"

"Ilena!" Ilena stopped. It wasn't often Leah used her name alone. "It *was* necessary. You may be grumpy for being thoughtlessly woken, but Ore has been trying very hard. You nearly died twice because of the experimental surgery. He has been very lost, and the rest of us haven't been much better.

"We've all been able to sleep these last three nights because he was with you, and we've been supporting him in return as best we could. Do not say things you do not understand! I have told you that often enough!"

Ilena had stared at Leah through the whole lecture with wide eyes. In a panic, she tried to answer. "Ah...ah! ...I'm sorry, Leah. I'm sorry I frightened you. I didn't mean it."

"Then don't do it again!" Leah's voice was still angry, but it held tones of the fear now as well.

"Okay. I won't," Ilena said, frantic to comfort Leah. She held out her hand to her long-time guardian and surrogate mother. After a moment of trying to decide just how angry she was, Leah's need for comfort won out. It had been a long hard three days for her.

She threw herself onto Ilena and held her, her tears of worry finally falling forth. Ilena held her in return. "I'm sorry, Nana," Ilena said again. "I won't let Elliot experiment on me anymore. But for now...I really need to be able to walk on my own again. You know that. But if it doesn't work this time, I'll give it up."

Leah sniffed and wiped her eyes. "I want to hold you to that, Mistress, but I know it's important."

"No! Really! I will! I'll find a different way." But now tears were falling from Ilena's eyes. Tears of anger and frustration. "I must, Leah! My enemy laughs in my ears continually, telling me that he's made it so. That he himself has rendered me impotent to fulfill my own plans."

She ground her teeth. "In my nightmares I'm bound chained to a throne while all of Tarc withers and the people groan and the horses writhe upon the ground - and he laughs. I look towards Selicia and it's flooded halfway up the mountains and the people struggle to remain above the water, then one by one slowly give up and sink beneath the waves and the desert people stand afar off and look in amazement - and he laughs. And, desperate to not see it, I turn to see Ryokudo and the people are bound in chains, being carried off to hell, while all of the land burns - and he laughs.

"Then he unchains me and says he will give me a gift." Her tears came in earnest. "He brings before me the people I love and thrusts a sword deep into their bellies. I rise to protect them, and my leg gives way so that I collapse on the ground, and I'm unable to move, and the hatred in their eyes stabs at me until I can no longer breathe.

"At my own tears, he laughs again, then leans down and whispers in my ears, 'Did I not tell you that it would be so much better for you to become strong before I met you again? See what I can do? What I have done to you from even this distance? I will take more than your leg, Ilena. See? I shall take it all.' ...I want to see him dead before me so badly, Leah. Dead before he can bring his plans to fruition, his laughter dead upon his lips and no longer in my ears."

Ilena bit her lip, her face a mask of misery. "I must find a way, Leah, but I can't think of one. All I can think of is how my plans have been warped if I can't do what it is I need to do. I want to just tell it all to Rei and Sasou in the hopes that they may at least protect Ryokudo, then run so far away across the sea that he can't reach me to use me for his purposes. All I can see is that if by my being here, it means he can prevent anything from acting against him, then it's me that I must remove.

"But he's already made even that move impossible." Now her voice was bitter. "Already I'm bound to my bed and to the very people he'll destroy, the people I'd hoped to use against him. They're as effective as the chains that bind me in my dream, for they won't release me to escape from his reach. In one move, he has blocked all of my plans. If I can't ride again, then he will have already won."

Ilena paused, then turned her head away, closing her eyes. "What use does Ore have of a flightless partner who can be nothing but a burden to him? You were all cruel to have made him be the one to keep me alive when it was the only way he might have been set free."

Leah collapsed onto the chair next to the bed, her hands over her mouth, not knowing what to say to comfort her mistress.

Outside the door, his forehead resting on it, Ore's hand clenched, dark emotions rolling in him. Then in one swift motion he was running, leaping, and up on the roof. Thayne watched him go sadly, very confused and hurting himself. He returned to listening, watching over his Mistress for his Master's sake. It was the only thing he could do.

-o-o-o-

Ore exercised himself. It was the only way he could get rid of the excess emotions that wanted to explode out of him. He ran until he found a hapless post and swung his sword at it viciously so he could vent on an opponent. Then sheathing his short-sword again, he shadowboxed, allowing the flowing movements to slowly calm his mind into coherence again.

When he was finally physically tired, he ran again until he found himself by 'his' tree. He was up it in an instant, the pathway already memorized by his hands and feet.

He leaned on the truck, as he'd leaned on Ilena's door, facing it with his head resting on it, his hands resting on the trunk. Hot tears stung his eyes, and his hands clenched again. He turned and dropped to sit on the branch, his arms crossed on his knees, his head resting on them. For a while he just breathed.

-o-o-o-

"Rei," Mina said quietly. He looked up. "He's in the tree again. It doesn't look good."

Rei quickly looked around. Across the courtyard outside his balcony, the place where Ore sat in the tree was almost directly level with the balcony. Mina was right. It didn't look good at all.

"I'll go." Rei walked out to the balcony, climbed on the banister and leaped to the ground. He didn't do it so much here, except when Ore was in the tree, but he used to do it all the time at Ichijou to escape from the walls of the castle there, so it was no trouble for him.

Mina and Andrew walked onto the balcony and watched from there in case they were needed. They were used to following Rei on the crazy paths he walked, and they were by now used to Ore. Mizi followed them out, her hand going to her mouth when she saw Ore huddled in the tree, Rei walking up underneath him.

"Ore," Rei called to him. There was no reaction. Rei leaned his back against the tree, in an imitation of what Andrew would do to him when he himself went to the trees for comfort.

After a while, Ore said, a bit coldly, "I didn't call for you, Master."

Rei thought about that, looking up at him again. He hadn't moved. "Is it something you think you should be able to solve on your own?"

"...Yes."

"Hmm," Rei crossed his arms and put a foot up behind him on the trunk of the tree, then he looked up at Andrew and Mina on the balcony. They recognized their cue and leaped over the banister, leaving Mizi to watch from a distance.

Having experience with Ore, they were careful to not hold any emotion and to just casually and quietly walk close to the tree on paths that would prevent his escape. They stopped at a distance they could hear, but not too close, and rested in balanced awareness.

When they were ready, Rei said to Ore, in a cross between casual and ordering, "Tell me anyway." He was looking up at Ore again and saw him shudder. That was a promising sign.

He waited. It was like looking at a cornered wild stallion who wanted to fight, but had been worn down enough that he knew he was going to have to submit, it was just a matter of time.

Rei could wait. He'd known Ore was like that a long time. Ore had given his reins to him over five years ago, had been his stallion and no one else's. Ore still held most of the wildness in him that made even Rei have to approach him again and again as if he was newly brought to the stable. That was what Andrew and Mina were for. To remind Ore he was under restraints, too.

Rei had learned that Ore actually found it somehow easier to be obedient when they were there. Not a reluctant obedience, either, but rather it eased the burden of being obedient. That was why it had been so difficult for them all the time Ore had run from Ilena and Mizi in Osterly. It was like Ilena made him even wilder, made him forget he was now a horse of the stall. It didn't look like it would be a repeat of that this time, though, thank goodness.

But then, she was come to them just as wild as Ore had. How could he not feel that pull again, be confused by it? He was to help her, but her wildness would also affect him. Rei suspected it was that conflict Ore was struggling with. It was true that Ore had the responsibility to calm her, but he wouldn't be able to do it if he wasn't calm and settled himself - and that was Rei's job.

Ore shuddered again, then actually groaned. All three on the ground were surprised. Then he was on the ground in front of Rei, one knee and a fist on the ground, his head bowed before him. They could tell it was taking all of his formidable self control to prevent himself from doing anything other than hold himself completely rock hard still.

From her angle, Mina could see Ore's jaw clench several times. She glanced at Rei, worried. He caught her look and nodded faintly. He stood up straight and looked at Ore, his own stance becoming one of relaxed readiness. "I'll hear it now," he said quietly and firmly.

Ore's formal reporting voice flowed from him as if he wasn't present, just the words were. He retold what had happened from the time his fingers had become tangled in Ilena's hair until he had left Thayne outside the door. Ilena's anger at him and sending him away. Leah's scolding of Ilena. All of Ilena's words to Leah about her dream and her despair. When his voice clipped off after her last words about him, Andrew and Mina both briefly flared in worried surprise.

Rei looked at Ore's back. He'd shown his master the burden and was waiting on him. That was good. Rei considered. Ore was right, it was his to answer as he saw appropriate. Rei had given that to him. What could Rei take, or give, that would help Ore to do what he needed to do?

"She does indeed see her opponent as very formidable," Rei said. Ore nodded once. "But we already know about him. When I'm ready, I'll hear her plan against him. He's not in a hurry - his plans have already been many years in the unfolding. In my time, I'll decide what I'll do about it." Ore barely shivered, but it was a releasing of a burden, leaving it to Rei. He seemed to breathe a little easier. That was good.

"I've said it to you already: I'll see that her rough plans are made smooth, and the way possible. My board isn't set yet." Ore took a deeper breath and nodded. Rei narrowed his eyes. He'd taken his part. The rest would be up to Ore. "She's yours, Ore. It's up to you to teach her what that means."

Ore resisted, his back tightening. "She is Master's."

Rei sighed within himself. Ore still didn't believe him from that night before, was still struggling with his position. "You are mine. Until you've trained her, she won't be mine. She is yours only, until then." Ore's back caved to the burden, but he wasn't happy.

"Yes, Master," he answered quietly, his voice much more as it should be, but that didn't mean the others relaxed. Ore stood. His face was set into controlled neutrality that gave it a coolness it didn't often have. He bowed to Rei, and Mina moved closer to Andrew to give Ore space to leave the courtyard. He turned away from them and left the courtyard, his shoulders carrying a burden he wasn't carrying smoothly yet.

Rei sighed, relaxing finally. Mina looked at Andrew, then Rei. Andrew shifted into a more relaxed posture. "*Haah.* He's still having difficulty with it, isn't he?" he said.

"She isn't an easy partner to have," agreed Rei. "I expect it will take quite some time, actually."

"Perhaps he needs to give her what she understands, first," Mina said.

The men looked at her. "I wonder if he'll see that himself?" Rei answered, and walked towards the stairs that would take him back up to his office. He could jump up to the balcony, but he wanted the excuse of a little more time to calm down and think himself.

-o-o-o-

Ore went back towards the medical wing on the ground, thinking very hard about how to teach Ilena as he went. He stopped at the infirmary first. "Ryan?" He looked around.

"Back here!" the young man called from his office.

Ore walked through the outer receiving room then the first inner patient receiving room and into the back offices of the medical staff. Ryan's was the first one so he as Head Medic would be closest to the patient room in case of an emergency. Ore leaned against the office door frame and pasted on his public smile. "Would you have a bit of time to make that tea for Ilena again? I've made her angry and I need a peace offering."

Ryan looked up surprised. "Sure." He got up. "I've also been researching medicinal aids for her emotional changes. I think I should have a tea you could give her by tomorrow."

"Oh? Ryan has been busy. It would be very nice if that would work, but we should probably keep its purpose a secret from her, neh?" He winked at Ryan.

Ryan grimaced. "Yeah, probably. I'll bring it by to try it, but you should let her maids know they can come order it any time they need it."

"You could just give them enough of the mixture they could make it up anytime they wanted." Ore looked through a pile of bagged leaves on Ryan's desk, careful not to rearrange their order.

"Well, no, it should only be given once per day, or less. I could tell them to experiment with which time of day is best." He had his head buried, looking for a component of the tea he was making for Ore.

"I'll be right back," Ore said to him and disappeared into another room in the infirmary. He was a common fixture there, so no one paid him any mind. He was back just before Ryan had the tea ready for him. He thanked Ryan, then left with the tea, stopping briefly in the empty front area to add something to it, then continued on.

When he reached Thayne and the door guards, he ordered, "When I send Miss Leah out, don't let her back in until I've said it. You aren't to enter either." They nodded. He knocked once and entered the room.

Leah was back in her corner, and Ilena was resting in her bed. Ore walked up to the bed, his expression unreadable. "Ilena, I'm sorry I made you angry. I've brought you some tea, will you drink it?"

She turned her head and looked at him solemnly in the eyes. "I'm sorry to have been unnecessarily angry with you, Ore," she said. "I'll drink it."

He sat in the chair and lifted her head to help her drink it. He had the cup just pressed to her lips, about to pour it, when he stopped and took it away. She looked up at him in surprise. "Perhaps I should taste it first to make sure it isn't too hot still." He lifted the cup to his own lips.

"No!" she reached for it. "You mustn't!"

He paused. "Why not?" he looked at her coolly.

"It...it's been poisoned," she was almost afraid to admit it. Leah looked up in alarm.

"Ilena, why would you willingly drink it then?" he asked her.

Her eyes were very round. "Because I have immunity," she said almost breathlessly.

"Ilena, that isn't right. I've told you already to be aware of yourself. You are not to put yourself in danger. I won't tolerate it again." She lowered her eyes and apologized. "...And why would you prevent me from drinking it?"

"Because it's safer to assume you don't have immunity," she answered.

Ore leaned back in the chair. "Ilena, what would you do if you saw my unprotected back and couldn't move?"

"Aahhh, I would call out to you, or send someone to defend you." Her eyes were still round when she looked back at him and she seemed confused.

Ore stood and carefully poured the poisoned drink into the vase, then turned the cup upside down on its saucer. "Miss Leah, please see that this is properly disposed of and clean them very well." He handed her the vase and the cup and saucer. She took them, bowed, and left the room.

When Leah was gone, Ore walked over to Ilena and stood over her. "It has never been necessary up until now for you to protect me upon your own two feet, with your presence. Yet you have done so anyway, very capably, from a distance and without my knowing. Why is it you believe that being in the place where I am changes that?" She stared at him, no answer forthcoming.

Carefully placing his words together, Ore continued, "Master explained to me that you've worked very hard to become what you believe my perfect partner would be, but you haven't been here to learn it yet. I don't know what you believe you now lack because you've been injured, but I don't see anything lacking before me save one thing.

"That one thing I've promised Master I'll teach you. It isn't acceptable to me that you attempt to learn it on your own." Ilena blinked. "It's your duty to learn it from me," Ore told her with finality. She nodded. She understood what he was saying, even though she didn't know yet what he was going to teach her.

"I wish you to understand another thing," he continued, and his voice became hard. "I'm a very selfish partner. I didn't watch over you because I was ordered to. I watched over you because Master knew I would defy him if he didn't allow it. *I* have made you to stay alive because *I* wished for you to stay alive. Because I wish for you to be my partner, you'll not run from it." Ilena shivered and tears began to form in her eyes.

"You chose to live so you could answer Master's questions. In his own time, he'll hear you and make the way smooth and will defeat his enemy and yours. It's your responsibility to allow him to do that." Ilena's hands clenched, then she forcibly relaxed and nodded slightly. Even if it was her plan, she'd already decided before even coming that she would have it be Rei's test. It wasn't something she didn't already know.

Ore hesitated. There was one more thing that needed doing, but it would likely complicate matters for a time. One more restraint needed to be laid. He looked at her closely. No, it would need to be done, or she wouldn't understand.

Firmly pushing aside his own doubts and fears, he bent over her with one knee on the bed and put his hands on either side of her head. Putting his lips to hers, he gave her the passionate kiss he had threatened her with earlier. He held it just until he felt her body respond, then he let it go and lifted himself enough to look into her eyes.

She looked as miserable and lost as he'd felt when she was slipping away towards death. "You are mine because you've already given yourself to me," he said, stating the fact her body hadn't been able to deny, "but until you've learned what it is I'll teach you, I can't accept you." He stood back up and looked at her, his own emotions still a very deep river flowing swiftly, although calmer now.

Ilena's face slowly crumpled and tears began to fall. Her hand clenched at her heart. "Is-is that...a promise, Ore?" It looked like it hurt her to breathe.

He put his hand on her head, then ran it down to her cheek to wipe the tears from her eye. "Yes," he said gently. He sat beside her on the bed, not touching her, while she held her hands over her face and sobbed.

When Ilena recovered, she was also calmer. Her own immediate worries and fears had been addressed and settled, even if it was with promises of future resolution. Ore had taken her recovery time to work out how to put into words what he wanted to help her learn.

As he spoke, Ilena gave him her close attention. "Ilena, you came here before you were ready, forced by the circumstances you were put into. You've said that your goal is to stand behind Master at the side of Ore, supporting Mistress. Was that your goal even if you'd come of yourself?"

Ilena paused, considering. "On the board of nations, that's the most effective place for me to stand in order for there to be peace in Ryokudo and between the surrounding nations." Her face wrinkled in sorrow. "There are few places for me to stand, and many of them are places of dark sorrow and loneliness. In that place, I can give what I have to give to all the people of the nations.

"If I can't be given that place, then I would wish to be set free of what I am so I can hide myself in a place of my choosing where all the world can continue to believe the princess died with her family. Death is my only other option, because I can't abide any of the others available to me."

Her eyes looked sorrowfully into Ore's. "I can't be a trophy wife tied to a lord who will answer to Sasou and refuse to let me act, nor can I be a prisoner in a far castle. I was born to be a princess and to lead, and I have my Grandfather's intelligence and capacity."

She bit her lip. Not really wanting to say it out loud, she told Ore, "Sasou knows even better than I what dangers I bring with me. This position is one he's willing to allow me to work in and live. I'm not sure he *would* let me live if we can't make it happen, although I'm sure he's thought of what alternatives he would find acceptable."

Ilena closed her eyes and turned her head away from Ore a little. "Even so, perhaps I didn't really believe it when I believed I would be able to walk through the castle gate on my own. Perhaps I still held onto a belief that I would be able to find another way." She breathed quietly for a few breaths. "I've been trying to accept that this is where I am and that I can only walk forward from here. ...It's still difficult."

194

Ore let her rest for a bit. "Master's already said it, that you'll stand in that place. There's only the one thing you need to learn." Her eyes turned to look at him again.

"At Tokumade, we were made to be, forced to serve, punished for the slightest wrong, silenced. That isn't how to learn proper service. When I chose to serve Master, and follow after Mistress, I learned that service offered is light. Because I *want* to serve, and have chosen for myself, it isn't a burden.

"I need to know that you're choosing to serve." He was very serious. "If you decide you're still being forced to serve, you'll never understand. In not understanding you'll eventually do harm to yourself or others."

He tipped his head a little to consider her, to see if she was understanding what he was saying. "Master's heard you. He's willing to let you serve in the way you've *asked* to serve. If I go to him and say that you can only serve unwillingly, he'll let you go. He's not the kind of master who desires to force others to serve him. He wishes to have his friends and companions surrounding him."

Ilena looked down briefly, then back into Ore's eyes. "I have learned that," she agreed with him. "It's different, and preferable most certainly, to serve someone like that. Still...I'm not confident."

Ore shook his head a little. "No. After serving Pakyo where you of necessity had to be strong and fight against him, I would imagine you wouldn't be." He blinked at her. "That's what I must teach you, what I also had to learn: how to properly serve a master that's worthy of service.

"There's a time to hold your tongue and allow them to learn by their own mistakes. There's a time to speak your words so they don't fall and cause great harm to themselves or those who are beneath them. Always you must be obedient, but it comes from your own heart's desire to see they're strengthened to the best ability you have to do it."

He smiled gently at Ilena. "You already know those things, but you haven't been able to practice them. If you'll trust me to, I'll teach them to you, since I also had to learn them late, after I was already willful and strong. It isn't difficult if it's a thing you desire to learn. It only takes the time of practice and understanding the finer points that aren't obvious."

Ilena blinked at him and ran her hand over her blanket a little, as she did when she was feeling impatient and closed in by her circumstances. "It's okay if you only learn to serve Master and Mistress," he reassured her. "I also only serve them.

"But," he wouldn't let her eyes turn from his, "if I'm to be your teacher, you must practice with me first until you understand. You must trust me, that I won't lead you astray. You're my partner, so I wish to see that you reach your goal. What are you willing to do to reach it?"

Ore sat patiently for another minute, then rose to his feet. Kindly he said, "I'll give you the time to think on it. It isn't simple to come to the answer when the heart must be the one to agree, and the mind must see the way for all of you to settle to it."

He moved to the other bed, removed his boots, and lay down on his back in his thinking pose - one leg resting on the other raised knee, hands clasped behind his head. He'd also been allowed time, more than once actually, to decide it for himself, that he would follow Rei. It was right for Ore to practice what Rei had done if he wished for Ilena to learn what he'd learned. He would have to do that a lot, actually.

He spent his thinking time going back over his own lessons remembering what Rei had done to help him. Ilena would be different, and even Ore would be different from Rei, so he would learn new things as they worked together from now on. Still, he knew what the important things were, the things he cared about Ilena knowing so she could stand properly in her place behind Mizi strengthening Rei and even Ore himself because strengthening them would be a strength to him.

Ore fell asleep thinking, but then Ilena did as well since she was still recovering. When the dinner cart was announced with a knock on the door, Ore woke up and brought it into the room. The scents of the meal woke Ilena up. Ore took care of her as usual without commenting on their earlier conversation.

After they'd both eaten, the cart returned outside the room, and Ilena properly cleaned and the wound inspected (it was still fine), Ore sat down on his bed, cross-legged, leaned against the wall, and closed his eyes. He remembered many things from his past and he wondered many things about Ilena's past as well.

"Ore," Ilena said quietly after some time had passed.

He opened his eyes and unfolded himself to rise from his bed and walk to her side. "Yes, Ilena?"

"Please, teach me. To have come this far and not tried my best ...it wouldn't be a faithful effort for all of what I've done until now," she requested.

Ore gave a single nod. "It's okay to have to learn it again and again, what it is you want to do, until you remember it. Tell me, what is it you wish to do?"

Ilena looked at him calmly. "I want to learn to serve Master Rei and Mistress Mizi as Ore serves - with peaceful joy."

Ore smiled. "I would be happy to teach you how to do that."

-o-o-o-

For the remainder of that day and all of the next, Ore let no one into the room, and he didn't leave it. Rei wasn't surprised when Mizi arrived at the office instead of Ore. When she told him Ore had gone into seclusion with Ilena, he nodded and said that Ore would come when it was time.

The third day, Ore appeared briefly in the Rose office in the afternoon to read his reports from Falcon's Hollow and write the summaries for Rei. He wouldn't speak unless directly asked a question that related to the work, and he refused Mizi's request to speak with Ilena, saying when she was ready, he would let her know.

Before he left, but a few hours after he'd come, Rei put down his pen and asked Ore if he'd allowed Doctor Elliot to check on Ilena. "It isn't necessary. She's recovering. This morning the tendon showed signs of proper grafting. He'll see her when she's ready." Ore said briefly, then was gone.

"It's been two days, Rei," Mizi said, worried.

"That's not very long for Ilena," Rei said. "I wouldn't be surprised if it should take longer than a month, although I can't give him longer than a week at this time."

"But, I don't understand," Mizi said, her frown deepening.

"Mizi," Andrew said, and she turned to him. "It's because she can't leave the room. The reason Ore sits in the tree outside Rei's balcony is because when Rei taught Ore what it was to walk with Rei, he was in his quarters at night, and during the day he was in the office or in the courtyard outside - somewhere he could hear Rei's voice and answer him."

"When Andrew was teaching me to accept the service I needed to learn to give," Rei added, "he followed me everywhere until I learned to want to not be away from him, and over time I was able to settle for fewer trips away and for less distance."

"But it wasn't until Mizi was here that you chose to be serious about staying where you should," Mina added.

Andrew nodded. "You've never needed such training Mizi. You already see your goals and have great personal capacity to serve where you best can."

"If Ilena weren't injured, but could walk, it's likely she would be here with us in the office," Rei took up the explanation. "She would already be helping you as your secretary, but we would keep her close to us until she was comfortable with how to be in the castle. Even with Ore sitting with her this week, she'll still need that help when she can finally move about.

"Up until now, she's only been the power in her own House. While learning to exercise power responsibly has been good for her, she's only had the practice of constantly working against the lord set over her. We need her to learn how to work *with* us. When Ore left the tree last, Mina said that he needed to give Ilena something she understood first. That's what he's doing. He's giving her one man - himself - to look to. He'll be able to broaden her capacity, and help her to become stronger for her duties here.

"When I send Ore to collect the last set of witnesses and we go to confront Earl Shicchi, it will be you who'll need to sit in his place and help her understand that what she's learning for Ore also applies to you, and by extension to each of us. In that thing, you must overcome your own tendency to be overly obedient to all others. Her way of being makes you want to relate to her the way you relate to my brother, the King.

"You can't allow it. She must respond to you as if you were me or Ore. You've done well so far, but we'll be gone for weeks. You must have the strength to maintain it until we return. Her ladies, Leah and Rio, and Grandfather also, already know how to help her, and you may turn to them for assistance, but you yourself must show her your strength always, as you've done for Ore. However, Ore doesn't resist you. Ilena will continuously test you.

"I would like you to consider it carefully before Ore allows you to be with her again, so that you know how to face her." Rei stopped and looked at Mizi. She was looking a bit overwhelmed. It was a request that would usually end up putting her into a panic, of the sort she usually needed help with. But at the same time, she already had practice with that sort of thing with Prince Amiran of Yamanzar, and somewhat with Ore and Rei themselves.

"If you like," Mina said, apparently thinking along the same lines, "you may consider it as if Prince Amiran has come to visit and his aide has asked you to give him some intensive training while they were here."

"Ah, she's as bad as that?" Mizi was doubtless thinking of her first experience with that prince who'd demanded she show up in his castle just for him to put her on display next to him because of her hair. She had run away from Yamanzar, leaving only a length of her hair behind, saying that if he desired her for her hair, he could have that only.

That was how Rei had met her just inside the Ryokudo border from Yamanzar and she'd come to be with them. Prince Amiran was now much better after she'd visited with him several times, but most especially after the time Rei had come to him and they'd rescued her from her kidnapping.

"Well, it's different, but yes," the other three all agreed.

"*Hahhh,*" Mizi sighed. "Well, then, yes, I'll consider it properly. ...Although so far she's behaved properly with me."

"That's because she was training you to understand her, and walking carefully. You must determine if what she's doing is training you properly, or testing the boundaries of proper behavior. You do remember what she was like the times Ore wasn't with us, don't you?" Rei raised his eyebrow in question.

"Ah...yes." Mizi did. While Ilena had done good things, it had often been without restraint. "I'll help her understand."

"Good," Rei smiled at her. "I'll leave it to you, then, when we're gone."

CHAPTER 11 Preparing for the Final Act

On the fourth day, Ore let Doctor Elliot in to inspect Ilena. The surgeon pronounced the graft a tentative success and stitched the incision closed so that it would begin to heal properly. Ore wouldn't allow him to stay and visit, however, making it a business trip only. When asked to report on the visit, Doctor Elliot said Ilena had been quiet, only answering his questions about the graft and her health in general, but she'd been alert.

On the evening of the fifth day, Ore appeared at the balcony of the Rose office just before the dinner hour. As he walked into the room on his own, he looked at Rei and said, "Leah is feeding her dinner tonight. We'll see how she does."

"That's good," Rei looked back at him, "because your time is getting short. I need you to be ready to go soon."

"Hehh. Well, it might be enough for now. When?" Ore stopped by Rei's desk.

Rei answered, "I'd like to send the order for the first clandestine wave to move out tomorrow. That puts your time to move out in two days. If necessary I can wait another day, if Grandfather can get them all collected as fast as the last set."

"Two days.... And how long will we be gone?" Ore asked.

"I'm planning on three weeks. It depends on how much clean up there is, though."

Ore's eyes widened a little. "That's a long time for Mistress to be in charge, isn't it? Well, I have a thing in place to help with that. ...But Master! We'll be gone for your birthday! That will be a sad thing."

"What? My birthday? Eh, I guess so." Rei hadn't even considered it. He wondered briefly if he was going to be stepping on any lord's toes and sensibilities to skip any celebrations at the castle for his first birthday there as Regent - although he didn't mind it himself.

"Well...maybe that could be another incentive to help Ilena." Ore turned to Mizi. "Mistress, if she behaves for you, when we return, we'll have a birthday party for Master in her room. You may tell her when it seems best to you. If you decide she may have it, I'll use it to test her resolve." He looked at Andrew and Mina. "And, shall we have it anyway?"

"I think so," Mina looked pleased, her chin in her hand, already plotting.

Andrew nodded. "It would be good to have a short break before we must become very busy with the final preparations."

"Then, Master, if the time is that short, I'll go have dinner with Grandfather. I shouldn't be away for too long."

Rei nodded and handed him the list back. "Do you understand the plan well enough to coordinate with Grandfather?"

"Has anything changed?"

Rei shook his head. "We're still expecting the flood to hit right after you deliver them. Make sure you're not caught up in it. If you come by before you head out, we'll give you an update on the full-scale plans."

"Okay," Ore said, and headed for the balcony door. "I'll send for you soon, Mistress, so we can see how Ilena will do. If there are things that need correcting before I go, they shouldn't be left undone."

-o-o-o-

Ore headed out the Pelican gate and started walking in the direction of the Scholar's Tavern. He put his hands behind his head and gave a whistle. Shortly a middle teen girl popped out from the usual crowd walking the broad street between the outer wall of the castle grounds and the buildings of Nijoushi. She walked with him, her hands behind her back, humming a jaunty tune.

He listened to it for a bit. "That's a good song. Is it new?"

"Yeah," she said. "The traveling entertainers were here last week. They brought it up from the coast. Said it was a new one from one of the places across the sea, translated of course. It's pretty popular in town right now."

"Ehhh...do you think you can remember it to sing it later, after we get back? I like it."

She tipped her head. "Yes. I can remember anything."

"Well, then remember to tell Grandfather to come meet me at the Scholar's Tavern. I'll be in an upstairs room. And tell him I'm sorry to make him come in a hurry - I've not got much time."

"Heh. Yeah, you've got a pretty bird in a cage that will miss you too much if you're gone too long."

Ore reached over and tweaked her ear. "Maybe."

The girl laughed and skipped away. "Let Ma and Pa know I'm on my way, too," he called after her. She waved at him without turning to look, then disappeared.

Ore stretched. He'd been inside a long time. He'd take the upper route and exercise some. At the next shadowed section, he was up on a roof and running. It felt good to stretch on the jumps between houses and shops and get the blood pumping on the runs in between. The climbs up and down the sides of the buildings between crossing the broader streets used his arm and back muscles in good ways as well. It also felt good to know Ilena might actually be able to do it with him, maybe within the year even.

Although she wasn't allowed to flex her leg for these six weeks, whenever he put his hand over the graft site to see how the recovery was going, the tendon and muscle both reacted together. Oddly enough she never complained about it, even though he was sure it was still painful. The last time he'd done it, he'd watched her face to see why. It had made him smile to see the look of triumph in her eyes.

He was pleased with her progress. It had taken them the first full day to understand each other, but she was a willing student, perhaps a little over-eager, even. She was going to be unhappy with him leaving in such a short time, but really it was about right. It would force her over-eagerness to be moderated as it should be, and give her proper practice.

He just wished they weren't going to be gone quite so long. It would be better if he could pick it back up when he returned, but Rei wouldn't let him take any more full days or weeks off just before the Lord's Court.

Ore stopped across the street from his goal and looked around the ground below him. No one was watching, so he slipped down into the space between the buildings on his side of the street, then walked out and across the street to the Scholar's Tavern.

He walked in and Ella met him. "If you'll come this way please," she turned and led him up the stairs to one of the smaller conference rooms.

It was his first time upstairs and he looked around, interested. The rooms were all around the outside, so that if you had neighbors it was to either side, but there weren't many common walls like there would have been if they were all centrally located. There was a center area and when he asked her she said it was a large party room that could be reserved for special occasions.

Ella explained that usually entailed reserving the entire tavern in order to keep the noise from filtering downstairs, so it wasn't done often. There were occasional small weddings there, though. Most scholars who got married didn't have loud raucous weddings after all, but if they thought they might, they made them reserve the whole place.

She ushered him into his room and took his drink order. He kept it light, to a single large beer. He wanted more, but he had lots of reasons to not do that tonight. While he waited, he pulled out his list again and re-read it. Rei had made a few notes on it and Ore took note of them.

Grandfather arrived with the food and drink, and Ella brought enough for him, too. Ore thought that was pretty fast for an old guy to show up. Either he was more spry than he let on, or the network was fast. Or perhaps he just lived close by, but somehow Ore suspected that wasn't it. It had taken him quite a while to show up the last time Ore had called him out at the castle without prior warning.

"Good evening, Grandfather," Ore said. "Thank you for coming to visit with me on short notice."

"Good evening, Father." Grandfather settled at the table in the chair opposite Ore. "I'm glad to be able to see your face again."

Ella finished setting the plates and mugs before them and walked out, closing the door behind her. Ore waited until he heard her footsteps walking away, taking the opportunity to begin eating.

He could see Grandfather taking note of why he paused. He was looking a little worried, but it was no wonder. He hadn't heard anything official out of the castle since before Ilena had gone under for the beginning of the experimental surgery.

"What do you know, unofficially?" Ore asked him, spearing another piece of meat and adding it to the potato already on his fork.

"That the first surgery failed and the second has apparently taken, and that you've got her in seclusion." Grandfather answered easily, but a little uncomfortably.

"Umhm. That's the official word, too." Ore didn't look up at him, but was monitoring his responses. "We nearly lost her during the second surgery, and again later that night, but she was good and came back for us. She's quite triumphant that the tendon is responding well, although she isn't to test it until the six weeks of bone healing are completed." Ore paused to eat and think about what he would say next.

"I've told her if she does well while I'm gone, she can begin to have visits with you again." This time he did look up to watch Grandfather's face. It was tight. "Is there a thing I should know?" Ore asked without appearing too interested.

The old man looked down at his plate, trying to decide how to respond. He took another slow bite. "Are you sure she'll be able to succeed? You'll be gone a long time, no?"

Ore considered. Grandfather was right. It wouldn't really be fair to Ilena if it was going to be too long for her. Finally he said, "I'll ask Miss Leah to keep watch for me. If it looks like Mistress isn't strong enough to help her succeed, I'll allow Miss Leah to call for you." Ore looked him in the eye. Grandfather nodded, looking relieved.

They ate in silence a moment longer, then Ore pushed the last list over to Grandfather. Grandfather picked it up and looked at it, also carefully reading Rei's notes. He put the list back down, and tapped it, his face creased in concentration. "When are you expecting the flood?"

"Right after I deliver them, but I'm not to get caught up in it," Ore answered.

Grandfather nodded again. "That's what we're figuring, too. Are you taking the direct route in?"

Ore shook his head. "The logging path detour. Can you send a decoy group down the direct route?"

"Done. Shall we cross paths at the join?" Grandfather took a bite of his dinner.

Ore shook his head. "We can't afford to go through the ambush spot above there. Can you hide your group in the rocks at the North Road-Castle Road split, then as soon as you hear us coming, head down that way? We'll pause there for fifteen minutes, then follow your group down."

Grandfather tipped his head, thinking. "Yes, that should work, although we could just remove the roadblock for you. Then you wouldn't have the opportunity to get jumped during those fifteen minutes."

Ore shook his head. "The ones who are waiting fifteen minutes aren't us. They're another decoy, from the garrison. We're trying to lead as many south as possible so the northern enemy forces won't get reinforcements. We expect one group to follow your first group down and the ambush spot will only have token resistance, meant to feel out the strength of your group, and weaken it a little.

"Our decoy will be bringing in another group of them. We don't want them to cross, that's why we'll wait. Your group will need to pull both sets on down the road, preferably with no evidence left behind, before our group gets to that spot." He paused to see if Grandfather understood. He nodded a tight nod.

"Take them out as far down the road as possible, even to the safe house if you want. We'll keep coming up behind you and take out what's between us before we turn and take out what's coming behind. But we'll want your help for those, or we'll be sandwiched. That could be bad." Grandfather had a speculative look in his eye.

"What we need to know is where I'm to pick everyone up from and coordinate a starting point." Ore paused pointedly. "The closer to the castle I can pick them up, the longer I'll have with Ilena. I have to leave no later than three days out if I have to go collect them all myself. Master wants them at the safe house by six days from now."

Grandfather pursed his lips. Ore drank from his mug as he waited. The old man shook his head. "The farthest out will go to the closest garrison, but that's as far as they'll go without seeing your face. The next set will only go so far as to meet you at an inn at the same town they live in so they can go back home without anyone being the wiser if you don't show up.

"The last set I can get out and to a temporary safe home here. I can even get them down to the safe house itself if you'll let us take them early, and don't mind breaking the required coding. They've already seen you, so they're all ready to go, without you saying anything to them." He smiled a little ruefully. "Sorry it's easy the wrong direction, but that's because of the protections they need."

Ore shrugged. "That still cuts out some of the travel time." He handed a pen over to his dining companion. "Write down the total number and ages coming with each one. We'll need to know for the decoys. It would help to have the number of blades, too, just so I know." While Grandfather wrote, Ore considered the last set.

It would be convenient to let them go on down, but it didn't sit well with him. If he didn't hear their answer, he wouldn't feel right letting them in with everyone else whom he'd protected. If someone slipped through that shouldn't, that would be a problem. He was already worried someone who shouldn't have had heard the code, and would get through. The only thing that helped with that was that he now knew how to see them. However, that still meant he had to see the last set, too.

"Could you have the last set meet us on the logging path? The guards watching that path won't be friendly to anyone but who I bring in, so your folks shouldn't come down it too far, but I can let them know that we're rendezvousing there. Do you think you can get them there without being followed?"

"We'll take out anyone who does follow," Grandfather shrugged. Ore was reminded of Foster when he'd told them they wouldn't keep anyone alive unless they made a special request. They all seemed so mild and friendly up until they casually mentioned protecting themselves so completely.

"Ah, I should say, even though we're letting your outside help the inside, don't mix, and don't assume you can be neighborly afterwards. That will have to wait until after the Lord's Court. We want to keep things nice and clean up until it's all over." Grandfather nodded and Ore reached for the list.

Ore was glad to see the number of children was minimal, two teens and one youngster, with two of them coming from the closest group. He'd only have one teen from the second group. Everyone else was adults, and really only single adults, the exception again being the family with the two children.

So there would be two males to meet up with at the garrison, then a single male, a single female and her teenage son at the second location. Then they would meet up with the family of four and and another single male at the logging trail. Perfect. The decoys could all be from the garrison and useful blades.

He pointed to the second group. "Can they all ride, or do we need a carriage?"

Grandfather read the names again. "She can't ride, but her son can. They could double up. All of the others can, and are anticipating it."

Ore looked up at him in pleased surprise. "We can ride hard from the top?"

Grandfather nodded smiling at him. "If you want, we'll give you waypoints to trade horses at. You won't have to stop except for quick meals and short naps that way. On the way out, too. If you want, the first place will keep your horse for you to finish with on the way back, although I know he likes to run as much as you do."

"No...," Ore was thoughtful, "that would be good for him. He'll have to run hard from when I get him until I get up north. If he doesn't have to do the full thing it won't ruin him. I like that idea. How long from start to finish, then? When do I need to leave the castle?"

Grandfather pulled a piece of paper out of his jacket and handed it to Ore. It was a map with locations, dates, and times marked on it. "This is your itinerary. Just update the dates to when you want to arrive and work your way back. Don't lose it or let it out of your sight. You know what will happen if you do."

Ore nodded. He'd get everyone killed is what would happen, including the waypoint families. He looked carefully at times. They were pushing him hard on the way out, but that's what he'd done the first time. They even knew how long he could go and how long he napped for.

"You were keeping a good watch the first time, weren't you?" he asked, appreciatively. Grandfather said nothing, just took a drink from his mug. Ore felt a bit of smugness from him, though.

He put his finger on the garrison farthest out. He'd send out his first decoy there, a duplicate of himself to continue on, then disappear. They'd make it look like he'd left a message and a small squad was being sent back along the route he'd come. He pointed it out to Grandfather and told him how much time he expected to stay there and when they would leave, asking him to update their notes so that they were on the same page. Grandfather nodded and Ore looked at the return route.

He was pleased the only public place they would be during the whole trip was the tavern he would pick up the second set from. "Is it run by Family?" Ore asked.

Grandfather shook his head. "You'll have to lay low in that town. The whole place is owned by the enemy. The first two will wait for you outside town. We do have people that will help you get in, and help everyone get out, though.

"As soon as you get into town, pause by the well. A child will take your hand and ask you to help find his mother. Go with it and he'll lead you to her. They'll hand you off to each other in like manner until you get where you need to be.

"Let them come to you once you're in the tavern. If each of you are happy, they'll leave first and meet up with you at the other side of town. You'll be led out in a similar fashion to how you were led in, but each one of you will be going different routes. The first two will collect them if it looks dangerous for them before you get there, so you'll just have to find them. Look for the two headed cat.

"The next distance is short," Ore looked at it and saw it was so. "That's because you'll have to ride double to get there. The horses won't be able to go as far, but you'll get more horses there." Ore saw the next napping point was the following stopover. It would be very early in the morning. Then riding hard all the way to the safe house. So still roughly two and a half days.

That didn't cut off much time, but it meant he'd have one last night with Ilena and could get his final orders the next morning, instead of having to get them in the afternoon and leave by sunset in two days. That would be easier. She still needed him more at night than during the day, and he wasn't any different. Ore sighed. Grandfather looked at him. "Is it not okay?"

"Ah, it's not that. The itinerary is fine." Ore folded it up and put it in his jacket along with the list of names. "It's what comes after that."

Grandfather looked at him with a commiserating smile. "Yes. Long battles are always horrible things that are just necessary and nothing else. Always takes fortitude to get through them. ...Are you taking Thayne with you?"

Ore considered. He hadn't thought of it yet. "I won't, but Ilena will make it happen somehow anyway. He's a steadying influence for her, but she all but told me when she sent me to get him that she'd be sending him with me up north. When he meets up with me, I won't send him away."

Grandfather looked approving. "It's always good to have someone watching your back in larger battles like this one. And...," his face got very serious, "if Father falls, Mother will follow."

Ore stopped and looked at him sharply. "Even if I've been training her not to?"

Grandfather looked at him as if he were a young child who understood nothing. "Ore," It was the first time anyone in the Family outside the castle had used his first name and it surprised him. "Don't you know yet what you are to her? What she is? What her ultimate goal is?"

"...You know?" Ore asked him. Grandfather nodded, still looking him in the eye. That's right, he was one of the Immediate Family. That made sense, that he would know. Ore blinked and considered the other man's words. "*Haaah.* Yes, she will, won't she? ...I'll be careful." In their role reversal this week, he'd forgotten. He was hers.

Ore leaned back, holding onto the edge of the table with one hand, his other hand draped over the back of his chair. The tips of the fingers holding the table tapped quietly on the table as he looked at Grandfather appraisingly. "One last question." Grandfather nodded. "How much support is the Family going to give Master's forces?"

Grandfather didn't look quite surprised at the question. He did grin to let Ore know he'd won points. "Rather a lot, actually. We were hoping to learn what the sign was to be known as friendlies so there wasn't Family caught in the crossfire."

Ore reached into his jacket pocket again and drew out a simply drawn falcon with its wings spread wide, white on black, with a half waxing moon over it's head, three arrows in its claws. "That's the symbol of our falconess we fight for. Put it someplace easy to spot, but keep it covered until the battle is joined. You know what will happen if it's discovered early."

Grandfather took it and touched it a bit reverently. "It's a message to *him*, isn't it?" He looked back up at Ore his eyes round.

Ore nodded. "Master is very angry."

Grandfather slowly grinned a big and very predatory grin. "We're looking forward to that hunt. He's been hurting Mother for a very long time."

"Hmm," Ore leaned forward to rest his elbow on the table. "Scary. An entire household out for revenge. Twice." But his eyes were the same as Grandfathers, and his grin matched as well. Then he stood. "Well, I'll be glad to be able to run with them, then. I'll be going up late, with Thayne I assume. So tell them to be looking for me to come from behind, but end up first in line.

"Earl Shicchi is mine, though I'm not fool enough to take him on alone. The uncle is Rei's. Make sure he's not alone either, although he'll have Mister Andrew and Miss Mina along, of course. Watch over them, too. They've finally decided to get married and we'd like to see it actually happen."

Ore set his payment down on the table and started to walk towards the door. He paused and looked back. "Oh, by the way, I'm officially Father, but until she's finished with her training, we're not a couple. And until King Brother okay's it, we're not married."

Grandfather looked at him, then nodded. "I'll let the rest of the Immediate Family know."

Ore nodded back, then let himself out. On his way back to the castle, he wondered who else was in the Immediate Family. He only knew of the four, Mother, Father, Leah, and Grandfather, and he still didn't know Leah's title.

Maybe it was time for another lesson with Thayne...or maybe it could wait until they were on the road together. As he ran the roofs back to the castle, he was thinking he would like that bit of the adventure waiting ahead.

-o-o-o-

Ore stopped by at the Rose office first, although he could feel that he'd already been gone too long from Ilena. He quickly showed Rei, Andrew, and Mina the map he'd been given. He summarized the conversation, including that they could expect decent support from the household in both locations of battle. Then, telling them he'd come get his final orders the third morning from then, he headed back out the door and hurried to Ilena's room.

As he expected, Ilena glared at him in annoyance, but she was good and didn't say anything. He asked Leah for her report, then excused her.

Ore sat on the bed next to Ilena and looked at her mildly. "Get used to it."

Her look changed to one of confusion, then she sighed. "Master Rei's ready then?" Ore nodded and rewarded her with a small smile. Ilena looked at him sadly for a moment. Then her eyes went hard, and he was again reminded of Foster and Grandfather and thought that the symbol they'd chosen was very appropriate. She was the falconess in that moment.

"Kill them, Ore. Of all the people, in all the chaos, make sure *they* don't leave the mountain alive." She looked at him a moment longer, her expression unwavering. "I know Master Rei has thought of the option of keeping me alive by treating with uncle. Don't let him do it. I won't live. I'll choose death first, killing him first if I can."

Ore, remembering what Grandfather had reminded him of, changed what he would have said. "Yes, My Lady." She looked at him surprised, then with gratitude. "Ilena, I'll be having Mistress come in briefly tomorrow while I'm here. She has a thing she's been wanting to talk to you about."

Ilena's eyes widened. He could tell she was excited to see Mizi. Then her eyes narrowed. She kept her mouth shut, but he could see she was fighting to not speak. He made her wait until she had her impatience under control, then he nodded. "You may say it."

"That means you're leaving within three days. That will be difficult," she complained calmly.

"It amazes me how you already know all of this. Are you sure you haven't had to learn it all before?" It was a light tease, meant to be more practice for her in curbing her impatience.

She was able to let that pass acceptably. "Of course I have," she said calmly. "I've lived in a castle before."

Ore was puzzled. "How old were you when you left?"

"Seven...going on forty, or so they told me," Ilena answered.

"So is it a problem with you being too young at the time? Or too much time between then and now?" he asked.

"If it was a problem with age, they wouldn't have called me Mother from the beginning." That was true. He'd experienced that himself. "It's that I've received too much training from my enemy, but that's a story for when Master Rei is ready for it."

Ore was taken aback by that answer. "Is that why you're so eager to be retrained?" he asked slowly. Her eyes became blank slates. He sighed. She did that when she had too many answers and didn't know which one to pick. He reworded it. "Is that one of the reasons you're so eager to be retrained?"

She waited an appropriate amount of time to recover and then even took the time to word the answer thoughtfully. "Yes, Ore, it is," but he could see the fires of hatred burning in her eyes. That had been a difficult success.

He rewarded her by brushing her cheek with the back of his hand. She half-closed her eyes and rubbed her cheek on his hand, in a good imitation of a raptor interacting with its handler.

He lifted a lock of hair between his fingers and, as he slid his hand down it to return his hand to himself, he answered her. "It will be three mornings from now. I hope you'll continue to do your best."

Ilena shivered and closed her eyes. He could see her in his mind's eye, a distressed falcon with its feathers fluffed, its head turned away and down. If she could have moved, she would probably have curled up.

He encouraged her, knowing that she didn't want to have him gone that long. "What will you use to reward yourself for doing well, Ilena? What will keep moving you forward?"

She opened her eyes and looked at him, the falcon in his mind turning it's head to look at him, although it was still hunched. After thinking for a moment, she answered him, "When I miss Ore, I'll run with him in my mind. When I need a reason to keep moving forward I will soar above the army and smell the blood of my enemies." Then she sighed. "And when I need to throw a tantrum, I'll warn Leah in advance so she can be prepared."

He raised his eyebrow. "You won't promise to not throw tantrums?"

She turned away from him. "How can I promise such a thing when you'll be gone so long? This room is already too small. Even the falcons in the aerie

208

will scream for the sky when kept in the dark too long." It was true. Allowing her to vent would prevent her from slipping into depression, which she might do anyway, given her recent surgery.

"All right." Her ears perked up. "I'll let Miss Leah know that if you warn her in advance then a tantrum won't be punished. But, you can't use that as an excuse. If you abuse it, that will be punished." She looked back at him and nodded. "And, what do you want from me if you're able to last the whole time with good reports to me when I return?"

She trembled. He already knew the answer. He waited for it. "I want Ore to sleep with me that night. So that I'll know that you're really still alive, and really back here in the castle. ...That you haven't gone away for good. That I didn't send you to die." There were tears in her eyes.

"I'll do it," he said. He'd known it because it was his answer as well. They were partners, and being separated during times like those were the hardest, for both of them. And there was another time. "And I'll sleep with Ilena two nights from now, so that I may have the strength to leave again." That statement was not a reward. That was her responsibility as his partner.

Ilena's tears spilled over, the relief on her face nearly painful. She lifted a hand and covered her eyes. He sat quietly by her side until she was sleeping, then he moved to the other bed and readied himself for sleeping. She'd done very well tonight, given the news he'd had to bring her.

CHAPTER 12 Preparations for Battle

The next morning, the Regent of Suiran sent out secret orders, and the forward spies secretly disappeared into the north. Grandfather sent his voice down its courses. The Children of Mother raised their heads to listen and began preparations.

Two nights later, as Ore lay holding his healing partner, Ilena turned her head to him and said, "Father, ...love my Children."

"I will, Mother," he promised and ran his fingers through her hair.

Her hand reached up and clutched at his shirt. "And, Ore, love me more.... Come back. Return to me as alive and unharmed as you'll leave."

He kissed her forehead gently and held her to him. "I will." He knew she wept silent tears of frustration at her inability to protect him herself.

The morning of the third day, he carefully and tenderly cared for her as he had for the last week, even as he had for the first month they'd been reunited. Ilena watched every move and trembled at every touch as she memorized them, her heart beating wildly to be set free of her bindings so that she wouldn't have to be separated from him. When he was done he fed her the last breakfast they would have together for weeks, and she still didn't take her eyes off his face.

When he turned to take the cart out of the room and call Leah to sit with her, she called him, raising her hand. "Sir Ore!"

He turned towards her, surprised. At the look of fierce ownership in her eyes he turned and went to her side, took her hand, and knelt on the floor beside the bed on one knee. "May your arm be strong, your sword swift, and your horse never stumble. May your sight never dim, your companions never fail you, and only the blood of your enemies stain the ground. Go forth conquering, and bring me the heads and left hand of my enemies."

"Yes, My Lady," he said solemnly and kissed the back of her hand. He stood and looked at her, then tipped his head. "Selician?"

She shook her head. "The battle blessing of Tarc." He looked at her a moment longer, then nodded and went to fetch Leah.

He gave instructions to Leah in Ilena's hearing that he wanted her to know of, then he took Leah out to give her private instructions. When Leah returned to her mistress, Ilena had her head turned away and wouldn't answer her. Leah sighed and let her alone. Mizi would arrive after lunch, and that would be soon enough to cajole Ilena.

Ore stopped by the infirmary and spoke briefly with Ryan, who promised to help take care of Ilena. He told Ryan what the best time for his emotionally stabilizing tea had been, and asked if it could have the leaf that boosted a sorrowful mood increased for the time he was away. Ryan nodded solemnly, then wished him well.

When Ore reached the Rose office, Rei and Andrew were already at the maps. Ore looked around the room. "Where's Mistress?"

"Next door," Mina answered without looking up. "Morning is when she sees the petitioners."

"Ah," Ore said, remembering she had talked about that with Ilena, who had been very pleased. He walked over and joined the two men at the maps. Mina joined them shortly after.

At noon, when the sun over Ryokudo was at its highest, a lone rider left out of the Sword gate and ran his horse hard from the east to the west along the North Road following the feet of the rocky mountain northern border of Suiran. As he rode through that day and into the night, and then again into the next day, he carried with him the orders of the Regent of Suiran and the garrisons began to prepare for the march against Earl Shicchi and his allies. The echoes of the voice of Grandfather sounded throughout the Children of Mother and they began to rise up to do her bidding.

The morning after Ore left, when Thayne and Leah had completed caring for Ilena, and Rio had finished feeding her, Ilena called Thayne to her. She held her hand out to him as she had to Ore. In unknowing imitation of his master, he knelt beside her bed and took her hand, knowing what was coming. He was both itching to follow his master, and sorrowful that there would be none to stay with his mistress during her long, lonely vigil - or so it felt.

"Father goes into battle with none to stand at his back. That is not acceptable to me. As his man-at-arms, it is your responsibility to protect him in all things. Go to Grandfather and learn where you may meet him so that you can journey to the north at his side. Stay by his side and return triumphant with him.

"But if he should fall, stay to witness how it was done, then return to me and tell me you've seen it with your own eyes so that I must be required to believe it. Of yourself, you may not fall, nor avenge his blood until you've reported it to me, for I will believe no other's word." Thayne nodded, hoping mightily he wouldn't ever have to report such a thing to her.

"Speak my words in Grandfather's ear, that I require my First Son to stand by your side behind Father as his second until Father returns to me here, but he is not to disclose his identity."

Thayne's eyes widened, but somehow, he wasn't really surprised. "Yes, Mother," he said solemnly. She gave him the Tarc battle blessing, and he rose, bowed, and left to do her bidding.

Thayne spoke Mother's words to Grandfather, and the words he sent out along its courses in response sent a thrill through all of her Children and they moved as if it were a silent unseen flood toward the north, with eddies swirling towards the lands southwest of the castle, The battle lust in their eyes - normally so calm and kind - was kindled by her own.

One day after Grandfather sent his word out to the Children, a disguised Ore was leaving the farthest west garrison with two others, also disguised as soldiers on an errand, returning from the west to the east. As they ran hard along the road, the preparing soldiers began to load their wagons. Also at that same time, Rei called Dane to the war table. "Where is he?" he asked the aide.

Dane looked over the map carefully, then considered the time. "Here," he placed a finger east of the garrison that was the first pickup spot, "...returning." Rei nodded. "And where will he be tomorrow at at noon?"

Dane drew his finger eastward on the map from that location towards Osterly, then slightly beyond, then tapped it thoughtfully. "He will likely be on or close to the hidden route."

Rei was pleased. He looked at Andrew. "Please let the troops know we'll leave Nijou Castle tomorrow at noon." Andrew made a note in his schedule, then left the room to inform the castle garrison.

-o-o-o-

Rei confirmed Ore's location one more time with Dane the next day a half-hour before noon, then gave the order and Andrew rolled the maps up carefully. These were the waterproof maps that were taken on campaign. He placed them in their containers, and then into the bag he flung onto his back.

Rei looked at Dane and Tairn as Andrew and Mina waited for him at the door. "This will be the test of the Malkin family. I leave the Rose office in your hands." The brothers bowed to him and the three turned and left, going over to the Lotus office.

"Mizi," Rei called her. She was preparing for the next day's petitioners before going to sit with Ilena. He paused, then said, "You could have her help you with this part. Then she would already be prepared to help you when she can move about."

Mizi looked up at him, a little startled. "Ah, that's true isn't it?"

Andrew smiled at her, "You're used to being very self-sufficient, but it's a strength to use the strength of others."

Mizi nodded. She remembered that Ilena said the same to her when Rei had finally decided to open the Rosebud office. She set the papers aside and rose to greet Rei. "You're going?" she finally noticed the bags the others were carrying. Rei nodded. She quickly put her papers together and stuffed them into her folder. "I'll come see you off, then."

They walked down together to the garrison grounds where a stand had been set up for Rei to speak to his men from. The soldiers who were going with Rei were gathered together in companies on the parade ground. Before entering the grounds proper, Rei made Mizi stand between Andrew and Mina, telling her to come on the stand with them and stand behind him. She looked at him a little startled, but nodded, then made sure her folder wasn't sloppy, since she didn't have anywhere to put it but to hold it.

They walked across the field and up onto the stand. Mizi noticed that there were three horses standing ready beside the stand, including Rei's white horse. It made her heart clench. They were really going, without her, and for three weeks.

She took a deep breath. She had plenty to do. She would be helping Tairn and Dane in the office, doing her own work with the petitioners, and sitting with Ilena, not to mention learning all she could that Ilena had promised to teach her. It would go quickly. But, still, it was the first time Rei was leaving her behind in such an obvious way.

She listened to Rei's rousing battle speech, feeling the excitement of the soldiers who were looking forward to showing him what they could do. She smiled, thinking of the respect the soldiers had towards Rei. They'd often been her staunchest supporters as well. She looked out over them and felt pride for their strength they lent him. It helped her have strength also, to know that they would be fighting for and with him.

As Rei completed his speech, the soldiers shouted with one voice, "Regent Rei! Regent Rei!" Then he turned, but instead of walking down the stairs to his horse, as she expected, he motioned her forward.

Mizi jumped as Andrew turned and bowed to her and offered her his arm. As she took it, he said to her very softly, "You can just wave, but if you'd like to give them some words of encouragement, it would be helpful." She looked up at him, her eyes wide. She looked at Rei again, and he smiled at her. She looked into his eyes, then smiled back.

Andrew placed her on the stand next to Rei and bowed himself back to his position. Somehow he'd slipped the folder from her arm and she didn't have it any more. She clasped her hands in front of her skirt and thought back to what she'd just been feeling.

"Thank you for supporting Regent Rei. The strength you lend him is the strength of Ryokudo and Suiran. You make all of us who depend on you proud and give us the strength to continue to move forward also." She bowed to them. "Thank you." The soldiers roared their approval.

Rei looked at her, his brilliant blue eyes sparkling. He reached up to put his hand behind her head and pull her to him. He kissed her with a long kiss to keep them both until he returned. She was vaguely aware beyond the blood rushing loudly in her ears that the soldiers were cheering.

"Well, that seems appropriate," Mina said mildly as they escorted a reeling Mizi off the stand after Rei. "Announcing his intentions to the soldiers first."

"It's excellent for morale, too," Andrew grinned back at her.

"Well, but it puts her in the middle of things all by herself though," Mina frowned back. "To announce it then cowardly run away."

Rei looked back at them as they arrived next to him by the horses. "I'm not running away. I'm giving everyone time to get used to the idea. After all, it's only her they're going to find at the Rose office while we're gone. Oh, and do use my desk for your work while we're away, Mizi. It's available. You don't need to work alone in the Lotus office. I'm sure Dane and Tairn would welcome your company."

Mizi nodded, completely missing his ulterior motives behind his offer, her head still spinning. Andrew and Mina stared at him for a moment, though. Mina hid a laugh behind her hand and Andrew shook his head. To cover they turned and put their burdens on their horses. They'd recovered by the time Rei finished giving Mizi a hug, and they turned to hug her as well.

"Take care," she told them, hoping they understood she meant all of them, but especially Rei. They all swung up into their saddles and the Regent of Suiran, her beloved Prince Rei, with his faithful knights and friends at his back, rode out the Sword gate at the head of the castle soldiers.

The battalions of soldiers began to roll inexorably forward towards the north, and for a time it appeared that the army was being raised because of the Children of Mother that ran before it. The Regent himself rode with the army, coming from the east to distract enemy eyes from the rider who was returning from the west.

-o-o-o-

Thayne stood waiting, holding the reins of two horses in his hand: that of his own horse, and that of his master's. The way-station house had been informed that Father, with his Children, were on their way and would arrive within the half-hour. He'd just finished saddling the horses and was walking them to the courtyard to tether them for leaving.

It was the last stop before the group would turn off the main road and take to cover, allowing the decoys to lead any enemies farther along the main road. That meant it was the last place Thayne could meet up with Ore easily.

The courtyard and house grounds were surrounded by woods, like all houses of northern Suiran, so he wouldn't see them first. Instead he was using his ears. When he heard faint hoof-beats coming towards the house, he called to the house to let them know of the imminent arrival, and went and stood out in the middle of the forest-lined drive that came from the main road.

When he saw the five horses coming, steaming and sweating, he grinned. Father always loved to run as fast as he could, but he never ran first when he was escorting Children. Still, Thayne was sure he'd been seen.

He heard the other members of the house coming out, now. The lady of the house and her daughter would be carrying food and drink. The husband and his sons were coming to help take the labored horses.

Four of the five horses passed him, stopping farther into the courtyard. The fifth pulled up next to him and he held the reins as Ore lept off the horse, then stumbled slightly. Thayne wordlessly caught him, then decided to hold onto him just a moment longer. He raised his eyebrow. "Mother would be furious if she knew you've been skipping out on sleep this whole time."

Ore nodded, resting his hands on his knees, waiting for the world to stop spinning. "Master's scarier."

"Then you haven't seen Mother mad yet. I thought they'd planned in sleeping stops?" Thayne asked him.

Ore just looked at him darkly. Thayne held his tongue. Ore finally gave up and dropped to the ground, sitting cross-legged. Thayne took the horse he'd been riding to the large stable for the others to take care of, then went and fetched food and water for Ore and took it to him, since he wasn't capable of moving still. The others were also sitting on the ground near where they had dropped off their horses, eating and drinking and being waited on by the ladies of the house.

"Have you learned to sleep in the saddle, yet?" Thayne asked him.

Ore nodded as he hungrily ate. "Can't when protecting them, though."

Thayne nodded. "Then you sleep, I'll protect." Ore looked at him around the edge of his mug, then nodded wearily. "Or would you rather sleep here for a few hours?"

Ore shook his head. "They're closer than we thought they would be. They seem to want to herd us. The only thing I can figure out is that we aren't bringing in one group, but are getting fresh groups that are trading out."

Thayne looked worried. "Have you told the other way-stations?"

"Yes. They each have said they'll handle it."

Thayne nodded. "I'll go tell this one. Is there anything else to it I should mention?" Ore shook his head. "No patterns?" Ore shook his head again. Thayne stared at him. "It's not Earl Shicchi's orders then."

Ore looked at him with bloodshot eyes. "Apparently not."

"And did you say that to anyone else?"

Ore shrugged. "Probably, but I stopped paying attention to what was coming out of my mouth after we had the second set with us. We barely made it into town and almost didn't make it out. It's taken everything to get us this far ahead."

"How long do we have?" Thayne was alarmed.

"Just long enough. Like I said, they're pressing us to keep moving. They aren't attacking...yet."

"Any thoughts on where they might?"

Ore shook his head wearily. "I'm just hoping the next part of the route isn't compromised."

Thayne chewed on his lip. "Will you let me lead us in?"

Ore looked at him long and hard. "I still have to collect the last set. You know where?"

Thayne nodded, still thinking out a plan. "I'll be right back."

Thayne went and talked to the man of the house, James. He told him what Ore had said, and James looked worried. "That doesn't sound good at all."

"I think someone's either leaked our communication system, or someone's working for their side that's been on our side." Thayne said.

James was thunderstruck. "That's the worst possible."

Thayne nodded. "We're going to have to test it. Don't send out word we've left until we've had enough leeway to get ahead. Then watch to see who passes. Grandfather needs to know immediately if it's a traitor." James nodded. "If it isn't, then we need to delve deeper. If more than one person knows the code on that side we'll have to scrap it, and it's the best one we've had yet."

James sighed in agreement. "Alright. I'll use the local code to send out the general gather after I send out the move-along code. If they swing back around, they're with a local person and we might be able to weed it down. If they don't, we'll just take them out and see who's in the mix. Once we've got it narrowed down I'll send word both directions."

Thayne thanked him, then went and introduced himself to the Children coming in this trip. They were nearly as tired as Ore. He was going to have to take it slow enough they stayed in the saddle, but fast enough they could get to the safe house and rest. Then he had a thought and went back to James. "Have you got a wagon we can have? I'll leave the horses with you and you can trade them for another, except Father's and mine."

James looked at him in surprise, then grinned. "They are pretty wasted, aren't they. Mixing it up might just be the thing to do. Give me a bit. The boy's and I'll get things set up. But I'd like the wagon to be a loan and have it back before harvest time. Do you think that's possible?"

Thayne considered. "Yeah, I think that could happen. Might have to have the soldiers stationed there bring it by, though."

"That'd be okay," James said, and he turned and headed back into the stable. Thayne took the other fresh horses back into the stable and started unsaddling them, ignoring the surprised looks from Ore and the others still sitting on the ground.

He carefully kept his and Ore's horses separate, put their gear near the door, and added the gear from the other Children. When James and his sons pulled the wagon out of the barn, Thayne was very satisfied. It was indeed the standard way-station wagon Mother had requisitioned.

The way-station wagons were built to be harvest time wagons - high sides, large capacity, and very sturdy. It took two horses to pull them when they were loaded down. But what only a very few knew was that they were also stow-away wagons.

Each had a false bottom with entry from above and exit below for emergencies. There would be enough room for the six people to lay out and sleep, but not much for wiggling. Thayne didn't expect much of that. There was room in the box under the driver for the gear, and a false bottom there as well.

While the two sons stowed the gear, Thayne and James worked on getting the horses into the traces. Since they were battle trained, it was a bit difficult. They weren't very eager to all of a sudden be draft horses, but Thayne didn't want to have them stick out by being halter led at the back. That would be too suspicious.

He was able to finally talk his horse into it. Ore eventually had to get up and come talk to his before it would acquiesce. They decided it was only because he was promised a good two day run after it was over.

"So...where are the rest of us going so that we aren't seen?" Ore asked.

Thayne looked at him speculatively. "Do you want me to tell you, or do you want to find out on your own when you wake up?"

"Wake up?"

Thayne hauled back and hit Ore so hard he spun nearly a full circle and fell to the ground in a heap. "Right then," Thayne said and hauled Ore back up and over his shoulder. "I'll likely pay dearly for that later."

"...I ...should think so," said James rather weakly. "Was it really necessary?"

"He's as bad about small spaces as Mother, James. You know what it was like." Thayne didn't look at him.

James had been one of the Children at Tokumade. He paled. "He's going to kill you if he wakes up in the box. It would have been better if you'd told him first."

"Nope, then he would have fought back - and he's the one we need to hide the most." He heaved Ore onto the edge of the back of the wagon. "Get the rest of them over here." He checked to make sure he hadn't done too much damage to Ore's face, or killed him - he'd spun rather dramatically. He was alive and the skin hadn't broken, but it would bruise up good.

As James' sons opened up the box in the back, he turned to the others, who were looking at him with a bit of fright in their eyes, not quite sure what he was planning. "Let me introduce myself again, now that he's out. I'm Thayne of Wexford, Father's man-at-arms, one of the first set of Children taken to the safe house, but called out by Mother to walk behind him.

"You'd all know me as Fourth Son." They all looked at him, shocked, then nodded and relaxed just a bit. "Father's filled me in on what's been going on. I think we've got either a leak or a traitor, so we're changing it up. You all need sleep more than anything, so here's your bed. It will be a bit bumpy, but for the time you're all out like logs, it won't matter. There are soft beds in quiet rooms waiting for you, so the comfortable sleep will have to wait until then."

"Do any of you know how these work?" Two raised their hands. "Great. One of you get over next to the escape hatch. We'll put Father on it. If he wakes up and panics, drop him. He won't like that any more than being punched, but it will be better than leaving him stuck in the box. His horse won't leave him behind.

"The other one of you, get under the door knob on the opposite end. The rest of you, in between. Don't think too hard about it. Just close your eyes and imagine you're in your nice cozy bed. You'll fall asleep soon enough. We get enough from the main house that Mother had them made special so it isn't dark and closeted. It'll be light and airy enough during the daylight, for all that makes it dusty. You'll want baths by the time we get where we're going."

He turned back to the escape hatch man, Oren. "If you can cover his eyes and talk him into believing he's not in a box, you don't have to drop him, but I don't know how long he'll last that way."

Oren nodded. "I was at the house when he was. I remember."

"Good, that makes you the best man for the job, then. Let's get going before he wakes up." Thayne waved the collected witnesses up into the wagon.

The teens had already lifted Ore into the box over the escape hatch after making good and sure the latch wasn't going to let him drop accidentally. It was made to open suddenly, dropping the person on it, then allow each of the remaining passengers to roll out of it one by one.

If they held still just long enough, the wagon would pass harmlessly over them, then they could jump up and run off the road and escape. It wasn't glorious, and the drop could be painful, but it was usually well worth it compared to what the alternatives were.

The top door was actually almost the whole of the false floor. It was easier to get them into because it didn't feel like crawling into a cave. The psychology of it all had been extremely important to Mother, but that didn't mean she would have ridden in one, any more than Ore would have chosen to. They'd been locked up at Tokumade as part of their "punishment" more than anyone else in the household.

Thayne had actually been pretty amazed that they'd lasted in the small rooms Ilena had been in at the castle. He'd learned pretty quickly it was only because they stayed together, and it was why he'd been called in to stay with her at night during the second pick-up of witnesses. He'd been very glad when he spent those nights with Mother that he'd not had to endure that particular punishment, but then, he'd never been at Tokumade anyway. He'd just heard all the stories.

When everyone was in, the boys shut the door and made sure it clicked shut. There were hidden latches on the outside and obvious ones on the inside. The two men on either end would be able to find them just fine to get the door open when they got where they were going.

The boys threw in straw to make it look like Thayne had just made a delivery and was on his way back home, although the high sides and back, which James latched closed again, made it difficult to tell anyway. A man on horseback would be able to just look in and see that it was empty of cargo. Thayne reassured the horses one last time, then climbed into the driver's seat.

"Since we're going by wheel, give me twenty minutes head start, but only wait until they're just past to call in the reinforcements," He didn't want the traitor to get very far ahead, if there was one. "I'm going to go to running calls. If Grandfather gets worried, send it back by the old one-three code. He'll know it's from me. But otherwise, keep it hushed. I know the local code where I'm going so they'll pick me up when I get there."

218

James nodded. "Good luck. We'll find out who it is and make sure it gets fixed."

Thayne nodded and got the horses going. It took about a half-hour to get them used to pulling, but by then he was off the main road and long gone from the places the enemy behind them knew about.

-o-o-o-

Thayne followed narrow roads that were bordered closely by the woods and not traveled often. They were the dirt-rut roads cut by wagon wheels the farmers used to get from field to field. The fields weren't very close together here where the woods had to be cut back and fought against to prevent the fields from turning into woods again. They were also the roads used by farmers and woodcutters to get from their outlying homes into the small villages to deliver their crops or woodland gleanings. He didn't see people hardly at all on these roads.

When the sun was getting low in the sky, Thayne finally heard the noises he'd been waiting to hear. There was a cry, a thump, then a crash. Ore's horse stopped pulling and the wagon bumped into it's rear. It took a bit of clashing between the horses and the wagon to get it to stop - they hadn't practiced that yet, after all.

By the time that was done, Ore's cursing was winding down. Thayne turned to kneel on the driver's seat to see over the sides of the wagon and smiled down at him standing behind the wagon about twenty feet. Orc was not at all pleased, and Thayne was pretty sure that was his murderous look. He heard the click that said the others had pulled the escape hatch closed again.

"Good evening, Father. You slept longer than I thought. That's good. Climb in the back. I've thrown in a cloak. Wrap it around yourself and keep the hood up over your head and face. You've just bummed a ride from a farmer headed home with an empty wagon. Come sit up in this corner," he pointed to the one beneath him inside the wagon, "and I'll explain as we move. We're late as it is since our two horses aren't used to this kind of work."

Ore, anger bordering on rage still on his face, ran, leaped. and vaulted over the high back of the wagon. Thayne kept watch for one of his throwing daggers to come his way, just in case, but one didn't, which was a good sign. Father was in control at least a little bit. Thayne sat back down and got the horses going again, although they looked at him affronted first. He promised them apples at the safe house when they got there.

"We're not going that far," Ore said coldly.

"Well, actually, we are. Listen to what I have to say." Ore listened while Thayne explained that their communication system had been compromised somehow, that he'd made the decision to change the travel plans, and travel silently because of that.

So far it had paid off in that they hadn't been discovered, but it did mean they were running with no protection. Thus the trade-off was so far a neutral.

He expected to reach local friendlies soon, though, and then they might find out some information about what had happened.

"As soon as we reach the local communication network around the safe house, I'm going to have them move the last set of Children and have them meet us elsewhere. If their location is known by the enemy because of the communications breach, it's possible they're planning to attack at the time we pick them up, getting them all at once, and close enough to the safe house to take it out, too. ...Assuming there are still Children left alive to pick up, that is."

"But, why are we going to the house?" Ore still hadn't heard anything to say they should yet.

"Because this wagon's a loaner. The only way to get it back in one piece to it's owner is to take it through the front gate."

"And how are we going to do that in the middle of a battle?" Ore had moved from cold to testy. That was a good direction, Thayne thought.

"Oh, I expect it will be all over by the time we get there," Thayne said lighter than he felt.

"It's taking us that long?" Ore was surprised.

"No. The plans changed because the enemy did something unexpected, right?" Ore was silent. It was a rather frightening thought. "But that's okay. We're used to that kind of thing. If our side had to go out hunting, they went hunting. Like I said, when we're in range, we'll learn what happened."

"Just why are you guys used to this kind of thing?" Ore asked, suspicious.

"We're trained to it," was all Thayne would say.

Ore was quiet for a long while after that. Probably nursing a headache. Thayne actually hoped he'd gone back to sleep.

CHAPTER 13 Getting the Final Witnesses to Falcon's Hollow

"Thayne, I've got a question. ...These Children didn't feel they had the authority to answer." Ore seemed to have woken up again back in the wagon bed.

"Go ahead." Thayne was willing to talk as they went. It was still a bit of a drive before they reached the next Children, apparently.

"They're all horsemen, except Miss Maise, am I right?"

"Yes."

"To train and care for Mother's herds?"

"Yes."

"Do you know how she knew who to put where, even from so long ago?" Ore asked.

Thayne blinked and smiled to himself. "That's the kind of mind she has. It's pretty amazing to watch, actually, although you've got to have the patience of a king to see it sometimes. We're pretty lucky to be at a point where a lot of her effort is coming together at once."

"...Yeah," Ore said quietly. It sounded like his head was resting on his arms, his legs tucked up in front of him.

There was a sound in front of the wagon, made by something hidden up in the trees. Thayne answered it and a lithe body dropped into the seat next to him. "Hey, Ox!" the young man said cheerfully to Thayne.

"Hey, Slim," Thayne said back. "What's happening these days around your house?"

"*Haah.* Loads of stuff, actually. I'm not sure where to start."

"Hoh? Well, tell me about the Children."

"They're doing well, but we've had to move them from the chicken coop to the barn. They've been growing so fast, you know." He winked at Thayne.

"Well, when you've got that many, I suppose you have to make allowances. Will your da' let me take some off his hands yet to help in my fields?" Thayne asked.

'Slim' thought about it. "Well, he might. They're pretty skittish at the moment, but they'd like to get to a place they can feel more secure. Want to see?"

"Yup. That's pretty important to me right now. I'd be willing to take them tonight, if they'd be willing to go."

"Well, then just keep going straight for now. I'll keep talking while we go. I've just run a long ways and could use the rest."

"Oh? It's that far?"

"No. It just took me a long time to find you."

"Hitching rides is your thing, isn't it, Slim," Thayne said as if bored.

The young man smiled. "Why not, when all you've got is your own hooves to run around on normally."

Thayne grinned back. "Well, I like being able to hitch a ride now and then, too."

They sat quietly for a moment, then Thayne asked, "Have you heard from your Grandfather yet?"

"He was asking after you," Slim said solemnly. "There's been a bit of a panic, actually."

"Tell me about it," Thayne said. It was hard to tell if he was asking, or if he was being sarcastic.

"The river's been compromised. Only the tributaries are flowing right now, and that's apparently upstream and down. The Family's got a work-around about in place, but I left before hearing the last word on what it was. Grandpa wants to talk to you before you head out again, though."

"I'll be sure to do that," Thayne said quietly. "I'm not sure we'll be able to make it to the next stop, elsewise, given what I've heard. Tell me about your Father's mousetraps."

"*Haahh.* Well, that," Slim was reluctant. "Well...maybe someone else can tell you about that. But there aren't any mice where I'm taking you, just some friendly watch dogs."

"All right."

"You know what the stream around here sounds like?" Slim asked.

"Yes," Thayne answered.

"Then, this is my stop. Listen for it."

"Thanks, Slim."

"No problem, Ox. See ya!" The young man jumped down from the wagon and disappeared into the woods again.

When the wagon had gone a few more wheel turns, Ore landed on the seat next to Thayne. "Hello, 'Ox'. Okay, I know how to see, but how do you know the names?"

Thayne grinned at him. "We just make them up based on what the person reminds us of when we first lay eyes on them. He was pretty skinny, so 'Slim' worked. It actually works pretty well. Someone else might see something different, but if they already have a word given to them their own mind will fill it in nicely. It rarely ever gets mistaken when combined with knowing how to see."

"So... roses and a thorn?" Ore asked from the time they'd picked up the first set of witnesses.

"Sallie, Miss Freida, her maid, and Dane," Thayne answered.

"The hare and the tree...that'd be Peter and Foster?" Ore confirmed.

"Yup."

"Yeah, I can see how it works. And the conversation you just had...it's a pretty handy way to communicate since everyone is already labeled with family titles. In the main no one would know you were exchanging information."

Thayne looked at Ore. "Yes, but it only works when you're speaking person-to-person. It's the long-distance communication that's been compromised, and the main one, too."

"You break it down into both area-speak, and then a common one across the Family as a whole. I assume for reasons just like this one?"

Thayne nodded. "This would make it the third time. Mother's enemy keeps us busy, and his men. He usually lets us know they've broken it at times like this, too, just when we're trying to do something important. We've learned how to deal with it, though."

Ore looked at him wide-eyed. "How's that?"

Thayne glanced at Ore. "We have new codes waiting to use. It's possible it's in place now, but Slim didn't know if the test run had been successful yet. That means it's gone out but not back in yet. We'll only start using it once everyone checks in.

"We're probably still waiting to hear back from everyone that went north. They're a little farther out, and a lot of them at that, and of course we haven't checked in yet. We'll have to do that before we get to the house or they can't start using it."

"It can keep track of every individual?" Ore was amazed.

Thayne nodded. "Else we don't know who we've lost."

"Does that happen often?"

"Sadly, yes," Thane said. "Especially at times like this." He sat quietly for a moment, then said, "Can you tell me what Slim really told us?"

"Well...," Ore said thinking back. "He said the rest of the Children I need to collect have already been moved to a safer location where there aren't any enemies around and they have guards to protect them, but they're worried and looking for us to arrive." Thayne nodded.

"And, the river being compromised was the main communication line, with only local lines working as of his last knowledge." Thayne nodded again. "And he isn't the right one to ask whether or not my plans to deal with the flood and the ambushers worked, although obviously the ones I'm involved in haven't yet, so it's probably safe to assume they had to be scrapped."

"Mmm...no, I didn't ask about the flood. Just the ambushers," Thayne corrected.

"Ah, because you asked about 'traps'," Ore got it quickly.

"Yes. I would have asked him more about what we could expect up ahead but he wouldn't answer the ones I thought he should at least have known about. It's one way to keep communication short. Shorter means less time for someone who shouldn't be listening to figure out what's going on."

"I understand," Ore nodded. That was common practice in the underworld too, as was coded speaking like that, so it hadn't been all that hard for him to pick up on. It was a lot easier to understand if you knew the underlying code - in this case, who the Family really was. "Has the enemy not picked up on the Family code, the person-to-person code?"

Thayne grinned at him. "Of course they have. It isn't that hard to understand, but he doesn't know who anyone other than the top name is. And there are lots of people who have mothers, fathers, sons, daughters, sisters, brothers, uncles, aunts, and grandfathers. So the information comes to him piecemeal and mixed with misinformation all the time.

"It's harder to sort through than the long-distance code. So he occasionally gets things he wanted to hear from the person-to-person stuff, but Mother's said to not worry about it too much. He's getting even more from his spies, so it's mostly useless to him by the time he gets it."

There was a sound from in front of them. Thayne answered it with another sound. A second sound came from in front of them. Thayne frowned, then made the same sound he'd made before Slim had dropped into the wagon with him. A young girl popped up with a question on her face. She jogged beside the wagon as they rolled along.

"Hello, Little Bird," Thayne said. "That was really sloppy. Try again."

"Sorry, Big Brother. It's just come out this morning," she pointed into her open mouth. There was a hole where a tooth should be. "I've been practicing, but it still won't come out right."

"Well, then it can't be helped, I suppose," Thayne relented. "But you'll have to say it then."

"Just keep going. Everything's still clear ahead."

"Thanks!"

She waved and disappeared.

"Can you teach it to me?" Ore asked.

"Probably not. Nor do you need to learn it, yet. It'll be better for you to learn the main line one first and get used to it. The branch lines are offshoots of the other main lines, so are like dialects. It's easier to learn them if you know the main line, and even easier if you know the old codes, which I will teach you when you get high enough level. The higher ranks use them for emergency communications that are kept very brief, and usually one-way, since the enemy knows them."

Ore nodded. He'd still need a translator for long distance communication for a while, then. It was probably a very good thing Ilena had sent Thayne after him. The group he was bringing in wasn't willing to consider themselves authorized to tell him anything useful, although they would have done as the other two groups and at least told him when to go left or right or such. "How's my partner?" he asked.

"Fine when I left two mornings ago."

"Waited a whole day, huh?"

"Yes. Kept waking up the first night. I made sure she knew I was there." Ore was quiet for a moment. It wasn't unexpected. "But it's the news about Mistress Mizi you should like to know, I think."

"Eh? Mistress?"

"Yes, it happened after I was sent after you, but it went out on the main branch and I heard it before you got to the way-station. She went to see Prince Rei off, but he surprised her and had her stand with him for the rousing send-off speech for the garrison soldiers. He asked her to give some last words, which were obviously unrehearsed, pure, and exactly what the soldiers needed to hear.

"...And then he kissed her on the stand in full view of everyone on the parade grounds and in the stands." Thayne couldn't keep the grin off his face.

"Ehhhh?! Did she faint on the spot?" Ore could just see it.

"Apparently not. Mister Andrew and Miss Mina managed to get her off the stage still walking. She was loopy though and missed her destination and went to the infirmary instead. Mister Ryan had to turn her around and walk her back."

Ore laughed. "I can imagine. ...Wait, that much detail can go out on the river?"

Thayne looked at him out of the corner of his eye. "Father, how would we ever know anything if we couldn't converse in detail?"

Ore took a while to digest that news. "That seems very...advanced."

Thayne looked back at the road in front of them and said, without much emotion, "It's the most advanced in the near continent, if not farther. That's why it galls that her enemy keeps breaking it. ...But I've got a suspicion it isn't modified too much beyond what he comprehends each time on purpose.

"Sometimes it feels like it's changed just enough to be teaching the rest of us something...like the code we'll end up using, the one he won't be able to break, is so difficult we need to be brought to it, or something like that." Ore didn't know what to say to that. He knew it would only come to light when Ilena wanted it to. Otherwise it was just speculation.

"Ah, there's another thing about Mistress Mizi. She's been sitting at Prince Rei's desk in the Rose office, apparently with his permission. Dane says that she's doing very well with what she can do, including fending off offended lords, although he and Tairn, acting as her assistants, are stepping in when it gets out of hand or overwhelming.

"Apparently Marcus has a pool going for how long it takes Mistress Mizi to realize what Prince Rei did to her. Dane says she's still clueless and just going about doing her work as she normally would. Your partner approves of what Prince Rei did and has offered to give, in addition to the pool take, a minor bonus to the person who comes the closest to guessing it. But it's only open to castle personnel." He looked up as he said it, and there were a few sighs and groans from behind them.

"Ah, that's too bad," one of the younger men, David, said. "I've been waiting for one of those to come down."

"You've got a dream, then?" Oren asked.

"Yeah. But since we get to be at the new House, I figured there might be some good opportunities coming soon. I'll have to keep waiting, I guess."

"Good morning," Thayne said to them all, now that they were awake and had the door open so they could sit up. "I think we should be to the last set of Children soon, and if we're lucky, dinner will be with them. Otherwise it will be a late night one at the new house, as you say."

"I'm hungry," the teenage boy said.

"You're always hungry," his mother said fondly.

"Well, he is a growing boy," Ore said mildly. "Will you explain about bonuses and dreams, while we've got the time and are having a lesson?"

The men in the back took that up and Thayne let them. They explained that Mother didn't usually pay in coin, she paid in the fulfillment of dreams. Whenever she introduced a new member into the household, she asked them to give her three dreams of theirs, a minor, a middling, and a major. When they did something of value for her, she would grant them a fulfillment of an equivalent value dream.

Occasionally she would have fun "bonus" fulfillments. This was a "minor bonus" so the winner of the take of the new castle pool would get their minor dream fulfilled. Most of the time people did things for her because they wanted to, so most minor fulfillments were fun grantings like this.

Middle and major fulfillments were usually reserved for the larger or important jobs. If someone did something for her that she hadn't asked for, but which she felt was deserving of reward, she might also grant one.

Thayne looked over to Ore. "Everyone who is coming to the house to stay is getting one of their major dreams fulfilled by it."

Ore was surprised. "Everyone? They wanted that badly to be there? ...I'm afraid I don't understand."

"No, I don't suppose you would just yet. Mmm. Anyone back there want to tell him which of your dreams is being fulfilled by it and all the details around it?" Thayne asked.

There was silence for a while, then the teenage boy, Edward, spoke up. "I will. I'm still young enough that my dreams are new." Ore wondered at that language. "Mother found me at that House in the stable. I was trying to calm a new horse that had just come to us. No one else could go near him, but that was because I was the only one that understood it'd had a traumatic experience before it came to us.

"It had gotten loose and everyone else was standing at the front and back of the stable to prevent it from leaving, but they'd left me to go in after it and get a halter over its head, or at least backed into a stall and locked in. Mother walked up and asked what was going on, although I wasn't paying attention to that, then walked on into the stable. Our men called her back saying the horse was crazy and when she wouldn't go back, they called her crazy, too.

"They say her men just stood and watched and a quick bet was taken as to how fast she'd have the horse tamed. The first I knew she was there, she was near beside me, leaning against one of the stalls, her arms crossed, as if she'd just come for a pleasant visit. My eyes felt like they were going to pop out.

"She calmly asked me what I thought was wrong with the horse. The men said that since my attention had been moved from the horse, it was then it lunged to bite me, but she looked away from me and at that horse and it stopped stock still. She kept her eyes on it, but asked me again what I thought was wrong.

"So I told her. She nodded her head and told me I'd missed one detail. When she told it to me, I knew what needed to be done. So I turned back around and did it. I was able to get the horse into its stall easily that time, and train it correctly within a week.

"She and Earl Shicchi were visiting for that whole week, so before she left she came by the stable again and watched me handing him off to its new rider. She called me over and said I had a natural aptitude for horses and asked what I wanted to do with my life.

"I'd been thinking about it since I'd talked to her before. I immediately told her I wanted to be able to handle horses the way she did. With a single look she tamed that horse. With a single understanding, she taught me to tame it as well, although it took me longer. I wanted to be able to do what she'd done.

"She smiled at me and said she'd love to take me on as an apprentice, but I'd have to do some work first. I'd have to keep learning more and more about taking care of horses where I was, and to come when I was called for."

He stopped, finished with his story. Ore looked questioningly at Thayne. "That doesn't sound much different from the 'how I met Mother' stories I've already heard."

"Well, in this case, Edward is a 'natural talent'. Mother scouts them in all fields - you'll remember from Robert's story." Ore nodded. "So he hasn't done anything - yet - to earn it. In this case it's a dream awarded before the action, also like Robert. That's what Edward means by having new dreams. Those are the easiest to talk about, I suppose.

"For those of us who paid the price before receiving the reward, that's more difficult. Those of us who are awarded old dreams...well, those are pretty precious. ...Maybe someday I'll tell you mine, but not yet. Though, in truth, they're not much different from the stories you've already heard either. After all, isn't it that all of us dreamed of being freed from our miserable circumstances? But the thing she's bringing most of us here for, that's another dream."

Ore leaned back, thinking. Ilena had never asked him what his dreams were. She was asking him to fulfill hers. But...she had already fulfilled several, or was fulfilling them. She was still alive, after all this time. She had protected him from his brother's rage, for many years. She was presenting him the opportunity to remove his brother from his life, and with that remove his fear permanently. She was protecting the most important things to him - Master and Mistress and their path together.

She had even tried to fulfill dreams he didn't know he had. She'd presented herself as a perfect partner to him. She'd given him a family, if he wanted it, and even further purpose for his life that would provide more strength to Master.

Ah, and even a man who would punch him unconscious, tease him mercilessly, and run with him, and watch over her for him. He wondered for a moment how she could not be jealous of Thayne.

No, she was relying on Thayne, the same as he did when he had to leave her. It was the same. The same as Master and Mistress and Ore. But now it would be Master and Mistress and Ore and Ilena and Thayne - and of course Mister Andrew and Miss Mina.

But somehow that felt lonely. ...Had he been lonely? Even though he had them? It certainly wasn't lonely any more. Now it was very busy. But...when she wasn't there with him...that was a new loneliness. ...Or rather, a very old loneliness from a different point of view.

"Thayne?"

"Mmm?"

"It isn't Mother's way to let people stay lonely, is it?" Ore asked.

"Not if she can help it. Poor Peter was one of the few exceptions, although he isn't any more. I'm sure that she feels much better about that now," Thayne agreed.

"If that's the case, who is it she's chosen to be Thayne's partner?" Thayne froze in shock. "Do you not know it yet?" Ore asked, rather gently.

A shudder went down Thayne and he almost wept. "Ah, Father," he finally said when he was under control again, "you see so deeply into the oddest things, and at the least expected times. Truly you are like Mother." Ore waited.

After a moment more, Thayne answered, "Mother hasn't told me yet if or when I may have a partner." To Ore, he did indeed sound lonely. "But for now, that's as it should be. Father only has need of one to follow him at this time. When it's the right time –," he shuddered again and had to breathe through it, "– Mother will give to Father another." It took Thayne a long time to recover after that.

-o-o-o-

It was dark when Thayne's head snapped up. The woods were still just as thick around them, but the noise level was suddenly something more than wind and wild animals. "You lot, get back underneath. Stay hidden 'til we're

228

at the house and I say you can get out. Father, you're my brother. You were born deformed. You can see and hear, but can't talk too good. Keep your face and head covered. Can you show a deformed hand?"

Ore nodded.

"And work for a deformed leg and foot in your walk, too. Practice it while you're getting the straw back there where it needs to be. Don't move from your corner unless I tell you to." The door behind them clicked closed. "Keep down while you head back there. Ah, and the kids we're picking up, are they girl or boy?"

"Two girls, fifteen and eleven." Ore answered back quietly, then slipped over the high side of the wagon with barely a ripple showing over its edge now that the sun was just down over the horizon. He shuffled around the wagon, pushing straw with his feet to practice his walk.

"Peter! Stop being so restless back there! We're just about to the place I told you we were going to get some help at home. Settle down, now. They'll have to ride back there with you. You be good, now, hear? and leave them alone." Ore shuffled to his corner and sat huddled in it. Thayne had noticed Ore's face was beginning to swell finally. He sighed. Maybe one benefit would be Ore wouldn't be quite so recognizable after all.

A minute later, Thayne pulled the wagon into the yard of a house with a large barn. There was quite a bit of activity going on at the place, for a country home. His eyes darted everywhere. It looked like this was the area central command. He shifted uncomfortably. It was too many people to expose Father to at a sensitive time like this. He'd thought it might be something like this, though.

The horses managed to get the wagon to stop mostly where he wanted it, but that was because they stopped by his leading them by rein, instead of suddenly on their own. A balding wiry man came out of the house to the call of one of the people in the yard and came up to him. Thayne climbed down from the wagon.

"Ox. Slim said you'd be stopping by." The man ran his hand through his remaining hair, looking frazzled.

"Ah, yeah. Sorry. He didn't say you were hosting this many guests, though, or I'd of waited."

"No, it's alright. He said you were asking after help again. I'd help me to have a few extra beds tonight."

"All right, then. I was hoping to get a couple of your girls to come help around the house. Ever since Eveline died, Peter and I just haven't been able to keep up. With his hand the way it is, he drops more dishes than he helps clean, and he can't sweep."

The balding man called to one of the lads standing nearby, "Go fetch Christie and Kate. Tell them to bring their things with them. I'm sending them with Ox for a while." The lad bobbed his head and ran off towards the house.

"Ah, I've also got Mattie and Paul here. You know my wife's the area midwife...well Mattie wasn't doing too good, so Paul brought her over. She miscarried early this morning, but I haven't got a proper place for her to rest, and you've got a wagon. Could you put them up tonight, then take them on home tomorrow?"

Thayne looked around the busy yard. "Sure. They can have my bed. It's the only one big enough for two. Peter doesn't mind sleeping next to the fireplace, so I'll take his bed. Ah," Thayne interrupted before the area captain could send another order, "Peter fell out of the wagon hard when we were unloading. Would your wife have some time to take a look at his face for me? It's swelling up pretty bad."

The captain gave Thayne a horrified look. He'd just been potentially told the equivalent that Father had been attacked and injured in a fight. "Certainly. Is he alright?"

Thayne hurried to reassure him. "Yes, yes, it's my fault. I'd placed a bale he wasn't aware of, and he tripped over it and tumbled out. I feel real bad about it."

The captain gave him a scathing look for being so careless as to let *Father* get hurt, then sent another youth scurrying to fetch the couple and a medic. Thayne didn't let it bother him, but he was starting to wonder why he hadn't heard about the last man they were supposed to be picking up.

"Ah, Fred, why's your place so busy tonight, but the woods so quiet? It's been almost spooking me. Am I going to be able to make it home? And Slim said his Grandpa wanted me to contact him as soon as possible. Should I try to stop by tonight?"

The captain, newly dubbed "Fred", shook his head rapidly. "Don't you worry about Grandpa. Maybe you can think about that when you get home, but you should be as quiet tonight as the rest of the woods, I suspect, as you're headed back. You might run into a couple bully boys on your way home, but if you're polite, I think you'd make it okay. We've got strangers in the area and its spooked everyone."

He'd been looking closely at the wagon, and decided Thayne's ruse should be sufficient. Then he looked at Thayne with a serious expression on his face. "I've got a thing in the barn I'd like you to take a look at. It's one of those things only you can fix for me. I'd be obliged if you'd at least look at it while you're here and waiting."

Thayne nodded, and as he passed the spot where Ore was sitting in the wagon, he said, just loudly enough for Ore to hear, "Peter, I'll be right back. Just sit quietly and wait for me."

As Thayne followed Fred into the barn, he could see it was a medic station. A number of men and youths, and even a few women, were in various stages of being tended to. He was glad to see that the majority of injuries were relatively minor, although sufficient to have had them removed from battle for a time. He grabbed Fred's sleeve to pull him close so they could converse quietly. "The flood?"

Fred nodded. "That's going as expected. It's the rest that's not, and with the river down we're not sure what to do about it but run quiet with our eyes and ears wide open."

Thayne nodded. "That's what I'd do, too. I'm blind, and confused, so we'll follow your lead."

Fred looked at him concerned. He'd hoped to hear the news from Thayne, apparently. "We'd like some direction, if possible."

Thayne considered it. "Is it that there isn't anything to spring the traps?" Fred nodded. "How many traps are there?"

"One on the main road, and you're going to have to go through it, but looking like that I think they'll just inspect it. If they pull out your passengers, they'll trigger the defense, so you can just hide under the wagon 'til it's over like good locals. ...There was another on the secondary road, but we took care of that one some time back."

It was Thayne's turn to look concerned. The logging road had been compromised early on. He'd been afraid of that. Fred turned and led him farther into the barn to a place that was quiet. There was a stall there with two obviously armed men sitting outside it. Fred stopped a bit of a distance away from it, then nodded his head at it. Thayne walked stealthily up to the stall. The two guards looked at him, but let him pass silently.

Looking into the stall, Thayne saw a man lying on the straw, he was bound, hand and foot, and gagged. That was unusual. He must have been trying to make noise to give away his position. The man felt Thayne's presence and lifted his head to look up at him. Thayne looked at him stonily for a moment longer, then turned and went back to Fred. They went back to the hospital area before speaking quietly again.

Thayne's eyes burned. "Get him to the castle. Alive."

"Not Grandfather?" Fred was surprised.

"That one is Mother's jurisdiction." His words were cold and hard. "He can sit there in the dark until she can see him proper herself."

Fred nodded. "We'll be sure he's delivered properly."

They could see Thayne's passengers arriving at the wagon. As they headed out of the barn, Thayne said, "Tell Grandfather what you've found, but do it with a mouth. Keep it private. He likely needs to know tomorrow." Fred nodded. He'd see a messenger was sent into the castle city to talk directly with Grandfather.

Thayne put a mild expression back on his face to show his guests. "Hello, I'm glad you young ladies can come help me in my house. Peter and I are just not enough to take the place of my Eveline. I hope you can help us with the housework, and maybe a little cooking, too. I'm only passable, I'm afraid. You two can have the attic room."

Thayne was unlatching the back wall of the wagon as he spoke. "With Peter's leg as it is, he can't get up ladders, and because of the fall I took last year that had me out cold for three days, I only go up the to the barn loft carefully when I have to. You should feel safe enough there.

"Peter's going to be more scared of you for the first while than you are of him. It would be good for me to introduce you before we get going so he's calm on the trip home. He wouldn't do anything but make noise, but Fred says we should try to keep quiet."

Thayne looked over at the group. The healer had arrived as well. "If it's okay, I'd like to have his face tended to first." The others nodded, and Thayne pointed to a spot just outside the wagon, indicating to the medic to wait there. "I'll go tell him you're coming so he'll stay calm."

Thayne climbed into the wagon and walked over to Ore. He crouched down next to him and very quietly said, "The last man is a traitor to the Family. I'm having him sent to the castle to rot in the dungeon until Mother can deal with him herself."

Ore's eyes glittered. "Is that going to be long enough?"

"Probably not. But Doctor Elliot can have as much fun with him as he wants, as far as I'm concerned." Then more loudly he said, "It's okay Peter, Fred's wife will be gentle. She's going to make that feel better, okay? I'm going to let her come help you now." He turned slightly and waved the healer over.

He shifted back out of the way, but stood so that Ore couldn't be seen from outside the wagon. The healer was also careful to not move the hood too much out of her way, keeping his hair covered as much as possible. She was quick with practice, and soon had Ore's face poulticed and bandaged.

"That feels much better, thank you," he told her quietly as she put away her tools.

She bobbed her head. "Be well, Father." Then she was hurrying out the back of the wagon to return to her duties in the barn.

Thayne bent down next to Ore again. "They want to know what to do about the enemies in the woods. The flood's going as planned, but there's been nothing to trigger the traps."

Ore shrugged. "Whatever the Family wants, then. We don't need captives from them. The ones from the flood will be sufficient. We don't want strays left, either."

Thayne adjusted the hood over Ore's face so it could be seen by someone standing just next to him. "Peter, Fred's let us have two of his girls to come help us. You're to be nice to them, okay?" Thayne waved the girls in.

They glanced at their parents a little worried, but they nodded and the girls climbed in and walked shyly over to Thayne and Ore. Thayne kept between the rest of the world and Ore, but motioned for the girls to come around where they could meet Ore. "Peter, this is Christie."

They looked at each other, then the teen nodded. "Hello, Peter," she said. "That looks painful, but I'll bet the poultice feels good, doesn't it?" Thayne was proud of her. She'd played her part very well. Ore nodded at her and Thayne smiled.

"This is Kate." Thayne introduced the younger sister.

Kate nodded and said a shy, "Hello."

Ore tried to smile at her, but winced in pain. He glared at Thayne. "I'm sorry," Thayne said contritely. Then he turned and pointed to the opposite corner at the other end of the wagon. "You girls can sit over there. That way he'll sit quiet while we're on the road. You'll need to also be quiet, okay?" They nodded and went to sit down next to their bag that had been put in by Fred.

"Peter, we're also taking Mattie and Paul to our house for the night. They're going to stay in my bed. Mattie's baby died so she needs a comfortable place to stay tonight. We'll take them home tomorrow, okay? Do you remember them?"

Ore shook his head, playing his part. Thayne looked over his shoulder. "You should come get reintroduced, too, I think. Just so he isn't worried."

The couple climbed into the wagon, Paul helping Mattie solicitously, and her moving slowly and carefully, also playing their parts. They walked back to the pair of men. "Paul" crouched down in front of Ore and looked at him. "Well, that is a bad bruise," he said kindly.

Ore asked quietly, "Josh Drexel?"

Josh answered, "I am waiting to hear the words of Father."

Ore responded, "Mother has sent me for you. ...And I'm sorry it's taken so long."

Josh shook his head and answered as he pulled his wife closer to him, "Complications were expected this time. Peter, this is my wife Mattie. You came to visit us last fall, do you remember? Thank you for letting us stay at your house tonight."

Mattie nodded at Ore. "Hello, Peter. It's good to see you again." Ore nodded back.

"If you two will go sit with the girls, please, we need to get moving. I'm sure you're very tired, Mattie. We'll be to my house soon, I should think," Thayne instructed, then to Ore he said quietly again, "I know you're going to want to talk to them, but don't. We have to go through a trap."

As Thayne headed to hop out and close up the back of the wagon, he said just loudly enough for the passengers to hear, "If we set off the trap, sit still. If they make you come out, the defenders will attack. Hide under the wagon and keep playing your parts." He carefully closed and latched the back door of the wagon.

Turning to Fred, he shook his hand and thanked him, then very quietly passed on Ore's instructions regarding the enemy. Fred's eyes lit up. "We'll clean out the area starting immediately, then. Maybe you won't have to be bothered to stop."

"That'd be nice. We're already behind schedule." Thayne turned and walked up to the front. The horses shook their traces to jangling. "One last pull," he told them, and they moved out.

He kept a careful eye on everyone and their movements in the yard as he pulled out. He was happy to be finally out of the bustle and have his master away from the multitude of eyes. Everyone had gotten into their parts well, but still..., he sincerely hoped they wouldn't be stopped on the way.

In the end, they made it to the guard station unhindered, but he could hear the struggle going on in the trees around him as they passed the ambush location, and the horses danced as they passed through, recognizing the sounds of battle.

He did have to pause at the guard station. There, guards were blocking the road. He pulled the horses to a stop early to give them room to get the wagon stopped.

"Brad. James. Tom." He nodded to them soberly. "It's good to see you again. Will his horse be enough to get us in?" He pointed to Ore's horse in its place to his left.

Brad walked up to the horse and looked him over, then shook his head. Thayne slid over. "Then come up here and look over."

Brad, watching Thayne cautiously - so that Thayne left his hands carefully in front of him, loosely holding the reins - climbed up on the seat next to him and looked over. Thayne heard Ore shift so the guard could see his face.

When Brad jumped back down, he said, "That bad, was it?"

Thayne shook his head. "It looks a lot worse than it is. Everything but his face and one casualty is fine. The captain will explain it later. Do you know if the fighting up ahead is done?"

Brad shook his head. "You should be able to get to the barn and house just fine, but we haven't heard anything recent." Thayne nodded and got the horses moving again and the other guards moved out of their way.

Once Thayne was out of earshot of the guards, he quietly told everyone to shift so the trap door could be opened. "We aren't really interested in the general soldiery knowing about these wagons, Father, but you can tell Master Rei in your report. I should've had them come out before we got that far. That's my error."

"No," Ore answered just loud enough Thayne could hear. "That was better than putting everyone at risk by having them come out too soon. And it would be still better to have them sit until we're in the barn. I know you're thinking the more blades available the better, but they can likely be more effective if they come out the trap door. They won't be trapped in here and they'll have the element of surprise."

"Alright," agreed Thayne. They were quiet until they arrived at the barn. As he went ahead and pulled right on into it, Peter came running up and grabbed the halters of the horses.

"Thayne!" He was also quiet. "And this is Father's horse!" It was nuzzling his pocket, looking for the promised treat. "Is this them?"

Thayne nodded, feeling all of a sudden very weary. "The horses were good sports. See that they're well fed and watered, and I promised them treats. Then saddle them for me. The gear is underneath me." He heard the trap door open as he stood to open the space he'd been sitting on.

The first man out went around to the back and unlatched the back of the wagon, opening it for the topside passengers. The remaining people dropping from the hidden compartment came around to Thayne and collected their bags. He handed down the heavy saddles to the other men, then pulled out the last of the things and closed it up. He hopped down and made sure the last one out had latched the trap door again.

Thayne nodded to Peter, who began the difficult process of getting the horses to put the wagon where he wanted it, since they had no idea what he wanted from them. Edward saw the trouble and instead of following Thayne into the house, he turned back. "I'll stay and help," he said.

Ore nodded. "Peter, that's Edward. See he's brought into the house safely when you're done."

"Yes, Father," Peter said.

Ore and the rest ghosted across the space between the barn and house. The faint sounds of battle could be heard occasionally, but it wasn't the full blown sounds that had likely been heard when the flood had begun. If all was going well, it should be nearing completion.

They went to the closest door, Ore first. Thayne brought up the rear. Ore poked his head in and said, "It's me, can we come in?" A sword clicked back into its sheath, and the door was pulled open. He recognized the face. That was good enough.

Ore slipped in, then counted his followers until they were all in. He turned to the guard. "Peter's going to be bringing the last one in after they get the horses seen to. He's about the same age as Peter, but he's had more to eat. Name's Edward."

The guard nodded. "Take them to the dining hall. Bill's waiting there for them."

Thayne turned and led the group onward. Betty joined him and asked how many rooms would be needed. "Three singles, a double for now, and a family foursome." She flitted off saying she would come get them when they were prepared.

The dining hall was the first bright lighting they'd had all evening, and they stood blinking a bit when they entered. There was food and places set waiting for them on the table. It wasn't long before everyone was tucking in, including

Ore and Thayne. Dinner had been a long time coming. Edward entered when they were about half done eating and caught up with them quickly, then passed them as he started in on seconds while the rest were starting to settle into digesting.

Ore stood up and walked around the tables to stand in front of them. Bill, who'd already been introduced, stood nearby. "I'm glad you've all made it here safely. You should be able to rest now, but keep watch until the all clear is given. Bill and the rest of the Family will take care of you. I'm going to let him give my little speech, since I wasn't supposed to be here in the first place. But there is one new item only I can pass on. Bill, if you'll pass it on to everyone else?" Bill nodded.

He gave the summary of what had happened to Ilena quickly to catch them up. "As of now, she's recovering well, the second graft seems to have taken, and we have signs that the tendon and muscle are working together correctly. Because the bone also needs to heal again, we won't know for another five weeks if it's been truly sufficient, but it looks promising.

"She's been made Director of Intelligence to Prince Rei, just for your information." He frowned and looked at Thayne. "Was there anything else?" Thayne shook his head, not thinking of anything either.

"We expect about another five weeks or so to the Lord's Court. Once the sentencing has been completed, you're free to come and go. We'll let you know when that is. Until then, stay put and follow the house rules Bill will explain to you next."

The dining room door flung open, and a dirty disheveled Foster rushed in, followed by Captain Garen, not looking much better. "Father! Good, you haven't left yet."

Ore looked at them, his good eyebrow raised. "Both of you? That means the battle's over, then?" They pulled up short, staring at his face. It looked like they weren't sure which questions to ask first. "Your son decided I needed a sudden, forced nap," he said coolly to Foster.

Foster looked darkly at Thayne, who looked mildly back at him. Foster shook his head, "While I'm sure it isn't pleasant, he outranks me, Father. If he decided it was necessary, then it probably was."

Ore snorted, affronted. "Then who do I appeal to?"

"Given where you're located, to Mother."

"I'll be sure to." He looked at Captain Garen. "Is there anything these folks need to know right now?"

The captain looked around the table at the newcomers, then shook his head. "We've pushed them out of the valley and are holding the boundary. The outside family is handling clean-up now. It would be helpful if we could count on some of you to take a patrol shift in the early morning so the fighters can get some sleep."

"Actually, we came by wagon," one of the men at the table said, "and got some sleep on the way. We could take an earlier shift."

Foster and the captain looked at each other. "We need to talk to Father, then we'll see."

Ore started to move towards the door. Thayne joined him, and the four retired to the office. On the way, Ore sighed. "It would be awfully nice if this place came with drinks. I could use one, or many." Foster slipped away and rejoined them after they'd settled in the office, bringing alcohol and four glasses with him.

This time Ore took the head seat among the comfortable lounging seats of the room. The dark leather was worn enough to be comfortable, but wasn't shabby, and the padding was still supportive but also soft. The darker wood frame was sturdy and was of simple rectangular structure that matched the masculinity of the room. Thayne lit the gas lamps in the room but didn't bother to light the fireplace. They wouldn't be long, and it was warm enough now that spring was getting late.

When a sufficient number of lamps were lit, Thayne gratefully slumped down into the seat to Ore's right, the second's chair, and rubbed his forehead. He was wishing he could talk his master into taking another four hour nap, but he knew it was worthless to try. Maybe he could be the first to sleep in the saddle on the way. He took the drink his father handed him with gratitude. "It's good to see you again, Da."

"Same here, Thayne. I thought it wouldn't be for a while."

Ore slightly grimaced, trying to not hurt his face while he did it, as he took the drained cup from his lips and held it out for more. "It wasn't supposed to be."

Foster looked at him. Thayne smiled. "It's okay, Da. He doesn't get drunk. You remember." Foster did remember that Earl Shicchi had never once gotten drunk at the hunting lodge, and the Viscount had had to ban drinking games with him, and overspend on alcohol, then complain loudly after the Earl left. He poured Ore more. This time Ore only drank half the glass at once.

"I'll start, then," Ore said. "The trip out went as expected. I sent out my decoy, continuing on towards the west, and we got started back. About four hours into it, the enemy showed up behind us, saw us, and started heading towards us at a fast clip. We panicked and ran. They never did catch up to us, but they also wouldn't let us rest.

"We were afraid to take them to the way-station, so we bypassed it. That put us in town too soon. I sent the Children I'd picked up already on around to the meetup point, but they came back and met me by the well before I could meet up with my contact. They said the meetup point was being watched."

Ore shook his head. "All we could do was wait together by the well, although we took up different stations. They tailed me to the inn, then when the Children I met came out, they interrupted the pick up and let the Family in town know they needed a new escape route. But the Children were being watched, so it gave the first set away, too."

Foster drew in a sharp breath and Thayne sat up straight. "The enemy knew who the Children in that House were?"

Ore nodded. "I tested all four of them before we continued on too far, but we were being surrounded quickly by unfriendlies and the town Children wanted to move us out. They did bring into the network some who could test them by Family means, and they were all vouched for, but I think you need to watch them for a while.

"I wouldn't recommend using any of them for guard duty for a while. Use the excuse that because they haven't given their testimony and been integrated yet, they aren't free to wander around and help much."

Ore continued, "We got on the road, and again they were quickly at our heels. But this time, since we were doubled up and still on the original horses, we weren't going far or fast. We had to stop at the next waystation. When I turned off the main road, they slowed down, then turned away."

Ore shook his head. "I knew then they knew everything, but there wasn't anything to do about it but keep going and see what they wanted. I made everyone sleep, but I didn't. If one was a traitor, I wanted to be awake to see who it was. If they were going to ambush us when sleeping, I wanted to be able to give warning.

"Neither happened and we got back on the horses four and a half hours later and got going again. An hour out and we had a fresh batch behind us, making sure we kept moving east." Ore looked disgusted. "I like to run, I hate to be pushed.

"I was glad to see Thayne when we rode into the last way-station. I was hoping he'd have an explanation. I wasn't thrilled at all to be knocked out so rudely." He was back to cold again.

Thayne took a breath. "Father, would you have gone willingly into the safety of the place you woke up in?" Ore stared at him coldly. "My thinking was that you wouldn't, but would argue to either sit next to me or in the back. Until I understood what had happened, I couldn't afford to let you be exposed, or target practice at the bottom of a barrel.

"My responsibility is to keep you alive. That was the best path I could see at the time to be sure I was carrying out my duty." Thayne stood, setting his glass down. He bowed to Ore. "I'm sorry for doing an outrageous thing to Master Ore. I'll accept responsibility."

"Then you'll explain to Master when we arrive what it is you've done. We'll see if he'll allow you to remain," Ore's voice was still cool, but was tinged with less anger. Thayne paled, but it was his responsibility. He stood upright again and sat back down. The air in the room remained a little cool as well. "Captain Garen, please summarize what's happened here."

The captain explained that about an hour after noon their positions had been simultaneously attacked from three main locations around the rim, but there hadn't been any attack from along the main road. They figured that was being watched for Ore's group to come in on, but they had no idea why the attack came at that time.

The second wave had come right after the dinner hour. The soldiers positioned along the logging trail had come and found him after the second wave saying that the second wave had attacked the Children waiting to be picked up at that path. They'd helped defend them, but because Ore hadn't come yet, they couldn't be brought in, so the outside Children had taken them elsewhere saying they would help them meet up with Father.

One of the Children had been angry and demanded to be taken to the safe house immediately, saying he didn't need to see Father, he already had. The outside Children had quieted him and taken him with them. A third wave had come only a short while before Ore and Thayne had arrived with the witnesses.

"We're one person short because he's a Family traitor. I saw it with my own eyes," Thayne said stonily. Foster was very troubled at that news.

Captain Garen nodded. "It felt that way to me, just from their description. Off. Not like what one of Mother's Children would do."

"Grandfather had mentioned that, unlike the other four to pick up, some in the last group were ready to come without seeing me. I wonder if he already understood?" Ore swirled the cup in his hand once as a frown passed across his face.

Ore considered what Captain Garen had said. "...Their first attack came as soon as they received word Master had left the castle. Perhaps the second was because they'd lost us and couldn't push us into the hollow any more, so they came to push at least that one in." The others nodded. That sounded feasible. "And the third...?"

"That was probably the order to let the Children clean out the woods." Thayne supplied. He told his story from the beginning, too. "I knew the horses were a sign of the group to the enemy. I figured the way-station would have one of the modified wagons, so I decided if I could convince the two horses we needed to pull it, and Father to take a nap, it would mask our progress.

"I brought the wagon to the area using the local routes I'd memorized the afternoon before, rather than take the main road. I wasn't able to get very much information when we got to the area, just get the line on where to go for the pick up. They did confirm my guess that the main line communication has been breached. Local lines seem to still be intact." Foster shook his head. That was always a low blow to the Family for a while, and a disadvantage to Mother.

"We were taken to local central, which I'd guessed we would be. They showed me the last Child to confirm what he was and get orders on what to do about him. They also wanted to know what to do about the enemies still hanging around the woods. Father gave them permission to clean them out.

We collected the rest and headed for here. By the time we reached the main road ambush, the outside Family was already taking them out, so we managed to get here cleanly."

Thayne turned. "Captain Garen, if the outside Family asks for assistance in taking the traitor to the castle, will you help? He needs to be directly questioned by Mother herself. He can wait for her in the worst cell there. If we all forget about him for a year, that won't bother me, though she'll probably want his information before then. But he can't die or escape before she knows what he knows." Thayne looked soberly at Foster, then Ore. "He's from out of country."

Ore sat up straight and stared at Thayne. "Which one?"

"He's marked from Selicia."

Ore thought about that. He wasn't Master to understand everything, but he did know enough. "He's a roundabout spy then?"

Thayne nodded. Ore thumped back into his seat. "Why bother? Doesn't he know she knows it's him either way?"

Thayne shrugged. "He's probably telling her something like where the next push is going to come from after this one. Like I told you about the main communication line breaches - he sends messages to her that way." Ore looked up at Thayne slowly, his face going very dark.

Thayne was very glad Ore hadn't looked at him like that after he'd hit him. "She's said it this way: 'He watches to see what I'll do, and then he pokes his finger into my cup to create ripples to show me he can still affect what I do. He is both laughing at me, and testing me, to see if I'm strong enough'."

Ore held himself very still. "What will happen when she's strong enough?"

"We assume he'll come himself."

Ore's eyes flashed. He didn't move for a while longer, however, except to grip the arm of his chair very tightly. When he relaxed, although he didn't very much, he downed the rest of his drink and stood. "It's time to go. Help them get that spy to the castle. Master will also want to hear what he has to say, when he returns. Send the word that he's to spill everything he knows. Both Mother and Master get the report, with a copy coming to me.

"If any of the others we brought in today are traitors, they get the same treatment. If you can't figure it out, I'll bring Mother before we let anyone go. She knows all her Children." He didn't see the shocked expressions on their faces as he was already walking to the door. Thayne had to hurry and jump up to join him, almost forgetting in his shock he was supposed to be leaving also. Father would actually bring Mother out.

CHAPTER 14 Unexpected

Two horses sped up Castle Road to North Road then westward. They stopped at the easternmost way-station to sleep, but they didn't trade horses. The five hours was sufficient for man and beast who loved to run. They ran the rest of that day and into the night.

They stopped for a late dinner, then turned and ran northward along the road that led into the mountains where the hiding holes of Earl Shicchi were located. The woods were still present, but often they were interrupted by patches of grass that barely grew from the rock that was too close to the surface to allow tree roots good purchase. They'd run until nearly midnight when one of the riders reached out and grabbed the reins of the other's horse and slowed them both.

Thayne motioned for silence, then he took the lead, at a somewhat slower run. He listened to the noises around them carefully. He took the next left. When they reached the next crossroads, he stopped them, listened to the near silence there, then took Ore off the road and into the woods until they were hidden, but could still see the road.

He carefully pulled his sword from its sheath. Ore followed suit. It wasn't too long before they heard hooves, first one set, then behind it multiple, as if three or four sets. Thayne whispered almost noiselessly, "Protect the one." Ore nodded.

They watched as a single rider sped past them, then four in hot pursuit. They crashed out of the woods and took off after the four. In an open grassy area that would make fighting on horseback simpler, three of the four turned to stand against them. Ore took out one rider with his throwing dagger, then the two were on them.

At the clash of sword on sword, the lone rider out front swung his horse around and clashed with the remaining horseman coming up behind him. It didn't take long for Ore to figure out the opponent he was fighting was a Little Death user. He hissed, striking even harder. He hated that drug, and now had a double personal vendetta against it.

He pulled his sword out of the neck of his opponent and turned to see if Thayne was okay. He was also pulling his sword out of his dead opponent. Ore double checked to make sure the third enemy was dead. The dagger had hit the man in his eye and continued on through. That was pretty final. They turned and looked in the direction the lone rider had been running. He was coming up to them. Ore was a bit surprised he hadn't kept going.

"Thank you." The man, who couldn't be seen clearly in the dark, had an interesting accent Ore hadn't heard before. "Sir Ore, I am your guide for the rest of your stay in these mountains."

Ore, wondering how the man could see him well enough to recognize him, cleaned off his sword and put it away, but didn't bind it. Since Thayne had led them here, the news of his arrival in the mountains was probably known to the whole Family by now. Except...he hadn't been addressed as a Family member. "Is it common to pick up stray enemies on the way?"

"Of course. The battle in the mountains has just begun, and hasn't reached the houses yet, even."

"Good. I would like to get to the front before it does, but speaking to the Regent must come first," Ore requested.

"Of course." The man led them back the way he'd come, going at a pace Ore found completely acceptable: fast.

The breath of dawn was on the wind as they came up to the edge of a protected mostly tree-less valley and looked over an encampment. They'd had to fight off two more small enemy patrols, and ran from another three that were too large to fight, although they'd seemed to get distracted before too long with some other foe that came out of the woods behind them.

The main part of Rei's fighting force was already much farther up the mountain and moving like raiders. The goal was to whittle down all the enemy forces, hedging in the houses so that no one could escape, then Rei would attack the houses at once. The reports were supposed to be in when Ore arrived at the battlefield as to which house held which Earl Shicchi. Those reports would be from Rei's spies who had been watching the houses for several weeks now.

The encampment was beginning to stir as the eastern sky was just beginning to lighten. Ore, Thayne, and the guide with them left their horses with the horsemen at the outside edge of the encampment and walked to the main battle tent that sprawled in the center of the encampment, it's pennants flapping lightly in the dawn breeze.

When they entered the main tent it was well lit. Rei, Andrew, and Mina were already breakfasting at a small table set to the side of the central large encounter table that held the maps. Canvas walls bordered this main room, cutting the sides and back of the tent into smaller rooms that held equipment and other things necessary for a mobile office and war room.

Ore walked up to kneel before Rei. He felt the other two who were behind him fall behind a respectful distance and stand at attention. "Here you are Ore." Rei paused, then said, "Lift your head." Ore hesitated, then did as he was ordered, knowing what was coming next as Rei took in the bandage on Ore's head. "Ore...you weren't supposed to get involved."

"I didn't," he said simply.

"Explain, then," Rei said, slightly impatiently.

Ore stood, turning ninety degrees and slightly to the side so that his escorts were in Rei's view. His formal report was going to have to wait. "No. That's Thayne's responsibility." His words were cool. Rei raised an eyebrow and turned to look at Thayne. His eyes caught sight of the third man and he stared at him a moment, then continued on to Thayne.

Thayne took a step forward and bowed to Rei. "I'm sorry, Regent. In order to prevent potential harm to Master Ore's life, I made the outrageous decision to knock him out and force him into a small dark space without his permission.

"However, I also gave the order that as soon as he was aware again, he could be released from that same small dark space, and an alternate protection determined so that his sanity might be preserved. The fault of his injury is mine."

Rei considered Thayne a moment. "And why would you consider it necessary to force your master into such protection without his permission?"

Thayne straightened up. "Because Earl Shicchi, the elder's, favorite punishment of Master Ore was to lock him up in a coffin for three days at a time. It was, on average, repeated every three weeks. His brother, the current Earl Shicchi, remanded the sentence to two days, and only when he was angry with his brother, Master Ore."

Even Andrew and Mina froze. "Was that common practice for the Shicchi family?" Rei asked horrified.

"Yes," Thayne answered. Ore was looking rather dark at having to be reminded. "Mistress Ilena was locked up for seven months straight after Master Ore ran away. That was the most severe case known. Most of the staff were only locked up in such manner overnight."

"I thought they were punished with beatings?" Rei said, even more horrified.

"They were. When the beatings were done, they were taken to the coffin room. On occasion, they were thereafter buried in those same coffins in the morning, the combination having been too overwhelming."

"How did Ilena not die?"

"Earl Shicchi ordered her fed once per day. He wasn't particularly interested in her death, only in punishing Master Ore vicariously. Overcoming the madness was her own strength."

Rei looked over at Ore. He looked like he was about to pass out. Rei rose out of his chair, but Thayne reached Ore first. He carefully helped him sit down. "She never said...," Ore moaned faintly.

"I'm sorry, Master Ore," Thayne said. "I didn't know you hadn't been told." Ore put his head in his hands. Thayne kept his hand on Ore's shoulder.

"That's why they can't sleep in the castle, or be in enclosed spaces?" Andrew asked.

"Yes," Thayne answered. "I was very surprised they hadn't gone mad in the first room you had them in at the castle, when I looked in to see it, although it soon became apparent to me that it was because they'd stayed together. Those who've lived through the Shicchi House punishment have said that if multiple of them were in the coffin room at once, they could communicate with each other and it staved off the madness."

Rei's eyes were wide. He'd had no idea, although he knew Ore had mentioned that the small rooms might be problematic. "Ore, why didn't you say?"

Ore shook his head. "It isn't Master's fault, and even a small room is better than a coffin. It's only when falling asleep or waking up that it's most difficult, in the in-between time. Master let me be with her during those times.

"But I didn't know it was that difficult for her. Before I left, she'd been careful to not be punished, although the elder Earl Shicchi had scolded her once before banishing her from the main house."

When Ore had recovered sufficiently, Thayne rose to finish his report. When he was done, Rei blinked. The report had a lot of important information in it. "The enemy knew the plan?" Rei asked.

"Yes."

"And Ore hadn't slept in two days? Long enough to get so tired he couldn't react to a blow?"

"Yes."

"And you only kept him in that place for as long as he was asleep?"

"Yes."

"And you went all the way to the safe house?"

"Yes. ...The wagon was ours only on loan and could only go into the Hollow by way of the main road. Because the Children needed to be delivered safely, I chose to take us all directly to the house. We've come directly from there," Thayne explained.

"I see. ...Why did the enemy know the plan?" That was Thayne's to answer to as well. That had been a breach of the Family.

"Mother's enemy has broken the code twice before, although it's difficult; however, I can't answer the question sufficiently as I haven't been able to communicate with Grandfather myself since I met up with Master Ore. " It was the best answer Thayne could give.

Rei motioned to Ore. Thayne went back to stand by their guide. Ore rose to his feet again and stood at his usual relaxed attention. He gave the full report, from the time he left the castle until their arrival at the encampment. He included all the reports he'd received at Falcon's Hollow.

Part-way through the report, Rei turned and finished eating his meal, listening closely. When Ore was done, he motioned for Mina to take the food cart over to the three men. "Eat," he ordered them. While they ate, he put his thoughts together and narrowed down his questions. "So, they did unexpected things?" Rei mused.

"Yes." Ore answered.

Rei looked at Andrew and Mina. "They've done other unexpected things as well." He looked back at the three men in front of him. "Let me ask a question not really related to your report." Ore looked at Rei curiously. "How is it that you keep appearing with new members of your family surrounding you? Is your guide another cousin?"

Ore whipped around and stared at his guide. It was the man from the Black Cat. The one who Thayne had told him to make note of. That looked like he could be a prince. That looked like Ilena and him, tawny gold eyes with his long black hair now bound for fighting. He smiled at Ore and bowed formally.

In his soft, foreign accent he said, "Sir Ore, Regent Rei, I am sent by Princess Ilena to follow Sir Ore at the side of Mister Thayne until the battle is over and you arrive safely at Nijoushi again. I apologize - she has required that I ask you to name me for the duration of the time I am here to assist you. I am a native of Selicia, but I am not related to Sir Ore nor to Princess Ilena."

Everyone in the room sat stunned. "He's palace trained, at least," Mina seemed to recovered first.

"If he knows what she is, he's part of the Immediate Family," Ore was next to find something to say. He itched to know who. That particular comment made Rei relax somewhat.

"...But we aren't allowed to know who, and he's from Selicia," Andrew was always the one who pointed out the potential drawbacks.

Rei very graciously said, "I'm grateful that Ilena has asked for someone she thinks highly of to stand to protect the things most important to her at this time, and that you've come. We look forward to working with you.

"Here, in my councils, please refer to me as Rei. Also, please do not refer to Ilena in that manner to any other persons. Her title is still secret within Ryokudo in order to protect her. I would prefer to call you by a name you approve of. Is there one you can recommend?"

"While I am not of any royal line of Selicia, I would be pleased if you would call me Grail," the man requested.

Rei and Ore recognized the name. "Is there a particular reason you would choose the name of one of her cousins if you aren't related?" Rei asked.

As dry and sober as Andrew typically was, "Grail" answered, "Mistress Ilena's first personal order to me was to see his death was avenged."

Rei blinked. "... Ah, I see. Thank you for telling me."

The newly dubbed Grail bowed slightly. "It is my pleasure to serve." He'd very neatly placed himself as a highly favored personal servant to the young Princess Ilena, come from Selicia. And supported his own claim with evidence they could corroborate themselves immediately. Ore was impressed.

Rei turned to Mina. "The generals will be here soon. Please tell Ore and his men what's gone on here while Andrew and I prepare."

Rei and Andrew turned to the maps and conversed quietly while Mina told Ore, Thayne, and Grail what had happened in the north over the past two days. They had, of course, marched and arrived and set up encampments. This was the first morning of serious consideration for the castle group.

The reports they'd received from the past evening and into the night had been as unexpected as what had happened to Ore. The main news, received late in the night, was related to the Houses that were current allies of the Earl, the ones the Children had been retrieved from by Ore.

Separate military groups had been sent to arrest the lords of those Houses. When they arrived, they'd found the houses and grounds burning, the members of the households dead. No survivors had been found by the time the messengers had been sent, although searchers had been looking.

Tokumade was also burning, but there were no persons on the grounds at all, living or dead. The soldiers were combing the lands around the households for signs of the persons who had caused the massacres.

Ore looked at Thayne. "I wonder if the ones who did that were the ones who also hounded my heels?"

Mina nodded. "I was wondering that also."

Ore frowned. "It wouldn't be good to have the dogs running loose in northern Suiran. Should we clean them up also?"

Mina shrugged. "Rei will decide. We've also received the reports from the houses up here. There are a sufficient number of men who serve Earl Shicchi, perhaps increased by members of the other Houses, that all of the houses are of necessity occupied, but we've found it odd that the report says that both Earl Shicchi and the uncle are together at the farthest north house. Ilena expected them to be in separate houses.

"Rei feels that if they're together, either Earl Shicchi needs the restraint of the uncle, or the uncle is indeed planning on turning against him at the last minute and offering him as a peace offering...or both. He's already sent word to clean out the southern houses and close the noose on the north house so it's prepared for his arrival."

"Prince Rei will go himself?" Grail was astonished.

Mina nodded. "That's his way. We'll all go with him."

"Has a fourth location been found yet?" Ore asked.

Mina shook her head. "Many of the searchers have returned with their reports already. There's a way through the mountains to Tarc, but the way to Selicia is impassible from this location, unless they should go back south to the North Road and around the mountains in this area. The way to Tarc is being watched very carefully, as it's possible the uncle, at least, would try to escape in that direction."

Ore turned to look at Thayne and Grail. "Is that pass being watched by the Children of Mother?"

Grail nodded. "It has been for a very long time. There hasn't yet been a report of anyone going north on it."

Ore nodded. "I think, if anyone goes north along it while we're hunting, or even after, a capture would be preferred, but we should confirm with Master."

"That's preferable," Rei's voice came from the table. "Spies would be just as useful as the uncle or Earl."

Grail bowed his head slightly. "I'll see the request is sent."

Thayne asked, "Is the communication network here in the north still integral?"

"The battle network is, yes." Grail answered him and Thayne seemed content enough.

"Come see this, Ore," Rei said. The four walked over to the map table. "I saw it last night as I was falling asleep." He had the map of Suiran open on the table, on top of the other maps. There were four red markers below three blue ones, and a white line.

Rei pointed to the red markers, all in a row in the center of Suiran and along the north border. "These are the four Houses that were part of the alliance, and are all now burning. The largest of the sections of land they represent are the lands of Tokumade, closest to the castle, on the west of it.

"Here," he pointed to the three blue markers that made up an upward pointing triangle, "are the escape houses of the Earl. To both sides the mountains split around them, and to the direct north are even taller mountains. This," he pointed to the white line, "is the passageway from Tarc into this area."

"Here," Rei pointed to the northeast of the white line, at the very edge of the map, "is Tarc. The normal route between Tarc and Suiran is here," he pointed to the upper edge of the map, east of the castle.

Rei looked at Mina. "And here," he pointed to the lands just south of that passage and east of the castle, "is Yosai." Mina saw it quickly and went pale. Ore drew his finger along both lines. Even Thayne and Grail looked concerned.

Rei said to Ore, "You said that the spy who was captured was marked as if from Selicia, yes?" Ore nodded. "Thayne, you said that the enemy in Tarc sends messages to Ilena in the things he does, the people he sends." Thayne nodded. "Then would you say that I might be right in saying that he's just told me what he intends to do when he comes?"

Grail and Thayne looked at each other. Thayne bowed to Grail ever so slightly. Grail wasn't happy being given the higher role in this case, but he took it anyway. "Because I have a longer time of experience with this enemy, I shall answer you, Regent Rei. However, I would first like you to tell it to me, what you think he is saying."

Rei looked at Grail and nodded once. "I think he's saying that he has on purpose opened up a hole for his forces to come down and encircle the castle from the west. That he will use a distraction, within or from Selicia to draw our attention to the far west, while at the same time actually undermining and secretly attacking Yosai and the other holdings to the east.

"By the time the distraction from the west has been settled, he'll have opened up a hole in the east in addition to the one in the middle. Once both openings are completed, then is when he'll actually move to bring his army down from the north to pincer attack and besiege the castle."

Rei looked at the map again, and pointed to Kouzanshi in the far west. "Here," he drew his finger to a pass in the mountains north of Kouzanshi in the far west, "and here," he put his finger on another pass just east of the the first one, "are the passes from Suiran into Selicia, with the second one also having access through a long hard pass into Tarc.

"If the Lord of Tarc wished to pin down the forces protecting Kouzanshi so they couldn't come to the aid of the castle, he could send in the forces of Selicia, or bring in a portion of his own. If he wanted to do that, he would need to attack Kouzanshi during the summer months, as the western passes aren't accessible in the winter.

"With the weakening of the four lands to the west of the castle, and if he should be able to weaken those to the far west this coming summer, I would lose the troops those lands would have otherwise brought. That would be a very great loss.

"Even still, the Lord of Tarc wouldn't be able to stand against the forces of all of Ryokudo if I called upon my brother for aid. However, if the Lord of Tarc came against Nijou Castle in the winter, my brother would find it very difficult to bring his forces to assist until the spring, and the Tarc forces are nearly equal with what I would be able to bring to bear.

"If he should then arrive to attack the castle next winter, having removed the strength of Kouzanshi during the summer, the forces I could defend the castle with would be minimal indeed. I believe that he has already declared war on Ryokudo."

Grail looked at Prince Rei for a long time. Then he bowed. "Mother will be very disappointed it was not her you told this to first."

A cold breeze blew into the room as the tent flap was lifted and two older gentlemen and a younger aide came in from outside. The matter of the Lord of Tarc was set aside and the matter of accomplishing Rei's goals in regards to Earl Shicchi and the uncle behind him began in earnest.

As the battle planning meeting wore on, Ore and Thayne became rather tired. Eventually Ore asked if they could remove to the sleeping cots in the antechamber of the battle tent long enough to get a few hours of sleep. Grail asked Ore if he might as well, as he'd been up nearly as long as they had.

Ore allowed it, and Rei approved the three of them resting for a time, saying he would have Mina wake them. Ore shuddered and warned the other two that it would not be a pleasant awakening if they were not prompt to obey. His last thoughts as he passed into sleep were of Ilena.

-o-o-o-

"Ryan? Ryan?"

"Yes, Rio? What is it?" Ryan poked his head out from around a cabinet. When they met by chance at the Scholar's Tavern on their mutual evening

248

off, he'd asked her to please call him only by his given name. She'd insisted that he must do the same as well. It had been an enjoyable evening, to have a companion.

"Miss Leah has sent me." Rio was wringing her hands. "Mistress Ilena refuses to eat her breakfast this morning. She didn't eat well all yesterday, and this morning when I went to feed her, she wouldn't.

"Usually she will always be obedient to Miss Leah, but when she also tried, Mistress Ilena looked at her and only said, I'm sorry, Leah,' and turned her head away. She won't speak with us nor open her eyes."

Ryan had come over as Rio explained and looked at her in concern. "What can I do?"

"Miss Leah feels that perhaps if you'll make the tea she took the first day after she woke up from her surgery, and come feed it to her, she won't be able to reject Ryan."

Ryan looked a little surprised, then nodded. "I'll do it."

"Thank you very much," Rio was very relieved and left hopeful.

-o-o-o-

Rio entered the infirmary for the second time that day at lunch time, and stood waiting as Ryan finished helping his current medical patient. He glanced at her a few times while he worked. She didn't look good and he wondered briefly if she'd come for herself this time. Her arms were folded tightly in front of her and she was slightly hunched, as if in fear or pain.

He was finally able to excuse his patient and turn to Rio. "What is it, Rio?" he asked her in his best "calm the patient" voice.

"It's Mistress Ilena again, Ryan," her eyes were so sad. "She tried so hard to eat, but it wouldn't stay down."

Ryan put his hand on her arm. He'd been taught that physical touch was also calming. "It's okay, Rio. The body can do that on it's own when it's trying to recover from difficult circumstances, and with a little help the body can repair it as well. I'll make more tea for this time. Then I'll come and we'll try together at dinner, if you'll fetch me."

As Rio took courage from his words and looked up at him, he noticed suddenly, now that they were standing so close together, that he could nearly look into her eyes. With another year of growth or less, he would stand at least as tall as her. Because he had three more years, at least, of growth, he would likely in the end be slightly taller than her.

For some reason, that pleased him. He let go of her before he blushed, and turned away so she wouldn't see. "You'd be welcome to come with me while I make the tea. It won't take long."

He walked towards the herb room and was mildly delighted when she followed him after a slight pause. As he worked, he wasn't sure what to say to her, but she didn't seem distressed by his silence, rather it felt like when Mizi would be in the room with him - a comforting companion.

He realized that he would like to know Rio's age, but was embarrassed to ask. It somehow didn't seem too appropriate, but the voice of Ilena saying he wouldn't learn things if he didn't ask was nudging him to ask it anyway. "Ryan." He jumped a little.

"Yes?" He put the last herb into the mix and picked up the hot water that constantly sat over a small flame since such tinctures and teas were common remedies for the castle staff.

"I've heard that you're the youngest Head Healer in the history of Ryokudo, but I was wondering what that meant. ...How old are you?" Rio had asked the question first, and he was somewhat relieved.

He carefully poured the hot water into the cup. "I'll be seventeen in three months."

"Ah! Seventeen! I thought you were much older! ...But that's like Mistress Ilena. She was seventeen when she became Steward of Tokumade. It must be because you're both very intelligent so as to seem many years older than your age. My birthday isn't much further from your own. I'll be nineteen in five months."

Although she was running on, Ryan didn't mind. He'd been captivated by her statement that he seemed older. He'd never been told that before, always being called younger because he was short for his age. "Thank you," he said softly, giving her a shy smile.

She paused, blushed slightly, then smiled back. "You're welcome, I think."

Ryan startled, "Ah, the tea's ready. Shall we go?" Rio had such soft features when she smiled. He thought he'd like to see that more frequently.

On the way out of the infirmary, he asked her, "Do you know when your next holiday is? I haven't yet been able to go out and see the city since I came. I'm not very good with crowds the first few times I go places, and Ore and Mizi seem to be very busy these days. I would enjoy it if you could possibly keep me company."

Rio stared at him in surprise. He hurried to add, "I can go whenever your holiday is. After all I am the Head Healer. I can set my own schedule to some degree." He smiled again, knowing that he was being a little funny.

Rio laughed lightly. "I should think you would be able to. ...I'd be happy to go with you, but I'll have to ask when Master Ore returns when I may have a holiday. I hope that won't be too long for you to wait."

"No, that will be fine," Ryan said, the smile still on his face. She'd understood he was being humorous. Having always been around people who were older than him, it never occurred to him to question the fact that she was almost two years his senior. They were close in age, that was enough.

-o-o-o-

Rio came to get Ryan for dinner. He was glad he'd asked her to. She said it took four tries to pull him out of his deep thoughts, and apologized for interrupting him. He reassured her, saying it was quite normal behavior for him, and he didn't mind it at all.

He didn't tell her that he'd missed the dinner meal for the last four nights in a row and eaten it cold nearly at midnight each night. Not having Mizi around to remind him to take care of himself was becoming a bit problematic.

As they walked to Ilena's room, Ryan asked if the meal cart had been delivered yet. Rio shook her head, then pointed. The cart was just now being pushed towards them. "Good," Ryan said. He walked over to meet the cart and asked the server to wait just a moment. He looked over what was on the cart, both for all of them, and for Ilena. "Please go back and bring us an orange," he requested. The server nodded and dashed off for the kitchen.

"An orange?" Rio asked.

"They're Ilena's favorite," Ryan answered. "I noticed it when I was helping take care of her when she was first brought to the castle. If we can entice her with her favorite food, then she may be able to hold the required food as well. There are a few other foods here that we may be able to encourage her with, but the orange will be most effective. Watch how I feed her, then you may be able to better encourage her yourself tomorrow."

Rio nodded enthusiastically. "I'll watch carefully, Ryan. We're very concerned to be able to help her as best we can. It's worrisome to see her this skinny. She's been this way before and it took many months to get her to eat again."

"She has been?" To Ryan that was actually important information. "How long ago was it?"

"Ah, she's twenty-four now, and was about eleven at the time."

"That was very young to be that way," he was surprised. "What caused it then?"

Rio became very sober. "I...I'm not sure Ryan would like to know."

"Rio," he said in the voice he had learned would get his patients to tell him the things they didn't want to tell him, "this is very important. If her body has already learned once to not eat, it may be more difficult for me to get her to eat again this time. If I can understand what happened the first time, I won't make mistakes."

She still paused, but her concern for her mistress won out. He was relieved. "Ryan, Earl Shicchi is very evil, although his father before him was worse. I think the story will be too much for you, but I will tell you that he locked her into a small box, the size of a coffin, for seven months without letting her out. She was allowed to eat one meal per day.

"When she was finally let out, she was only skin and bone, and very weak. If you want more medical details, you must ask Miss Leah. She was there for it, and was the one who nursed her back to health.

"Mistress Ilena and Miss Leah came to Tokumade from somewhere else when she was about nine. The rumor is that she's somehow related to the

Shicchi family, and came when her parents died, with no other family to turn to. It was a terrible place to have to stay, and most of us, given her situation, would have stayed alone in whatever place we'd been before.

"But without her, we would all have died much sooner and not be her Family now. She kept us all alive through the pain and horror of that place. The fact that she mentally survived her time in the coffin was a miracle. We all respect her greatly and would do anything for her. Ryan is gentle with Mistress Ilena, and I'm glad."

Ryan had never heard of such evil, and was reeling, even though he could tell she was trying to soften the story as much as possible. "Does Ore know?" he finally asked.

"I don't know if she's told him or not, but I suspect she hasn't. Master Ore was also in that House. Earl Shicchi's father punished him regularly with a similar punishment, although only for days at a time, so he understands that she finds it difficult to sleep at night, but I think she's spared him the knowledge I've just told you, knowing it would be too difficult for him to accept it."

"I think," Ryan said slowly, "that Ore should know."

Rio shook her head. "Perhaps she'll tell him, or she'll decide it's too large a burden for him to carry and will keep silent, I don't know."

"Why would it be his burden?"

Rio was reluctant to answer that question as well. "...She received the punishment because he ran away from the House and Earl Shicchi blamed her."

Ryan's heart stopped for a moment. He knew Ore well, and knew that the knowledge he'd just received would be indeed a great burden for the kindhearted man who always had a smile and ready word for him. But at the same time it seemed to him, who was always not being told things, that it would still be better for Ore to be told.

Ryan said, "Well, it's her's to tell, but I think it's not fair to Ore for him to not understand her well enough. There are things that one would do much differently if all of the knowledge is presented. I've learned that well with our medicine. Not knowing one important detail can change everything in how we treat an illness, and in the potential recovery of the patient.

"It's for that reason I asked you to tell me. There are some things I'll do differently now that I know she's lived through her body rejecting food because of starvation once before. While it sounds like a very terrible situation to have been in for her and for all of you, thank you for telling me that much. I hope all of you are much happier now."

Rio smiled. "We are, very much so. To see Mistress Ilena arriving at the possibility of achieving her goals makes us all the more so. We want to help her succeed."

The server who'd brought the food cart came running up with the orange Ryan had requested. Ryan thanked him, hid it in his pocket, and he and Rio took the food cart in together, Ryan working out his plan to help Ilena as he went. He pushed the food cart up close to Ilena's bed, then turned to her smiling. "Good evening, Ilena," he said. "Are you feeling well?" He ran through his usual check of her health. Keeping to patterns was soothing.

She smiled slightly, although she looked just a little unsure at having all the smells around her. He was watching for that. He nudged the cart a little farther from her, under the pretense of moving it out of his way. She seemed to recover just a little. "I'm feeling well enough. The pains are mostly aches at this time. I'm still feeling weak, of course." She'd learned he wanted to have details when he asked her that question.

"And are you keeping mentally healthy as well?" he asked her, sitting down on the chair between her and the cart. He surreptitiously pricked the skin of the orange in his pocket, allowing a little of the scent of it to leak from it. It didn't take her long to get an extremely interested look in her eyes. He smiled.

"Ah, well, that's more difficult, of course," she admitted. "Being at loose ends with nothing to do but lie here always makes my skin itch and my muscles wish to be exercising, but I'm coping with the help of Leah and Rio. It helps that Mistress and Ryan can come visit." Her eyes were keeping a close watch on him, and were growing hungry. That was good. He was looking for that.

"Well, I'm glad for that. Be sure that you do let them, or myself, know if that's becoming difficult. We want for you to be as healthy as possible, after all, mentally as well as physically. It will make for a better recovery all around. Shall we work together to get your body to eat something real tonight?" Ryan asked.

Ilena shied away from the thought, then looked at him hungrily again. "You seem to have brought something with you to bribe it with. I hope it will work."

"Do you want some?"

"Yes."

Ryan smiled. "That's good. It may work then. But first, can you tell me if there's anything else on the cart that you find smells good?"

Ilena gave him an apologetic look. "I'm afraid you'll have to move. I can't focus my sense of smell on anything else than what you're carrying with you."

Ryan smiled. "Very well. Rio, will you please offer Ilena each dish one by one. We'll test to see what her body is interested in eating tonight."

"Even if it's not on the approved list?" Rio wasn't sure.

"Yes. What her body needs and what we can give it are different in some cases, but not all cases." He moved and Rio began to pick up dishes. He continued to explain as Rio would hold up a dish and Ilena would nod or shake her head. "The body has a natural ability to tell by smell what nutrients it needs. It's easier to feed a starving body those things."

Rio was separating the dishes according to Ilena's preferences. There was one in particular that she reacted very badly to. Then she and Rio laughed, once it had been placed far away. "That was one I never have liked," Ilena told Ryan. "It's made me sick every time I've been forced to taste it."

Ryan looked at it closely. "It contains a vegetable that some people's bodies find intolerable, although we don't quite know why it happens. Miss Leah, you should let the kitchen know. They won't send it to her again, although if you like it you can let them know that also." Leah nodded. She was watching the proceedings with great interest.

Ryan looked at her a moment, then said quietly to her, "Miss Leah, Rio told me about the time before when Miss Ilena was like this. Is there anything in particular that stood out to you when you were nursing her back to health that I should be aware of?"

Leah clasped her hands together in front of her waist. "She'd also been given only minimal water to survive. It was necessary for me to re-teach her to drink, not just to eat. That's why I sent Rio to you for the tea. I didn't want her to get so bad she couldn't drink again. It was like having an infant again for quite some time. I was able to get her back to eating using that thought."

Ryan nodded. "That was a good way to do it in that situation. Here, she already has those basics. We just need to add back in the adult food, if you will."

Leah nodded. "That's my understanding, also, but I hadn't thought to use smell to do it. Her sense of smell is particularly high because of the first starvation, I've always thought."

"It's possible," Ryan mused. "Is it the source of her excellent hearing as well?" He was remembering Ore's comments when she had lost her hearing for a time.

"No, she came to that much earlier."

Rio turned to Ryan. "We've sorted all the food on the cart, Ryan."

He walked up to the cart and took note of all the foods she was needing. "She's definitely had enough breads." He smiled at Ilena.

She smiled back. "Yes, very much so."

"Vegetables, in the main, and simple meats." He nodded. "That's about what I suspected. I'll send a specific menu to the kitchen that we'll try for a week, maybe two depending on how you're doing, then we'll do this again."

Ilena's eyes went wide. "I can eat real foods?"

"Well, you may not like the fact that they'll be processed for very young children, to still prevent choking, but yes. We need to feed the body what it will eat in order for it to be willing to work with us. For now, we will choose...," he picked out a chicken dish in a sauce, and a dish with only vegetables that had been cooked to soft. He handed them to Leah who carried them to the desk. "Rio you may make up our plates while we work on Ilena's."

They made up a plate for Ilena that had the chicken shredded in the sauce, in a small portion, and mashed each type of vegetable separately, such as would be made to introduce new flavors to very young children just learning to eat them, but he limited the foods to four total. "Just as we introduce new flavors slowly to children, we don't want to overwhelm her body too quickly. As I wish to also have her earn her special treat, I want to be conservative tonight."

Ilena was looking at them as best she could, her head craned to see them. To Ryan, that was another good sign. Her interest in eating was continuing to increase. That was important to getting the body to accept the food and keep it down. "We're ready," he said, and Rio put the pillow behind Ilena's head.

Ryan went and stood where Ilena couldn't see just yet. "Miss Leah, Rio, we used smell first. The body has asked for what it needs. We are going to offer those things to it, and it will tell us what it needs the most. That is done by using the eyes. Ilena, when I show you the plate, I want you to tell me the first food you see that your body desires to eat."

Ilena nodded and he walked around to stand before her and hold the plate where she could see it, although that was not so easy from her position. "Carrots," she said simply. He immediately put a small amount on the spoon and fed it to her. She tasted it slowly, savoring the flavor.

"Feed it quickly, while the body still craves it. The reward is important. But here at the beginning we'll only use small amounts at a time so as to not overwhelm."

"More," she said. He again immediately gave her a small amount. After she swallowed it, she pondered. "One more." He again kept it small. She nodded. "That was the right amount. I was afraid I would get too much."

Ryan nodded. "That's important. The body needs to trust that it won't get overwhelmed when it's getting what it needs. The portions must stay sufficiently small for it to begin to trust the food again. It will take the next week to two weeks to work up to even a half spoonful on most foods. Do you want more carrots, or would you like something else."

Ilena frowned. "Something else, but it isn't on the plate."

"Would it be a drink?"

Ilena was surprised. "Yes, that would be nice."

Ryan nodded to Leah and she poured a glass of water and walked around to the other side of Ilena and helped her to drink several sips. "Separating the flavors is desirable at this point, but later we'll mix them. For drinking, sips are acceptable while eating, since the body in general is only accepting very small amounts of anything right now. As the portions on the spoon increase, so will the amount you drink.

"But when you take your tea, you should be working to make the amount you drink each time a normal amount to remind the body that it is an adult body, and it can perfectly well handle that amount. That will help you to be able to eat larger bites at your meals as you go along as well."

Ilena and Leah both nodded. "Chicken," Ilena said next. Ryan again fed her very small bites until she was done, again only a very few bites, but more as she was able to eat five of them before needing to stop. They continued the process until she'd eaten as much as she could keep down. In the end, she had alternated each vegetable with the chicken, although the first five were the most bites she'd been able to eat in one run.

"You're quite meat deficient," he said, "but that's to be expected. I would think that you are also milk deficient, which is why I chose the chicken that was cooked in a sauce in which milk was used."

"The flavor was very good," Ilena said.

"Then that's probably the case," Ryan said. "I use flavor last of all, because sometimes what we need and what we taste are not the same. But if it tastes good, it's still an acceptable indicator you need it." There was still food on the plate, but Ryan handed it to Rio to put on the cart.

"Now," he leaned back, "at this time there's no point in forcing the body to eat more than it can. But soon, if you don't begin to eat greater amounts on your own, we'll need to encourage it to eat the correct amount for an adult body to survive in a healthy manner."

Still leaned back casually, he pulled out the orange and began to slowly peel it. "You are, I imagine, feeling rather full, and not like eating anything at all, so I may have to eat this by myself, but we'll see if we can tempt the body into acknowledging it might have enough room for something it really wants." He watched her eyes, which were watching the orange in his hands. He was looking for a specific reaction.

"When we're ready to help your body increase the quantity it's willing to accept, we'll use your favorite food of the day to encourage it. We'll feed you what you think is a sufficient amount, like the three bites of carrot at the beginning. Then we'll offer a bit of, say orange, but you won't get to eat it until you eat three more bites of carrot. If you can eat them, you'll get your reward. Then we'll repeat it for the next food, and so forth.

"We'll be unable to use only oranges, sadly, as the body will eventually need something different to interest it, so if there's any other thing that could tempt you in the same way, it would be very useful to know." She didn't answer, she was so fixated on the orange.

Ryan smiled. That was where he wanted her to be. He put one of the peels in her hand. "Just hold that for a moment," he told her. He put the remaining peels on the plate on the cart. When he turned back he watched what she was doing.

Ilena was rubbing the outside of the orange peel, then she lifted it to her nose and smelled the interior. He had a sudden idea. Later, if he ever needed to win her favor for something, all he would have to do would be to make a tea for her that included orange peel.

He'd learned while working with the head healer at Ichijou, Parmenia, that the right tea could calm and make pliable strong women who never chose to relax on their own. He would never forget Ilena would likely be calmed by orange tea. He couldn't after all. That was his gift, that he remembered everything he saw or read.

He walked up to Ilena and put his hand on her head. She looked up at him. "Are you feeling like eating might be a good idea right now, if it could be what you want? Or is just having the peel sufficient?"

She paused in thought, then said, "Just one, please?"

"If I give it to you, you have to chew the entire piece and swallow it. I won't give it to you in small pieces, nor can you just suck the juice out of it." She looked at him in surprise. "Decide," he told her.

She considered just a moment, then her eyes flashed. "I'll eat it."

He immediately held one section out to her, but he made her take it. She reached up slowly, then in a flash it was in her mouth and she was chewing on it, her eyes closed in pleasure.

He watched her closely. This was a bit tricky, this part. Once the part of the orange that was easy to eat was gone, the body was likely to reject the outer skin. It was the other hard part of getting young children to eat proper foods. Texture. Her body had to be able to process the fibrous parts of foods.

It would be a problem with unshredded meats as well. The orange was perfect to teach it. If it didn't go well she would choke on that part today, but to explain it before she'd performed it would interfere with her being able to do it.

She was reaching that point and he watched what she would do. He was surprised when she swallowed it down suddenly, likely still mostly whole. She grinned at him. "I learned to do that with mikan before, so I've practiced that part. It was probably the thing that frustrated Nana more than anything else - teaching me to chew and swallow real food again."

Ryan sighed in relief. "That's good. If we don't have to fight that part, the rest will come easily and naturally." He paused, then asked casually, "Do you want another?"

"Nope." She was actually cheerful, finally. "But it was very good."

"Hmm," he said thoughtfully as he sat back down in the chair. "Well, I haven't had my dinner yet, so I'll go ahead and eat it then." He took one of the slices and ate it, not too fast, not too slow, as if he was just casually eating it. It only took getting to the second slice before she looked like she was regretting her decision.

As he peeled off the third section, he looked up into Ilena's tawny eyes. She was almost begging with them. His eyes turned up into a smile and danced. She made a face at him. "Ah, you're teasing me!"

"Yes," he said mildly, and ate the third slice.

"Arah!" She bit her lip, looking concerned. He knew she was trying to weigh what her body would do with what she really wanted to do desperately. Then she took a deep breath, and closed her eyes and relaxed. "If you'll save me the last piece, I may be able to eat it in a few minutes. But right now, I can't." She sounded sad and he wasn't surprised, but he was pleased she was willing to try.

"All right. I'll save it for you. Let me know when you want it." He set all of the remaining sections on a small plate on the cart and picked up his plate to eat his own dinner. "You've done very well, Ilena. I'm pleased. I hope you'll continue to work this hard on each meal from now on."

"Thank you, Ryan," she said.

When he was done eating, he set his plate on the cart, then took the little plate of oranges off the cart and set it on the desk. "Rio, we're done with the cart," he said. She took it out of the room to leave it for the servers to retrieve. "Ilena, do you think you can eat the last piece of orange?"

She sighed. "Not a whole one. Maybe a half. But I'm not sure it would be worth it at this point." She sounded like she was already falling asleep. He wasn't surprised. A weakened body with food in it that it needed would not stay awake long.

Ryan nodded. "You're full enough, then. I'll leave it for later." He looked at Leah and motioned to the orange sections. She smiled and bowed her head, understanding that she was allowed to use the remainder of the orange slices to reward Ilena.

"Thank you very much, Mister Ryan," Leah said. "I've learned some important things this evening."

Ryan nodded. "You're very welcome, Miss Leah. I'll send the menu to the kitchen when I have it written up. You won't have to test the foods for the next while, but you will likely have to tempt her to eat them." Leah nodded and looked resigned. She'd already had to live through that process once, but this time Ryan had made it easier.

CHAPTER 15 Correspondence

Mizi sat down in the chair at Rei's desk and sighed. She'd just finished sorting the day's mail into the proper piles, and now she had this to decide what to do about. Sitting before her was a message tied with a gold ribbon. Likely, at most King Sasou would wait three days to receive a response.

"Dane?" she called.

"Yes, Mistress Mizi?" he looked up from his work.

"Would it be possible to get a message to Rei?" Mizi asked.

Dane had seen the letter come in, "One could be sent by courier. If you were willing to use Mistress Ilena's network, it would arrive to him over a half-day sooner than if you used the military network."

"Surely you boast, brother," Tairn said, looking up.

"No." Dane looked at him seriously. "Mistress Ilena's goal is to decrease it again by another half, at least, once she's finally in the position to do so."

Tairn raised his eyebrow. "Will the method be shared?"

Dane answered, "I should think so. She plans to have it be one of her businesses."

"She'll market it?" Tairn was even more surprised.

"She needs to earn money to support her household somehow," Dane shrugged. "Right now, use of the messenger birds is reserved for military and castle use, and a few lords who can pay the high prices for the few available birds. Mistress Ilena would like to see her method be able to be used eventually for any who wish to pay for it."

"Ehhhhh." Tairn was impressed with her ambition.

Dane turned to look at Mizi to see if she had any other questions for him, but she was already at work, her head bent over a piece of paper, her pen moving rapidly.

Mizi put down her pen and reread the letter she'd written, then decided Rei should know what she'd done. She pulled out another piece of paper and began writing again.

Dear Rei,

A private letter arrived from King Sasou on the fifth day after you left. I've sent him the following response, by way of the messenger birds, so that I might know what he wishes for me to do. I hope the campaign is going well,

Mizi

Dear King Sasou, she copied from her first letter.

Regent Rei is currently on campaign in the north to bring Earl Shicchi to face justice at the Lord's Court to be held within a few month's time. I have received your private letter to him. I don't intend to read it myself, but wish to know what you desire for me to do. He's not expecting to be at his desk again in the Rose office for another sixteen days.

If you're willing, I could have it sent to him by way of the Director of Intelligence's courier network, with his response coming by the same way. That will make his response come to you later than you anticipated when you sent it.

I await your response,

Lady Mizi

She placed her note to Rei in a message folder and placed it underneath the folder that had come from King Sasou, put the original to go to King Sasou on top of them both, and set them aside. Then she went to the door and stepped out briefly.

She motioned to a paige sitting in the ranks of those assigned to the Regent who waited outside the Rose office. He leaped up to speak with her. "Go to the message hall and fetch me some of the ribbon used to tie up personal messages. It must be of the color red." She paused, then added, "And I think it should be of sufficient quantity to last me for some time. You may go." The paige ran off.

"*A-hem.*" She turned to her right and sighed internally. "Miss Mizi, I really don't think it's appropriate for one such as yourself to be doing the Regent's business." It was Marquis Preston, here in the hall for the fifth day in a row, and apparently for the same purpose.

Mizi took a deep breath and turned to face the marquis. It wasn't her first time. There had been a marquis like this at Ichijou castle, too. "Lord Preston, as I said before, Regent Rei has requested that I continue to work in his office while he's away and do what it is I can do. I intend to be obedient to his word. If you wish to question him, you must do so when he's present.

"I would think that allowing your own duties to languish for the remainder of the three weeks he is gone would only be a sign to him that you are unwilling to do your own duties as required of a minister to the crown. I have business to attend to. Excuse me." She ignored him when he would have spoken to her again and closed the door to the Rose office against him.

She'd tried to reason with him politely the first two days. When he actually followed her away from the Rose office the day before today as she was headed to Ilena's room, berating her all along the way, she'd had to desperately request help from Marcus to deflect him so that the Marquis didn't learn of Ilena or her location. She'd been very glad Marcus had shown up just at the right moment.

She'd been so flustered that she'd finally asked Ilena for advice on what to do in this situation. So far, she felt much better at having had her say and then refusing to stay and listen to him have nothing but wind to say again. She took a deep breath, then returned to Rei's desk, taking up her own work.

Perhaps longer than she was expecting, there was a knock at the door and the paige she'd sent was let into the office. She looked up and waited. He walked up to her and said, "I'm sorry to be so late, Lady Mizi. The message office doesn't have red ribbon at this time; however, they've sent out to get some.

"In the meantime, I was able to find a servant girl who had a red ribbon that she was willing to give to you for your purposes." He held out a length of pretty red satin ribbon. "When the message office has obtained the ribbon necessary, they'll send a portion up to the office here."

Mizi was loath to take someone's hair ribbon they'd likely purchased for their own purposes, but she was short on time. "Thank you very much," she took the ribbon and the paige excused himself.

Thinking that she might have to wait several days before receiving the message ribbon, she cut just the necessary length she needed off the ribbon she'd been given using the little knife Rei used to cut his own blue ribbon. She folded her message to the King, rolled it up to fit into a message bird's message tube, and tied it with the red ribbon, then carried it out the door.

"Henry," she called a paige she knew she could trust, "please take this message to the message office. Tell them it's to be sent by message bird immediately to King Sasou. Wait there to receive his reply and bring it directly to me. That is all."

"Yes, Lady Mizi," he took the message, bowed, glanced to her right with a telling look, then disappeared.

Mizi closed her eyes. She'd had it with the marquis. She'd originally decided she wouldn't do it, but Ilena's final bit of advice was all that was left.

"Miss Mizi," the Marquis began. She didn't let him finish.

"Marcus, please go down to the Secretary to the Minister of Public Works and let him know that his Minister is loitering about the hall in front of the Rose office again, for the fifth day in a row, and needs to be reminded of his proper duties to the crown. That is all." She turned and walked back into the Rose office, closing the door tightly behind her.

Marcus, a big grin on his face, dashed off. Marquis Preston stood in the hall astonished, then remembered that he didn't enjoy scoldings from his secretary and decided he would like to be elsewhere when that man appeared in this hall.

-o-o-o-

Mizi was supposed to be going down to visit with Ilena now, but instead she was staring at the letter that had arrived from King Sasou, another gold ribbon on it, directed to her. She was sure it wasn't written by his own hand, although she wouldn't know as she'd never seen his handwriting before. But he most assuredly had at least voiced the words:

Dear Lady Mizi,
It was quite shocking to be handed a message with a red ribbon on it. Has my little brother finally understood what to do with you? Or was the office staff too busy to deal with my message itself, that it had to ask the infirmary

261

for help? I do hope Tairn is doing his work properly. I trust Director Ilena's couriers sufficiently.

Sasou, King

"Ah, now what do I do?" she sighed.

"Mistress Mizi?" Dane looked up at her.

"King Sasou responded to my question, but if I don't answer him again, it won't go well. However, it doesn't seem to be something that needs to go by message bird. Yet at the same time, I'm not able to tell sufficiently. Which should I choose?" she asked rather plaintively.

Dane cautiously asked, "May I ask, what's in his letter that he needs to know?"

Mizi looked at the letter again. The king had maligned the entire office, so perhaps it would be best if the entire office answered it. She handed it over. Dane read it, then questioningly looked at her as he moved to hand it to Tairn. She nodded and he passed it over.

Tairn sighed when he finished reading the letter. "So, you still have an adversarial relationship with the King?" Tairn asked sympathetically.

"Well, I don't think it's quite that," said Mizi. "It feels more like he enjoys teasing me." She sighed. "Andrew says he enjoys teasing Rei, too, and that Rei hates writing letters to his brother the most."

"Well...," Tairn decided to leave that alone, "I would say that for this letter, it wouldn't be necessary to send it by message bird, unless you wished to send him a particular, unwritten message."

Mizi considered that. "You mean, if I wished to express an immediate answer to his criticism of the office?"

Tairn smiled at her. "There are many things an immediate response can say, the same as a message sent slowly on purpose. How you send this response can say as much as the words themselves." He handed the letter back to her.

Mizi took the paper, considering what Tairn had said, and walked over to the door. She poked her head out. "Henry, go tell my next appointment I'll be late. I need to write a response to this letter from the King." She shut the door still preoccupied.

"Ah," Dane interrupted her as she moved back to the desk, "what about the message to Rei?" he reminded her.

She shook her head. "No, I want to send him a copy of my letter to this one, too. I think he'll need to know what I've communicated to the King so that if he needs to answer to it as well, he's not unaware."

-o-o-o-

Less than one day later, Rei, preparing for the final assault on the house of Earl Shicchi, sat holding two message folders, the first one thin and bound with gold. The second one was somewhat thicker and bound with red. A messenger stood before him.

Rei blinked and looked at Andrew and Mina. They were as bemused as he. He opened the first one, from the King, and read it.

Little Brother,

I hear you've allowed Mizi to sit in your office at your desk. That seems as bold a move as the kiss on the platform just before leaving was cowardly. I look forward to seeing what your healer can do in that place.

Happy Birthday,

Big Brother Sasou, King

Rei had a sinking feeling. He looked at the red ribbon binding the other folder. "Mizi?" guessed Mina.

He nodded. "Yes, we talked about it when she first came to the office, remember?" He handed Sasou's letter over to them to read.

"I thought so, too," commented Mina after she read it.

"But why did she send it on?" Andrew asked.

Rei looked down at what was still in his hand. "I'm a bit afraid to find out," he admitted. He slowly slipped the red ribbon from the message folder, placing it carefully in his jacket pocket.

Andrew knew it was going to join Rei's growing pile of "Mizi first's" memorabilia in the Rose office desk drawer. He hoped suddenly she didn't go looking through the desk while they were gone.

Rei opened the folder and began reading. He handed the first two letters over to his aides - the response she'd sent to the King in the first place, and his response to it. When he read her second response, Rei began to smile.

Dear King Sasou,

Prince Rei has asked that I sit at his desk in the Rose office while he's away so that I might accomplish that which I can do to make his own burdens less. Thus it was to me that your first message was brought. I felt it best to respond to you promptly at that time.

I'll send your message to Prince Rei via Director Ilena's courier, then. However, in order to not place an unnecessary burden upon our message service, I shall send this missive to you by the normal route.

Tairn and Dane Malkin are both performing their duties for Miss Mina most admirably while they are also kind enough to assist me with mine. The Rosebud office is keeping up with the remainder of the necessary work sufficiently.

I should think it would be as obvious to you as it was to Rei that my messages would come by way of a red ribbon.

I look forward to hearing from you again,

Mizi

Dear Rei,

I've sent this response to the King by way of standard mail. If he wishes to have me as a correspondent, then I'm happy to oblige. Likely there will be another set of letters for you to read when you arrive back at the castle, if he's not too busy to continue teasing me. I do think that allowing you to be aware of what he's saying is important, so I'll continue to keep copies.

Ilena has been as great a use to me in the office as Tairn and Dane, although it's through the advice she gives me when we visit in the afternoons since I can't have her presence. The paiges Marcus and Henry also help me, both with the office work, and when I am out and about in the castle. The small hurdles of the first few days seem to have been worked out and things are going smoothly now.

Please take care. I'm thinking of you often. ...And Happy Birthday. I haven't spoken to Ilena about your party yet, but she is doing well.

Mizi

P.S. Ilena says she would like black, because if she has to send a written message to you or the King, it will most assuredly contain dire news, and you should therefore be prepared before you open it to read it. I'm in disagreement, still. We'll wait to hear what your preference is before deciding.

"Mizi is as solid as always. Andrew, please prepare to write for me," Rei ordered. Andrew went to his field desk and took out pen and paper, then waited for Rei to be prepared to give his dictation.

Elder Brother,

Mizi has been my Adjunct for several weeks now, in charge of handling all petitions brought before the Regent. The lords have become used to seeing her face in that capacity. As she has also been helping, when she has time, with duties about the Rose office, I felt it best to leave her in charge of both while I was away.

The kiss was not cowardly. It was calculated to both bring high morale to the soldiers before bringing them out to battle, and to send the message to the lords of the castle that I expected them to be obedient to her while I was away. It also was a message to all of Ryokudo that I intend to announce my intentions towards her very soon, as I'm sure you already understand.

Mizi's unrehearsed speech to the soldiers was well received and thoroughly acceptable. I expect responses to have been prepared by the time I return. I look forward to answering them, although I expect Mizi is already answering many of them on her own quite admirably.

We're preparing to engage Earl Shicchi directly. I would hold this message until I had a positive report to send you, but then it would arrive to you later than the promised time. I shall send that report to you when we've accomplished our goal. I'm spending my free time considering the matter of the Lord of Tarc.

Prince Rei, Regent Suiran

P.S. Would you like to weigh in on what color ribbon Ilena should send written messages tied with? She says black so that we'll be prepared for the terrible news that will inevitably be contained therein. Mizi favors the more optimistic violet, or green. You may let Mizi know in your next letter to her if you have a preference.

As Andrew brought it over to Rei to sign, he said, "I do believe that's the fastest, and perhaps longest, letter you've ever composed to the King. You're growing stronger."

"Ah, well," Rei handed the signed letter back to Andrew to be prepared for sending, "actually I've been composing it since I decided to kiss Mizi that day. I knew he'd be asking. It did help to read their communications first. Somehow I'm always able to draw strength from Mizi in all things. Ah! Before sending it, please copy it, then I'll add on a note to send to Mizi."

Andrew took the letter back to his desk and copied it, then tied the original with blue to go to the King. "I'm ready, Rei." His pen was poised over the copy to continue writing.

Mizi,

Thank you for the kind birthday wishes. Your letter was a perfect present. We're well, and nearly about to confront the Earl in his hole. I'm hopeful we can return home early. The help of Mother's Children has been invaluable for keeping the enemy from escaping outside the boundaries we set for them, so the clean up afterwards should take much less time than I'd anticipated, although it's perhaps too soon to say that just yet.

I've sent you a copy of my response to my brother. He merely wished to send birthday greetings and to let me know he'd heard that you were working in the Rose office now, and wondered what my intentions were. I wish I could tell you how to differentiate between the letters he sends that are important for me to answer right away, and those that may languish, but it's not always consistent. You would have to read them yourself to know.

I wouldn't mind giving you that permission, but you should seek his also. It's unlikely he'll grant it. Perhaps now that he's your correspondent he'll know to ask you directly next time when I'm unavailable.

I'm glad to know that Ilena, Dane, and Tairn are being helps to you and that you have other allies within the castle. I trust that things will continue to move smoothly for you. I also think of you often, and Ore also thinks of Ilena. Tell her that the second she sent for him has been very invaluable, although at first he was surprising. I'm looking forward to her story about him when we return.

He signed the letter, then tied it himself. Andrew handed both letters to the messenger who bowed and left. Ore, with his men, walked in the tent as the messenger left. "You're using Mother's messengers, Master?" Ore asked, recognizing him as Family on sight. "Where are they going?"

"What do you think, Ore? Should Ilena's messages be sent with a black ribbon, or a purple ribbon?" Rei asked him, putting all the letters he'd received together again.

Ore looked puzzled, then looked at Thayne and Grail. In one voice all three said, "Black."

Rei looked at them surprised. "Why?"

"Because Mother has no need to send written messages, Master Rei," answered Thayne. "All of her messages are by voice."

"If she wishes to tell you a thing, she'll tell you herself," answered Ore. "...And it matches her hair."

Grail answered last in a very dry voice, "Be prepared to plan her funeral if you receive such a message. She'll have sent it just before her own death."

"That would indeed be most distressing," Rei said. "But I won't hold her to it, rather I would hope it never happens."

"Will you give Mizi an opinion, Rei?" Mina asked.

"And have to choose between the two of them?" he answered, horrified. "I'll let my brother decide."

"Is that cowardice?" she asked.

"Wisdom," all the men in the room chorused.

"What's brought this about, Master?" Ore asked.

Rei handed over the stack of letters. "Mizi is now a correspondent with not just a prince, and a vagabond, but also a king." Ore began to read.

"Mmm, quite the opposite of Mother, then isn't it?" Thayne mused quietly. Grail smiled his faint smile in agreement. "What color does Mistress Mizi wish for Mistress Ilena?" Thayne asked.

"Purple, although she says green is still obviously available," Rei answered.

"Rei, must it be a solid color?" asked Grail in his soft voice.

"It's simpler for the eyes to see, but no, I don't believe there's a restriction."

Grail reached into his jacket and pulled out a medallion upon which hung a length of cording, braided from three colors. He handed it to Rei for his inspection. "These are already her colors."

Rei held the medallion in one hand and ran the fingers of his other hand down the cording. It was braided with black, green, and gold. He liked it. The medallion had on one side the crest of her father, the lioness rampant with three roses beside it.

The other side was the crest of the Touka family with the modification for the Second Princess, her mother's crest, though of herself she was still the First Princess until Rei married Mizi, if he had his way. He reverently handed the medallion back. "You are indeed someone special to Ilena, if you carry this," he said.

266

Ore slipped his hand in and took the medallion to see it before Grail could obtain it. Grail didn't protest. After Ore was satisfied, he handed it to Grail silently, gave him a look that promised he was going to have to tell him sometime soon who he was, then returned to reading the letters.

"What did you say in your response to King Brother?" Ore asked as he gave the letters back to Rei, who handed them to Mina for safekeeping.

"That Mizi has been his Adjunct, rather than a healer, for weeks, and exactly why he kissed her and put her in the Rose office at his desk," Mina summarized. "And sent a copy of that letter to Mizi with further encouraging words."

"Ah, the Children of the castle are going to be disappointed then, I think," Ore said a little wistfully, and Thayne smiled.

"What is it?" Mina asked.

"They had a bet going as to how long it would take Mistress to figure out what it was Master has done to her, and now he's told her himself. That will surely take the fun out of it all." He turned to Thayne. "Will she still award the minor dream?"

"Mmm, perhaps, but it's not certain. Likely she'll be just as unhappy Master Rei let it out." Thayne answered.

"What?" Rei was having a hard time with Mother's Children having fun at Mizi's expense.

"Mistress Ilena was also part of it, in that she was offering an additional reward to the winner of the bet," Thayne said.

Rei's eyes narrowed, then he gave up. "Then perhaps it's good I've ended it."

"Indeed," agreed Grail.

"Isn't that agreement because you've already lost the bet, Grail?" Thayne grinned at him. Grail looked at him stonily. "He has great faith in your Princess, Master Rei."

"Thank you for that," Rei said to Grail, who relaxed a little at his gratitude, but refused still to admit he had participated at all. "However, I wouldn't have voted for her to have understood it at all until either myself or Ilena had explained it to her."

Thayne and Grail both straightened in surprise he would say that. He continued for their sake. "She still really knows nothing about palace politics. It's a field Ilena is planning on teaching her, but hasn't yet had the opportunity to. So if I had participated, that would have been my answer."

Thayne looked chagrined. "Then I've lost as well."

Ore put his hand on Thayne's shoulder in mock sympathy, then changed the subject to the report he had for Rei.

CHAPTER 16 Battle

It was dark on the mountain and the sunset was fading from behind them in the west. Ore, Thayne, and Grail were hiding among the rocks and scrub above the last house to be breached. They were resting, waiting for the full moon to rise over the mountains to the east. That would be the signal to begin the attack. The soldiers had tightened the noose to just around the final house for two days now, preventing anyone from entering or leaving.

During that time, the soldiers not needed for that duty and Mother's Children had swept through the mountain, ensuring that there were no enemies remaining anywhere else. The other houses had been attacked, cleaned out, and burned to the ground earlier. Rei didn't want anyone using them for bases of attack in the future. All that was left was to confront the Earl and Ilena's bastard uncle.

They'd been seen going in, and the third doppelgänger that Ilena had told them about had been found in Kouzanshi and taken into custody. Nothing had been allowed to leave the clear ground around the third house, although Rei had given orders to allow the people in the house access to the outside unharmed, if they cared to come out. He wanted to know if they were still inside, and still alive. It had been pretty quiet.

Thayne was sitting up on a small rocky ridge looking down into the bowl the house was in, taking his turn to watch from their position. The house was in a small clearing, likely cleared by the men who'd built the house itself, since it was completely surrounded by the last fingerling of woods that refused to let go of the rocky heights until that rock escaped and rose at steep altitudes around three sides of the trees. The lights in the house glowed through a few windows around the curtains that had been drawn so they couldn't see what was going on inside.

There were torches set around the perimeter of the clearing by Rei's forces. They'd been placed there as soon as the net had reach that distance. They wanted to be sure that the men inside didn't try to slip away at dark, and they didn't much mind the Earl knowing they were there. They'd kept their distance other than that.

Rei had decided to wait to see if the Earl would make the first move. He'd come out of his house each morning and demanded that if he was guilty of a crime, that he be given due course of the law and not be kept penned up like an animal. None had answered him, and eventually he'd given up and gone back inside.

He'd been quite angry this morning when he hadn't received a response, but the morning before, his response had been more mild. A large number of Mother's forces had been household members at Tokumade. They confirmed for Rei that the first 'Earl' had been the uncle, and the second had been the Earl himself.

Rei was satisfied they didn't need to wait any longer. One or the other wanted him to know they were there and wanted to talk. He was willing, as long as he held the advantage. He'd sent one set of soldiers up into the rocky mountains above the third house just at dusk, including Ore and his men.

"*Hahhh*," Ore's nerves were alternating between his usual before-battle focused calm, and sudden moments of the old fear he'd carried with him for so many years now. He was controlling them by remembering Ilena and the anger and desire for revenge he had for her sake. That cycle was getting old already.

He stood from where he'd been crouched, in a relaxed waiting stance, and stretched. Moving would be preferable at this point. They still had about an hour or more to go before they moved up to a closer position to the house.

He turned to look at Grail. Grail was watching him, as he had been for much of the evening, from where he was leaning up against the rock Thayne was sitting on. As they'd left Rei to come here, Rei had called to Grail and said, "We can't afford any hesitation tonight. Whatever it is, fix it, or step aside before we engage." Grail still hadn't said anything, although Ore had been waiting for him to. It was time to get it out of him.

Ore stuck his thumbs in his pants pockets and rocked back on his heels. "Let's have it then, Elder Son. I'm tired of feeling like you're trying to decide how you'll eat me. If it keeps on, I'm going to have to assume you're actually working for the uncle in that house over there."

Grail pushed off the rock with his back and strode a few steps closer to Ore. Ore stayed in a relaxed ready stance, not threatening, but not unaware either. He'd been having a hard time getting into the skin of the older man and wasn't sure if he would suddenly attack or not.

"Not all of us approve of what you're doing." Grail paused, wanting to be sure Ore understood that he was voicing a concern that more than one member of the household held, and more particularly, himself. "Why is it necessary to put Mistress Ilena into seclusion? Are you attempting to moderate the Princess when her independence is her strength?"

Ore paused. He hadn't considered that would be what Grail would be concerned about. Grail himself was very well trained to serve under a master, even a king or prince. Ore rubbed the back of his head and wondered if he was the right person to answer the question, although of course he was the one who needed to answer to it.

"Elder Son, you knew Ilena before she came to Tokumade?" When Grail inclined his head, Ore asked him another question. "Did she ever serve a master before then?" Grail thought just a moment, then shook his head. "At Tokumade, she didn't either. Rather, she strove to master the lords of that place, and won."

Ore paused, trying to collect his thoughts. "That was a thing I couldn't do. I wouldn't serve out of fear or because of anger, but I also didn't care to master them. So I chose to run and live independent, serving only myself.

"When I found Master, I saw in him what I'd seen in Ilena: someone who could lead with kindness, inspire others, and who invited others to serve them. It was the latter that I'd never experienced before - only being forced to serve. Because Master has never forced me, I've learned that service is not a burden, but is light, and I've chosen it for myself.

"Even so, because I'd only fought serving others, I hadn't learned how to serve properly. That's something that you have learned, likely from a young age - like Mister Andrew." Ore looked at Grail, knowing it was true, and wondering if he could comprehend what it was like to have to come to it at an older age.

"Even after many years of training, I'm still considered 'wild' by those who grew up to serve, though from my own understanding I'm far from the wild I was. Can you understand the difference?" He tilted his head questioningly.

Grail looked at him with a bit of superiority. "Of course."

"Can you?" Ore asked unbelieving. "I think you need to consider it harder than that. Can you stand in my shoes?" He waited. Grail was looking impatient. "It's important to understanding Ilena's position, Elder Son," Ore said gently.

Grail tried to consider it, his face furrowing. Ore tried harder. "You aren't forced to serve blindly, nor are you bound to silent service. Both of those were required at Tokumade. But those who must serve in that way never serve with their hearts. Your service is one you continue to offer because you choose to. In your service, you may give, strengthen, and if necessary, even rebuke without fear." Grail nodded. He understood that much.

"How do you do it?" Ore asked. "How do you know what is the proper way to say what needs to be said, and what the proper time is? Or when it's the proper time to hold your tongue and bow your head? Can you teach me?"

"Ah...," Grail, in thinking about that, was beginning to see the difficulty of it, although of course it was done.

"Certainly gentle training beginning as a young child is much simpler, is it not?" Ore asked him. Grail had to admit it probably was. "But when one who isn't used to it asks you, it becomes difficult." Grail nodded.

"Ilena has learned to serve in the same way Master and King Brother have learned - by offering strength, inviting others to serve, and always minding the lives of others. These things are good and they are strengths to her, but they are not the service you offer." Grail understood.

Ore took a breath. "Ilena isn't being punished. She's asked to learn to serve as Grail and Ore serve. ...You understand her goal, to stand behind Master at the side of Ore, supporting Mistress?" Grail reluctantly nodded his head. He'd heard it, what Ore was saying, but he wasn't ready to accept it yet. Ore spelled it out anyway. "None of those things is to lead. She'll continue to lead others, that won't change. But to be able to accomplish her goals, she must learn to serve as you and I serve.

"Because in this thing she is as 'wild' as Ore, Master has made me to be her teacher. Because I have lived the same path she must walk, she trusts me to help her understand. Because she has a goal and is impatient, she's working very hard to learn it. Because I'm her partner, I wish to protect her path." Ore stopped, and gave Grail time to digest what he'd said. Then he asked, "Have I answered you?"

"Because I cannot see the results of what you're doing," Grail said carefully, "I find it difficult to accept."

Ore studied him. "What position are you in that it should need to be acceptable to you?" Ore was merely asking for information.

"Truly do I wish at this moment to tell you, but the Princess has forbidden it at this time," Grail answered.

Ore looked at him, then up at the shadow of Thayne above them, blocking out the stars. He'd been watching the two of them for many days now. Thayne always answered when there was a question about the Family, but Grail was too careful. When they interacted with each other, Thayne always took the younger brother position, thus Ore had called Grail by the term Elder Son, not really liking calling him by a false name assumed just for this mission.

Grail was Selician and he carried Ilena's princess medallion. Ore believed Grail had brought it out on purpose, to give them a sign. And there was the time in the Black Cat, when Grail had come to test him. Ore looked back at Grail.

"Then I shall say it, although I only partially understand. You are someone that Ilena values so highly that she is still even now not willing to tell her partner nor her cousin and master, but continues to protect you. You come from Selicia and have known her childhood. Thus, like Miss Leah, you have been with her from the beginning. If you can't be properly convinced, you will be able to remove her from this path."

Grail answered, "Your understanding is sufficient. I guard her footsteps."

Hah, Ore sighed a puff of air. This Eldest Son stood behind her the same way Mister Andrew stood behind Rei. Thus, he would indeed be very concerned about those Ilena surrounded herself with and the influence they had on her. "It must be very difficult to be placed far from her." Ore said sympathetically. "Mister Andrew cries if Master is gone from his sight longer than a few minutes."

Although it was difficult to read Grail's eyes in the dark of the stars, for just a fleeting moment Ore felt a raw pain emanate from the Eldest Son of Mother. "...I have not –," he cut off, then turned away abruptly. "When she is ready and calls me, I will come." Grail's voice was thick. Then he said very dangerously, "I will see what you have done."

Ore sighed inside. This Child of Mother's would be much more difficult to convince than any of the others. Why had Ilena kept him so far from her? Surely he should have been kept the closest of all?

-o-o-o-

When the moon rose sufficient to reach their higher position, Ore, Thayne, and Grail moved down into the valley, staying just ahead of the light itself as it reflected off the grey stones. Ore was headed for a position at the back of the house, near the torch that was directly across from the back door.

Rei expected the uncle to come to the front to parlay, and would meet with him there to hear what he had to say. He had one of the Family waiting with him that knew how to distinguish between the two men so that they wouldn't be mistaken, although at the beginning, and in the end, it really didn't matter which one was which. They just needed to do away with them both.

Ore gave the sign that they were in place. The guards in front of him put out the torch. Running around the house to both sides of him, each of the torches were also put out until only the three in front of the main door were lit. Then the center of those three was also put out. Rei was in place and ready.

They'd been up in the dark of the mountain in order to adjust their eyes to the darkness and they'd been very careful to not let that be damaged by the torchlight. The soldiers who'd been on watch around the house were already used to the light, so they could get close enough to the torches to put them out without compromising their sight.

Now the group that had come from the mountains switched places with the ones who'd been closer. The original soldiers watching the house would have time for their eyes to adjust while the first part of the battle was fought by the new line.

It didn't take long for the front door to open and the Earl to come out. "Have you come as a coward in the night to fetch me, then?" he roared.

"That depends on who you are," Andrew was the Voice of the Regent, and he answered coolly.

The Earl stopped. He squinted in the darkness, trying to see if there was a person who might be talking to him, or if that person was hidden. Not seeing anyone, he answered, "Who I am may depend on who you are, and who you seek. Show yourself!"

The back door of the house opened. Ore tensed. Men flowed out and encircled the back of the house, facing outward, but they didn't show themselves to the front of the house. Ore's instinct, and Ilena's description of the Earl, told him the one in the front was the true Earl Shicchi, and the one coming out the back was the uncle, preparing a way to escape if the trade didn't go well. But he was to wait.

Grail stepped into the space between the lit torches, but in a place he couldn't be seen clearly. The message ran around the house and Thayne whispered in Ore's ear. Ore nodded. He'd been right. If the person who came out the front was Earl Shicchi, Ore's double would show himself. If it had been the uncle, Rei would have stepped out.

"Kase!" The Earl in the front roared. Then he laughed loud and long. "Have you finally come for me yourself, then? Has your owner let you off your leash long enough to come hunting?" Ore's reaction was less than even Grail's was. He could care less what the man said.

"I've already let Ilena go, you know. But then, you were the last one to see her, weren't you? Did she die still speaking your name? Or was it mine?" He laughed evilly. "Her words at night contained my name as frequently as yours." Ore wondered if they should have told Grail about the sleep talking, but it was too late now, and he probably already knew.

There was movement at the back door, and another Earl Shicchi came to stand just inside it, covered in a cloak, and just partially visible. Andrew's voice could be heard again, taunting the Earl as if he were Kase. Grail played the puppet.

It had been decided that Grail's accent was sufficient to give him away as not being Kase, so he wasn't to speak himself. Ore suspected he'd have choice words of his own to voice if they exchanged blows. Once they crossed swords, it wouldn't matter any more.

Andrew voiced a challenge to the Earl. The Earl answered with a scoffing laugh. "Do you think you're finally ready to face me? Have you grown strong enough, then? I would be happy to test you. ...But only you and me."

Ore felt a hand on his back. He turned and looked into Rei's eyes. They smiled predatory smiles at each other, then traded places. Ore left Thayne with Rei and Mina, and headed around to the front of the house to meet up with Andrew and Grail. Grail, using Andrew's voice, was accepting the personal challenge. The uncle, having heard the challenge and its acceptance, was stepping away from the back of the house.

As Ore moved stealthily around the house through the trees and rocks, he could see the men in the back tightening their formation in preparation for breaking through the blockade. It looked like the uncle was going to try to make a run for it to Tarc, not having a Prince to negotiate with.

Grail was wearing a hood and scarf to disguise his slight differences in appearance. He carried himself differently, but with the number of possibilities of who Kase could have become, it perhaps wouldn't have been unusual for the Earl to wonder if there was yet another potential Kase he had somehow missed. Grail stepped out into the clearing, carrying his sword, and the Earl stepped up to meet him.

Ore carefully inspected the windows of the house for signs of watchers at the side windows, then ghosted to the side of the house and hugged it where he wouldn't be seen, keeping low to the ground.

As soon as he was in place, he heard the first clash of steel from the front of the house. Only a few blows into the battle and another signal was given. Four arrows shot through the two torches still lit. Pitch on the arrows caught fire as they passed through the flames and the lit arrows stuck into the front of the house.

Ore counted to five to let the arrows catch the side of the house on fire. Then, before the men still inside the house could come out the front door, he looked around the corner and quickly assessed the fight.

Ore ran silently up behind the Earl and thrust his sword deep into his enemy's unprotected back. Ore twisted the blade and pushed it up towards his brother's heart. "You're facing the wrong way, Brother," he said as Earl Shicchi twisted in surprise to see who had interrupted the challenge and was killing him. He grinned into the wide eyes. "You see, you aren't the only one with a double from Selicia."

The Earl, this time himself also on the maximum dose of the Little Death, roared and hammer swung his sword around to chop at Ore. Leaving his sword in his brother's back, it having gone in too deeply, Ore nimbly lept back. Grail, now with the unprotected side facing him, swung his sword with great strength and cut through the Earl's neck severing the head from the body. Ore decided that form of death must be a Selician thing.

But now he wondered if he had a problem. He was facing an armed Grail and his own sword wasn't within easy reach. Grail reached down and yanked Ore's sword out of the corpse and tossed it to him, then turned to face the house. Ore, somewhat grateful Grail wasn't going to turn on him, at least not yet, caught up his sword and also turned to face the house.

Their defenders arrived at the same time as the men fleeing from the burning house did. Ore was once again fighting men who had been taking the maximum dose of the Little Death. He hoped desperately as he fought side by side with Grail, Andrew working to reach them, that it would be his last time.

-o-o-o-

Rei waited until he saw Ore flit across the open area to the side of the house. Then he moved to stand just inside the clearing, knowing his pale hair and cloak would give him away in the moonlight that now flooded the courtyard at the back of the house. Mina and Thayne were close behind him in dark clothes that wouldn't be seen.

He'd had Ore look up the name of Ilena's uncle in the history of Selicia that Ore was keeping in his room. He called that name now, just loudly enough to be heard by that man, but not by anyone in the house or in front of the house.

The uncle froze briefly, then asked, almost too eagerly, "Who are you? Do I know you?"

"No, you don't know me," Rei answered. "But you've called me, so I've come."

The uncle furrowed his brow, "Is it the Regent, then?"

"Will you negotiate with me?" Rei said, neither confirming nor denying his identity. The uncle looked unsure. "You've already given me Earl Shicchi. What is it you want from me?"

The uncle scowled. "I've given you more than the Earl. I've given you the treasure of three kingdoms. I don't believe you've let her die, but if you have,

274

then I wish for you to give me your life. If she lives, then give me an army to retake my rightful place."

"The only army I'll give you is the one I've brought with me." Rei said. "You would only be a pretender to that throne for you have less claim upon it than the one who took it from you."

The uncle went into a silent fury. At the same time, the men still inside in the back of the house suddenly came pushing out of it, fleeing the flames that were burning through the front of the house.

In the chaos, Rei slipped back into the outer perimeter within the woods, but he kept his eyes on the uncle, as did Thayne and Mina. He was their goal, and they expected him to run. When he did, they would be waiting for him.

-o-o-o-

Taking advantage of the chaos at the back door, the waiting soldiers rushed the men there, pinning them between the burning house and their own blades. There, also, they found men who had taken the maximum dose of the Little Death. Even though they'd prepared, they had to fight hard to preserve their own lives.

It wasn't long before the second wave of Rei's troops were needed to help fight. As they moved in, the first wave slowly disengaged to be treated and recover. Rotating in that manner, eventually all of the Earl's men were defeated.

The uncle defended himself and directed other men to defend him as well. He carefully looked for openings to slip through until he was finally close enough to the boundary to see an opening and slipped through. He looked back once to be sure no one had seen him, then turned to run.

He ran into a sword that pierced him through the belly. As he stared at it in surprise, another sword took his head. Unknowing, a third took his left hand shortly after his body had fallen to the ground.

-o-o-o-

When the battle in the front of the house was done, Grail collected the head of Earl Shicchi, then followed Ore and Andrew to sit between the lit torches. Not long thereafter, Rei arrived with Thayne and Mina. Andrew made a fuss over Rei, as expected, and Rei let him, just long enough to be satisfied, then scolded him into quiet.

Ore smiled to watch the familiar interplay, enjoying also Mina's dry barbs that said she, too, had been worried about not being by her partner's side. When it looked like they were about comforted, Ore sent Thayne and Grail to find proper carrying things for the parts of their enemies they would be taking home. When they had gone off, Ore called, "Master!"

Rei turned, and seeing him sitting alone and looking sad, gave him full attention. "What is it, Ore?"

"Grail is to the Princess what Mister Andrew is to Master. ...He can't see where she stands, so doesn't trust and is very pained. ...But so far he's obedient," Ore reported what he'd learned up on the mountain.

Rei nodded. "I thought it must be something similar to that."

"But, if he's in that position, then why doesn't he stand with you in the castle?" Andrew hurt just thinking about it, if it were him.

Ore shook his head. "I don't know."

"That must be the source of contention between them, Grail and Thayne." Mina said.

Ore raised his eyebrow. "There's contention between them?"

She shook her head. "Because they stand behind you, Ore, you can't see it. But we who look at the three of you see it in them, the rivalry."

Ore sighed. "The rivalry of siblings I've noticed. I don't understand why Mother would allow such a thing to exist."

"When you're answered by her, then you'll understand it," Grail's steady voice answered them. "Until then, pay it no mind."

Thayne, coming up behind Grail, grinned. "If you *mind* such things in vain, you will have to *pay* more than it's worth. It can be a difficult thing to do sometimes, but it's worth it to trust that Mother knows what she's doing." Thayne gave Grail a significant look and Grail turned away from him coolly. Thayne grinned at Ore and slid his thumb into his belt loop.

"Until she goes rolling for the edge of the cliff," Ore amended absently. The others looked at him, not understanding. He didn't elaborate. He looked at the two who followed him. "Are the two of you also vying for the position of Mother's favorite, like Marcus and Henry?" Grail and Thayne looked at each other, then looked away from each other and Ore, and wouldn't answer.

Ore sighed. "I think I must speak with Mother on this thing very soon." He shook his head. Then he rebuked, "Thayne, don't provoke your Brother. Mother has need of both of you, and it makes both of you less able to perform your duties."

Thayne looked down. "I'm sorry, Master Ore, Grail," he said and bowed briefly. Thayne said to Grail quietly, as they were all moving to return to Rei's encampment, "I've noted it before, that Master Ore's mind suddenly moves in unexpectedly deep directions. Be aware that this will happen again." Grail didn't answer him, but he'd definitely heard him.

-o-o-o-

Several days later, the encampments were taken down and the army moved out of the mountains. Rei left one garrison worth to build a guard station to monitor the pass to Tarc and man it. He wanted to know if and when the Lord of Tarc was going to come by that way.

They set up camp for the night half-way between the battlefield and the castle, at the foot of the mountains where there wasn't a horrible slope, but the woods couldn't get so close, making a natural broad grass field the tents could be set up in. In total they were too large a group to stop at towns and villages along the way.

276

Mina caught Ore's attention and gestured with her head. He looked that way and saw Grail and Thayne talking a distance away. He sighed. They were obviously arguing. He walked over. It really wasn't a good thing to have them at odds. "No!" He was close enough now to hear Grail's angry answer to Thayne.

"Then let us meet with Grandfather, at least. I'll introduce you." Thayne was wheedling.

"It isn't time yet. It will bring confusion to the Family." Grail shook his head.

Ore was close enough to join the conversation. "What? That Grail is using an alias and is allowing Master to believe he's an agent working out of Selicia? Since when is bending the truth with such stories confusing to the Family?" Thayne and Grail startled guiltily, then looked at each other, Grail with anger, Thayne with stubbornness. Grail finally looked away and Thayne turned to Ore.

Before Thayne could answer, Grail said in frustration, "Thayne wants to make Grandfather's life simpler, his own as well, and have the four of us meet at the Scholar's Tavern to get his report and give ours instead of chain communicate them. We can't get Mother's approval before arriving because the main communication line is still down. He wants to ask for forgiveness after. I'm against it."

"There's a problem with you meeting with Grandfather, Grail? I thought you already knew him?" Ore asked, surprised.

"That's not it," Grail shook his head, but didn't elaborate.

Ore thought about it. It sounded like it would be simpler to him, too. "Well, I'd be okay with it, if Grandfather approved. It isn't like Grail would be telling me who he is there any more than he has here. And you're approved to stay with us until we reach the city, aren't you?"

Grail shook his head in frustration that Ore was agreeing with Thayne. "Yes, but there are things the Family is looking for, and it will confuse that."

Ore put on a knowing expression. "Oh! You mean that to be seen with you is a sign of my acceptance into the Family. Hmm...yes, that would be confusing, perhaps, particularly since you don't like me yet. Well...what to do, then?"

"Ask Grandfather if I may come also," Rei said from behind them.

Ore turned and smiled, liking the surprised expression on Grail's face. "Oh, I like that idea, Master. Shall we make it a pre-arrival party, then?"

"No, Ore. Not a party." Rei rejected him.

Ore's face fell. "I can't drink then? I really need to, you know. It's been so very long...since I went to fetch the surgeon." He got no sympathy from any of the other five.

Andrew finally took pity on him. Putting a hand on Ore's shoulder, he said, "Well, there is always the Welcome Home Birthday Party." Ore perked up a little.

Now it was Rei who faced Grail. "I've no interest in taking sides in a petty quarrel, but I do want to know why the communication line of my Director of Intelligence went down at a critical time, what was done about it, and why it still isn't up. As Grandfather is acting in her stead at this time, I'll hear it from him."

Grail hesitated slightly, then bowed. "Yes, Regent. I'll send word to Grandfather to have him prepare to meet you."

CHAPTER 17 Reunion

Ilena was crying for a bath again. "I'm sorry, Mistress," answered Rio, distraught herself. It would still be a little more than two weeks before they could let her sit up to take a bath. She had only recently been able to be sat propped up slightly in the bed.

"It isn't the bath you want," Leah said firmly, "it's the *who*. He'll be here soon enough. But you don't want this report going to him, I would think." Even she'd just about had all she could take.

Ilena shook her head. "I don't. It's not. I itch! I want to be scrubbed clean so I don't itch anymore." She sobbed, completely miserable. She'd been lying in a bed longer than she could take any more, and had, for today, just given up. She'd been trying so hard to be good, to be respectful and exercise restraint, but today she couldn't do it. Today she wanted everything she couldn't have, and that was making her even more miserable.

Rio looked between her and Leah. Finally she said, "Miss Leah, please will you let me take care of Mistress Ilena today?" She knew Leah wasn't in the mood to reward Ilena today, but Ilena wasn't going to be able to perform for them at all. Leah also needed a break from Ilena and the little room. She'd taken her responsibility very seriously and had been the one to stay with her every night and most days since Thayne had left. "For your own sake?"

Leah blew a great breath of air, then suddenly nodded curtly. "You may deal with Her Highness today. I'll return when I'm ready to see Mistress Ilena again." She turned on her heel and left the room.

Rio put Marcus and Henry to work, sending them to call several maids who were in Ilena's Family, then to collect a large basin and lots of hot and cold water. When the small army of maids arrived, she explained her plan.

As soon as all the water arrived and they had all their tools, they had Marcus and Henry remove the desk and both beds from the room, the women lifting the sheet Ilena was lying on straight up, then placing her on the floor as her bed was removed out from under her. By the time the army of maids left, the room, the bedding, Ilena, and they had all been cleaned, and a special lotion applied to Ilena to ease the itching.

Even though treated as if she was just an object to be dealt with, having the chatter of people around her and their busy-ness, being thoroughly scrubbed and lotioned, and having the room smelling clean instead of like a sick room, made Ilena much calmer.

She still wanted to be able to get up and walk, but she could deal with that. She was already exercising in the way she had learned so many years ago. This time, she was sure she was going to walk so wasting time when she should be strengthening her body wasn't acceptable.

"Thank you, Rio," she said humbly. "I'm sorry."

Rio smiled at her sympathetically. "You must say that to Leah, who's been working hard to help you, but I know it's hard. You've done very well to make it this far. I hope next time you can go further." She considered. Mizi was supposed to arrive soon. She really wanted to help her mistress succeed, and it would be important that she be good for that visit. "If you can properly practice while Mistress Mizi is here today, shall I invite Ryan to dinner tonight?"

Ilena lit up. "Can I be Mother to him a little? I'll watch you."

Rio considered it. Ryan actually liked Mother quite a bit, but she wouldn't tell Ilena, not today anyway. "If you'll watch me and if you're good for Mistress Mizi's visit."

"I'll try hard," Ilena said happily. Rio wasn't so sure. She knew her mistress tended to be more excitable when happy. It wouldn't be so easy, she thought.

-o-o-o-

When Mizi came, she gave her report to Ilena on how things had been for her since the last time she'd come. They'd agreed that Mizi would tell her in detail what happened in her days, then if she had questions or concerns she would ask for Ilena's help. Often she'd learned of something she was lacking and asked Ilena to teach her, or had looked through her list or the list Rei had given her again and found a thing she wanted to work on.

On occasion they were able to just visit. If the visit became too relaxed, Ilena would find a topic she thought Mizi was lacking in and ask her to expound upon it, thus showing her the holes in her understanding. Often she would then send Mizi to read and study it for herself, suggesting ways to practice, if it was something she needed to do for herself. Always, Mizi was to come back and specifically report on her progress for those things.

At the end of this day's report, Mizi said to Ilena, "You've been doing very well for quite some time, haven't you?"

Ilena looked ashamed. "Well, until today, Mistress. Today I itched so much that I couldn't help it. I'm afraid I had a tantrum. Rio was very kind and let the maids scrub the room, and me with it. I made Leah angry with me, though. I'm very sorry."

Mizi looked a little surprised. "Miss Leah was angry? I wondered why she wasn't here."

"I told her to take the day off," Rio said to Mizi, "and that I would deal with Mistress Ilena myself. She's been working very hard."

Mizi nodded. "Yes, she has. I'm sure after a day to recover, she'll be able to be with Ilena again. But Ilena, you're doing well now. Was a scrubbing sufficient, really?"

"They also rubbed me with some cream. That has helped very much. ...And Rio has promised me a gift if I'll be good for the rest of the day." Ilena was embarrassed.

Mizi laughed. "Well, then I'm glad you're being good. ...Would it help you to make it the next length if I could offer you a gift as well?"

280

Ilena looked at her, curious. Mizi continued, "It isn't a terrible thing to be irritated by skin that won't behave. It's when you won't try that it becomes a problem. If you can continue to do well until Rei and the others return, then shall we have a welcome home party, and wish Rei a belated happy birthday, in your room with everyone?"

Ilena's face blossomed. "If I can behave at a party, I may actually have learned something." Then her face fell. "But Mistress, I'm struggling with understanding a thing."

"Please ask me," Mizi said, wanting to help her.

"I can't find the right balance. Ore was training me strictly in order to help me understand the depth of the difference of what I understood and what I need to understand. Because he isn't here to tell me, I don't know how to tell when I may be free to..., well, I don't even know how to say it.

"It's like, I'm not able to be myself at any time, that I must hide away who I am under a strict mask." Her eyes misted. "It's like I must become something completely different. I want to understand, but I don't want to lose myself. It's very lonely."

"Ah!" Mizi was surprised and waved her hands. "No, you don't have to do that. That *would* be very lonely." She considered. She wasn't sure she could explain the balance either, since she'd always had it.

"Perhaps he was going to allow you to slowly build to an understanding. It's unfortunate that you've had to have this gap in the timing of your training, although it's surely been good for you to practice that long. ...I think it might be best for Ore, who's been through it, to continue to show you. Rest assured he'll help you understand it. You won't be required to lose yourself."

Ilena nodded, having to be content with believing Mizi, finding her words to be of some comfort, even though it was true that she was beginning to feel a bit rebellious. Particularly today. She took a deep breath. She wanted to have dinner with Ryan, and she would really like to see everyone when they returned, if she could. "Well, then I'll continue to try hard and maybe when Ore returns I'll be ready to behave at a party."

-o-o-o-

At dinner that night, Ilena was delighted that Ryan seemed smitten with Rio. She wasn't sure Rio saw it, but she certainly did. Just watching them together kept her occupied nicely for quite some time, and soothed the Mother in her, but there was a thing she'd been waiting for.

"Ryan?" she called when there was an opportunity near the end of the meal.

"Yes?" he turned to her.

"May I ask you a thing?"

"Yes," he answered kindly.

"Before, when I first came, you were lonely. Are you happy now?"

Ryan smiled. "Yes, I am. When I first was able to go to the Scholar's Tavern with Ore, I took the opportunity to ask him my questions. It was comforting to me to have him answer them, and to know he was willing to answer them. I've been practicing asking my questions, as you suggested. There are many who talk with me easily now who come to the infirmary."

Ilena smiled back. "I've noticed that even when you come here, you're able to talk more easily. It makes me happy to see it. You've become stronger."

Ryan blushed a little. "It was the strength of Ilena that helped me to become so."

"If I've been able to help even a little, I'm glad." She looked at him, then looked at Rio, not sure how to go about broaching the next topic she wanted to talk about. "Rio come help me," Ilena requested.

Rio went to Ilena and bent down to her. Ilena held her hand up by her mouth and whispered into Rio's ear the thing she wanted to say and do. "Ah," Rio said, "begin it with 'May I help you to' and allow him to make the decision as to whether he'll hear it or not."

Ilena nodded, and looked to Ryan, who was waiting patiently. "Ryan, may I help you to increase your strength, as well as practice your investigative skill?"

Ryan considered it, then nodded. "It would be good for me to be able to talk to many people," he said.

Ilena smiled happily. Rio gave her a warning look, and she considered her words with care. "You know I'm the Director of Intelligence?" Ryan nodded. "What that means here in the castle is that it's my responsibility to make sure that the Regent is secure within his own home. Therefore, I have many eyes and ears here in the castle that watch and listen for me. In order for you to become stronger, may I suggest we play a game?"

Ryan tilted his head. "That sounds intriguing."

Ilena liked the light in his eyes. "When you believe you've identified ten of my operatives, whom I call my 'Children', return to me and tell me their names. If you're correct, I'll reward you one thing that you desire that is within my power to give." She paused.

"There are difficulties, however, that you should be aware of. I'm not the only one with operatives in this place. The King and the Queen Mother also have operatives here, and perhaps others do as well whose intentions are not so kind. You must tell me ten of mine. If you like, we can keep it simple and be done. But if you wish to increase your capability, we can increase the difficulty of the game over time."

"In what way would we increase the difficulty?" Ryan wanted to know.

"I believe it will be your natural inclination to wait for them to come to you. One way to increase the difficulty is for you to have to go find those who don't come to you. In that way you'll learn to converse with others in different environments than you're accustomed to." Ryan nodded his understanding.

"Also, I have Children in each level of the castle - servant, staff, and lord. For the simplest level of difficulty you would bring me the name of ten of the servants. For the next level of difficulty, from the staff, eight names would be required. For the lords, six, although they will be very difficult to determine as they must hide the best. I'd be willing to reward even four names from the lords.

"Once you've been able to do those things, then I'd move to seeing if you can determine who are the operatives of anyone other than myself, but that's very advanced until you've learned to see my Children with ease."

Ryan considered. "I like the challenge you present. I'll accept it. Is there a time limit?"

"No. I'll be watching to see what you can do." Ilena was very pleased. "What will you start with?"

"I'll begin by seeing if I can learn to see them in my own place. Then I'll see what I can do elsewhere," Ryan decided.

"Will you please keep me informed as to your progress?" Ilena asked. "Ah, and when one is confirmed, you can't ask that person for any help to see another. I'd like it to be done with your own strength. Although at the beginning, if you're unsure, you may ask me."

"Okay," Ryan smiled. The gentle growing appealed to him, it seemed. Ilena was content.

-o-o-o-

That night, Rio praised Ilena before they slept. "You've done very well today, Mistress. You handled yourself with Mister Ryan properly."

"He's easy to practice with," Ilena said sleepily. "The same as he's easy to talk to."

"You like him, Mistress?"

Ilena smiled a secret smile at her woman. "Yes, Rio. ...But not the way you do."

Rio blushed. "Will you apprentice him?" Rio asked, trying to turn the conversation away from her feelings for him.

"I just did," Ilena said happily, wiggling a bit down into her sheets. "He'll be one of my best sets of eyes and ears in this place." She looked at Rio again, straight on. "After all, everyone comes to him."

Rio chuckled. "Indeed. You are very sly, Mother."

Ilena chuckled happily to herself, then allowed herself to relax into sleep. This reward she'd been able to earn herself had been the best yet.

-o-o-o-

It was one of those rare occasions when the central room of the upper level of the Scholar's Tavern was in use. There were two castle guards at the door to the room, and several others below in the main room. In the room itself were Rei, Andrew, Mina, and Ore. Opposite them were Grandfather, Grail,

283

and Thayne. The unevenness of the sides made them feel the missing presence of Ilena.

They'd been served a delicious meal with tea, while sitting on comfortable pillows in front of individual low tables. The meal had just been removed and they were now ready to begin the discussion.

Grandfather shifted positions to sit kneeling, and bowed to Rei. "I'm sorry, Regent, that I made an error in judgment in choosing to delay changing the code for the main branch." He sat back up. "However, while it made it more difficult to communicate across long distances, it didn't prevent us from knowing what was going on, nor from being able to act."

"I understand that each area may act independently," Rei answered, "but if the communication across the distances is broken, how may they receive needed instructions from the head?" He'd decided to do his own speaking in this forum.

"In the usual way, Regent Rei - by runner and physical message delivery. It's still effective, though slower."

Rei was confused. "How else are messages sent?"

"Ah...," Grandfather paused uncertainly. "By sound or sight. The Regent should ask the Director for those details at a more appropriate time, as they would take some time to explain."

Rei sat mystified, then decided he would accept that answer. "How much longer will it take to get the main line functional?"

"It already is, Regent." At Rei's confused look, Grandfather looked at Grail.

Grail answered, "Because I couldn't trust the information on the main network in the beginning, I made the decision to keep the battle line independent for the duration of the campaign. That ensured that your actions wouldn't be known by the enemy that had broken the main line. Also...," he stopped and looked at Grandfather.

"Keeping the line down until the end of the campaign allowed us to keep the enemy in confusion," Grandfather took the lead again.

Ore shifted slightly, a small frown on his face. Rei asked his question for him. "If there had been trouble here, how would we have heard of it?"

"I would have immediately sent a runner, such as the one that delivered the King's message to you, if I weren't able to attend to it myself."

Rei raised an eyebrow. "So, was there trouble that you attended to yourself, then?"

Grandfather smiled reassuringly. "Truly, it's not something to concern yourself about. But it will come out in my report to Grail, that is if you're still wanting to stay for our internal reporting."

Rei nodded. He was very interested in observing that. He wanted to learn more about the inner workings of the information-gathering Family that was now his Department of Intelligence.

284

In the end, it was quite long. Thayne asked Ore to give his report first, then gave his, from the time he left Grandfather until the current time, leaving out no detail including a word for word repeat of Ore's report. Grail then gave a long detailed report that contained all of the reports of his underlings - everyone in the Family that had gone to the fight, as he'd been the equivalent of their general - and included all of his own experiences following Ore.

The castle contingent came to understand why their meeting had been scheduled to begin shortly after sunrise and the first meal had been breakfast. Lunch had come and gone by the time Grail was finished. He'd remembered and passed on every detail that had come to him, the same as Ore would give a fully detailed report to Rei. When he was done, Grandfather asked if they could recess briefly, and Rei gave his permission.

As they were walking around to stretch their legs, Thayne went to Ore. "This is your day's lesson, Father. You also must be able to do that when you're finally at the level of Immediate Family. You were able to give your report acceptably."

"It's how I already report to Master," Ore said shrugging. "But I've never had to remember the reports of others to that detail to also give them, not without having them in writing."

Thayne nodded. "In Mother's network, a written message is a message the enemy already knows. Information can only be protected when it's within the head of a man that will choose when to open his mouth. Information can only be trusted when the person saying it can be trusted, and it can be verified."

Rei had walked up to listen. Thayne stopped and looked at him. Rei asked him to continue, so he did. "When you report, or receive a report, it must be done that way every time. Every word must be exactly said. When it's a critical message, those who are in the chain always repeat back what they've received to make sure that every word is correct before they pass it on. An error of even one word is not acceptable, at any level.

"The local lines, or 'streams', 'tributaries', or 'branches', report all their doings at regular intervals. That's to maintain order within the river, and to confirm that all is well in each area. If a report isn't received at its time, a request is sent back down that they be checked by the next closest area to confirm their integrity and well being. If an area has an emergent message, the river is interruptible, although it's not always busy.

"Grail's report was long because he needed to report an entire campaign's report. If the main line had been integral, it would have been much shorter. It will now be the same with the reports coming in from the streams. It will take quite some time to receive them all and restore the regular flow."

"Ah, like the same as us in the Rose office," Ore sighed. "We'll have great mountains of papers to swim through for some time."

Thayne smiled and nodded. "Yes, the same. There are some people here who'll not get to sleep for at least another week, if not more, as reports will come in night and day."

Ore thought about that for a moment, then asked, "How many days will it take Grandfather to give his report to Mother, when she's finally able to receive it?"

Thayne stared at him, then turned to Grandfather. "Grandfather, he's done it again! Will you answer it?"

Grandfather smiled benignly at Ore. "You aren't ready yet for that answer, Master Ore. Some day you'll receive her reports with her, and give yours as well. Then you'll understand."

"Doesn't she get them the same as we give them to Rei?" asked Andrew. "All of you are like us, in that you receive all of the information, but then we summarize it for him so that his time may be put to better use. Don't you do that for her as well?"

Ore shook his head and Rei agreed with him. "No, Mister Andrew. Ilena knows every detail. Even without me having heard her say it, I know it."

"Ah," Grandfather cautioned, "but it is similar. There are things that we don't have to tell her."

"Like when it was a problem resolved at a lower level?" asked Rei.

Grandfather nodded. "The problem and it's resolution is passed along, but not the details, unless she should ask for them."

The four from the castle blinked. "Then that's it, isn't it? She only receives the information she asks for."

The two from the Family grinned. "Indeed."

Ore glanced over to Grail. He was standing apart from them, his arms crossed, watching them. To Ore, his eyes were shadowed with pain. When he saw the expression on Ore's face, he turned away from them and returned to his cushion and sat. Rei decided he was also ready to continue and returned to his place as well.

When they were in position, Grandfather spoke to Rei first. "As you've seen and heard, the reports are very long. Out of respect for your time, I'll only give my report of what's happened here in this place, as I believe it's what concerns you the most, and I'll give a summarized version, such as you're used to. You are, I'm sure, anxious to return to your own house." His eyes sparkled. "However, you'll go into it much more informed than normal."

-o-o-o-

Less than three weeks after they left, the soldiers of Rei returned to the castle, save the ones left behind to clean up the burned noble houses and build the new garrison. From the Rose office balcony Mizi saw them coming over the hill in great streams. She struggled briefly with whether she should stay and do her work, or go and welcome them.

Seeing her indecision, Tairn said, "Lady Mizi, to welcome them when they enter will give them as much reward as sending them off did. They find strength in knowing that we're happy to see them return after their great efforts for us."

Mizi, trying to not look very happy, said, "Then I'll go down to the garrison grounds. Please let anyone looking for me know –"

Tairn cut her off, "– that they can come back at a later time. You have a Prince to greet. Your time is his." He grinned.

Mizi flew as quickly as she could to the stands that looked over the garrison parade grounds. Not knowing where she was allowed to stand, she went to where she would be able to see them best and first, straining to see Rei. Unbeknownst to her, she ended up standing exactly where the Regent would have stood to look over the soldiers if they had been standing for him to inspect them, or address them.

When Rei entered and saw her standing there, he grinned. "See, she's even able to welcome us properly."

"Do you think she knows what she's doing?" Mina asked.

"No," Rei answered happily.

Ore laughed. "Likely you're right."

Rei rode up right underneath her, watching her the whole time. She looked at him only, also, as if they had been apart for many years. Then Rei turned directly underneath her to sit on his horse and watch the men finish entering the grounds. She looked up also at that time, though first she looked at Andrew, Mina, Ore, and Thayne riding behind him to take up positions to his left and right.

They gave her smiles, and Ore waved. She waved back. A ripple of noise went through the men, who were unusually lining up in their parade stations instead of immediately turning to work - a reaction to Rei and Mizi's interaction and movements.

When everyone had entered the area, and seemed to be waiting for something, Mizi glanced down at Rei. He nodded to her and she remembered what Tairn had told her. She took a deep breath. As loudly as she could, she said, "Thank you everyone, for your hard work. Welcome home." She bowed briefly to them.

As the men cheered, Rei grinned a huge grin. He leaped off his horse and handed the reins to Ore. He went to the stairs, ran up them two at a time, and reached her side. There, he gave her another kiss, as he had when they left, and the men roared. He looked into her green eyes and said quietly, "Thank you, Mizi."

Rei turned to the men and held up his hand. They quieted and stood at attention. "This day we have returned successful and proud. You have my gratitude. ...You're dismissed."

As Rei took Mizi's hand and began to lead her back down to be with Andrew and Mina, she said, "Welcome home, Rei. I'm glad to see you again."

He smiled. "I'm glad to be home. And even more, I'm glad to be welcomed home by you, Mizi."

"And will you welcome me home too, Mistress?" Ore said, looking at her with his signature grin from the bottom of the stairs.

"Welcome home, Ore," she said smiling at him. "It's good to see you again also." She turned to the others, who had also walked over to the stairs, leading their horses. "Welcome home, Andrew, Mina, Thayne. I'm glad to see you're also well." They returned her greeting, smiling at her.

"You've done well, Mistress," Ore said to her. She tipped her head, wondering what he meant. "You have won the hearts of the soldiers of Suiran. They will follow you anywhere." He'd put his hand to his heart theatrically, then flung it out as if to say "to the farthest reaches".

Mizi laughed. "I hope I won't ever need to do such a thing, Ore. If I've helped them understand our gratitude, that's enough."

-o-o-o-

As Rei and the others worked to complete the things that needed to be done, Mizi watched them from the stands, wanting to be out of the way. Ore was going to leave Thayne with her, but Thayne forbore and said that it was Ore who should be with his Mistress and he that should serve his master by doing the work. Thus Ore was standing behind her when one of the lords who'd seen the welcoming came to talk to her.

Ore listened quietly as the man reproved her, watching what she would do. Mizi listened politely, then called him by name and said, "If there's a thing I may do to support Regent Rei, it's my duty to do it. If by welcoming the men who fought bravely and gave him their strength I may do a small thing, or a great thing, then it's mine to do. If Rei had felt I'd acted to remove strength from him, he would have immediately corrected me.

"I've done no wrong. If you wish to express a concern, then it should be directly to the Regent, who's already made his decision." She looked him straight in the eye, no fear in hers as she spoke to him, the same as she always did, even to the King.

Even though he'd heard her say similar things in defense of Rei before, Ore was very proud of Mizi. She'd learned the strength to not only defend Rei, but herself as well. He smiled at her back as the lord she stood up to left in frustration. He would enjoy reporting that to his master. "You've become stronger, Mistress, while we were away," he complimented her.

"You think so, Ore?" she asked. "I've certainly learned many things, sitting in the Rose office and being supported by those around me. But I still have many more things to learn."

"I'm sure you'll continue to be strong," Ore said. "Master was very pleased that you came to greet him."

288

She turned and smiled at him. "Tairn said I may. I wasn't sure."

"I'll be sure to thank him, then, for Master's sake." Ore made sure to remember it.

"Ah!" Mizi remembered, looking at him again. "Will you go and greet Ilena?"

Ore smiled a soft smile for her. "Yes, but it isn't time yet. There are things I must do first. Will you let me surprise her?"

Mizi tipped her head, then shrugged. "If that's what you wish."

"How has she been doing?" he asked her.

"She's been learning her lessons well, even as she's been helping me with mine. ...She isn't sure she wishes to have the party at her room," Ore was surprised, "at least not until she can speak with you. She's still unsure because Ore hasn't seen her yet."

"I'll go soon," Ore reassured Mizi. He could tell that at least she very much wanted to be able to include Ilena. That was a good sign.

-o-o-o-

Ore paused outside Ilena's door and took a moment to steel himself. He'd learned already when training Ilena that he found it just as difficult for him to learn to be a master of the sort she needed as she found it to be obedient. When he was strong, she found it easier to be strong herself. Just as he, on this side of the door, found it hard to think of her on the other side of it without being overcome by his need to be with her, he knew she would find it difficult to think of him having returned.

Before they could be together as partners, first he needed her report and to prepare her to receive Rei, who was nearing ready to come and complete his business of retrieving the Earl by hearing her witness. It was necessary that they both be strong a little longer.

He knocked a single knock and entered the room. Ilena, Leah, and Rio looked up at his entrance. Leah and Rio were for just an instant very pleased to see him, then closed their faces as they should.

Ilena took a little longer, going from shock, to a tangle of emotions she couldn't face, to regal in order to regain her composure, then finally to ready humility. He was pleased she'd been able to make the process flow smoothly. He found it interesting that she used her normal court behavior to help her get to the behavior she wanted.

By the time she was ready, he'd walked to stand by her side. He folded his arms. "I'm ready to receive your report, Ilena," he said, letting her know this was a business visit from the beginning.

Her eyes went to the slightly unfocused look of remembering that he recognized from his own reporting. It was the first time he'd required this kind of reporting from her. He was pleased, but not surprised, when it was the same as what he'd heard at the Scholar's Tavern - very detailed, down to the

289

conversations, of everything that she'd done. Already she was used to giving, not just receiving, these kinds of reports. He wouldn't have to teach her.

It took some time, just as Grail's report to Grandfather, although not quite so long as it was just her own report. Ore listened carefully to the entire thing, judging as he listened. It was also his first time to receive this detailed a report.

He had to quickly learn what things to hear and release, and what things to take note of for talking about when the report was completed, and what things he would need to report to Rei on, as - in their case - he could give Rei a summary. He was glad he could learn one thing at a time here. To have also had to memorize everything she said would have been too much for him this day.

Still, by the time it was done, he was wishing he could have asked her for the summary. To have his first time contain weeks of living was overwhelming. He stood quietly, trying to put together what it was he needed to say. She was still, waiting for him. Somehow, her eyes showed understanding. *Ah. She's trained others to receive this kind of reporting before. Of course.*

He relaxed into the knowledge that had flowed into his brain through his ears. "I'm glad you've been able to learn to eat properly, and that you've been properly helping Mistress. That's good," he praised her successful efforts. "What have you learned from your tantrum?"

"I've learned that if I let a thing that is difficult continue too long without asking for help, then it will overwhelm me, and that's not good."

What an excellent answer, he thought, surprised. "And what will you do in the future?"

"I'll try to find the source of my distress early and bring it to the attention of one who desires to help me. If I can't find the source on my own, I'll ask for help to find it early."

Ore nodded acceptance of the answer. She'd already said she'd properly apologized, and been helped to find acceptable ways to distract herself from those things she couldn't change. He thought of a question that came out of her report. "Why was Grandfather not called to come?"

Ilena's eyes crinkled up slightly in a smile. "I knew Grandfather was very busy, and didn't wish to disturb him. Even still, it was not me that would have called him."

That was true. He'd left it to Leah to make that decision. He turned to Leah. "Why did you allow yourself to become overwhelmed?"

She looked just a little surprised to be called for her own actions. "I'm sorry, Master Ore. I also found myself not understanding that I needed to reflect upon my own limitations and seek assistance when it was needed."

Ore nodded. "And what will you do in the future?"

"I will also consider my own needs and ask for help when I'm beginning to be in distress," Leah answered.

Ore looked at her for a moment, then softened for her. "It's understandable when it's been only you, with the help of Rio, to see to the needs of Ilena for many years. Please remember that you have many who can help you now."

Leah bowed. "Yes, Master Ore."

Ore turned to Rio. "Thank you for being a strength to both Miss Leah and Ilena." Rio quietly accepted the praise.

Ore turned back to Leah. "Is there anything else you would need to add to the report?" He really didn't want to hear her give a fully detailed report like Ilena's.

Leah thought back through the time, then added simply, "Mistress Ilena has grown stronger. I'm pleased with her progress. I hope our efforts are able to be accepted."

Ore nodded. "Thank you for your efforts in her behalf. I hope the same." He turned back to Ilena, trying to think of if there was anything else he needed to say.

Her eyes held a plea. There must be something she needed to hear still. Then he remembered. It was part of the tantrum, and perhaps the reason she was unsure about participating with everyone yet. To answer it, the formal report needed to be over. He confirmed one more time that it could be, then relaxed his pose, moving to sit next to her on the bed, as was his way when he moved to a more relaxed teaching time.

He sat as usual, one leg tucked up under him, his hands relaxed in his lap, not touching her, just being near in a position that was easy for them both to see each other. He finally noticed that she was propped up into a reclining position. He smiled slightly. "So this much time has passed, that you're now able to sit up a bit."

She smiled back. "Yes. It's made the handwork Leah's been teaching me to keep me busy much easier. It was hard to do the stitches with the cloth held over my head, although that kept my attention very well because it was so difficult."

"Later, I would like to see how you've been doing with that as well," he said. He paused briefly and noted she waited for him very patiently. That was good. She'd overcome her over-eagerness. "You asked Mistress if it was necessary for you to lose yourself in order to learn what you need to learn." He could understand her concern.

"She was right to tell you that it isn't necessary, and that I'm training you to come to understand through progression. If you've practiced being fully restrained at the beginning, it's easier to understand where to go to if you're unsure. Full restraint is never wrong." He could see she could understand that position.

"How Rio helped you when you had dinner with Ryan that night is the next step to understanding. While we may give advice, we must first learn to offer it, allowing the master or mistress to reject it. If they reject hearing it, that is theirs to decide, to learn strength from it however they will.

"You've done it before, when you asked Master if he would pay the price to hear how to make my way easier the first time I went out to collect the Children. Because he wouldn't pay the lesser price to hear your words, I was made to pay a price, and thus his own price in the end was higher.

"You must do it from now on. It's your next lesson." He looked at her solemnly. "While you've done it before, I expect it will likely be a difficult lesson for you to learn, given how you behave when you're Mother."

Ilena paused as if she had a thing to say in response. He nodded to give her permission to speak it. He was glad she still remembered that kind of exchange. It had been the hardest for her learn at the beginning. "When Rio helped me understand it, it seemed to be a natural thing, and not difficult at the time." Her brow furrowed. "I think it may be because I do it often that way when I'm teaching."

Her brow cleared. "If I can think of any advice I might give as an offering to teach, rather than a thing that needs to be told, it will be simpler to do. ...Although of course the practice to remember it will take time," she added very practically minded.

"I'm glad you have a way to think of it that will help you," Ore praised her, a bit relieved himself. He would still have to be very vigilant until it looked like she was finally remembering it automatically, mostly because it was an area in which she had so far shown very little restraint. He looked at her to see if she was done with her questions. He could see she'd paused to think. Then she looked sad. "What is it?" he asked her.

"Ore...," she looked up at him questioningly and very sad, "I understand that it's necessary to contain my emotions. I already learned that when I was young, and practicing it again was necessary, but...," she bit her lip, "...am I never allowed to laugh again?"

Ore was stung. "Is that what you meant by feeling like you were losing yourself?" he said gently. She nodded, still biting her lip, although not even that was quite keeping her from tearing up.

He gently wiped the tear threatening to fall from her eye. "If Ilena couldn't still laugh, she wouldn't be Ilena," he said simply. "The same as if Ilena couldn't cry, she wouldn't be Ilena. I'm still Ore, although I've also had to learn restraint, and am even still learning it. It is true that we must learn when it's appropriate to relax and be just Ore or just Ilena, and when we must show the greater restraint."

He paused. "Is that why you're unsure about having everyone come? Because you haven't learned the balance yet?" Ilena nodded. It made sense to him. At a party, one would normally expect to be able to relax. If she didn't understand how much and under what circumstances she could relax, she would be constantly watching her own actions.

If she couldn't relax, the others wouldn't be able to either. It wouldn't be good for anyone. "*Hahhh.* Well, I wonder. ...How was it you were able to make it through the dinner with Ryan the day you had your tantrum?"

"I watched Rio," she said slowly. "She was able to tell for me when I needed restraint, and I was obedient."

Ore smiled. "Then shall we try that? You watch me. I'll help you know when you need to restrain yourself. That way you can begin to learn when it's okay to be just Ilena, and when it's necessary to practice restraint."

Ilena looked at him with great trust. "If it's you, Ore, I'll be able to do it."

Ore sighed to himself. That was all well and good, but it meant he wasn't going to be able to relax quite as much as he'd hoped, because he would have to remember it was his duty to help her.

Being able to have the party in her presence would be a good thing. There would be very few opportunities for her to practice when she could relax and by how much until she was able to be present with them. Though....

He turned to Leah and Rio. "In order for her to be able to have more practice, it would be acceptable to me if Ryan was invited to dinner whenever he could come, if you'll help her learn the proper balance. When they can, I'll also invite Master and Mistress to come to dinner as well."

The pain in his own heart lifted as the gratitude in Ilena's eyes grew to make them overflow again. He leaned over and kissed her forehead as she wiped the tears away. "It's a thing you can learn to do, Ilena," he said.

"Thank you, Ore," she said.

He waited until she was in control again, then stood. "You're ready now for Master to come. He desires to have your witness to the matter of the Earl and your uncle. I'll go and give him my report, then you may expect us...all of us," he smiled at her encouragingly.

She looked at him surprised as if not sure she was quite ready for it really, then she calmed, looking into his eyes with trust again. Then she looked quite flustered and concerned. He raised his eyebrow. "*All* of you? Princess Mizi, too?" He nodded. "Ahh, will she be okay?"

"Aren't you the one who said she shouldn't be protected from the things that she needs to understand?"

"Yes, but...is she really ready for something so extreme?"

Ore paused, remembering that Ilena's own first experience with death had been at a young, impressionable age, and had been of the brutal murders of her own family. She had a right to question it. "I'll ask Mistress if she's ready. She may choose."

Ilena calmed down and nodded. If Mizi chose to see, then she would learn, and it would be a hard lesson. "Am I able to help her, if she can't bear the lesson?" her eyes pled again. She wouldn't be able to bear her mistress' pain if it couldn't be shared.

Ore half-smiled a little sadly. "You may ask her, and if she accepts, then you may. It's part of your own lesson."

Ilena nodded. "I remember doing that before."

"Asking if you could give comfort? You've asked before?" He'd never seen it, had only ever seen her give whether the person would or no.

Ilena nodded soberly. "It was when Master Rei needed help carrying the burden that is Ilena."

Ore's eyes widened this time. He remembered that time, when Rei had turned to look at him and had been full of Ilena's light. She hadn't forced it on him, but had asked, and he'd accepted. Both concepts were completely outside Ore's range of understanding.

Then he knew. It was because they were family, and they were a Prince and a Princess. There was no other combination like it, not until Mizi could be married to Rei. Ilena was able to fill a position for Rei that had been empty until she'd appeared. Ore felt very warm all over. He was suddenly glad, for Rei's sake, that Ilena had come to the castle.

-o-o-o-

Rei had finished his preparations and was waiting for Ore. While waiting he turned his attention to Mizi who'd been patiently waiting for him. He wondered a bit as to why, but was glad for her presence. He began walking his little troupe towards Ilena's room. "So, Mizi, what have you been doing since we left?"

Mizi opened her mouth, then shut it again, looking like she'd just thought a new thought. "Um, Rei, I've been giving daily reports to Ilena and was just about to give you the same kind, but it's perhaps too much information. To what level do you wish me to answer?"

Rei smiled slightly. He was pleased Ilena had been teaching Mizi to open her mouth. "I don't need the daily details." He'd heard enough of that already. "The summary of each day will be sufficient." He did want to know how she'd handled herself and what she'd been learning.

From the beginning, she'd indeed been accosted by the lords of the castle. He recognized from the names that many of them were those who'd been trying to protect their daughter's interest, but a few were those who had taken it upon themselves to be his shepherds, and one was a man he himself didn't like. It seemed she'd had the most trouble with that one. He was pleased that she'd finally, with the advice of Ilena and through the continued support from Tairn and Dane, been able to overcome.

He was also pleased with her progress report as to how much more she was able to do in the office and that her duties as his adjunct had become routine. The fact that she, with the help of Ilena, had been able to solve over time even the more difficult cases, was an indicator of her typical dedication to resolving problems that came up before her. He found it interesting that Ilena had let her do her own research first, then in the end, if even her advice had been unable to

294

resolve the issue, her help had been to help Mizi as the Director of Intelligence and give her a way to attack.

He wondered, but it sounded like Mizi had chosen to only use such attacks when she'd exhausted all other options and her patience besides. That was good, and confirmed his own opinion of her. Those cases he asked for more detail in. It was likely they would still try to come to him and he needed to know how to answer. Andrew and Mina also listened closely to those details. They knew they would need to help him discover if there was more that Mizi and Ilena couldn't see.

Once Rei understood the cases for himself, he would train Mizi further on how to handle them, both in research and in understanding when it would be appropriate to more quickly move to attack. She didn't always need to exhaust herself upon those who were being malicious from the beginning.

Mizi was learning many good things as well in regard to becoming a Princess. She'd been studying the history of Suiran and its governance, saying that she wanted to branch out into Ryokudo as a whole, but that Ilena had recommended that for now she focus on the area that Rei had jurisdiction of, although Ilena also agreed that understanding how all of Ryokudo was governed was necessary to learn. Rei nodded his agreement. That progression was logical.

Mizi had been memorizing all of the lords, landed and in staff positions, and was currently working on memorizing the details of each one - family, length of service, and other facts that could only have come from the Department of Intelligence. Rei knew Ilena was preparing her to be able to speak to them from a position of strength and understanding.

Ilena was also having Mizi do one more thing that interested Rei. Mizi had been tasked with learning to observe everyone in the castle, from the servants to the lords. When Mizi talked about what Ilena's questions were to her about her observations, he came to understand that Ilena was trying to help her begin to see how courtly conversations were each a calculated game. That even the smallest facial expressions were clues. He was pleased Ilena was focusing on that specifically and in the best possible way, but he couldn't quite understand why she was also having Mizi do the same with the servants, so he asked Mizi.

"Ilena says that it's because I must be able to have allies in all places and levels, and I must understand what they expect me to be. Often when I tell her I've observed a number of servants, she'll ask me what I overheard them saying as I was approaching. It was an odd question to me the first time, as I usually don't listen to what others are saying, but she said it was important what people said to me, and what they said to each other. She reassured me I didn't need to judge harshly, just understand."

Mizi blushed remembering. "I remember the first time I overheard them talking about me. I was so embarrassed I couldn't listen to anyone else's conversation the whole day until I was with Ilena again. She told me that those would be the most important for me to listen to, because then I would know if I was on the correct path to my goal or not. So I tried again the next day.

"Some of the things that were said did help me understand that I was on the right path, and I was pleased to hear them, but some of the things were painful to hear," her eyes held the remembered pain, then cleared somewhat. "Ilena explained to me that it was the other side to the coin of jealousy. Because someone was jealous of where I was standing, they were doing what they could to attack."

Mizi looked at Rei. "Women are frightening, especially when jealous. It's been a hard lesson to learn that there are some who will not be turned, regardless of what I try. ...I've learned what it is to have enemies, and Ilena is helping me learn how to maneuver around them." Rei waited while she recovered. He was sympathetic, but he also knew that was a thing that he experienced differently.

She took a breath. "She's also helped me understand that if I know who a particular servant works for, I may know what their master or mistress really thinks by what they say to another servant, or how they react to me - coldly or with warmth." She smiled at Rei. "Many of the castle servants who work for Rei are beginning to see me with happy eyes."

Rei smiled back. "Your own work is doing that. Even I've had to win them over since I came. They were my mother's before then, and they have great respect for her."

Mizi nodded. "Ilena says that the ones that will not warm up to me are either spies that don't belong in the castle or are so firmly entrenched in their regard for the Queen Mother that there's nothing I can do to sway them, but to continue to do my best, and they'll continue to be harmless."

"Well, the latter is true, but Ilena actually told you the first?" Rei was surprised.

"Yes. She says that it's important for me to understand who may be a potential spy so that I may be able to use that knowledge to my advantage if an opportunity presents itself and that even some who seem to be kind are also spies.

"Knowing from my research that it should be her responsibility to see to them, I asked her why they were allowed to remain in the castle. I thought she would tell me to not mind it, but she answered me directly." Rei tipped his head. He wanted to know her answer as well.

"She said it's because a house will always have 'cockroaches' and 'mice' within it. Once she's identified who they are, she can use them to pass on information she desires to pass on, and if information is gathered that she doesn't want an enemy to know, she can capture and be rid of the one that knows it.

"To constantly be vigilant in removing them means that she must constantly be worried about who will be sent next to replace them. She also said that she keeps the total number manageable, and those who send them have finally understood what her limits are and there is currently a truce between them."

Mizi paused, then smiled ruefully. "At that point, I'd reached my limit of being able to comprehend her answer, and let her rest, trusting that she knew what she was doing." She looked up at him to see his keen interest in the topic. "If you wish to understand more, you must ask her."

Rei nodded. He understood Ilena's reasoning, but he would ask her for a more detailed explanation at a later time. It was the first time he'd had presented to his face that there was such vermin in his own house, but he couldn't be surprised.

Ore opened the door to Ilena's room and walked out. Rei was sitting on a low wall that was part of the outside of the hall that went around the inside of the medical wing. Mizi was standing in front of him just within the courtyard. Andrew, Mina, and Thayne were standing around them companionably. Ore shut the door behind him and walked up to them.

"Ilena's ready, but is being prepared by her maids." He smiled at Rei. "It's still a big thing for them to receive Master in his official capacity, but it shouldn't take long. There isn't much they need to do."

"How was her report?" Rei asked.

Ore slipped into semi-formal to report himself. "She was able to practice what I taught her before I left and has held onto the knowledge well. She seems to have an acceptable grasp of the basic level of restraint and I've explained to her why that's important.

"I was pleased to hear that within all this time she's had only one tantrum, and it was easily handled. She learned her lesson well from it. ...Also, she was able to have an experience already in the next area I wish for her to study in, and I've set her to that task." Rei was pleased that she was willing to work hard, so she could stay with them.

"And what task is that?" Andrew asked. Having been the one to train Rei, he was curious as to what Ore had picked next for Ilena.

Ore quirked his mouth and eyebrow at him. "The proper restraints to giving advice."

Mina and Mizi both looked very relieved, Andrew looked of two minds about it - both relieved and humored, and Rei was having a hard time not laughing. "Master Ore," Thayne quipped dryly, "I think you have taken on a monstrous project."

Ore smiled at him, "Actually, she thinks she'll be able to approach it easily, although she admits the practice will likely be difficult."

"Oho?" Thayne asked, disbelieving.

Ore nodded. "She says if she thinks of it as teaching instead, it should be easier."

Thayne actually got serious, thinking about that. Rei watched his reaction. He also agreed learning that restraint would be difficult for Ilena. "No, that might work," Thayne finally said. "She's very good at asking to see what a person is ready to learn when she's teaching."

The door to Ilena's room opened again, and Rio stepped out and bowed to them, standing to let them know they might enter. Rei stood and the rest fell into place behind him. "Ah, Master," Ore said, "there's one thing I've forgot."

"Yes, Ore?" Rei said slightly impatiently. Ore often forgot very important things until the last minute when he was reminded of them.

"Is this a thing that Mistress should decide to see?" Rei looked at Ore a little confused, although now that it had been brought to his attention, he was also wondering at himself that he had assumed her presence. "Ilena was concerned that it may be overwhelming."

Rei stopped and turned to Mizi. "Mizi, you've said that you don't wish to be protected unnecessarily; however, Ilena herself has said that this may be more than you're prepared for. Do you know what I'm here to do?"

"Ahh...," Mizi shook her head, and her hand went to rest before her heart as it did when she was concerned.

"I'm here to have Ilena confirm for me that the men we've beheaded are the ones who I meant to find." Rei decided the words must be sufficiently hard to hear given that the sight to view would be even worse to someone who'd never been on the battlefield.

Mizi paled. After a great pause, she finally said weakly, "I'll wait out here for you." Rei reached out and held her shoulder briefly to give her strength as he nodded. Releasing her, he turned and entered the room, the other four following him.

Mizi sat hard on the wall he'd just left, trying very hard to recover. She was glad Ilena had protected her for that moment. She hadn't thought to question the burdens the aides were carrying with them.

-o-o-o-

"Welcome home, Master Rei," Ilena said calmly as Rei entered the room. He looked into her eyes. He could see they flickered between calm, worry, and a smile. Her general demeanor was one of a calmness he hadn't seen before. That was very good.

He was here for business, but he wanted to reassure her as well. "Thank you, Ilena," he answered her. "It's good to be home again." He stayed firmly in control, but allowed his eyes to also gently smile. Her smile flitted across her face, and the worry eased. He was pleased. He stepped aside and motioned to Andrew.

Andrew brought his burden up to Ilena. He stood where she could both see and reach it, then removed the covering from it. Upon a wooden plank was Earl Shicchi's head. "Please, will you confirm who this is?" Andrew requested of her.

She'd gone very still at first, and now she grew very, very cold. The silence in the room rang. She reached up one hand and brushed the hair away from the right ear of the man's head to look behind it. She looked up at Andrew. "Do you see the scar on the head and the nick in the ear?" He nodded.

"Please turn it for me." He obliged. She searched through the hair on the back of his head, then said, "Do you see any mark or sign in this place?" Andrew shook his head. She dropped her hands. "This is the head of Pakyo Shicchi," she declared. Andrew replaced the cover on it and moved away.

He took the head to Rei, removed the cover again and showed him the identifiers that Ilena had pointed out. Rei nodded and Andrew re-covered it and stepped to the back of the group of people who had entered. Rei motioned to Thayne, who brought a similar burden. "Please, confirm also who this is," Thayne asked her.

Thayne removed the cover and Ilena shivered and bare her teeth ever so slightly. She was unable to keep the predatory look from her eyes. She motioned for Thayne to lower the plank and examined the left hand first. "You see this nick in this fingernail, ...this unusual bend in this joint," she turned it over, "and this scar going from the palm into the wrist?" Thayne nodded. "This is the left hand of the exiled son of King Melick of Selicia."

"Please turn the board for me." She searched through the hair on the back of the head until she found the mark then looked at Thayne, "Do you see this mark?" Thayne nodded. "This is the head of the same man." Her mouth couldn't close over her silent snarl, and the look in her eyes was triumphant.

As Thayne carried it over to Rei, Rei asked, "Did he never tell you his name?"

Ilena shook her head. "No. I was only ever to call him Earl Shicchi, the same as all the others. I don't think even Earl Shicchi knew his real name."

Rei nodded, then looked carefully at the evidences she had pointed out to Thayne. When he was done, Thayne re-covered it and also stepped to the back of the group.

"I only have need of the head of Earl Shicchi," Rei said to Ilena. "As you're the closest representative to Selicia within my castle, what would you have me do with the head and hand of the other man?"

Ilena's eyes flashed and everyone in the room tensed, having already dealt with her before. Ore shifted and Ilena looked to him. He looked at her calmly, holding her eyes with his. She was struggling very much.

They let her have the time to get under control again, and it was long in coming. Finally she drew in a hissing breath, held it, and let it out, but she wouldn't let Ore's eyes go. She had calmed the emotional storm, but now she had to figure out how to properly say what she wanted to say.

Her eyes suddenly snapped from Ore's to Rei's. Rei wasn't quite prepared, but he remained externally calm. She waited until he was ready and gave her the signal. Very carefully, she asked, "Prince Rei, will you hear my words of advice on how to begin the next phase?"

Keeping his surprise hidden deeply that she would already be at the point of acting on the next phase of the war against the Lord of Tarc, he said to her calmly, "I'll hear it." He could see her struggle. She'd already been that way with him before, but now she was trying to bring it down to support level.

She closed her eyes, choosing to hood herself momentarily. "Master Rei, your next conflict will come from Selicia and the puppet king. Because it was he who destroyed the previous regime, you have in your hands a means to send him a message, thus gaining the upper hand before he can even move.

"It's possible in the same move to gain him as an ally, and to protect a thing you wish to protect." She took a breath and her eyes snapped open to look at him again, to see if he'd understood or if he would ask her for more information.

Rei considered what she'd said. The King of Selicia had claimed to have killed all of the family of Polov. But one, even though bastard, had remained to cause trouble. That trouble had been caused on Suiran - his - soil. He could lay the blame at the feet of that King, and send him a message, by sending him the head he'd missed. That would give him the advantage of having already been offended a second time - the first time for the death of his aunt.

It would give the King of Selicia extra pause before considering a push against them. To gain him as an ally - even if it was one of neutrality - against the Lord of Tarc, would be of benefit. If the King of Selicia thought that Ryokudo was sufficiently strong to stand against Tarc such that even Selicia could be freed from their puppet status, he would do it. "Is the King of Selicia sufficiently strong enough to stand on his own?" he asked Ilena.

She nodded once. "He's been learning properly since he was put in that place. Guidance from Ryokudo will aid him as well." Rei nodded.

As to the protection of that which he desired to protect.... Ilena was as much a princess of Selicia as she was of Ryokudo and was yet another of the previous King's house the current King had missed. If Rei wished for her to be able to remain in Ryokudo and not be used as a pawn by Selicia, or murdered for her potential claim, he would need to make it clear to Selicia that any attempt of either would be met with the same anger he would be expressing from the previous two offenses.

Rei looked Ilena in the eyes. "Then I will send him my message." She calmly held her tongue. He was pleased, as he was sure she'd already composed many messages to that man in her own mind. "If I send him the head," Rei asked, wanting to know what she'd been thinking, "what would I do with the hand?"

Her eyes crinkled. He knew he'd scored a point she'd been watching for. He remained calm so that she could answer appropriately. "I...," she changed her wording, "if you wish to send a message to my enemy, I will have it sent to him."

He held still, then said slowly, "What message would that be?" knowing he might be treading on uncertain ground, both for her training's sake, and that he might push her over into the area where they must ask her for all of the information before he desired to know it.

"That you have accepted from him his right hand and have removed from him his left." While she was still controlling herself somewhat, her eyes were now completely the piercing eyes of the wild falcon again. He held himself steady against them, knowing his own control was her control, but he was pleased with the message that would be sent. He was already angry enough to send it.

"You may send it, but I'll provide my own words." He wanted the Lord of Tarc to understand that it was he himself that had been provoked, and the words were not Ilena's to say.

She bowed her head as best she was able. "Yes, Master Rei."

As Rei left the room, he motioned for Mina to take the burden from Thayne and said to Ore, "I'll expect to see you shortly in the Rose office."

-o-o-o-

Ore bowed slightly and watched after Rei until the door was shut again, leaving him and Thayne in the room with the three women. He turned back to look at them. He'd expected to see at least Rio look a bit faint at the sight of the evidence that had been brought in, but she was as resolutely pleased as Leah to have been able to see with her own eyes that the source of their long-time pain was no longer living. Ore expected any who had come from that House would be as well.

He looked at Ilena. She was just opening her eyes to look at him. They'd gone from flaming to merely smoldering and he could see that she was working hard to come down, but she wasn't settling well. He stepped up closer to her. When Thayne followed him, she flared in alarm, her eyes narrowing.

Ore paused. The mode in the room hadn't changed from the very formal it had been with Rei present, and to her that meant if Thayne followed him closely, he felt Ore needed protecting. She hadn't understood why Rei had left them here.

"Thayne, please stay by the door for now," he said quietly. Thayne bowed slightly and moved to obey. Ilena's eyes darted to him as he moved, then quickly looked back at Ore again. He didn't move until she'd focused on him again.

Teaching her to only look at him had been a difficult thing so far because he hadn't allowed others into the room with them much until now. He held her eyes until she understood that she should have let Thayne move without looking at him. She blinked and bobbed her head in apology. Then Ore moved.

Ore put his hand on her head, and while looking into her eyes said, "You did very well under extreme circumstances. Master is pleased." She held still in surprise briefly, then he could feel her relax under his hand. When she was sufficiently relaxed, but still in control, he removed his hand.

"There is still work that must be done, but we'll come again this evening to relax from the efforts we've come from and before we must begin the remaining work." Her eyes were happy. He turned to Leah and Rio. "From the time we arrive tonight until tomorrow morning, you'll be free to do as you please." He turned to Thayne, "Thayne also." The three of them bowed in gratitude.

His official business done, but needing to answer to his Master's call, he turned to leave by turning to Ilena and brushing her hand with the back of his as he passed, letting her know that he, also, was pleased.

Even that was almost more than he himself could bear. It was going to be a difficult afternoon and evening, waiting for the time they could be together alone again, finally as just partners for a brief time. He didn't look back at her, and she held her tongue, and together they were able to be a strength to the other.

-o-o-o-

Ilena looked at Thayne, who'd stayed behind. "I'll hear your report now." He stepped forward from the door and the same detailed report he'd given at the Scholar's Tavern flowed from him, with the addition of what had happened up until the moment they were standing in. When he'd completed it, Ilena kept him waiting on her for some time. "Please explain to me what your duty is," she finally said. Thayne paled.

He swallowed. "To follow Master Ore and protect him in Mistress Ilena's stead and do all things I am rightfully ordered to do. To instruct Father in the proper workings of the Family as he is prepared to receive such instructions. To watch over and protect Mistress Ilena in Master Ore's stead." Ilena waited to hear more. He searched frantically for anything else he might have missed, but he could think of nothing else and stayed silent.

"Thayne, what is my goal for Ore?"

"To become the person Mistress Ilena can stand beside." Ilena was silent again, allowing him time to consider what that meant. "...And to become a person who can stand beside Mistress Ilena," he added, and slumped in sorrow. "I'm sorry, Mistress Ilena, that I didn't properly understand."

"Thayne, it wasn't a small thing. By your example, you've caused conflict between Father and First Son that's damaging to me and my path." She was both upset and sorrowful. "Your conflict with First Son has caused not only Ore to have to speak with you, but also Master Rei had to open his mouth. I've promised him that my Family won't bring shame and dishonor to him, Thayne. Because he's opened his mouth, your fate is now in his hands." Her eyes glittered with sorrowful frustration.

Thayne bowed. "I understand, Mistress Ilena. I'll properly take responsibility."

"Tell me what you'll do," she required.

"I'll apologize to Master Ore and Regent Rei for my misbehavior and lack of understanding, and ask for Regent Rei's judgment. I'll inform you of his judgment and be obedient to it. Then I'll go to First Son and explain

302

my lack of understanding and beg that he forgive you - that the fault of his misunderstanding is mine.

"If Regent Rei has dismissed me," the pain within Thayne was very evident, "I'll let First Son and Grandfather know a suitable replacement must be sent, and shall return to Falcon's Hollow until the time the Regent releases the witnesses."

"And if Master Rei forgives your error?" Ilena prompted when he stopped.

Thayne considered it briefly. "After I've heard from First Son, I'll return to you for further education."

She looked at him for a while, as if to remember him, then said, "It's sufficient." He bowed to her then left the room, a miserable young man.

CHAPTER 18 Coming Home

Thayne walked out of Ilena's room, closing the door quietly behind himself, only to find that Rei and his entourage were just leaving the Medical department. They had likely been leaving the heads and hand of the Earl and uncle there in proper cold storage until Rei's letters were written.

Ore paused first, his eyebrow raised to see Thayne out of Ilena's rooms when he'd been expressly left behind. Rei paused second, waiting on Ore. Thayne couldn't decide if he would have liked the time to walk to the Rose office to come up with what he was going to say, or if he was glad he could get it over with quickly.

He walked up to Rei first and bowed a low bow, then changed his mind and went on down into the fully humble one-knee bow, one fist on the ground. He focused his eyes on Rei's feet. "Mistress Ilena has corrected me. Please accept my apology for my thoughtless behavior and my lack of understanding of my proper responsibilities to Master Ore in behalf of Mistress Ilena. Tell me what I must do, and I will do it."

Rei was silent for a moment, then he asked, "What has Ilena already said you must do?"

"After I've heard your word, I'm to return into Nijoushi to fix the wrongs I've done to Grail in my lack of understanding, and do all I can to repair Grail's misunderstandings towards Master Ore. Then I'm to return to Falcon's Hollow if you or Master Ore have dismissed me. If I haven't been, then I'm to return to my place and receive further instructions."

Thayne managed to say the words, but his heart quailed. It was hard to have faith in himself, even though he desperately wanted to stay where he'd been placed. His lack of faith in himself had been his undoing already. He needed to face it properly and do what he could to change it so that he could be where he wanted to be - if it wasn't already too late.

Rei shifted and folded his arms. "Thayne ...have you been in the castle before this at any time?"

Thayne shook his head, not looking up from Rei's feet. "No, Regent. Not until Master Ore called for me and brought me."

"Hmmm. Even so, I have noticed you're trying your best. It isn't surprising that you also have things to learn." Thayne blinked. In the world he came from, Rei was being very soft. At the same time, he thought that Rei wasn't really all that soft, not given what he'd seen of him these last weeks. "If you earnestly fulfill your requirements to Ilena and Ore, and Ore is also willing, I'm content with you remaining as long as you continue diligent in your own lessons."

"I will," Thayne promised. That part was easy. Dealing with the tangle of emotions the statement brought up wasn't quite so much easy.

Ore stepped closer. Thayne couldn't move, but he addressed Ore anyway. "I'm sorry, Master Ore, for not properly understanding and for not helping Grail to see why Mistress Ilena chose you and why he should accept you."

"I would also like to not have Eldest Son angry with me," Ore said. "Please do your best. And please do your best to learn how to properly stand in your place." Like Rei, Ore was willing to forgive, but behind it was the stern requirement to continue to become better at what he'd been chosen to do.

Because that was also his own desire, Thayne answered humbly, "Yes, Master Ore." He stayed in his bowed position until the footsteps of the Regent's small entourage had left the courtyard of the Medical wing.

The trip to the hiding place of First Son was long, however. For two reasons, actually. The first reason was because this was Thayne's first time being in Nijoushi. The second reason was because Thayne had thinking to do and needed to work out his own internal conflict before facing First Son.

Thayne wasn't just Family, but that was where he started. He walked slowly into Nijoushi and gave the proper signal until he had another man walking with him. "Is First with Grandfather still?" Thayne asked.

He got a look that didn't trust him completely, but he still got an honest answer for all that. "He's gone underground to confirm the House."

"Thank you," Thayne said very respectfully. The other man continued on his own way. Thayne knew he'd have eyes on him for a while. He walked the city, following the flow of foot traffic until he reached the market district.

He stopped a youth that looked like he was a messenger, or a runner as they were called in towns. "I'm new in town. Which way to find a meal?"

The youth pointed to Thayne's right. "That way." Thayne reached for his coin pouch and the youth stayed put rather than run on. "Third open shop has the best prices," the lad took the initiative to earn better coin.

Thayne pulled out one of the smallest coins, then after a pause pulled out a second making the youth raise an eyebrow. That usually meant more information was wanted. "I need to declare," Thayne stated.

The youth narrowed his eyes at Thayne. "Which House?"

Thayne answered, "The Queen's."

The youth relaxed slightly. "When?"

"I need to settle and rest first. On your way back is fine."

The youth gave a nod and held out his hand. Thayne put both coins in his hand, then walked away, headed for the eating district. He kept his senses alert and one hand on his belt over his coin pouch.

Thayne wasn't really all that hungry, given the churning his stomach was doing, but he needed the time and that was an openly honest way to spend it. He had both sides now to calm down until he was picked up by the runner and shown to the hiding place of the local heads of the House of the Queen of Night.

He didn't really want to be in public right at the moment. He looked around at the buildings that lined the street. The third eating establishment that had tables set up outside it wasn't what he was looking for, but what he was looking for wasn't too far, just another two places beyond that.

He bypassed the eatery and walked through the door into the inn. When the waitress walked up to seat him, he held up a hand. "I need sleep before food. Can I get a bed for only a few hours - from now until dinner? I'll probably need a wake-up call, too." He grimaced as if not thrilled. Such a request always cost a lot more than most cared to spend, even him.

The waitress considered, then finally gave a nod and named a price. Thayne pulled it out, then followed her as she stopped by a key board and pulled off a key. "Last one on the left, third floor," she said.

"Thanks," Thayne took the key, then headed for the stairs. The room wasn't a surprise. It was a small one, one they didn't rent out often because of it's location and size.

He confirmed the door and windows were locked tightly before he lay down on the bed. He put his hands behind his head and closed his eyes. He wouldn't sleep deeply - no one who said they might be a nightwalker did.

Thayne needed to work out the issues inside him that were all chaotic. Letting his body rest, his mind went to work. Ore's words to him on their journey to Falcon's Hollow with the third set of witnesses came back to him. "Mother doesn't let people stay lonely very long, does she? ...When will she find a partner for Thayne?"

That was at the heart of Thayne's doubt of himself, which was at the heart of his conflict with First Son. Thayne had lost his partner several years earlier. He'd been too young, too weak, and they'd been surprised and overwhelmed. Thayne had nearly lost his life. To be the living partner, weakened by the event, crippled in heart even if the limbs had relearned strength, was still very difficult.

First Son was actually in the same position, and from that same event, from a similar surprise. Still, First Son was famous in both the House and the Family. Everyone respected him and knew that he'd not been the least at fault for what had happened to his partner.

For Thayne to be faced with the prospect that Ilena would likely be making him First's partner, merely because Ore had randomly chosen Thayne to walk with him made him shiver and his heart quail, his courage wanting to flee with him back to Kouzanshi. At the same time, with all his being Thayne wanted to walk at Ore's back. He'd wanted it for longer than Ore had known him.

He'd not followed the initial calling up Ore had done to the final conclusion. He should have done it as soon as Ilena had given him the order to pass along for First to stand with him behind Ore during the battle. Instead he'd acted as a child and damaged what he should have been building up, all because he couldn't believe in himself properly.

Thayne took a deep breath, held it, then let it out. His requirement was to fix that in himself, and then to fix the damage done. He very openly and honestly looked closely at his desires, Ore's desire to have him by his side, and his own commitment to Ilena. That had already lasted since he was thirteen, twelve years now - as many as he'd lived not knowing her.

306

When those things finally settled into him, his doubt could only say that it would trust his master and mistress. If they saw in him something salvageable, then he had to try, he had to continue on the path he was on. Everything he did from now on had to prove to First Son that he was committed to following Ilena and Ore and to being the partner that First Son needed.

They would have to learn over time what that meant, but Thayne committed before he rose to his feet again to humbly do whatever it took to learn it, and to strengthen First so that he could also accept it and the place that Ilena was determined to place him in.

Once Thayne had figured out what he needed to say to First Son, he was able to leave the inn. He purchased a small meal from the place the runner had said to buy from and ate it slowly. As the sun was setting, the youth arrived at his table. Thayne rose to his feet and followed him, slipping into hiding in the shadows when the youth did.

Eventually, they reached a hidden house among nondescript houses of people who tried hard but didn't have enough for extra luxuries. The knock at the side door to enter the house the youth gave was the same one Thayne knew intimately. When the door guard opened it, he recognized the youth, then gave a bit of a glare to Thayne. "He's new. Coming to declare," the youth explained. Thayne gave a nod and the door guard let them in.

Thayne followed the youth's example on the way past the door guard and placed a coin of medium worth into his hand. That much was payment to get in, the promise he could earn more for the House. The main room in the basement of the house was the same as Thayne was very used to. Open and filled with men, boys, and a few girls and women sitting scattered all over the floor save a walkway from the door up to the raised stand at the back of the room.

On that stand were four men, sitting cross-legged. All four were staring at Thayne. He gave them a slight, wry smile. He knew them and they knew him. He didn't really have to declare, but it was the way of the nightwalker Houses. Three of the men, older than him by at least ten years, were giving him looks of surprise at his size and age since it had been a number of years since they'd seen him. They also were giving him some measure of welcome. First Son not so much. He wasn't pleased to see Thayne at all, really. Thayne wasn't surprised.

Thayne walked up to stand directly in front of the raised stand, at the center point. He bowed slightly, then turned to First Son. That was where he was required to start. He bowed more deeply. "First, I was wrong to doubt myself and tease you out of my own weaknesses. I've been scolded and sent away until I've received forgiveness from you for my thoughtlessness."

Thayne rose from the bow and looked First Son in the eye. "I've also been taken to task most firmly for standing in the wrong place and not understanding the seriousness of my task properly. What can I do to help you see that Father is properly placed at the side of Mother and only has her best interests at heart? He is being obedient to her in all things and is learning his lessons properly."

Everyone Thayne could see blinked at him in surprise. Because he'd directly addressed the Messenger of the Queen in his own place, the other heads, the Lieutenants, stayed silent. First Son's lips pressed together, and his look went a little hard.

"If it's because you can't see where they stand, I'm willing to tell you what I see from where I've been placed to stand," Thayne offered what he could. "Until you're called to come stand in your place, I'll tell you, so you can be reassured."

First Son folded his arms and his face went from hard to cool expressionless. "Then tell me everything you've seen until now."

Thayne gave a slight bow, changed position so that his feet were shoulder-width apart, clasped his hands lightly behind his back, and unfocused slightly. Reaching back one month, Thayne began his report from when he'd been picked up by Ore as a witness and told every time he'd had an interaction with Ore, with Ilena, and with both of them. He told it in the full detail required by the Family.

It was almost midnight when Thayne stopped talking. One of the Lieutenants motioned and a boy brought over a tankard and handed it to Thayne. Thayne drank from it gratefully and handed it back. They hadn't had to do it, but the Lieutenant that had done it was the one loyal to Ilena, and it was his gratitude to finally hear of the details of how she was doing in the castle.

Thayne waited silently while First Son pondered what he'd heard. He'd even seen some of it himself at the early part, and not been disappointed then. Thayne could only hope what he'd said would help to heal the damage he'd done, and that Ore and Ilena had done to themselves in going into seclusion, even though it had been the fault of the injury more than anything.

First Son finally came back and looked sharply at Thayne. He still had his arms folded, but his face was more testing now, than cool. "Who are you that you should walk next to Father? Merely someone that he found entertaining? Declare yourself."

Thayne sighed to himself. He'd on purpose not told anyone who he was, except when he'd had to tell the witnesses from the third witness gathering to get them to trust him. For all they had titles that were recognized all across Selicia and beyond, few people outside of the city one lived in actually knew the face of who they were. And Thayne hadn't acted properly for his station or title. He was ashamed to say it in this place to this person, but that was also his shame to bear for having acted wrongly.

"I am fallen until redeemed," he said first, "although both Father and his master have allowed me to return to earn that redemption if you'll also forgive me and promise to learn to trust Father and Mother properly."

He got a scowl, then an impatient wave of a hand. "Regardless, tell me."

Thayne drew in a long breath and went into battle-ready mode. "I am Fourth Son, the Messenger of Kouzanshi."

First Son's blow was so fast, Thayne almost didn't block it in time. In the nightwalker Houses, only strength was believed and obeyed. When Thayne was told that First Son had returned to the House to secure it, he'd been told that First Son had returned to this house to prove that he was still the strongest in the city, and that he still had the right to claim the title of Messenger of the Queen of Night for Nijoushi.

Thayne had in essence said that he was First's equal, or his slight subordinate. It was both a challenge, and a requirement that he be tested of that claim of level of ability and title. Drawing on his newfound commitment to his ultimate goals, Thayne protected himself, meeting speed with speed and strength with strength.

He was glad that blades weren't part of this particular fight. First Son hadn't chosen to use them. He'd seen Thayne's sword in action in the mountains. He'd chosen this time to see if Thayne's hand-to-hand combat skills were just as good.

Thayne had one thing in his favor when it came to that skill. Ilena had built two halls of competition and practice in Kouzanshi - one for the knife, the other for hand-to-hand. He'd had to stay the top competitor of that place to hold on to his own seat, so he'd already fought against so many different styles he managed to hold his own against First Son.

When First Son added in a few odd moves, Thayne kept up. He knew them from Ilena and from the Tarc that lived in Kouzanshi. Still, he only defended, slipping out of holds, preventing damage. He was sending his own message. He wasn't there to take First's place. He'd not been ordered to, for one. For the other, he wanted First to understand that he would stand strong for him in his place next to him, but he wouldn't fight against him.

The next set of different moves were from Selicia and still Thayne kept up with First Son. The second most common foreigners in Kouzanshi were from Selicia, just on the other side of the mountains. Mother had plenty of people who came from there come play in the ring as well.

Still, Thayne watched First carefully now. Would he be obedient to Mother, or would he become angry that Thayne wasn't fighting back and push him?

First Son pulled back and paused. "You won't attack?"

Thayne shook his head. "I'm not here to replace the Messenger of Nijoushi. That was not my order. I was ordered to stand at Father's back, to watch over Mother, and to teach First Son." That last did make First Son angry, but he held still. "I will say it again, First Son. I'm sorry I didn't properly understand the last until I returned and reported. Please allow me to redeem myself in your eyes also."

First Son went from a paused attack position to a firm standing stance that still scolded Thayne. "I will expect to hear from you daily, then, until I'm summoned."

Thayne gave a nod. "Please also send and tell me what more I can do to help you if you find that insufficient."

"I will." First Son pursed his lips at Thayne again. He would watch and test, then, but Thayne couldn't expect anything else at this point in time. He would have to build up the trust little by little. That would be hard from the distance, but he would do all he could from there. Having one standing next to Ilena tell First what he would be seeing if he also could be there would be the best thing for them both.

First gave Thayne a firm nod. He'd passed the test of strength that would allow First to trust him in that position as proxy for the strength he wished he could give to their mistress. Thayne was relieved. "Welcome the Messenger of Kouzanshi!" First ordered to the room. There was a unanimous cry in the room. Thayne stood firmly with the pride of a Messenger.

Then he tipped his head at First, turned, and left the House to return to the castle. This was not the time to visit or celebrate. He was still under orders, and still fallen until Ilena and Ore redeemed him.

-o-o-o-

It had been a long time since Ore and Mizi had an excuse to cook for everyone. Rei's birthday party seemed to be a good one. Andrew and Mina had agreed to bring the drinks: juice for Mizi who couldn't hold her alcohol and alcohol for the rest of them. When asked if Ilena drank, Ore had surprisingly said he didn't know. It seemed to them unlikely she drank alcohol, so they were going to bring extra juice just in case.

"This will be the first time for Ilena to eat your food, won't it, Ore?" Mizi asked as she slipped her current creation onto a platter.

They were using a corner of the castle kitchen with the promise they'd clean up after themselves, the meals for the castle as a whole already having been made and clean up going on around them. It wasn't the first time, but it also wasn't often they had the time to cook. They were used to ignoring the looks they got from the scullery maids and boys who had a hard time not staring at Mizi's hair, or giggling over her good looking guard.

Ore deftly flipped the food searing in his pan over the fire. "Yes. I wonder if she likes spicy foods?" The others wouldn't eat it when he made it to his tastes, as he was the only one in the group who really liked it truly hot and spicy. He tried to tone the spice down some for them in what he did cook - except for his favorite dish. "I'll have to make sure Ilena tries a bite of my curry."

"Ore - you'll warn her ahead of time it's spicy, right?" Mizi asked worriedly.

"Mmm," he answered noncommittally, pouring the ingredients of a bowl of spices into his pan on top of the vegetables and meat.

"That's mean, Ore," Mizi scolded, setting her next set of ingredients near the stove. "Don't fight with her your first night back."

He looked at her innocently as he added and stirred the liquid sauce into the mixture. "It's not fighting, Mistress. It's...getting to know her better."

"Ore!" Mizi brandished her spoon at him.

"I won't fight, I won't." Ore defended himself. He took his food off the flame and placed it into a deep bowl. "There are still many things that I don't know about Ilena. This will be a good opportunity to learn some of them."

"Is she feeling better about us coming?" Mizi asked, getting her next pan heating over the flame.

"Some," he answered as he set his dish on the cart they would be taking down with the other prepared dishes on it. He stood up straight, stretching his back. "It is, I think, she's nervous because she hasn't been able to relax with us before." He walked back to the cutting table to begin cleaning up, the curry having been his last of several dishes to make.

"Hmm...well, perhaps that's reasonable. But...I think everyone understands that?" Mizi flipped her searing meat over, preparing to add vegetables already marinating in a sauce.

"Well, it will also be a good opportunity for her to get to know everyone," Ore said as he carried his cooking utensils and pan to the sink to begin washing them. As he washed he thought about Ilena and what was next.

Getting to know her as a person - her likes and dislikes, her preferences - was as necessary as understanding what her motivations were, if he was to agree to take the final step she was hoping for. After all, if she hated spicy foods and wouldn't let him drink in the house - it would be a sad life to be together that way. He needed to know if there were things that he couldn't live with.

At least she didn't snore loudly at night. He knew that much only, it felt like. And, even though she said she loved to watch Master and Mistress, that had been from a distance. If she really couldn't get along with them on a personal level, or even Mister Andrew and Miss Mina, that would be a major problem for Ore.

He wondered suddenly if she might be nervous about being with him also, and be considering it a first date. He laughed at himself. It somehow seemed a little late...or at least backwards. Would their last activity together be finally a date just the two of them?

He entertained himself by considering what kind of dates he might take her on, if they ever were able to go on any. Maybe tonight he would ask her what kinds of things she liked to do. "How much time before Ilena can be up from her bed?" Ore asked Mizi, having rather lost count due to the battle.

She walked over carrying her dishes to be washed. "Mmm...a little more than two weeks. She says she wants a bath first thing again, understandably." She smiled at him.

"That does seem to be like her," he agreed, grinning back. "Ah! That's why Master set the Lord's Court to be in twenty days?"

Mizi nodded. "Although I think he should wait just a little longer. It will tire her out, I think, to have her sit up in public so long right away." She looked at Ore. "I hope you'll watch over her carefully there, and if she can't sit any longer you'll find a way to bring her back to rest."

"I'll be sure she's taken care of, Mistress," he promised her.

-o-o-o-

Mizi and Ore arrived at Ilena's room right about the same time Rei, Andrew, and Mina did. They entered after knocking and pushed the food cart in with them. "Hello, Ilena!" rang out in choruses as they crowded in.

"Welcome, everyone," she smiled at them. "I'm glad you can come tonight." There was general chaos as Leah and Rio excused themselves and furniture was rearranged to better fit the remaining people comfortably. When Mina had put her bottles down on the desk that had been moved into the corner, she walked over to Ilena and embraced her. "Are you home, Miss Mina?" Ilena asked her.

"I'm home, Ilena" Mina answered her.

"Welcome home. I'm glad you've come safely." They parted and as Ilena looked into Mina's eyes, she added, "Thank you."

Andrew took her place. Ilena looked at him warmly but just a bit shyly. "Welcome home, Mister Andrew."

"Thank you," he smiled his gentle smile at her that was as warm as any hug. "It's good to be home."

"Thank you for your hard work," she answered and held up her hand, palm up.

Andrew took it lightly, looking at her curiously. She pulled him to her gently, letting him resist if he wanted. He allowed her to pull him close enough that she could speak with him quietly.

"Thank you for your concern for Grail," she said to him. "I miss him as much as he misses me, but there's a thing only he's been able to do, and it's not completed yet. When it's done, he'll come be with me, and we'll both be very relieved." She released Andrew's hand and smiled gently at him, allowing her pain to show briefly.

"Thank you," he said. "It's helpful to know it from yourself."

Rei was standing beside her next. Ilena was a bit surprised to see him there, but recovered quickly enough to say, "Welcome home again...ah...Rei." His eyes smiled. "And, happy birthday."

"Thank you, Ilena," he answered.

"I'm afraid that this year I haven't much to give you for your birthday, not being able to get out and pick something for you," she said apologetically, "but if there's a thing I may give you?"

"Yes," he said, and bent down and wrapped his arms around her, "a hug would be very acceptable."

She wrapped her arms around him and held him. Then she whispered in his ear, "Thank you, Master Rei, for keeping your promise."

"Are you content?" he asked her.

"Yes - for now."

He chuckled. "As honest as always." He released her and she let him go, and they smiled at each other.

Mizi walked up next to Rei and took his hand. Ilena turned her smile to include her. "It's good to see you together again."

"Thank you for protecting me, earlier today," Mizi said to her.

"It's my duty," Ilena said seriously. "There are many things you need to learn, but there are some things you shouldn't have to learn unless you must. ...Or choose to learn," she amended.

"Come and get your plates before it's all cold," called Ore. Everyone moved towards the cart. He appeared next to Ilena with a full plate. "You're sitting up, and you told me you're eating well now, right?"

"Yes, but that seems like an awful lot of food, Ore," she answered him.

He sat on the bed, carefully so he didn't spill the plate. "We'll both eat from it," he said to her. "Mistress and I made it all, so you have to try some of everything."

Ilena's eyes went wide. "You made it? And Princess Mizi?"

Ore grinned. "Yes. It's become somewhat of a tradition for us to make the food for these gatherings."

"What will you drink, Ilena?" Andrew asked as he went to pour glasses for everyone.

"What is there?" she asked him.

"With dinner, there's juice or wine. There will be a few stronger drinks after dinner."

Ilena considered for a bit. "Let me start with juice for now, thank you."

Ore kept a neutral face. "What do you wish to start with?" he held the fork over the plate.

"Princess Mizi's, please."

Ore gave her a bite of one, then ate some himself. He repeated it for each of Mizi's dishes, asking Ilena's opinion of each as they went, and telling her his own. Ilena praised Mizi's cooking and Mizi explained that her aunt and uncle had run a tavern and she had learned to cook there. As Ore prepared to give Ilena the first of his creations, she asked him where he'd learned to cook.

"Oh, here and there," he answered. "After all, not all of my jobs were from the desk of the underworld. Can you cook?"

Ilena shook her head. "No. My cooking is inedible. Leah has quite despaired of me being able to be a suitable housewife, and has always said that my station would be obvious to anyone who asked me to attempt to be one, even if I should keep my mouth shut."

There were chuckles from everyone in the room. As Ore put the first taste of one of his more mild creations into her mouth, Rei said, "The man you sent as Ore's second, the one we called Grail, he said that you were given laundry to do as a punishment. From his description it sounded like it punished them more."

Ilena sighed. "Did he say that? I suppose it was true. Leah only made me do it twice. The second time not only was her shirt darker than when I started, her last pair of socks had holes in them - and she was watching me that time."

As everyone laughed again, Ore asked, "Was it worse the first time?"

Ilena looked at him miserably. "Of course! I had no idea what I was doing, even though she'd carefully explained it."

Ore shook his head and gave her the next bite. "Mmm. This is very good, Ore. It's similar to what I would have eaten as a child."

He was pleased. It was one of the ones he was proud of. It was spicier than the first, but he usually ate it even spicier when he made it for himself. Then he put some of his personal curry on the fork. Everyone in the room looked up and watched him.

"You're going to give her some of that?" Rei asked, a warning tone in his voice.

"Of course, Master," Ore answered blandly. "She should try some of everything."

Ilena looked from one to the other, not understanding. "Is there a problem with it?" she asked.

"It's too spicy for the rest of us," Mina told her warningly. "Ore likes to melt holes in his mouth."

"Oh?" Ilena looked back at him. "Did you by chance bring an orange with you?"

Ore looked at her curiously. "No."

"Then next time, bring one with you, and I won't be afraid to eat with you."

"Are you afraid now?"

"Yes, but I'll eat a bite anyway."

"That's very brave," Mizi looked at Ilena with big eyes.

Ilena looked at Ore, not sure she should be trusting him. "Well, but everything else so far has been good. And, it isn't proper to refuse what's been prepared for you." Rei and Ore both nodded - Rei because that was the way royalty was taught, and Ore because he wanted her to try it.

As Ilena accepted the bite and began to chew, everyone had their eyes on her to see her reaction. "Mmm..., I think...I need to try another bite." She opened her mouth for more. Ore looked at her in shock, much like everyone else in the room. Then he quickly gave her another bite. She chewed it slowly, savoring the texture and flavor. When she was done she nodded. "Yes, this is it. This was my favorite dish in my father's house. Your rendition is very good, Ore. May I have more?"

"You can seriously eat it?" Rei was amazed.

Ilena nodded, looking at him. "Most foods in Selicia are like this. Some of the flavors are just a little different, but I imagine that the seasonings we imported from the northern desert are difficult to obtain here." Everyone shook their heads in wonder. She looked back at Ore and saw his wide grin.

Ore very solicitously leaned in and gave her another bite of his curry. "This is my favorite also," he said. "Everyone else makes me eat this one alone, so I make it to my taste."

Ilena looked surprised. "You have to eat it alone? But it's so good!"

"I think you both must have Selician tongues," Mina said as dry as usual. "We always wondered why Ore could eat things the rest of us couldn't."

"It's possible," said Ilena. "We are distantly related, after all." She held her mouth open for another bite. Ore had managed to get in a few bites of his own, and he did have to admit it was very good tonight. He almost didn't want to share it, but at the same time he was very pleased Ilena liked it. He gave her the bite she was asking for, then ate a few more himself, ignoring the looks from Andrew and Mina.

"Just how distantly?" Mina asked with her eyes narrowed.

"Great grandfather," Ore said briefly as he gave Ilena another bite.

Mizi thought about that for a moment. "But, Ore, doesn't that mean you're descended from the royal line of Selicia, then?"

"If it still was the royal line, Princess Mizi," Ilena amended. "He has just slightly less a claim to the throne as I do, I think. We're from the same generation, but I come from the line of oldest heirs, save my father. Other than that, either of us could claim the throne, if we wished to press the issue - which I don't. Do you, Ore?"

"Hmm...well, given that I understand what that means now, having followed Master for more than five years now - no, I have no interest."

Mizi frowned. "But Ilena, as a Princess of Selicia, don't you have a responsibility to the people?"

"Of course, Princess Mizi," Ilena raised an eyebrow at her, "and I take it very seriously. I have many Children in Selicia, quite a number in the castle itself. I've been influencing the current King and many of his court for several years now. He's willing to be molded in ways that benefit the people of Selicia, and he's trying very hard.

"I've decided, for the time being, if I can help him be free of his own taskmaster, that the people of Selicia would be much better served by having him be their king than for me or any other potential rival to bring the country to civil war again. They're only just now beginning to thrive again, although there's still some prejudice against those who preferred the prior regime, sadly."

"Oh," Mizi said faintly.

"Hmm...does that mean I have spies in the Selician court, then?" asked Rei.

"Of course," Ilena said matter-of-factly. "Oh, Ore, are we done eating?" She was looking at the nearly empty plate in his hand. Rei sat bemused, wondering where else he, through her, had spies.

"Can you actually eat more?" Ore asked her, surprised.

"Well, no," she admitted, "although it was all very good. I'd eat the rest for breakfast, if it will keep. Really, I was wondering if it was time to move on to after-dinner drinks. I would like to hear the stories of everyone's journey."

Mizi nodded. "I want to hear, also." She stood up and collected plates, putting them on the cart. Andrew stood and poured drinks again. When he reached for Ilena's glass, she shook her head and he left it, seeing it still had some juice in it. But when Ore's glass had been filled, she reached for it.

Ore's eyes glinted. "Sooo...what happens to Ilena, when she gets drunk, eh?"

She looked at him innocently. "I don't know, Ore. It hasn't happened before."

"Oh? Well, would you like to try this?" he asked her.

"Is it one you like?" she asked back.

"Yes. Mister Andrew picks very good drinks."

"Then I would like to try it."

"Wouldn't you like your own?" Andrew asked her.

Ilena shook her head. "No. As a rule, I don't hold a glass of alcohol. If Ore holds it and doesn't let me have too much, it should be ok, I think." Ore looked like he planned on having fun.

As Rei, Andrew, and Mina, with occasional comments from Ore, regaled Mizi and Ilena with stories about their travels, most notably the final battle, Ore had an enjoyable time finally getting to drink, and at the same time watch Ilena enjoy each drink he gave her.

He got a bit carried away and gradually increased the strength of the type of drink as he went. He discovered he was doing it more to see if she liked what he liked. If he was right, their tastes in alcohols were about as similar as the food.

He rather suddenly discovered that Rei and Mizi had fallen asleep and Andrew and Mina were staring at them. He stopped and looked around in surprise. "Is it so late?"

"Yes, Ore, it is, actually," Andrew was sitting with Mina resting her head on his shoulder. They were holding hands and looked about ready to sleep as well. "We thought we'd let Mizi and Rei sleep it off a little before walking them to bed, but we have a bet going on. Please, don't let us interrupt you."

"A bet?" Ore furrowed his brow, then turned to look at Ilena, who looked back at him mildly. His eyes narrowed and he looked around to the desk that held the various bottles. They were, for the most part empty.

He counted. Mistress could take one glass before she was drunk. Rei could finally take just under one bottle, but he would hurt the next day. Andrew and Mina always restrained themselves to three glasses for Mina and four to five for Andrew. Between them, that accounted for just over two bottles, or at most two and a half.

Five bottles of wine were empty and the stronger liquors were all down three to four shots each, although there were only three of those. He held up his glass, then looked in Ilena's. Her's still held juice.

Ore sighed. "You aren't even drunk, are you?"

"No," Ilena admitted, "or at least not any more so than you."

"So you don't get drunk."

"I don't know. I've never drunk enough to know, but you've been careful to not let me drink as much as you. That's been helpful. I was already pretty full from dinner."

"So, why don't you hold a glass of alcohol, Ilena?" Andrew asked.

"Because, like Ore apparently, I don't know when to put it down or say no. In order to not out-drink my hosts, I learned to not allow myself to be served it to begin with. After all, it was bad enough when Pakyo was drinking their winter savings in one sitting."

"How do you know you don't get drunk, then?" Ore asked.

"Well, early on, before I was made steward and was still rather young, Pakyo enjoyed teasing his men. He would hold drinking competitions with them when they got bored, or needed setting straight. It didn't take them long before they wouldn't compete with him, so he would tell them that he would set someone else in his place.

"Then he would sit me down in front of them. Of course they agreed, thinking they had an easy win. Then he would laugh uproariously as the last one slid to the ground in disbelief." Ore shook his head at her answer.

"Did you ever have a direct competition with the Earl?" asked Mina.

Ilena shook her head. "It was often requested, but he always refused. It wouldn't have been so enjoyable for him, would it - to see all his alcohol drunk, but neither of us having failed? It was suggested once when the 'Earl' was my uncle.

"He looked about to try, so I whispered to him what the result would be, and what his reaction was supposed to be. He refused and said he wanted to see how they did against me again. He got just as much sport out of it that Pakyo usually did."

"Is that a Selician thing also? Being able to not be affected by alcohol?" Andrew asked.

Ilena shrugged. "I don't know for sure, but I do know I can hold more than Grail. He can drink more than any person from Ryokudo."

"You should drink with my brother, then," Rei said blearily from his position curled around Mizi in the second bed. "He can out-drink me, but probably not you two. So, who won the bet?"

"Mina did," Andrew said.

"What was the bet?" Ore wanted to know.

"That you wouldn't figure it out on your own that she couldn't get drunk any more than you." Mina said, rising to help Rei wake up Mizi. "We decided it about the sixth glass, and she wasn't showing any effects yet. That should have been about two glasses for her, and two of the six were already the heavy liquors. When did you give up trying to get her drunk?"

"Ah," Ore said, a bit nonplussed, "when I started wondering if she liked the same things I did?"

"Mmm...," Mizi was trying to wake up. "Is it time to go?"

"Yes, Mizi," Rei said as Mina helped her up. He was already sitting on the edge of the bed. "Though I wish it wasn't so." Mizi sat up next to him, then dropped her head back down on his shoulder. "...And it will be harder to go if you do that," he added.

"Hmm? Oh, sorry." Mizi stood up and Mina wrapped an arm under her.

"Did Mistress drink?" Ore asked, suddenly concerned.

"Only a couple of sips of Rei's drink," Ilena touched his arm to reassure him. "It was very cute to watch him blush."

"Oh? I'm sorry I missed that," Ore said, "but even a couple of sips has her this way, heh?" He shook his head.

"Let's go," Mina said to Mizi, and she led her out, while Andrew helped Rei up and walked close by him, ready to steady him when necessary.

"Thank you again for coming," Ilena said to them. "It was very enjoyable. And happy birthday again, Rei."

He raised an unsteady hand in farewell. "Thanks! It was good to be with all of you tonight."

After the good-night's were said and it was just the two of them in the room again, Ore looked around at the room, then at Ilena. "Let me clean this up just a bit, then the two of us." Ilena nodded and watched him silently as he walked around the room picking up stray bits and bottles and setting them all on the cart. He would have it sent back to the kitchen in the morning.

Then he prepared them both for the night's sleeping. He wasn't sure if it was the alcohol having a minor effect for once or not, but for some reason it was a bit more difficult to be nurse this night.

He was pleased to see the wound was healing very nicely. When he put his hand on the new tendon, it responded smoothly, and already seemed to have some tone. He was a little suspicious of that. "Have you been exercising the muscle and tendon already?"

"...Yes," Ilena said apologetically. "I'm sorry I'm impatient, and bored, but I'm being very careful to not strain the bone."

He had a sudden suspicion and he checked the muscle tone of her other leg, then her arms, which she normally didn't move much either. Compared to the end of the first six weeks after her initial injury, she had quite a bit of muscle tone all over. He stood up, folded his arms and looked at her. She looked very guilty, but not really very apologetic. He finally sighed. "Did you learn to do that during those seven months?"

It was her turn to look suspicious. "How did you find out?"

"Thayne said it to Master. He didn't know I didn't know yet."

"However, it's not his to tell. He will certainly need further education when he returns, if you'll still have him?" Ore nodded. "Then I hope you'll provide it to him," she said it with finality - an oblique order for Ore.

He tipped his head. It was obvious she'd had Thayne report to her after Ore had left him in the room to return to Rei, given his apology so quickly afterwards. They'd all appreciated she'd been quick to understand and pass her judgment, but Ore still had questions.

"What do you mean when you say that Marcus and Henry are competing to be your favorites? And, when I asked Thayne and Eldest Son if they were also competing to be your favorites, why did they look away from each other and me and not answer, but look guilty instead?"

Ilena sighed. "It's two different things, but similar. Marcus and Henry wish to be part of the Immediate Family. They're working hard to show me that they can be partners and provide that sort of support, and do the level of work required." Ore nodded. That made sense.

"For you to ask the others if they were competing for it, even though you didn't understand what you were asking, they still understood it to mean they were acting as if they were one level lower than they've already proven they can perform. ...However, there's a thing they didn't understand, that I've explained to Thayne today and he's already explained to First Son.

"In effect it was that they were, indeed, being tested for the same position again. In that, they've failed, for it's one of the requirements that you be able to work with your partner. The failure was because Thayne misunderstood. If he can't repair the damage he's done, then I won't accept him, and you'll have someone else by your side."

Ore was quiet for a moment. Carefully he said, "I understand why you wish to have Eldest by your side, but I still wish for Thayne. Will my desire have no effect?"

Ilena considered and answered just as carefully. "If you can win First Son, and can help them repair their breach, I won't reject Thayne. It's as important that they be able to be partners as it is that you and I are. Your life will hang in the balance on more than one occasion on their capability to work together, and likely so will mine."

"I understand," Ore said quietly, then asked, "Were they not already partners?"

Ilena shook her head. "Thayne is Fourth Son."

"May I ask who Second and Third Sons are, then? Was Eldest partnered with Second and Thayne with Third?"

"Yes, that was the partnerships." Ilena's eyes filled with pain. "Both Second and Third died during difficult operations. First and Fourth Sons still blame themselves for being the weak member of the partnership, when it was only a matter of the difficulty of the work.

"In this they also struggle together. Neither trusts themselves to become a partner of any other person, and perhaps they do not trust the other to be able to be a partner to them, because they can't trust themselves."

"That sounds like a rather difficult pairing, then." Ore said. "Why have you chosen it?" He remembered Thayne's pained look when he'd asked who his partner would be. Now he understood it.

"I haven't," Ilena said, looking him in the eyes. "You did."

"Ah," Ore said almost as a sigh. He'd chosen Thayne, so he'd chosen the responsibility to see that he and Eldest could work together. That was going to be a rather large responsibility, but he really did want to keep Thayne by his side. "I understand," Ore bowed to her slightly. "I'll do my part."

Ilena nodded. "If there's a thing I may do to help, I'll do it."

Ore was mildly surprised, then nodded gratefully, "Thank you." He paused. There was another niggling question in his mind, but it wouldn't come to light. He gave up and went to the candles and blew them out one by one. He walked back to Ilena's bed and climbed up next to her, as he'd promised he would. "May I tell them both that they're demoted a level until they've learned to work together?" he asked her.

"If you wish," she answered, "but First Son must still perform his duties. There's none that can replace him at this time."

Ore considered. "Is there a time where he could be excused from those duties, even if only briefly enough?"

"...You must ask Grandfather."

"Will he be my ally in this?"

"Yes. He also wishes to see them both healed," she answered.

Ore put his arm over her to hold her and touched her head with his. "I'm home."

"Welcome home, Ore." Ilena put her hand on his cheek. "I've missed you. Thank you for coming back safely."

"Thank you for being here to come back to, and for being my strength to overcome my past and face forward again," he replied, his gratitude filling him with greater peace than he'd known for a very long time.

STRENGTH RETURNED

ORE'S NAME POEM

O, the ore oré
Olo oloré
This dolore –
Missing you
My dolore oloré
For olo oré.
-Ore

Translation: "O, the hours I prayed/Feeling frozen/This pain –/Missing you/My ache frozen/For feeling I prayed/-Ore (naming himself, the poet).
It's said he could be heard chanting it under his breath as he walked the roof peaks of the cities of Northern Suiran in the nightwalker era (533-539). – B.-R.T.

Strength Returned

Ore worked his way south. It was a slow, painful process. He'd only waited in Nijoushi long enough for the deep wound over his heart to not bleed every time he rose to walk to the privy. He was fortunate that he was liked in the underworld. He had a healer who wouldn't sell him out when he was easily killable and would wait to get paid.

The pain of the wound made him start his journey in the bottom of a farmer's wagon and not wake up until said farmer was home, rudely waking Ore up with loud cursing. A few coins had purchased the ride without a beating at the end, but he'd had to go two farms more to find a country daughter who was willing to be charmed out of a brief meal, and another three to escape the father and steal a night in a haystack.

He picked a haystack still standing in the field. He didn't want to be chased out before he was ready to move. Waking meant having to move healing flesh and muscles that didn't want to stretch. That was slow and painful work.

Hunger wasn't new, but a healing body needed food. He took the time most of the journey from then on to be nice to farmers for rides, not surprising them at the end of the ride. If he charmed them enough, he often could convince them to part with a good warm meal and bed in the hayloft. Sticking to the story he was traveling to the south to make his fortune in the capital city worked best.

Some of the farmers wanted work as pay for their hospitality. Then he showed his city bumbling and was released fairly quickly. That was the lie. He was protecting his wound. If they knew he was that injured, his cover story (which wasn't really a lie) would be uncovered. Respectable young lads making their way in the world didn't have wounds like his.

He paid in entertaining stories around the fire after the meal instead. He'd always enjoyed telling imaginary tales and stories to children. Adults liked them just as much, although they didn't often admit it.

The warm moist air of the south was difficult to breathe in, particularly with his healing wound stretching against his gasping breathing. His lungs were used to thin, cold, dry mountainous air, not the heavy wet blanket he was coming under the farther he went towards his destination.

He spent three days at one particular sheep ranch doing worse than that as he fought a fever, the moisture in the air making him ill in a way he'd never been before. He was openly and honestly grateful for the kindness of that farm wife. He promised himself he'd send her something from the city when he'd earned enough to properly buy and ship it to her. Such kindness shouldn't be repaid with stolen goods.

When Ore reached Ichijoutsu, he was relieved to be able to hide himself in a big city again, becoming "just one of the folks". It was tiring to have to put on a face in front of people for that long when injured. In the city he could sleep as long as he wanted in his chosen hiding place and be grumpy if he needed to be.

When Ore was awake, he sat casually on the steps of a not-very-busy warehouse that let him have a fabulous view of the bay and sea. The ships with their tall masts were as large as the warehouses or larger, a hard thing for a northern mind to comprehend. The largest moving thing northern eyes saw were the larger merchant wagons, and they were only twice the size of passenger wagons since the teams of four horses had to be able to pull them all day.

"Hey, Boy," a weathered voice growled at him, "you just goin' to sit and stare at them until yer grey? Or are you goin' to get proper work?"

Normally Ore would have lept four feet away, but this time he carefully stood and turned around, his heart racing nonetheless. The man looking at him was as weathered as his voice. His burly arms were folded, but his face was lit with his tease. He was too old to sail the ships and pull the ropes any more, but he didn't look weakened by age at all.

"I can't yet," Ore answered back. He got a raised eyebrow. "Doctor's orders. Have to finish healing up first."

The man looked at him for a bit, sizing him up. "Can you run figures? Count, write 'em down, check it against the manifest?"

"Yessir." Having come from a high House had its perks. An education in letters and numbers got him into places a lot of nightwalkers couldn't and being able to naturally be a noble got him even further.

"Name's Brok. A shipment's comin' in with the tide. Stay on the step and they'll think yer the person to talk to. See you talk to them, and bring them in. I'll give you the paper, ink, and counting to do. Keep up best you can."

Ore's slow signature smile came on his face. "You got it. Ore," he stuck out his hand. Brok took it, proceeded to squash it in his big one, then laugh at him for his weakness. Ore could tell he didn't mean anything by it.

Likely it was to prove just how much strength he would need to work the ropes and cargo of the ships and a warning if he tried anything shady. He was left alone on the steps again to sit and watch the ships, wondering which one coming in was going to be theirs.

-o-o-o-

"So...why aren't there any abandoned warehouses?" Ore bit into his third fish as Brok leaned back on the back legs of his chair and drank from his stein. The question had been bugging him. Now that the ship's cargo had been unloaded from the ship and counted and stored in the warehouse, they had time for him to ask.

"King's rule," Brok answered. When Ore looked confused, he went on. "Queen's father didn't want waste, nor a place for crime to sit 'n fester. Said both were signs the country wasn't healthy or prosperous. Did everything he could to make sure there was proper business to warehouse ratio, even going

326

so far as to tear down a few when he couldn't find proper shipping companies to fill them all.

"You seen the market and food district?" Ore nodded. "That used to be warehouse space as well. He turned it into indoor in-city profit building, and added inn space above the food district to draw in the ship's passengers as well. Been right prosperous a place as he could'a wished for."

Brok shrugged. "Course, he did his job proper, too, and made proper international connections and trade treaties, then made it so we businesses would want to come do business with Ryokudo. We aren't hit with high tariffs, so we can keep our costs low enough to sell but still have a profit. More business into the city means more prosperity. Royals keep the peace, too. International and in-city, if you get my meaning." He glared at Ore, a meaningful look.

Ore raised his hands in self-defense. "Sounds like a wise King. I know I enjoy the peace, and if your prosperity means I get paid, I'm good."

"Paid by whom?" It rumbled dangerously.

"You, of course," Obi answered innocently confused. Brok harrumphed, still suspicious, but Ore held the innocent face and Brok eventually gave in, figuring he'd got the message if he wasn't as innocent as he played at...and Ore had.

Three days later Brok appeared again. "Everythin' still as it's supposed to be? Or have you let the nightwalkers take it?"

"It's all still here," Ore answered honestly. It never paid to turn away honest work first when getting into a new town. He didn't have a reputation here like he did in the north. He'd have to build it up from the beginning, although he did have references when he was ready to get back into that work again. He'd not been troubled, though, as he'd slept in the warehouse and kept an eye on things.

"I've got a client coming. Let's see what yer best behavior looks like, eh?"

Somehow, Ore found himself after that three-quarters time working at the warehouse as guard and assistant, and quarter time being hired out for the strangest work he'd ever done as a nightwalker. He'd worked for nobles of Nijoushi, and across northern Suiran, but this was different. This was the information gathering side.

Somehow, he'd managed to get himself picked up by an information boss that used the warehouse as a minor business on the side. For the first several months his acting skills were always tested first at the warehouse as some client or other came along to inspect the wares at the building. If they liked what they saw, they bought something from Brok. It only took him thinking back on the first client once he got back from the job to understand that he himself had been purchased.

Once he understood the business Brok was in, Ore had fun playing the parts he was told to play. It was a help to his skills in that area, and was fun in the bargain. Most of the time it meant he didn't have to use his killing and thieving skills and that was just as good.

There came a day Brok surprised him, though. Ore had been slowly working his strength and speed back up, getting the protesting muscles to get used to movement again. Brok could move soundlessly, like he had that first day, a thing no one would suspect of an old seaman. He said it was a test, but Ore had injured him all the same.

Brok laughed a short dry bark as Ore wrapped bandaging on him, apologizing. "I figured you'd be good to set over the goods, but that's a hell of a lot better then I expected."

"Not really," Ore deprecated. "I'm sure I'd do my best, but I've a ways to go."

"Well, I can see that," Brok looked pointedly at his injury, "and you might knife someone I'd legitimately sent, if you'd knife me, but you'd still do it...protect the goods."

"I'm sure I can't be kept now," Ore said. "I'm sorry I didn't warn you before."

Brok looked away as Ore finished tying the bandage off. "Well, you probably should have. You didn't jump at my first approach, though, so I didn't know you had it in you."

Ore paused, then put the bandaging materials away, talking as he worked. "I wasn't lying. I couldn't then. I'd have torn it open again. ...But you did give me a fright. I'm sorry, I should have warned you then." He finished his cleaning up and looked Brok in the eye. "I've enjoyed working for you. Probably my most fun work to date, really."

Brok looked at him soberly and nodded. "You've got a good knack for it. I've not had complaints back." He rubbed his chin. "Is it just being surprised?"

Ore hesitated then nodded. "It's a survival thing. I'm not sure how to get it under control."

"You didn't kill me." Brok raised an eyebrow and gave Ore an appraising look. "You've been working on it?"

Ore gave him a look. "A long time and it's a lot better than it used to be."

Putting his chin in his hand, Brok said, "I've got a special job I want you on, but in that place you can't just up and pull a knife, no matter how surprised you are. How long would it take you to learn to not pull the blade? And to just threaten, not harm?"

Ore sat back and looked at Brok, puzzled. "You'd keep me?"

"Every nightwalker has a right to keep himself alive the best he can. Lives are short in the business." That was true, Ore well knew. The inability to control his instinct to protect himself before his mind knew what was going on had kept him alive this long on most of his risky jobs.

"It would take practice. And effort. I don't know how long. I don't get jumped by anyone but you in here, and I'd rather not do this again." Ore waved at the bound injury.

"Right, then. Off you go. When you've learned it proper, come back. The sooner the better. My opening won't last forever you know."

Ore paused just a little longer. "*Is* there an underworld in Ichijoutsu really?"

Brok laughed at him and made to kick him out. Ore got. He was mostly ready for the street again, anyway.

-o-o-o-

A fresh face on the streets and in the back alleys - again there weren't many of those in this squeaky-clean city at the feet of the main castle of the royals - was always call for sport. Ore knew it and wasn't starting green. It was still different than running in the north.

He got plenty of practice being jumped, and in places he would have never expected. Broad daylight, market zones, shops. It took him a while to understand that it was because the nightwalkers didn't have much other choice.

He learned quickly to not have a knife come out. The flash of steel, even if small like his hand knives that never left his palm hardly, drew cries from bystanders and guards from down the streets. Since he didn't want his face to become familiar to that crowd, he'd melt away as if one of those bystanders rather easily. That he'd learned before, and had only had more practice already here in this crazy town.

If he just went for the throat with his hands, he could quickly come back to himself and claim he'd been pick-pocketed and this scoundrel was going to pay up. Fisticuffs were, it seemed, expected - at least near the docks with the sailors who came off the ships to get drunk. The farther he got from the docks, the more he had to pretend to be an honest citizen protecting himself.

He was making his way back towards the warehouse when he finally got cornered on a rainy evening. That night he drew blood, but no one cried out, and no one but he walked away knowing what happened. He did get surprised looks the next day from eyes in faces he was starting to recognize. He sighed as he slipped into one of the establishments that catered to his kind. He didn't have the funds for anything better.

As he glumly looked at the plate of unidentifiable food, his elbow on the table, he suddenly felt the atmosphere change and the warning prickle between his shoulder blades. The man behind him was on his knees, his wrist near to breaking, before Ore looked into his eyes and actually saw him. The clatter of steel on the floor was loud in the stillness of the room.

"Who are you?" the man on the floor asked through gritted teeth. "And why haven't you declared yourself?"

"Name's not important, and Brok claimed me first. Hasn't been a need to declare yet." Ore answered.

"But he kicked you out?" The man seemed interested in talking.

Ore stepped on the blade and slid it away from the reach of the man, leaving his foot on it, and most of his weight. Only then was he willing to let the man go a bit, just lightly releasing his wrist. "No. You heard wrong. He told me to get training and come back. I'd declare but I'm about to go see what he had in mind. He's been giving me the first bit of fun I've had in a long while."

The man narrowed his eyes. "You'd have to declare to me."

Ore raised an eyebrow of disbelief. "Heads don't come test talent themselves. You lost. That means I'm the Head now?"

After a bit of hesitation, during which Ore was given enough clues to find the general area of the Head, who had properly come to watch the testing, the man shook his head. "You're not."

"Thought not." Ore was instantly on the floor, on his tip toes and fingertips, scuttling for the area of the Head, slipping from table to table as small pieces of very sharp steel rained down where he'd been.

The most protected person was the one he showed up suddenly behind, a knife at that one's throat. He looked at the man across the table from his hostage. "You know it's stupid to bring your precious treasures out with you to a testing when you don't know the skill level of your quarry? Perhaps I should be the Head after all?"

The man looked at him with wide eyes momentarily, then put his chin in his hand, elbow on the table, and smiled slightly. "Wouldn't have to test you if you'd just declare, would I? Let her go."

"Only if you grant me freedom of movement in the city and surroundings," Ore demanded.

"My territory."

Ore shook his head. "I don't have time to go declare to everyone. Not until I decide to freelance again."

"Can't very well pass the word if I don't have a name, can I?"

Ore considered it. He didn't want his brother to get wind of him down here. "Tei."

"You'll take a royal name?" Everyone was aliased in the underground. It was his audaciousness at taking a name from the royal line that was unusual. Ore didn't flinch, just stared at the man in front of him. Finally that one shrugged. "Fine. Your life on the line. You've been here long enough to have learned how strict the royals are on such as us."

Ore let the woman go, not letting down his guard at all. She'd stayed still, but not from fear. She'd known she was part of the test, and hadn't killed him. That didn't mean she wouldn't still get in a mark for touching her, if she'd been displeased.

He had to leave his dinner behind, sadly. One didn't stay in unwelcome environments, even if they had just promised truce. He headed to the warehouse, staking it out from a distance. He followed Brok home that night and surprised him, just to see what happened. He won, but then Brok got a hand on him and he was pinned to the floor, unable to move. He still wasn't able to overcome the seaman's natural strength.

"Yer still alive, at any rate. But why here?" Brok asked him, still holding him down.

"Wondering why you had your House test me that far." Ore didn't blink, his eyes fixed on the eyes of the man above him.

Brok went a little still. "Why d'you think I have a House?"

"Because your warehouse is a safe house. The nightwalkers don't touch it."

Brok smiled a little and stood up, letting him go. "Naw, that's a different thing. We've a truce, and sometimes we work together on the odd job."

Ore sat up, leaning back on his hands. "So why'd you ask them to test me? Just because of that?"

Brok turned away to pull out a crock of food from the cooling pantry. "They did that on their own." Before Ore could be on his feet to put the knife to the lie, Brok turned back slightly. "And they're goin' to be in trouble for it. The nightwalkers aren't supposed to touch things I protect."

"Even though you told them to make sure I learned my lessons well? You think they wouldn't have tried to go that far? Are you really so naive?" Ore was slightly irritated.

"No. Apparently they haven't learned their own lessons well enough yet." It was said so coldly Ore's spine shivered slightly.

"What House has claimed me?" Ore asked. There was silence. "You should at least give me that much, even if I don't stay."

"You foolishly gave me yer proper street name, Ore." Brok said quietly. "I hope you didn't make that mistake this time."

"I didn't," Ore answered back quietly. It was true that his surprise had made him not think things through that time. Brok being an information vendor might have found it out eventually, but he'd certainly done research since then, learning who his assistant was.

Brok was quiet until the food was on the table. He gestured at the plate across from him. Ore sat and they ate. When their bellies were full, Brok gestured again and Ore washed up their dishes. This meal the alcohol didn't come out. "Stay in the house tonight," he said soberly to Ore, pointing to a room.

"What House?" Ore pressed him quietly.

Brok stared at him for a while, then finally gave a slight nod to himself. "I'd have sold you to the highest bidder, but word came back from the north before I'd made up my mind." He looked at Ore, and without blinking said, "The Queen herself will come in a killing fit if yer touched by any hand but hers."

Ore's mouth dropped open. "...W-well, it's a respectable House, as far as they go, but I've never –!"

Brok shook his head. "They paid me to see you survive. They bought you. And now I have to go out there and make sure my claim's secure or I'll pay the price."

Ore put his hand on Brok's arm. "Let me come with you. I passed their tests, and won my freedom citywide. I'm a freelancer until I join with the House I choose to join with, regardless of what anyone says." He paused a second, puzzled. "Does the Queen have a House here, too? I know they're all over in the north, but this seems a bit far?"

Brok didn't answer, just turned away. "Come along then, if yer set on defendin' yer freedom from all Houses. If you survive, and I survive, I'll tell you what that next job is." His hand was on the knob when he stopped and asked, "What name did you give them?"

"Tei." Ore hadn't moved. At Brok's wide-eyed look over his shoulder Ore crossed his arms.

"And yet, you'll deny a relationship with the Queen?"

"I believe I said hadn't joined myself to the House, and you still haven't told me the name of your House."

"Why do you think I have one?" Brok countered. "I did just say I'd personally have to see you'd stay alive, didn't I?"

Ore considered that. "Well, true. I think it would be easier for the both of us to stay here, then?"

"Nope," Brok opened the door and Ore could feel it: the night's expectation and the crowd that awaited them. He sighed then nodded and followed Brok out the door and up to the rooftop.

-o-o-o-

"I said it, didn't I?" Ore said to the gathered nightwalkers. They were on every rooftop, crammed into every alley and what little dark corners of the street could be found. "I've also already proved myself. I'm a freelancer who's been taken in by Brok, until I'm ready to move on."

"Yet you'll go so far as to irritate the crown." It was hissed at him. They weren't happy with the name he'd taken, although he didn't care.

"Why do you think that will bring reprisal on you?" Silence met him.

Brok sighed. "Prince Sasou is following in his grandfather and father's footsteps already. He also keeps a tight fist on the underworld here. They say it's in the name of prosperity and peace. It makes life difficult. To take the name of royalty is to spit in their face."

"While I don't fear the Prince, that's not why I'm called that." The listeners shifted. Ore sighed. "Has only Brok heard of the House of the Queen of Night?"

That got a few hisses. "What has a northern House to do with the south? That reach is too far."

332

Ore shrugged. "True enough. But if you've heard of it, that's why that's my name. The Queen herself has kept me alive for her own purposes, although I've never asked for it. Because I owe her my life, I'll bear her mark."

"She isn't here, is she?" was whispered out into the night. A whisper that carried.

Brok shook his head. "Just because she doesn't claim territory doesn't mean her presence isn't felt."

"You have witness?"

"I am a witness," Brok agreed. "Since when have I held onto a treasure this long?"

"Bought or threatened?"

Brok laughed. "You need to ask me that question?"

"The Queen doesn't threaten," Ore scolded calmly. "The dragon and viper have no need to prove strength with posturing words. He's only just told me this night, although I didn't demand to know until now."

He was getting tired of this. "I've proven myself already. Go home and hold to the truce. I am just one. It isn't worth your effort. If the Prince has issue with it, I'll explain it to him myself. It's such a small thing."

The air was still, then Ore was ducking and turning to slice at the air behind him. He made light contact and his back was warm, Brok's back pressed lightly against it. Over and over they danced back to back with separate partners, but always the opponent moved away after a single mark, until one didn't.

That one was suddenly gone, however, after the third blow, sliding down the roof - unconscious or dead, Ore couldn't tell. Then there was no one facing him, but a ring around him and Brok, knives pointing outward. "It is sufficient."

The shadows paused then fought ferociously for five minutes and the circle never broke to let anyone through to Ore and Brok. At the end of the five minutes, the nightwalkers surrounding the group faded into the night.

"Idiots," growled Brok at the backs of the encircling men.

One looked over his shoulder with a wild grin. "Sometimes it's good to let the Queen's influence be felt a little more realistically."

"That's not it," Brok shook his head in frustration. "You didn't have to get marked before that, idiots."

The grin was gone in an instant. "We'd rather prove him for ourselves and see he's kept safe at the same time by the witness than let them have their way." Ore suddenly understood why his opponents had relented at first marking. It had been these - the few of the House of the Queen of Night who did reside as her men and spies in Ichijoutsu.

"Thank you," he said, "but really –"

"You don't get a say, Freelancer." The voice cut him coldly off. "You're required to stay alive. That's all that matters to us." They were suddenly gone.

Brok sighed. "Like I said.... Well, I think we can go to bed now."

They slipped down to the ground and carefully entered the house, searching it from top to bottom for assassins. When it was proven empty, they secured themselves in a room and slept until morning.

-o-o-o-

"Sorry to make you have to move," Ore said to Brok, as they shook parting hands.

"No. It's part of the business, too." Brok shook his head. "Good luck with the new job."

"Thanks for helping me get it," Ore said. Brok nodded and turned away, headed for business elsewhere.

Ore turned to face his next place Brok had assigned him to. He whistled softly in amazement, now that he could let himself do it in private.

He'd never in a hundred years have imagined he was going to ever end up in Ichijou, the main castle of Ryokudo. If he ever had to make good on his promise to protect the rest of the nightwalkers from his chosen alias, he'd certainly be in the right place to do it.

Then he wondered just how much harder it would be to not be caught by the Prince who would keep his country "pest" free so that it could be prosperous and peaceful. He sighed. He had his work cut out for him surely. And surely there would be little rest here. Already his vacation working at the warehouse was beginning to grow distant and dim, replaced by that awful thought.

Ore looked up at the high walls and the guards standing on them at regular intervals. He took a deep breath. It might feel like walking into a cage, one with lions in it, but at the same time he felt excitement. This was going to be his best performance yet. To hide in front of the very eyes of the royals.

His jaunty smile came on his face and his feet got him started for the lesser gate. The next few months, or perhaps year or so, were going to be very interesting.

-o-o-o-

"Dorian, come here."

"Yes, ma'am." As a very minor official, Ore was orderable by any noble in the castle. That meant if there was a lady he needed to charm to get information from, he could allow her that excuse to drag him off. Not that he let any of them take it past flirtatiousness. That would quickly cost him his job (he explained), a thing he couldn't afford.

That actually had made them flock to him in their turns. When he received a new order over the wall, he would change his affections until he could win a lady with sufficient closeness to what he needed to know.

He'd stayed as far from the eyes of the royals as possible, and so far had been ignored by them. There were others who had watched him early on, but he'd charmed the guards and soldiers the same as he charmed the farmers to get to Ichijoutsu. His face was as welcome in the barracks as in the gardens.

All was going well, until he was given the name of a lady he'd never heard of before. He was glad they'd also sent that she could be found in the medical wing, if she wasn't at the Second Prince's quarters. That last made his eyes bug out. No way did he want to be going anywhere near those apartments. Not only would that put him too close to royalty, but he didn't want to get the attention of a jealous prince.

He worked his way through his ladies until he finally heard enough gossip. The fiery red hair with golden gleams through it, the green eyes like the late summer leaves, the petite form carried calmly yet with self assurance (or thoughtless pride if the speaker was jealous), commoner from Yamanzar, and young. Younger than the Second Prince even.

That age gap made it all the more difficult. Ore couldn't woo a child. Still, he found excuse to visit the medical wing. Faking a simple illness wasn't that hard to do. Mizi was a recent apprentice, having just passed her testing.

She seemed young for it, but his surprise at the senior was greater. Ryan was still yet three or more years her junior. Shy, hard to get to open up, although certainly competent. Ore decided Ryan would be the one Ore would crack open for entertainment's sake.

Head Healer Parmenia wasn't too hard to charm. Intelligent - so flirtations were laughed at - but having a drinking buddy, that was acceptable - to both of them. She guarded her tongue, until she'd had too much to drink.

Ore kept the questions to one suspicious one per drinking night, surrounded by many others (casual) and only as a tease. Then she would answer it, playing along with the tease. Ore learned a lot of things from her - about the castle, both Princes, the Queen (a little), and of course, Mizi.

Then came the day his information brought a new order. *Discourage the flame. Put it out of the castle.* As much as he would rather not (she brought joy to those who worked with her and was a harder worker than most in the castle) a job was a job.

He started with simple anonymous threats, left where she would find them near her workplaces. He was surprised when not only did they seem ineffective, she didn't complain to the others about them. He moved up to more direct threats, but that was met with the same determination.

Finally Ore turned to forgery and lie. He sent it out that she was being punished and should have her movements restricted to only the medical wing and her castle servants quarters.

That did finally get someone's attention. However, it was not the attention Ore wanted. He suddenly began to find it difficult to be the one randomly in the medical wing on more business than was necessary. Nearly every time he did arrive, one or the other of the Second Prince's personal knights was already there. Often the Second Prince was there as well.

Rei, pale golden hair and eyes of startling blue the color of the high deep summer sky, was nearly as captivating to observe as Mizi. Their brilliant hair even more striking when side by side, Ore often had to tear his eyes away when he felt the eyes of the knights turning his way. He was discouraged. He was likely to be found out before he fulfilled his requirement.

In desperation, he finally went to back street methods. A threatening note attached to a weapon thrown to just miss the healer. "Leave the castle or your life is forfeit. Commoners aren't fit to stand at the side of Princes." Ore had to get rid of it nearly as soon as he wrote it. For the first time in a long time a lie ate at him, and he couldn't bear the guilt or he wouldn't get his job done.

But Mizi foiled him yet again. Her determination won out, and worst of all, Prince Rei found out about it. He was spending more time with her in her own places, so she couldn't hide it from him either.

Ore was completely at a loss, and perhaps he was lost anyway, his own heart betraying him when his head didn't understand it yet. The next time he checked in at the medical wing with Parmenia, the female knight, Mina, was there to drink with her also. Parmenia had been only too happy to introduce the two of them, particularly over whiskey and gin.

Ore finally was allowed to slap his hand over his face at the fifth drink of the healer, but it was at himself not her, not really. He'd been verbally dodging Mina's insightful barbs all evening and playing damage control with Parmenia, and was getting very worn out. The comment had been gaudy and terrible.

He took the glass from Parmenia's hand. "You've had too much, I think," he said firmly. "Time for you to sleep it off." He stood the healer up and escorted her to her sleeping alcove (she never left the medical wing). When she was tucked in, Ore sighed, then turned back to the work table to clean up.

"Do you have to do that often when you drink with her?" Ore froze, then cautiously continued on into the room where Mina was already cleaning up.

Just as cautiously he answered, "Yes, Miss Mina. I won't have to do the same for you, I trust?"

"If you touch me I'll cut your hands off."

Ore held up both hands in self defense. "Of course. I wouldn't dream of it. I just meant cut you off from over-drinking. The Head Healer is fun to drink with, but she never understands her limit, for some reason."

"You can match her well." Another insightful comment to dodge.

"I've a higher tolerance. It's one of the things that makes her fun to drink with. Not many can, you know." He very carefully steered away from the first thought that came to mind. Everyone knew men could hold more than women, but this was not the person to remind of that fact. "You looked like you were enjoying yourself, but also like you understand your limits."

"Indeed." The answer was short and dry, like many of her comments had been that night. She'd be nearly as fun to pry open as Ryan, the youthful genius of healing...except Ore didn't want to be that close to Prince Rei. They finished washing (him) and drying (her) the glasses and Ore took them to put them away.

When he turned around, his hands were moving on their own before he caught them, moving them palm up in front of him instead of for Mina's throat. She'd moved to stand right behind him. "Wha - what?" he asked, very flustered, and worried. If his eyes had given him away....

Her face had hardened, but when he continued to look at her innocently, afraid to say more, she relaxed slightly, looking away. "You're a strange one," she said.

"Ah, I think that would be you, coming up behind someone suddenly, boxing them in on only the first evening of meeting. Surely you didn't think I'd kiss you the first time I'd met you?" His habit of flirting was going to get him killed this night, he just knew it.

Blandly Mina stated, "You've never kissed a woman in this castle."

Ore blinked. "Would you know such a thing?"

"You have a high popularity among the lesser ladies, enough to make them swoon," her eyes went dully disinterested and it cut him, "though why I have no idea." She stared at him, then added, "Why you've left them for someone who isn't even interested in you...."

"If I've left ladies behind at all, perhaps I'm waiting for the right woman to come along? Are you come to tell me it should be you?" Her scathing look denied it strenuously and Ore slid his way sideways out from her cornering of him. "Well, if not, then I suppose you'd rather see yourself back to your rooms."

He raised a hand in farewell and headed for the door. "It was a pleasure to meet you," he said. "I'm sure I won't try to interfere with a ladies night of drink next time. Sorry to disturb you. I'm sure if the two of you...." He bit his tongue. What was next would have a knife between his ribs, he was sure of it.

He was surprised to get out the door, let alone to his room without being accosted. But he wasn't left alone. Not by the Prince's knights, and sadly, not by his employer. He received an impatient letter from the latter and wrote a frustrated response. He didn't send it, though. That would get someone else sent in to do the job. He burned that letter, and got down to some heavy thinking.

He was in the middle of such thinking a couple of days later when a shadow fell across him. "Just what department do you work for, Mister Dorian?"

"Interior Affairs, northern principality of Kochi." He answered it immediately and properly. The man staring at him would know. The First Knight and Head Aide of Prince Rei knew everything, nearly, about the workings of the castle. But this was a more dangerous situation than he'd been in with Miss Mina. "I'm sorry, Sir Andrew. Is there something I can do for you?"

"You can tell me why the Department of Interior Affairs forgot you exist."

Ore swallowed. "I'm sure they have many minor administrators, but surely they wouldn't forget one?" he pleaded, as if cut to the core by such a statement.

"You are better known by ladies and gardeners alike than by your own boss. He even questioned my sanity that you existed in his department at all."

Ore pulled out his identification tag and looked at it carefully. "I'm sure he gave it to me...," he muttered as if to himself, then pulled it off and handed it over. "It does say he did, right?" he stayed worried innocent.

Andrew looked at Ore piercingly, then inspected the identification closely. "It does appear in order," he finally said and handed it back.

Ore took it. He didn't have to feign relief much. He'd been afraid it was going to be kept on suspicion only. "Is there a reason?" he asked.

Andrew didn't answer, instead he asked back, "What have you to do with Miss Mizi?"

"Miss Mizi?," Ore furrowed his brow. "The red-haired Healer?" At Andrew's curt nod, Ore continued, "I've been treated by her once or twice in the medical wing when I've needed something, and I've seen her there when I visit with the Head Healer. She's pleasant enough if I greet her, but I've nothing to do with her outside of the odd professional moment. She's quite young you know."

"You're not that old yourself," Andrew rejoined.

Ore allowed a slow smile to come on his face. "I'm sure it's kind of you to say so. I'll likely still look youthful for many years to come, but I'm your age, most likely. Someone of her tender years is of no interest to anyone save her own peers." He let a knowing look out. The Prince was only a year or so older than her. "Though why he should be interested in a flower he'll be made to leave behind, I have no idea."

Suddenly that had been the wrong thing to say. The wave of cold anger Andrew gave off made Ore step back a half step. "Haven't I only said truth for a Prince?" he asked, desperate to get the man turned away from his anger, although perhaps it had been a sufficient distraction from his own person.

"Haven't you seen enough, just being there?" Andrew asked angrily.

Ore paused, then sobered. "I have." That gave Andrew pause and he looked at Ore closely. "I've seen they make a stunning pair. Those who see only with eyes of greed will either tear her from that place until she lies bleeding, or they will raise her up, determined to see them set together. Only those who see with eyes unclouded know why that should be so."

He turned away, unable to hold in himself his two opposing minds. "If you're done with me? I should go and remind the Head he really has hired me." Andrew allowed him to go. Ore almost wanted to yell at him to get him to do otherwise instead. It would be so much better to have the truth forced out of him, for his own sake.

Perhaps that's why he was less vigilant the next time he went to send his report. Perhaps that's what made him spend even more time near Mizi afterwards, worried for her safety. It was surely why he allowed himself to be surrounded by the two knights and listen in wonder as Mizi stood up to the Interior Minister herself, refusing to leave the castle just because she was common born and his eyes couldn't see any other trait that was good - although Ore knew she possessed many.

-o-o-o-

"Who are you really?"

"Dorian."

"Where did you learn to read and figure?"

"The house of my father."

"Why?"

"It was needful for running the business."

The questions were being asked for the fifth time, if Ore remembered that correctly. He finally did just what he wanted and put his head down on the table.

They'd still put him in prison, for threatening the Healer with a blade. He didn't complain. He understood he would have to pay the consequence of that. But he wasn't going to vary from his story to the guards. They didn't need to know more than they already did.

It was another two days before the door to his cell opened again, other than for food or guards asking questions, and three people entered. "Forgive me for not rising to bow," he said tiredly to the Prince.

Prince Rei frowned. "Why have they beat you?"

"Why indeed?" Ore answered, his swollen lip making it hard to say the words. But it had been because they'd discovered the scar and nothing would convince the guards his story was true after that, although he'd still never strayed from it.

The Prince let it pass. He could scold the guards if he wanted, but he couldn't change the past. "There is no Dorian. Why won't you tell the guards the truth?"

"Because that is the only truth that matters in this place."

"What name should you be called by?" Prince Rei insisted.

Ore toyed with giving him the newer name, but he wasn't the Prince to give that one to. He looked Prince Rei in the eye. "You aren't the only one protecting something important."

That brought the Prince up sharply. Ore thought he'd scold further, but instead he said, "Let me help you protect it."

Ore raised an eyebrow. "You'd protect a thing of a prisoner? Without understanding it?"

The Prince hesitated - a good sign he didn't rush into things unnecessarily. "I want you. I want you to help me protect what I'm trying to protect. Do that for me and I'll help you protect what you're trying to protect."

"Can we even trust each other?" Ore couldn't see it, the Prince trusting him.

A hand held out a tube. "'The flame cannot be extinguished. It is jealously guarded, and strong of itself. I respectfully decline and free myself of any further obligations.' Even if your orders were to make Mizi leave the castle, you've decided for yourself you won't.

"Mina and Andrew have both tested you as well. I can trust you. I want you to protect Mizi, to walk at her back, to help see she arrives at my side at the right and proper time." The face of the Prince was earnest and his words sincere.

Ore sighed a little. "And if you let me out of here, you wouldn't stop me from doing that very thing." Eyebrows went up on the two knights. "However, it isn't possible for you to help me protect what I protect. You do not need to know more than you know."

Prince Rei left that day unsatisfied. He came the same the next day and received the same answers. It was night when he came the following day, long after dinner, and he entered alone. He sat as close to Ore as he could get on his side of the bars.

"Tell just me, then," Prince Rei said. "You understand the importance of protecting one who is worthy of love and consideration. It can only be such a thing for you as well."

Ore closed his eyes, then finally sighed. "I'll tell you, but only because you've kept me in here too long already for wanting to know such a small thing." His look scolded Prince Rei when he opened his eyes again. His beloved was already the target of who knew how many assassins or worse, because Ore's message hadn't been delivered, and he'd not reported in time.

"In the north, I'm called Ore. There is one in the north who will kill me if he knows where I am and has stopped at nothing to do so for many years. I've come south because I was discovered finally. My death will bring about the death of the one I protect. I have promised to live."

"Then I shall see to it you live. Stay by me so I can protect you with my position."

"What can a Prince do? It is my own strength that will keep me alive." Ore stood and walked to the side of the cell Rei was sitting at. The prince rose to face him. "But if you will promise to protect that one with me, and for me if I should fall, then it will be enough."

"Who is it?" Rei asked.

"Will you promise it? Or will you turn that one into a hostage to be used against me?"

Rei considered Ore for a long moment. "As long as protecting that one doesn't set me against my brother, I will do all I can to do as you ask me."

Ore paused. "It might," he finally said, "but not at the moment." He looked at Rei, then tipped his head. "How about I say if it comes to that, I'll step in and remove that threat?" Rei held Ore's eyes, then nodded once.

"It is a cousin, held in the House of Shicchi. The Head of that House is hunting for me. It will mean the death of both of us if he lays hands on me. I'm hoping he believes I'm already dead.

"The last his men knew I lay insensible, bleeding from a great wound. The hands of the one I protect bound my wound and made me promise again to continue to live, but didn't stay. It wasn't time yet to bring that one out of the House.

"Someday that one will come for me. When that day comes, if I determine there will be no conflict with your brother, let that one stay also, otherwise I'll leave to be with that one."

"I'll do it," Rei answered and held out his hand. Ore reached through the bars and clasped his hand to seal the agreement.

-o-o-o-

Ore was in training to follow Rei in the castle for a month before he was set at Mizi's back. It was another month - when he'd seen her to her rooms, checked the courtyard, roof, halls, and finding nothing, gone to report to Rei - before they stole her away. He could only figure they'd wanted to know what had happened to him, and to confirm he was still in the castle and wasn't going to get the job done himself.

When he returned to check on her and found her missing, he immediately sounded the alarm and took off tracking her kidnappers. At least they'd kept her alive, although it was small consolation.

He headed into the town and immediately to the docks. They would take her far from the country to remove her permanently from the side of the Prince. She would fetch a high price with her coloring, and for that reason was why she'd been kept alive most assuredly.

None of the ships in port, nor information brokers willing to talk to him, had seen her or any such thing. He'd reached his first place of employment and was holding his hair in his hands when he was jumped by a silent walker. He managed to sift out of the fingers just before they closed on him. He'd already had proven to him sufficiently he wasn't able to escape that grasp.

"You fail in the job, then have the audacity to come back?" The scathing words actually hurt, a little.

"My last message to you was intercepted and I was thrown in prison. Who betrayed me? You?"

That brought the pause to the fight Ore was hoping for, although neither one relaxed. "What was your message?"

"That it wasn't possible because she was firm in her own resolve to stay, and protected by the Prince in that resolve. ...And I returned myself to being my own agent."

"Is that why you were protecting her then?" Brok's scowl hadn't really gone away at the news.

"It is. The Prince was willing to pay my price. Where have they taken her if this dock isn't safe for them to be seen leaving? Tell me and I'll be on my way, granting life for life because you protected me before. Stay silent and I will betray you as you betrayed me in the end."

"I didn't betray you," Brok said in his growl. "It was the work of the Prince himself...I suppose protecting that which he wanted to?" Ore didn't answer or change expression. Finally Brok answered, "There's a smuggler's fingerling north of here along the coast, but ships pull in only long enough to drop off or pick up. Likely they'll already be pulling out by the time you get there on foot." But he was talking to air. Ore was already gone.

Ore's preferred method of travel, when out of town, was by tree. He was pleased that the trees of southern Ryokudo grew tall and strong at the edge of the sea. He was able to move quickly. Had he been on the ground, his feet would have sunk in the miry bog. The tangle of vine was a bit difficult to get around until he learned, almost by accident, that the right vine grabbed could save him from a sudden wet entrance into said bog.

When he reached the narrow river entrance to the coast, and heard the near silent splash of oars, he knew he was too late to rescue Mizi on this coast. He relaxed and turned his ears this way and that, trying to determine if they were talking, but nightwalkers knew better, pirates even more so. Voices carried across the water, skipping along the surface to echo lightly all over.

Using his eyes to see the best he could in only starlight, he finally found the shadow of the great ship on the sea. Using that as his endpoint, he searched for the skiff that had been sent to pick up the package. He finally found it with only a quarter of the way left to go, headed towards the ship.

He watched as they reached the side of the ship and hoisted up an unmoving, slumped form. They'd knocked Mizi out, so she couldn't cry out. Ore was sure she would have, otherwise. And fought and kicked and bit if she could.

He stayed and watched as the anchor was taken up silently, memorizing the shape of the ship as best he could as the sails were unfurled. It turned slowly, creaking and groaning as it got underway. It turned for the south and a little east and then Ore moved, back towards the city and the port, keeping his ears and eyes as much as possible on the ship until it was over the horizon and gone.

-o-o-o-

"Master," Ore was on one knee in front of Prince Rei on the deck of the second of the royal ships, the *Gin no Sakura*. He'd made it back to the docks just in time for the ship's call, and to hear his summons onto it, the three looking anxiously down at him. He'd ordered the ship's captain to steer due south, pointing the direction to go, immediately upon landing on the deck.

"She's been knocked out with a sleeping draught. While I don't know what a pirate ship looks like, the one she is on has a shape similar to this one, and a

342

mark that is curly in design but not a simple one, like common folk. The men who took her paid for an informant, but know castle grounds and guards too well, and use sneak tactics regularly."

He could feel Rei's anger mounting. "Come," he ordered and spun on his heel. Ore and the two knights followed. When they reached the main conference room, Rei pulled out a map and pointed to a symbol on it. "Did it look like this?" he demanded.

Ore nodded. "The starlight made it less distinct, but it is like this, yes."

Rei swore. "That's her home country, Yamanzar. I came across her in a manor I would escape to when the castle walls closed in on me too much. She was hiding there from the First Prince of that country.

"Amiran has a harem large enough to satisfy him already, although he's younger than my older brother. Yet when he heard of Mizi's hair, nothing would do but for him to add her to his collection, as if she were a mere thing to set on a cushion and play with.

"She left the country when they told her to prepare herself to be presented to him. I had to fight him off myself, although we've both promised secrecy to it lest the countries become embroiled. We currently have trade and peace agreements with them. Neither his father nor my mother would look kindly on us for starting a war over a common girl, regardless that she is both beautiful and intelligent."

"He's stolen her back, even knowing that she's agreed to it?" Ore was surprised.

He was shocked when Rei turned red and looked away. "I wouldn't think it of him, but...she hasn't agreed to stay with me yet, only said she wishes to walk with me. I can't ask her to take my hand until I'm ready and I've made the proper place for her to stand. Until then she's free to stay or go."

"Master!" Ore scolded.

Rei scowled at him. "You know what kind of strength she has. If I were to claim her like that Prince did, I should also find her gone the next morning."

Ore leaned back. "At least you have the brains to understand it, then," Ore finally relented. It wasn't too dissimilar to his own experience.

Rei turned back to the task at hand. "Only if Amiran has learned it can I think he might have reopened the quarrel."

"Well, perhaps it's some other party, then," Andrew tried to soothe the prince. "Surely we'll catch up to them soon."

So they hoped, but so it wasn't to be. At the point they were sure they should have seen any ship, given speeds and directions checked and rechecked until Ore was drained (being the only one with that information), nothing was to be found.

They finally decided to go straight to the coast, then work their way down to the port and search to see if anything could be seen. When nothing was found and they'd still reached the port, they conferenced one more time.

Ore watched Rei, intrigued to see his mind working very hard. Finally he looked up. "Andrew and Mina will come with me to the castle. We'll see if Prince Amiran was behind it. If not, we'll see if the king will give us leave to search the coast and near country. Ore, you hunt through the streets and ask the other ships if they saw anything. Also find out where pirate ports are so we have some more certain locations to go check."

With that plan, they disembarked and entered Yamanzar. Ore would have liked to stay and enjoy the sights, sounds, smells, and women of this place, but not this time. This time they were distractions from the urgency he felt.

He managed to get declared fairly quickly and his geniality got people talking - really he'd gone about it the hard way in Ichijoutsu - and in not too much time he had the locations of the main pirate port of call, and a few other smaller fingerlings where smugglers ran like they had on his own home country's shore.

He'd sent some of the sailors from the *Gin no Sakura* to talk to the sailors on the docks, and now he headed back to see what they'd learned. There was a new ship limping into port. Ore headed to it. He made sure the person who snuck off the back side of it was in his clutches and quickly in a back alley.

"They may have promised you safe haven, but you've arrived behind us." Ore whispered dangerously in the ear that could hear him. The other was pressed up against the wall in front of them, as Ore had the informant's arm bent tightly behind his back so he couldn't escape. "Where was the package dropped off?"

The informant hissed, and Ore had to apply more force to convince him he really did want to sell his information for his life. "Wasn't. We were boarded half mile from sight of shore and everything of value stolen off the ship. The few of us left alive managed to make it here. We're lucky we were - that they wanted only the bounty and not every man dead. The paying passengers was what put up a fuss when they stole the main objective off with them. Talk is they've more of them on land and they'll be after that ship again."

Ore immediately marched the man to the *Gin no Sakura* and told them to hold him for questioning, and let the bosun know he'd be gone searching for Mizi, but if the new ship pulled out, they were to follow it again. He marked on the map where the pirate cove was, then slipped off the ship and headed to the other.

When he reached the ship the kidnappers had fled in, there was an argument going on. He stayed just outside the range of it and listened in. When the ones who had hired the ship and seemed to have caused the fight when it hadn't been necessary, turned to walk off in anger and disappointment, Ore stood forward to block their way. "It sounds like you need a ship ready to depart soon? I know of one you could use."

They looked at him suspiciously, but he held his calm open look, waiting for their answer. "We've got to get word to our comrades, but if we could hire a sound ship and a crew willing to wield swords, we'd like to hire it. There's a pirate who's stolen a thing important to us, and we're honor bound to get it back."

Ore fought to not look dark, or hit any of them. To have stolen away Mizi, these were not men of honor. "How long to get word to your comrades? And when will you wish to set sail?" He was worried a bit about the timing of it all.

"If we give your captain the location, will he meet us there? We need to ride out to meet with our comrades and it's on the way to the port we need to get to next."

"And what port would that be?" Ore raised an eyebrow.

They looked at each other, then named the pirate port, almost as a challenge. "You're in luck," Ore said casually. "That's the next port of call for my captain." They looked at him suspiciously.

"Tell you what, I'll let the captain know there's a job for him there, then come with you. Then if I've spoken falsely you can sell me at the pirate's port. Since I haven't, I'll be with you to correctly identify the ship you've hired and be the trusted face to get you and your comrades on it."

They were shaking their heads. "We don't need to be on it, we need for your ship to prevent the other from setting sail, or for giving chase if it's already on its way."

Ore crossed his arms and frowned. "Then I think I'll come with you to make sure you don't leave the ship to do all your dirty work for you. Don't need to have you run before paying your due. And I'll take a down payment with me to my captain, or he'll refuse the deal."

The men hesitated. "We haven't got it," one finally admitted. "We spent it all on that last one. There's more at the Village, but not on us."

Ore scowled. They apologized and agreed they should have to put something down for good faith payment. Finally one volunteered to act as Ore had offered, and would go on the ship, to be put up for sale to cover the costs if they weren't properly paid. Ore accepted that arrangement.

He found one of the sailors from the *Gin no Sakura* he'd sent ashore to help him information gather and turned the man over to him. "Take this man to the main conference room. He's collateral for the ship being hired to give chase to a pirate vessel. The ship is to meet me at the pirate cove as soon as it can get there. I'm going with his friends for the same reason, to prove we're willing to be hired for the job and to see they follow through on their end."

"You got it," the sailor answered and took the man off with him.

Ore turned to the others, mostly wanting to distract them from the ship their friend was headed for. "So is this urgent, or do you expect the other ship to sit at rest for a long time in that port?"

That got their attention sufficiently and they were willing to move off immediately, only stopping to pick up horses. They gave Ore the horse of the man he'd traded places with. As soon as they were outside the port city, they were galloping as fast as they could go west, parallel to the coast, though inland a few miles.

-o-o-o-

Ore was surprised to find that the trees and green along the coast gave way rather quickly to desert yellow as one moved away from the coast. The desert was spotted here and there with green: oases of tall frondy trees; scrub grass enough to give morsels of grazing to horse, goat, and camel; and pools of clear water. Soon enough he was lost, each oasis looking like the next and only the miles between telling which one was which.

The terrain was hilly, and as they entered one low valley, the men he was riding with turned into it and headed back up north towards the coast. The air was hot, but it was as dry as he was already used to. The scent of the sea came to them on the breeze as they neared the green that ran along the coast, and with it came the moisture in the air again.

Once they were in the trees again, there was a bit of zigging and zagging, and suddenly they were surrounded by armed men and sliding to a halt. Looking closely around him, he could see hidden houses and buildings among the trees.

"What is it, Darin?" an older man reached out to grasp the halter of the horse of the lead man of the little group Ore was with.

With a scowl, which was nearly perpetual on the scarred face, Darin answered, "We got boarded by the Gorgon and our purpose changed from bringing her home to having to go and rescue her all over again. Zayn's gone on a ship that will meet us at the pirate port, to bring it in and as a promise that we'll show up and pay our portion, since the ship we'd hired to begin with wouldn't go out again after the Gorgon."

Darin waved a hand at Ore. "He's the equal exchange who offered the ship and promised the captain would meet us there properly."

Ore gave as good an appraisal as he got. He could see now why they'd been good at sneaking into Ichijou. They were likely the equivalent of an underworld high House, based on the movements and estimated skill level - not to mention numbers of swords and bows - of the people around him.

Living like this, though, he wasn't sure how they would have found it simple to get into a castle, although he hadn't gone with Rei to visit the prince and king, so perhaps there were also actual buildings and castles in Yamanzar.

His appraisal done, the leader asked Ore, "Are the swords on that ship brave enough to face the worst pirate on the sea?"

Coldly he answered, "They won't let even you kidnappers go alive."

That got raised eyebrows and scowls. The leader looked puzzled. "Kidnappers?"

"You've stolen Mistress away from the place she chose to be. What else would you be, save kidnappers and slavers?"

346

The leader looked at him silently a long while, then turned back to Darin. "Did you know what you brought with you?"

Darin's scowl had deepened. "No. This is the first he's let on."

"Well, there are two to retrieve then, and," his eyebrow raised at Ore, "we're at least agreed on the one retrieval?" Ore nodded curtly.

-o-o-o-

Ore walked down the street of the pirate village built up around the pier of the hidden cove, headed for the pier itself. Pretending to be looking for work, he asked as he went about ships that were docked and who might be hiring. He was relieved to learn the Gorgon's ship was still docked, although no one thought they'd be interested in hiring him. He didn't care about that detail much.

He also tried to discretely get people to say if they'd seen or heard of a red-haired woman on any ship in recent dockings and the best he got was a rumor from a drunk sailor. He was frustrated, but couldn't be surprised that they would be keeping that information secret. Even the most famous of pirate ships could expect to be boarded and have their treasures stolen if they were too high in value.

He reached the pier and walked slowly down all the ships until he found the Gorgon's ship. It looked well protected and like they could leave as soon as the order was given. That was concerning. He was pretty sure the *Gin no Sakura* couldn't dock here, so would have to stay out far enough to sea to not be seen readily, and he didn't know how long it would take for them to get there.

He'd reached the end of the pier when he was hailed. "Oy! Give us a hand here!"

Ore looked down towards the sound, then smiled. He reached down and took the rope being handed up. He tied it to the pillar closest to him, then reached down again to help the first person finish coming up the ladder. "Hey. Good timing." He reached down for the next hand, then the third.

"Are they still docked?" the disguised Rei asked immediately.

Ore pointed over his shoulder at the large ship behind him. "They're keeping their treasure a secret. I don't have confirmation she's on board, but no one's seen her in the streets, so likely they plan on taking her elsewhere before selling her off."

Rei looked dark at the casual way Ore said it, but he hadn't said it lightly. Ore looked at Andrew, puzzled. He was looping a rope around Mina's wrists, behind her back. "Bondage play?"

"Not play," Rei corrected. "I want someone on board with Mizi to help protect her."

"Ohhh," Ore said, sort of understanding. He looked at Mina. "Good luck with that. The Gorgon has the worst reputation, and you're not necessarily the best goods, sorry." Mina shrugged.

"Have you learned in your asking who we can contact from the ship to sell Mina to?" Rei asked. Ore turned and looked down the dock, then pointed to a man who was leaning against a pylon, cleaning his nails with a knife. Rei nodded thanks and took Mina's arm.

"Ah," Ore interrupted him, "if you have time, or inclination, I think you might want to meet the Head man here, instead of later. Of if you just want to fight him next when we've got Mistress back, you don't have to. There was a bit of a disagreement in methodology, I think. It's not quite what it looks like, although I'm just as happy with getting rid of two groups as one."

Rei gave a nod. "Zayn explained it, and apologized for not understanding the situation rightly. Tell the Head I'll meet him at the appointed place and keep them penned in. We'll talk once Mizi is safe."

"Got it," Ore said and watched them walk off, keeping watch on the little boat below him, as if hired for that job as well as for the information.

He was a bit surprised when the sailor of the Gorgon paid for Mina and got her loaded on board the ship. He wasn't surprised when they set sail not too long after Rei and Andrew had left in their little skiff again. He headed quickly for the hiding place of the Raionmure.

"Master says he'll be there, to prevent their retreat, and he'll talk with you after. Zayn explained it. The Gorgon's set sail. Time to move." He swung into the saddle of his horse and waited for the rest of them to mount. They galloped off yet again, headed by land to rescue Mizi.

-o-o-o-

Ore was happy to finally have his knives bite into flesh. He'd been needing to get out his anger and worry. He and a few Raionmure snuck into the area around the lighthouse and silently slit throats in the evening dusk until there weren't any exterior guards. Then they gave the signal and the rest quickly ghosted to the building.

Entering silently, they went both up and down, carving their way through the interior. That got noisy since on the stairs up they couldn't silence the guards coming down as fast, although cries were cut off as arrows thudded into chests. The battle inside was heated for a while, but the attackers were determined and the defenders fewer and surprised.

When they arrived at the top, one looked out over the sea. "Ey! Ships inbound!" The cry went all the way down the lighthouse and down into the caverns below where the battles were just reaching their final stage. Those defending dug up renewed strength at the words, but the attackers were all the more determined to silence them before the ships arrived. They wanted no word of warning.

As soon as they could, they finished the battle and cleaned the bodies out of the cavern, hiding them behind piles of rocks as best they could. Those not dead were knocked out so they couldn't make noise. Then the attackers hid themselves and laid wait.

348

As Ore watched, the Gorgon's crew stowed the sails to slow down and enter the large cavern cave. The cave entrance was barely wide enough for the ship and would take masterful handling of the rudder. Behind it came the *Gin no Sakura*, running quickly with the wind. As he watched, the largest sail was taken down, then one by one, slowly the smaller ones, but at a pace the ship was still gaining on the Gorgon.

As soon as the prow of the chasing vessel was close enough, bodies began to leap from the *Gin no Sakura* onto the stern of the Gorgon's ship. He was quite sure the first person was Andrew and the second was Rei. Andrew would never have allowed Rei to go first, but Rei would have been determined to be first anyway, so would have grudgingly settled for second.

Ore had already gotten into position as close to the cave mouth as he could, standing precariously on the slippery rock. He watched and at the right timing leaped up and out and grabbed hold of the lowering anchor chain. He clambered up it quickly, put a throwing dagger in the eye of the sailor handling the anchor, then caught it long enough to not let it halt the ship until it ran aground.

As it did so, it groaned and threw everyone standing on it forward. He hoped that didn't kill anyone he wanted to have alive. He slipped towards the main cabins. He'd been on the ships enough that docked at Ichijoutsu to know that human cargo wouldn't be below in the hold.

Along the way he caught sight of Rei, beset by three pirates, and Andrew beside him trying to fend off them and two more as well. At least they were close to where they needed to be. Ore threw two more daggers on his way over, taking down one and wounding another so Rei could take him out quickly, then Ore was behind the two.

As soon as the space between Ore and the door to the cabins was empty, he grabbed Rei from the back, swung him around, and pushed him to the door. "That's where you need to be. Get going. We'll hold it here," he said, his knife coming up to block a wicked cutlass that had been going for Rei before then. He waited until he heard the door close behind Rei before losing himself to the sway, parry, and thrust of the fight.

Sometime, probably not too much time, later there was another body to his left, left-handedly swinging a sword with him and Andrew. "Sorry to take so long."

"No," Andrew answered from Ore's right. "It's a good time. You're okay?"

"Fine," Mina answered. "They cut Mizi, though. Gorgon got impatient with her." When Ore's next blow was particularly savage, she added, "Not badly - more a scratch. They didn't want to sell damaged goods after all." Still Ore wasn't happy and he took it out on the next five pirates.

The numbers of pirates coming at them was lessening, and the Raionmure and Ryokudo sailors had most of the remaining ones in hand. Suddenly Ore heard the sound of a whizzing coming from behind and he ducked, grabbing Andrew to push him to the side at the same time. With a thunk and quivering sound the blade on the end of the chain hit the wood deck between them. It would have taken Ore's head, most likely, and Andrew's arm if not for the ducking.

Ore immediately stepped on the chain, twisted, and grabbed it higher up and pulled for all he was worth, jerking sharply as he finished the twist. The body that followed it flipped in midair and landed on her feet.

Mina had turned and was now facing the woman pirate captain who was angrily looking at Ore. Not having her distance weapon any longer, she dropped the end of it and pulled a wicked and very long knife, almost the length of a short sword. The worst part of it was that it was serrated with wickedly long barbs.

Ore shifted his grip on his knife, but didn't let go of the chain he was holding. He didn't want her to get hold of it again.

His vision was blocked suddenly by Andrew stepping up to stand beside his partner. "Gorgon, give it up," Andrew said loudly.

"Get off my ship!" she retorted.

Andrew feinted, leaping forward a step and thrusting at her. She quickly parried, then swung her knife around to swing a blow at him. He stepped back out of the way and Mina went under the swing and sliced at the Gorgon's legs. The pirate captain lifted the leg, then kicked out following the blow. Andrew's blade intercepted above and the Gorgon was hard pressed to keep her balance and defend herself.

Then she was suddenly slumping to the ground. As she fell, Rei was exposed behind her, holding his sword with two hands on the hilt, the blade buried in her back, his face dark and his eyes hard. Ore froze for just a moment. Just in that moment of time, the Prince he followed was a High House Head. To have it shown to him so strikingly that the young man he'd chosen to follow during this time was worthy of his blade and skills struck Ore deeply.

The blade was removed from the back of the woman on the deck, and coolly cleaned on her shoulder, then replaced in Rei's sheath. "How goes the battle?" Rei asked just as coldly as his blade had gone in and out of the back of the pirate captain.

Andrew answered the question. "Final clean up, now that she's taken care of." Ore kept a eye on the ledge above them the captain had come from. They didn't need a last minute arrival of another pirate from the same position. When the head of a Raionmure poked up there, Ore made direct eye contact with him.

"Well, looks like I don't need to be worried about where she went, then, do I?" the leader of the Raionmure was pragmatic. He leaned against the wall, his sword held downward, bloodied but relaxed.

Rei turned and looked up. "Hell, most likely."

A quirk of the lips. "Most likely, indeed."

"Master, this is Hizaber, leader of the Raionmure," Ore made the introduction, not taking his eyes off the man. He might be the next person on the other side of their swords.

An eyebrow rose. "Master? So young." Hizaber's eyes were calculating and his face closed until he finally sighed. "Well if we don't make a truce rather quickly, we'll be back into battle again. What'll it be?"

"If you'll let Mizi return to where she wishes to be, then I have no quarrel with you," Rei answered.

"Well...I'd like to hear it from her own lips, if you don't mind it," Hizaber answered mildly.

Rei nodded and walked to the door. He opened it and held out his hand. Ore would have run, but he was the guard watching Hizaber so he stood still and did his job. He also would have moved the dead so Mizi didn't have to see them, but that was also not his to choose. He was relieved when Mina looked around the deck to make sure they were guarded from the rear.

Mizi did indeed have a cut on her forehead. It looked like they'd stopped the bleeding, but didn't have bandaging, of course. Ore's lips tightened at seeing it and his anger flashed again before he brought it under control. Those responsible had already been dealt with. It didn't need to come out again.

"Mizi, the group that helped us rescue you wants to know for sure who you want to go with, since they are also responsible for your first kidnapping, as I explained to you before, thinking you needed rescuing from Ryokudo." Rei led her out far enough, then turned her to look up at the man above them.

Ore saw the man react to the golden-burnished red hair, but by the time she was looking at him, his face said nothing. Mizi, on the other hand, froze and stared open mouthed. The hand Rei wasn't holding went to her heart, the fingers curled. "F-Fa-Father?" Rei and Ore both nearly collapsed on the spot.

-o-o-o-

Ore sat in a tree at the outer edge of the village of the Raionmure. The truce had been formalized into almost the equivalent of a treaty to be celebrated. The Raionmure were glad to have their leader's daughter safely brought home and wanted to show off for her, not to mention there was a group deeply sorry and trying to apologize for stealing her away without so much as even explaining to her why nor asking if she even wanted to be.

She'd been raised by an aunt and uncle away from the fighting life of those who'd been run out by lords of Yamanzar and made to live the life of fugitives. None of Rei's group had said he was the Second Prince himself, but Ore was sure Hizaber had figured out he was high enough, for having brought his own ship for the chase, and Mizi having been "rescued" from Castle Ichijou.

They would meet up with the ship again in the main port the following day. Ore would have gone with the ship, but Rei, reinforced by Andrew and Mina, had ordered him to stay with them. Ore was tired. It had been a long chase, with a lot of tension. He leaned his head back against the tree trunk, although his ears were carefully alert, and rested his eyes.

Ore wasn't quite sure how long he rested there before there were footsteps near his tree. He knew those footsteps. His eyes closed tighter as his heart constricted. He didn't want to see that face just yet, but she called to him anyway, and he couldn't disobey.

He landed lightly behind her and put a hand over her eyes. She stiffened. Looking only at the back of her head as her hands unconsciously went over her heart, clasping lightly, he said. "I'm sorry, Mistress. Because I couldn't protect you, you had to live through a horrible thing."

She paused and said nothing for a while, then she said. "You won't let me look at you, so I can know you're okay?"

"No," he answered. It didn't matter if he was okay or not. It mattered that she hadn't been.

She slowly reached up and took his hand, her fingers warm on the back of his hand and her thumb pressing lightly into his palm on the other side. She held him there, not moving his hand. "Then...I hope that the next time we come to Yamanzar I can see your face to see your smile. Please, let me show you the places I remember."

Ore stiffened in shock, rejecting her forgiveness even as his heart leaped at not being sent away. He sighed and slumped in defeat, almost touching the back of her head with his forehead, the scent of her rising to his nostrils and becoming part of the binding that her hold on him created. "I cannot win against you, Mistress," he admitted. ...And his heart yearned for another who was like this one.

With a twist and gentle slip to retrieve his hand, he was gone, back into the tree again, the double pain hard to bear. He listened to her return to the village to make sure she went safely, his hand she'd held lightly touching the scar on his chest over the place of his own pain.

If he couldn't protect this one, he still wasn't ready to protect that one, but it was hard, and only getting harder to not have her by his side where he could see her face and know she was safe.

-o-o-o-

Ore did his best to be somewhat sociable at the evening dinner party, drinking properly with the knights as they watched over Rei and Mizi from a distance to let them have time together again. It helped Ore to have companions that night.

There was a return to the castle of Yamanzar to visit with Prince Amiran - who didn't impress Ore very much, although it sounded like he was trying harder since this event. He lost himself in role playing the silent guardian and proper servant standing at Mizi's shoulder. When they were on board the *Gin no Sakura* again, he spent most of his time up in the crow's nest, letting the wind at that level brush his soul into calm, even though it was perhaps a sham.

The seabirds called as they soared in circles around the ship and Ore wished he could join them. The embrace of the wind lifting them was echoed by his memories of the embrace of the one he longed for, who had lifted him

352

up once again to be able to come to this place. He could only be grateful that he had come here, to be serving Master Rei and walking behind Mistress Mizi. To be with them was like being with her, although it made him long for her all the more.

The feelings he felt towards the two of them began to stir within him the strength and determination to be prepared all the sooner, to be able to demand that she come to him because he was finally strong enough rather than to sit passively waiting for her, or life, to decide it was time. When he finally determined that was going to be his path from this time on, he found the strength to stay on the deck again, looking out over the sea, leaning on the rail.

"You've finally decided, then?" a quiet tenor voice said next to him as warmth came up to stand to either side of him.

He looked out over the sea and took a breath. "I have," he answered.

The knights didn't say anything more, but they stayed with him, leaning on the rail as well, giving him their companionship and warmth, the unspoken approval and welcome filling him as well. He'd never had friends, so to speak, but he could tell this would be what others would call this - the beginnings of friendship.

He turned and leaned his back against the railing, resting his elbows on it, and smiled. "So, which of you wants to play at cards? Loser owes a bottle of red wine to the winner."

Andrew looked at him from the corner of his eye. "How expensive a bottle?"

Mina leaned backwards, holding onto the railing, to look at Andrew around Ore, her eyes narrowed. "Top quality, and I'll watch the two of you and share in the winnings."

Ore snickered. "You know how to play best of all, don't you, Miss Mina?" She just smiled to herself as Andrew protested then gave in and agreed.

-o-o-o-

Life in the castle settled back into patterns that were a dance of the seasons and activities and flow of Mizi, and when they could come Rei, Mina, and Andrew. Ore spent his time with Mizi practicing at becoming stronger. He was attentive, gentle, firm as necessary but in ways that didn't startle or make Mizi less of a person, but rather helped to lift her up like the air and wind had lifted the seabirds.

He found he was able to smile more, although he could also feel his inner core becoming harder and more tempered. With quickness he put down those who came to interfere with her chosen path. If she was present, he did it without frightening her. If she was busy, he just excused himself and dealt with it and returned.

He spent many hours tempering his body and practicing his hand-to-hand martial arts skills as well as his blade - the hand dagger. He worked on core strength and speed and at controlling his automatic instincts. That he found difficult and slow going without people to practice with, other than Mizi who he learned to feel and hear instinctively as well so that his instinct would protect her rather than attack her.

He did have tasks to do for Rei, being his Messenger, and then he set two he trusted to watch over her from the shadows. He was returning from one of those tasks, when he suddenly tripped on something. He kept his footing and quickly looked around, but found no one and nothing to have tripped over.

Even close inspection of the area found nothing, it having been pavement so no footprints could have been left. He found himself with a slight limp from it, though, that was irksome.

He stayed extra vigilant thereafter. If there was someone in this place that could injure him and disappear, he would need to become even stronger and better at what he needed to do in this place.

When he arrived at the place he'd left Mizi, he was told she'd been called away by the Prince. His two guards were gone with her, so he went immediately to Prince Rei's office, taking the outer path and landing on the balcony of the second floor office. "Master," he called, but was interrupted by a summons of the Prince.

"I'll be back," Rei promised.

"Mistress has been called as well," he called after, not seeing her with him. He saw Rei's back stiffen and the slight pause before he and the knights were out the door.

Ore stayed where he was and fretted. The flow of the castle had been interrupted, and it wasn't perhaps safe to wander off, although he desperately wanted to follow across the rooftops to see where Rei went and to be sure he was safe, and Mizi, too.

When Rei returned, he also was discontent. He went straight to the balcony and looked Ore in the eye. "Did something happen?"

"I was going to tell you when you were summoned," Ore said immediately. "I was tripped but there was nothing to do it, nor anyone there, and when I reached the medical wing, Mistress had already been called away." Rei scowled and even growled slightly. "What is it, Master?" Ore asked.

Rei leaned against the railing next to where Ore was perched, his sore ankle dangling down in front of him. "It's my brother, Sasou. He's returned to the castle and was testing you, and he's testing Mizi now."

Ore's heart fell. He'd failed that test, then, to not know there was someone there. Rei looked up at him. "No, it's okay, Ore. He's very, very good. If you believe you need to get better, he does too, but you won't be sent away. He tests everyone, but most of all those who I put next to me."

He scowled at the ground past his folded arms again. "It's Mizi I'm more worried about. To have someone like her next to me, in his eyes for a time it will be the same as in the eyes of the other lords. He'll test her most strenuously to see if she believes she can bed me and win favors, and he'll give her no benefit of the doubt, but have to have it proven to him every step of the way. Unlike me who chooses to trust first, he must see the proof of it before he'll begin to believe even a portion."

Rei sighed and looked up at the sky, not really seeing it. "He has to, or he'd not survive to be king, ...but it is so annoying, not to mention a slow way to go about it." Rei looked at Ore. "Do your best to help her show him what she can do."

Ore nodded. "I will, though she'll do it herself." Rei nodded agreement, but still was gloomy and fretted himself until Ore said he would go and see if she'd been released. Rei released him to go and Ore went quickly.

He found Mizi back in the medical wing, applying herself to the plants in the greenhouse. Ore had already learned that most of the time she went there merely to work and relax, but sometimes she went there when she had stressful things to work out. He carefully tested her and was sad to learn it was the latter. The older brother had not been kind at all, then.

Ore stayed with her, giving at least his companionship to strengthen her, until she finally sat on the floor and curled her arms around her legs, as if curling her hand at her heart wouldn't be nearly enough to contain her emotions. Ore almost panicked. "Ore...," her voice even was as uncertain as he'd ever heard it.

"Mistress, is there a thing you need to hear?" She finally nodded miserably. "Then stay here. I'll go and get him." He gave the sign to his two that watched over her and took off over the roofs again.

"Master, Mistress needs you." That was all Rei needed to hear and he was over the balcony railing, his own need driving him as well. The three flew after him, Ore taking them to the greenhouse, but they let Rei enter alone and only watched over them from outside. It wasn't a conversation to pry into.

-o-o-o-

Two weeks later, as Ore was about an errand for Rei, he was stopped. "You've been summoned to the Prince's office."

Ore stared at the messenger. He'd just come from there. Then he remembered. "Which Prince?"

"The First Prince."

"Thank you," Ore bowed and turned towards that wing, his heart suddenly beating faster. He'd spent a lot of time avoiding that part of the castle, and now he'd been summoned to it alone. Surely a harder test was coming.

Given that anyone could be watching him, he refused to show anything on the outside other than calm strength - the calm strength he'd learned to show to the underworld. With him, it included a level of exterior relaxed casualness that he would have to tone down a bit. He could do this if he thought of it as being called in for a job interview with a High House Head. It was just the highest House Head possible to be called in front of.

To think of it that way didn't make him afraid. It made him curious. What kind of person was the First Prince, really? He'd be doing his own testing this day, although not obviously, just passively so as to not make him angry.

Ore announced himself at the door to Prince Sasou's office, loudly enough to just be heard inside, but not so loud as to seem anxious. Just enough to let the First Prince know that he couldn't get away with saying he'd not come, nor had he heard the announcement. The guards waited just the right amount of time to almost seem insolent, but yet barely at the time to be obedient.

Ore nodded to himself on the inside. Even they had been instructed to test him. He bore it with patience, although he allowed just a touch of righteous anger to cross his face at the end as they moved to open the door and announce him. The First Prince kept him waiting even longer, but Ore bore that with complete patience.

When he was allowed to approach the First Prince, he walked to the precisely correct distance from the First Prince and bowed formally. "Ore, Messenger of Prince Rei, as summoned," he introduced himself, then calmly faced Prince Sasou, inspecting him without inspecting him.

He was young, but truthfully the age of Ore himself, and already looking like the king he would be soon, most likely. His lightly golden blond hair was spun straw turned to gold, beautifully brushed to shiny, and allowed to grow long enough to cover his eyes. At the moment all but the bangs lightly brushing the Prince's eyebrows were pulled back into a ponytail.

The face was a face that would be carved into marble it was so beautiful yet full of the strength of proud men and kings. Brilliant blue eyes studied Ore, eyes to match Rei's. Ore didn't allow himself to be pulled into them. He'd been with Rei enough now he could choose when to be lost in them. He stayed in a semi-formal relaxed pose, waiting to hear the words of the First Prince.

"My brother has kept a funny thing in the castle," Sasou finally said, leaning on one hand, "and he has set an almost funnier thing to watch over it." Ore refused to acknowledge the slight, burying his reaction far down.

Tests were to be ignored, not sparked at. If anything, such things were to be used as ammunition for politely barbed responses to teach the tester to not be rude. "But what I really want to know from Tei, is why he didn't finish his final job properly?"

Ore blinked and considered his answer. "I'm sure I don't know the Tei of which you speak. I know of no job ever given to one called by that name."

"Hmm," Sasou's eyes narrowed a fraction. "Is that because you accepted the job in your own name?"

Ore almost smiled. "Does one such as I have a name at all, to call my own?"

Sasou's eyes narrowed a fraction more. "Then tell me, Messenger of Rei, why have you protected the red-haired woman instead of seen her out of the castle?"

"If Prince Brother was my employer for the task, he would have received my answer to that already. I have protected her because she is worthy of protecting, and has earned it by her own efforts."

Sasou's eyebrow went up fractionally and he sat in slightly stunned silence for a moment. He finally put his hand to his forehead. "I'm not sure whether to take offense at the title you've given me, or to laugh at your response."

"It isn't wise to laugh at a thing you don't understand for yourself yet. I don't really care if you like what I call you or not." He kept a smooth, passive face and said it all very respectfully.

When Sasou stared at him with wide eyes, silent, Ore added, "And if you were my employer for that task, and heard my response to it, you would understand already. My answer today would not be any different."

"And if I were to place you in my employ today?" It was nearly cold.

"I answer to only one Master. I would not agree to it."

A brow furrowed slightly. "Even though I'm First Prince?"

"Even though."

"And after I am King?"

"Even still."

"Such touching loyalty." It was said with dry sarcasm, but Ore knew he'd scored a point in his favor - in his mind, even if not in Sasou's. "But have you turned your back on the Queen then?"

"I was never facing the Queen Mother," Ore protested slightly.

Sasou had a touch of impatience to him. "The Queen of Night, Messenger of Rei."

Ohhh, that Queen. It was Ore's turn to be impatient. "You lack even more understanding to even ask that question."

"But you gave her enough loyalty to claim a royal name in my own city," Sasou responded. "Would you not go to her if she called you?"

Ore took a breath to calm himself. "Please go back and study further, Prince Brother. I have a task you have interrupted for not knowing who you're talking to. If you will excuse me." He didn't bother letting Prince Sasou object or not, letting himself out of the room during the stunned silence that followed his comment.

When he arrived back at Rei's office, he was scolded lightly for arriving late. "Prince Brother kindly invited me to his office to allow me to test him," Ore answered mildly.

Rei was stunned to blinking silence for quite a while. Finally he said, "And...?"

"I found him lacking. But for Master's sake, I'll continue to watch him. Perhaps he'll be able to redeem himself." Mina was hard pressed to hide her snickering and Andrew and Rei stared at Ore as if their eyes would fall out.

Rei finally looked at Andrew. Andrew said, "I do believe he's being serious."

"Of course I am," Ore scolded them both. "Here's what you sent me to get, Master," he handed the item over. "Just in case, I'll go check on Mistress now; though having left Prince Brother as stunned as I'm leaving you, I suspect he hasn't thought of it yet."

He left out the balcony door and did, indeed, find Mizi working happily without interruption. He sat and watched over her that day with a small satisfied smile on his face. It had been gratifying to hear Mina's laughter as he'd reached the roof over the office. He'd been trying to get through that layer of her wall for some time.

-o-o-o-

Ore was supremely proud of Mizi when she was able to show Prince Sasou her full strength during the time of the plague at Kouzanshi. He'd done everything he could to support her so that the First Prince would see it with his own eyes, Mizi's full strength.

When Rei sent him to be with her during her two years of study, he'd gone obedient to the sending, willing to support her there as well, even if he didn't think it had been necessary. It wasn't his to decide, but to see the pain of separation in Rei's eyes had been hard.

Ore understood it all too well. His own pain came to the surface often then, being in the north again. He'd heard the voice of the Queen when he'd arrived and his heart had lept, though he'd not given it away. When Head Medical Researcher Shiotsu let him know that he was still being watched over by his own strength, even in that place, and had seen her with his own eyes recently and judged her worthy, Ore had to fight hard to not go seeking her out. It wasn't time yet, even then.

But having her there, knowing she was also watching him...it had been hard. So very hard. He wanted to go and claim her and make her his finally, but he would have left Mistress alone if he had.

When Mizi received her diploma and was tasked to visit all the lords of northern Suiran, he'd been willing to follow after her, but Rei had refused after the first half of the trip, calling him home. "I promised to protect you as well. This is that time. You will come so that he won't see you and kill you."

Ore had reluctantly obeyed, not wanting Mizi to be alone. He'd sent those he trusted to watch over her again, to see she also came out of that House whole and alive. He'd not questioned her. It wasn't necessary to ask if his own was in that House still. She was. Shiotsu had said it, for not knowing himself.

Once Mizi was safely at Castle Nijou that fall Ore began to work out a plan to retrieve her - his strength. He went with Mizi to Tokumade that spring, finding neither his brother nor his strength there - not on the way out nor the way back.

It confused him, but he remembered that she had been in Kouzanshi as well, so it wasn't that they were always at the manor. He was pleased to know

358

he'd remembered the layout of the manor correctly. When he was ready to go, he would know how to sneak through to find her. But he hadn't been able to lay eyes on her, to know what she looked like for sure, nor could he find out which room was hers, nor did he hear her name when he was there. There were still too many things keeping her frustratingly out of reach.

When Ore heard her name in conjunction with the assassination, and understood it was the very person they had recovered alive - the only one alive, he'd gone into shock barely able to hold onto sanity, slipping into automatic behaviors, holding to the patterns of daily life with Mizi. But it slipped when Rei came and they were alone.

It slipped again when he learned his strength was using the false strength of the Little Death and it only continued to slip - his hold on his sanity - until he finally couldn't face it any longer while so near her physical presence - a presence that demanded denial of all he'd been working towards. With bitterness he ran from Ilena, running from what his expectations had been that were so different than the reality; needing to understand, to reconcile and convert until he could see his way to move forward again.

He would sit and hold himself, his arms wrapped around his middle, forcing himself to stay put in his tree or on the castle roof where he could hear his master's calm voice speaking of everyday things, to give him an anchor to reality. The worry in Rei's voice when he called, the concern in the faces of Andrew and Mina - they forced him to try to think rationally.

At times he could begin to. Of course she would have changed, be older, be something he couldn't know fully just from what he'd known when they were young. He himself had needed to change dramatically to become strong enough. He probably wasn't what she was expecting either.

At night, he would see in the darkness what she looked like and would have to hold himself again. She was beautiful, regal without pride as if she didn't know it, although he was sure she did when he was angry again. Her words both drew him and repulsed him, as did her own latent desire for him as he had for her.

It was a thing he couldn't resolve and it tore him like nothing had before. At times he felt she would kill him, for all he'd worked so hard to become strong enough for this moment. Then he would berate and scold himself until he was weary.

When Rei finally ordered Andrew and Mina to drag him from the roof, from the tree, and force him onto his horse, he'd been in so much pain that he'd not been able to fight when they got serious. He'd already been beaten, his insides no longer able to take any more punishment. He could only face that ride as one who was headed to prison, knowing the gallows were next. Complete despairing resignation, closing his eyes to the scenery they passed.

By the time they arrived back at Osterly Garrison, there was nearly emptiness. The voice of his mistress pronouncing his sentence was the sentence of death, the chain that bound him to a thing he couldn't comprehend, and could no longer see he'd desired from the beginning.

Having Ilena state the same request had been the fire laid to the faggots at his feet as he stood bound to the stake, a thing he intellectually understood he should be afraid of, but there was no longer room for fear in the numbness he'd fallen into. He would have cried tears of despair and perhaps frustration but they were lost to the same numbness. He was lost to the dense fog and shadows.

His only escape was into sleep - and that they allowed him just enough leash to sit on the roof and stare at the sky unthinking, unfeeling save the few times strong emotions tried to burst his chest apart again, splitting the scar that marked him, that made him as much hers as the binding words of both women who had betrayed him.

But he couldn't be angry at Mizi. Only at Ilena, that she'd led his mistress to the thought that bound them together. He'd left them alone, though, so only he was to blame in the end. He'd close his eyes and ride the wave of darkness then, despair and bile rising at the same time, until he couldn't face being alive or aware any more and he returned to the room to sink into the escape of sleep.

In the end, it was the emptiness that allowed the first drips of life restoring water to plink softly into his pained heart and burnt soul. Before then, what little strength he had gave life to bitterness, the only thing he had left. But when Ilena had been earnest and insistent on learning anything she could, then had casually and without restraint given Mizi everything she needed to take a step forward on her path, to become even a little stronger, it was like the faint light of dawn lighting the darkness so that it held the possibility of interest, and he held his breath, not sure he could hope.

Her suggestion that had made so much sense and held even a hint of the playful delight he himself held when he made plans was like the first birds singing at the growing light of dawn. He'd still held himself, still in pain, but when she'd laughed and delighted in the little things that the run through the ambush had shown them, it had been like the first rays of the sun bursting over the horizon, showing his darkness to be a fog that could perhaps be burned off by the morning warming sun.

Although he hurt, it was pushed back a little by that light and warmth. Considering her words had also done that. This time her words had dripped into his heart enough to nourish it a little again and he'd not run from them, but looked at them differently. He couldn't face them properly, but he could do that much.

Arriving at the castle and seeing that small room, he knew he'd have to stay by her side and not complained. He'd have done that for any save perhaps his worst enemy if that one had grown up at Tokumade, and she wasn't that, however much he hurt and was confused. Being back in the castle helped too, although Ore was still under probation as far as Rei was concerned.

Ore was a little surprised to find comfort for once being inside the castle walls, as if getting up with the sun and walking to the barn to take care of the animals because it was what one did every morning - it fell over him softly. It wasn't different to leave the office late, it was just a different location to walk to. He never slept anywhere easily and wandered late at night, often taking night watch shifts, so this wasn't any different, really.

Arriving to find a besmitten Ryan had raised his eyebrow, but he already knew from Ilena's handling of Mizi that Ilena had a tongue that won others quickly. It was Ryan's report of Ilena's tears behind a closed door that caught him and somehow he felt pricked by it, his angry thoughts of her inhumanity lifting a reminder to him that he'd been unfeeling himself, disregarding any pain she herself had, perhaps even delighting in it as payment for his own. It wasn't kind, and it wasn't strength.

He'd repented of it before he walked in the door, his pain echoing hers, giving him a calm he hadn't had since he'd heard her name, as if the morning breeze had begun to blow gently, tugging and lifting at the fog, encouraging it to dissipate, to let go of the land it hovered over.

Under that fog wasn't a pretty scene, and it came to light eventually. There was scaring, sure enough, the hardness of the ground left bare to see, rocky places blackened by the scorching he'd received. They didn't let him be soft to her, made him judge her harshly even still.

But there was also uncovered the bare earth that was soft and the seeds that were planted there from long ago. The soft water dripping slowly into his soul slowly seeped into those places and began to awaken the seeds, although it was slow and hard to see at first.

Oddly, for all he found them outwardly uncomfortable and unseemly, it was the tears of others, after her own, that were the water that made the seeds begin to sprout and seek the light, pointing it out until he had to acknowledge it existed. They weren't tears of insincerity, nor of falsehood, but of unrestrained honest gratitude, of pains in the past re-experienced, but lessened by the softness they'd been gifted from someone who understood. And just how much she understood he couldn't even know until he finally understood who she really was.

The rising sun had finally shed enough light, slowly increasing over the days, until he was standing fully in it, no shadows left, and in that sunlight, he had to bow to reality and let go the pains of his confusion. Finally, he reached the point that he could begin to move forward, walking again along the course he'd set long ago, at his own pace, at the proper speed, the way finally made clear.

He taught her, then, what she needed to know to walk his path with him and she'd willingly listened and learned, anxious to understand. They walked under trees then, light dappling the way, the shadows sometimes confusing them, sometimes giving them relief from the heat of the sun's rays. Sometimes he made them pause and consider the path again, or rest until it was time to move forward again.

Then he left her on the path to see if she could walk it without him. That was hard, but it was still within his proper timing and order. And her sun continued to move across the sky in its proper path and when he returned it was still shining on his own path and she waited for him on it.

Then she showed him her own strength, increasing in intensity little by little into the afternoon and he had to learn to bear that increasing heat, learn to breathe a little deeper, to create his shade, to calm her, and to increase in his own strength even more.

That was when he wanted to reach out and kiss her, to pull her to him and not let go, to get lost in her and let himself be consumed by his desire - past and present - to have her always with him, to never let her go, never lose sight of her face. He had to fight that as it rose up in him and he finally had to warn Rei that he was going to be lost in it soon, the heat reaching it's peak and driving him to midafternoon madness or slumber.

He'd hid from her light, then, until he could hear what he was to do next, the brightness having blinded him to his path again, only knowing that he had to be obedient, to follow the voice of his Master to stay on the path. Even still, he had to be sure when he received the word he could call her to stay by his side on his path - had to sit hidden a little longer from the heat of the sun to think carefully and purposely, to seek out his guide posts.

Then, when he was set firmly on his path again, sure of his way, strengthened even more, he opened his arms and called to her and embraced her and was enfolded in her arms of warmth again. There were still things along the path they had to walk through and over, times of correction and learning, but now he was finally able to interlace his fingers in hers, to kiss her and hold her and feel her warmth against his own body.

And joy of joys, to watch her unfold into the calm, cooling sun of the late afternoon and evening, the breeze that blew then being cooling, a caress, a kiss. He delighted in watching her, and she followed after him, danced alongside him, ran ahead and called to him, only to return again and take his hand and smile, the work of the hard day done, the respite of evening approaching.

He sank down by the evening fire and pulled her with him, to hold her in his arms and enjoy the peace of the sunset. Life would be very full, and there was more path to walk, but now they would walk it together. He would anchor her to the ground, to his path, and she would warm him and light his way, and together they would keep one another company as they walked forward following Rei and standing behind Mizi, supporting those who they'd promised to help on their way.

And still, still, it was difficult to let her go, to not be lost in one another forever. During the nights they held each other closely and were warmed by each other's presence, sleeping deeply like they'd never slept before alone, finding comfort where there had never been any before - in the darkness of the night. And even in his dreams he was still kissing her and holding her protectively in his arms: his sun, his warmth, his strength, his Princess, his Ilena.

Simple Pronunciation Guide

To help English speakers, here's a pronunciation guide for the Japanese words. Japanese has a much smaller collection of vowel sounds than English. Many sounds are very similar to Spanish sounds.

Short Vowels:

"a" as in f**a**ther
"e" as in m**e**n
"i" as in s**ee**
"o" as in b**oa**t
"u" as in f**oo**d

Multiple vowels put together are each said. So in "Rei" you should hear both the short "e" and the "ee" of the i. In "Sasou" you should hear both the "o" and the "u" making a sound similar to, "**ow**, I hurt myself."

Long vowels of Japanese often merely sound like they just put two short vowels together. "R"s are rolled very slightly, "j" is slightly a "jz" sound, and such go the consonants. Anglicizing them is fairly equivalent. The "y" is soft and often swallowed or only lightly voiced and is never the forceful sound of "ee".

People and Places

Ryokudo The country our main characters are from and royals of.

Ichijou The main palace of Ryokudo, residence of the King and Queen, on the southern coast in the eastern corner.

- King Sasou Touka (Age: 28.) King of Ryokudo, older brother to Rei.

- Queen Aryana (Age: 27.) Queen of Ryokudo, Sasou's wife. Born in, and a noble daughter of, Kouzanshi, Ryokudo.

- Lord Michael Barret (Age: 37.) King Sasou's childhood guard, first aide, head nag, and Minister of Intelligence of Ryokudo.

- Parmenia (Age: 34.) Head Court Healer of Ichjou. Mizi and Ryan's superior before they moved to Nijou.

Ichijoutsu The bustling capital port city of Ryokudo that sits at the feet of Ichijou. Full of trade and people who smile because their kings work hard to make life simple and fulfilling for their subjects.

Region of Suiran The entire northern portion of Ryokudo. It's in the main dense woods with boggy soil, filling up the rolling hills that lead up to the north rocky mountains.

Nijou The secondary castle of Ryokudo, the head seat of the Regent of Suiran. Set near the tri-corner border of Ryokudo, Tarc, and Brulac so they can quickly defend the contested location.

- Dowager Queen Kata Touka (Age: 51.) Sasou and Rei's mother. She lives in isolation within Nijou, having given the rulership of Ryokudo to Sasou when he reached a sufficient age and education to take over the throne. She was Regent of Suiran before Sasou sent Rei to take over the position.

- First Prince Rei Touka (Age: 18.) Regent of Suiran, younger brother to Sasou. Our secondary male protagonist.

- Sir Andrew Marciel (Age: 27.) Rei's childhood guard, first aide and knight. Mina's partner.

- Ramona "Mina" Durand (Age: 24.) Rei's second aide and knight, Andrew's partner. Heir to Yosai Earldom.

- Mizi (Age: 18.) Court Healer of Nijou, assigned specifically to care for Rei's health. Rei's girlfriend and hopeful intended. Our secondary female protagonist.

- Ore (*See also Kase Shicchi.*) (Age: 27.) Rei's third aide and knight, Mizi's guard, Messenger of the Regent. Ilena's partner and guard. Our primary male protagonist.

- Ilena (*See also Thailena Touka Polov.*) (Age: 24.) Suiran Director of Intelligence for Rei. Ore's partner. Our primary female protagonist. As the number one witness against Pakyo, she's being kept hidden in secrecy within the castle to protect her until Rei can bring Pakyo to justice.

- Ryan (Age: 16.) Head Court Healer of Nijou. Mizi's superior.

- Tairn Malkin (Age: 28.) Rei's fourth aide. Heir to Nakaba Earldom, Dane's older brother.

- "Grandfather" (Age: 48.) Suspected right hand assistant of Ilena. He's only known by his code name in her intelligence network.

- Leah (Age: 43.) Ilena's nurse and secretary, who has watched over her since her birth.

- Rio (Age: 17.) Ilena's maid and assistant.

Nijoushi The capital city of Suiran, sitting at the more-protected western edge of the castle grounds.

Kouzanshi The university city of Ryokudo, set up high in the rough mountains of the northwest corner of the country.

- Shiotsu (Age: 33.) Head of the Medical Department of the University of Kouzanshi. Mizi and Ryan's Professor of Medicine.

Tokumade The Earldom of the House of Shicchi, the house of the line of the kings of Suiran. Lies to the central northeast of Suiran, west of Nijoushi.

- Earl Pakyo Shicchi (Age: 33.) Head of the House of Shicchi. Rei and Ilena are working together to bring Pakyo to justice for the crimes he's committed throughout his life because the Shicchi House, as a royal "untouchable" House, could get away with murder - literally.

- Kase Shicchi (*See also Ore.*) (Age: 27.) The youngest brother of Pakyo, and heir to Tokumade. He's been Thailena's support, the same as she's been his, while they've been in hiding and working hard to bring Pakyo down.

Yosai The Earldom of the House of Durand. Mina's home. Her father is the Earl and Head of the House. She is his only heir. Lies to the east of Nijou and is often on the northern front of the northeast corner battles when they occur.

Nakaba The Earldom of the House of Malkin. Lies in the center of the Region. An honorable House that is allied with Sasou and is becoming an ally of Rei's.

- Dane Malkin (Age: 23.) Youngest son of Earl Malkin, younger brother to Tairn. One of the witnesses against Pakyo, being kept in safety in a secret location.

Falcon's Hollow A small holding and manor located in the bowl of a large hidden hollow south of Nijou. Where Rei is protecting all of the witnesses being gathered as proof against Pakyo.

Yamanzar Nation across the Inner Sea south of Ryokudo. There is a small land access between the two nations, a bare roadway between a tall mountain and the sea. On the other side of that mountain is Brulac.

- First Prince Amiran (Age: 22.) The reason Mizi left Yamanzar. He was a lazy womanizing prince with a large harem from a young age. Since meeting the team of Mizi and Rei his goal has been to learn how to have the strength of true royalty.

Selicia The nation to the northwest of Ryokudo, accessible only through two harsh passes through the rocky mountains. Kata's sister, Tatiana Touka, was married to the third prince of Selicia, Raoul Polov. They were murdered in a coup in that nation about the same time as Kata's husband died.

   - Thailena Touka Polov (*See also Ilena.*) (Age: 24) Tatiana and Raoul's daughter. She's been missing, presumed dead, since the time of the coup. Rei and Ore have discovered she's been in hiding in no stranger or difficult a place than Tokumade. They're still keeping her existence a secret until they hear from Sasou what he'll allow the public to know.

Tarc The nation to the northeast of Ryokudo, accessible through low rolling hills of trees that give way to grassland. Tarc is one wide expanse of highland grassland, populated by insular nomadic clans of horsemen.

Brulac The nation east of Ryokudo. There are tall mountains between the two nations on the south end of the border, but only tall wooded hills separate them in the northeastern corner of Ryokudo.

Altherly The nation west of Ryokudo. Rough rolling hills and a wide river divide the nations.

CPSIA information can be obtained
at www.ICGtesting.com
Printed in the USA
BVHW041646250220
573162BV00015B/400